THREE MINUTES OR LESS

Life Lessons from America's Greatest Writers

THREE MINUTES OR LESS

Life Lessons from America's Greatest Writers

From the Archives of the
PEN/Faulkner Foundation

BLOOMSBURY

Published by Bloomsbury USA, New York and London
Distributed to the trade by St. Martin's Press

Library of Congress Cataloging-in-Publication Data has been applied for

ISBN 1-58234-069-2

10 9 8 7 6

Typeset by Hewer Text Ltd, Edinburgh
Printed in the United States of America
by R. R. Donnelley & Sons Company, Harrisonburg, Virginia

CONTENTS

First Love

Illusions

Obsession

CONTENTS

Heroes

Journeys

A Sense of Place

A Lesson

Confessions

Reunion

Endings

Introduction

O N OCTOBER 30, 1989 the PEN/Faulkner Foundation hosted its first gala at the Folger Shakespeare Library in Washington, D.C. Twenty-one writers had accepted an invitation to speak for three minutes each on the subject, "Beginnings." The host for that inaugural gala was Roger Mudd, for many years a mainstay on CBS News, a man whose profession had taught him to respect precisely the value of time. When the writers were being given their instructions for the evening, Roger was insistent about the time limit. "Three minutes," he kept saying, "you all have three minutes. Do you know how long three minutes is?"

He feared, of course, that fiction writers measured time a bit more subjectively, and he was right. On that evening, and in the galas that have followed, many writers have soared effortlessly beyond the three-minute limit. They are fiction writers, after all, and as one of them said, "Three minutes – that's a haiku." Nevertheless, the writers have accepted the limit as a poet accepts the limits of a sonnet, and turned the limit to advantage, creating short pieces of marvelous ingenuity and intricacy. You will find that some of the selections are more polished than others, since they have all been transcribed from the taped record of the gala; and some writers adhered exactly to a written script, while others permitted themselves small or large flights of improvisation.

Bear in mind as you read that the gala is a festive occasion, and that the writers – after a brief introduction by Roger Mudd, our first host, or George Plimpton, the incumbent Master of Ceremonies – take the stage of the Folger Shakespeare Theater. It is, every writer would agree, one of the most comfortable and inspiring settings imaginable.

The space is intimate, seating only 250 people. The speaking voice carries easily to every corner of the room, and – if you happen to believe that every spoken word creates an endless vibration in the air – the words are added to the great speeches of Hamlet and Lear and Prospero that have been spoken from this stage.

Such a thought might be daunting, especially since three minutes is hardly time for profundity. Most writers have approached the gala as an opportunity to divert, to enchant, to charm, to entertain. Still, the selections show just what kind of light a writer is able to shed on a given subject. Especially in a city like Washington, where abstractions rule and language is mostly institutional, the particularity and strong individuality of each piece is startling and welcome. Here are men and women who are willing to speak for themselves, and only themselves, men and women who do not hide behind abstractions and want no truck with institutions. Their authority comes from a more powerful source.

Year in and year out the audience for the PEN/Faulkner gala tends to be made up of the same people, who count themselves fortunate to have the first claim on the relatively few seats in the theater. We at the PEN/Faulkner Foundation include ourselves among the fortunate few, but we have often wished that a book would make the presentations available to a much broader audience. You are now holding that book in your hands, and we hope that the mood and spirit of the occasions will be conveyed along with the words.

From its inception the gala has been generously sponsored by the Ford Motor Company. The proceeds support the PEN/Faulkner Award for Fiction, the largest juried prize for fiction in the United States. Named for William Faulkner, who used his Nobel Prize funds to support and encourage other writers, the PEN/Faulkner is a prize founded by fiction writers, judged by fiction writers, and funded and supported to this day by those writers who continue to give benefit readings of their works. The readings assembled here are expressions of that spirit, which has guaranteed the PEN/Faulkner Award a permanent place in American culture.

The PEN/Faulkner Foundation

BEGINNINGS

October 30, 1989

William Kennedy

MY FIRST SHORT story I wrote for *Collier's Magazine*. *Collier's* didn't know this when I wrote it. It was called "Eggs," and it concerned a man who goes into a diner and orders scrambled eggs. The counterman doesn't want to serve him eggs and suggests goulash. The man insists on his eggs, and the counterman reluctantly serves him. The man eats them and leaves. End of story. I was eighteen, the first year of college.

After I wrote "Eggs," I showed it to my mother, and, as with everything else I had done in life, she thought it was very good. I also showed it to my banjo teacher. "Very good," he also said. He did not say "Very, very good," which is what he said when I played well during my banjo lesson. I showed the story to my father, and he read it at the breakfast table while eating eggs of his own. He liked soft-boiled eggs with a teaspoon of sugar on them and tea with three teaspoons of sugar. I never saw him eat scrambled eggs. How could he know about my story? He read it and said, "What the hell is this?" "It's a story, a short story," I said. "It's about a guy who goes in and eats eggs," he said. "That's right," I said. "What the hell kind of story is that?" he said. "It's a realistic story," I said. "I'm sending it off to *Collier's*." "They publish stuff like this?" "Every week," I said. "Who the hell wants to read about a guy who goes in and eats eggs?" "The whole world reads *Collier's*," I said. "The whole world eats eggs." "Is this what you learned in school?" My schooling had cost serious money. "I don't want to argue about it," I said. "You either like it or you don't." "Take a guess," my father said. Well, I'd show him. I sent it off to *Collier's* that afternoon and I've still got the rejection slip to prove it. I never showed any more stories to my father. This is known as writer's block. However, I reread the story last week for the first time in forty-five years, and my father emerges from that day as a masterful literary critic. A retarded orangutan could write a better story than "Eggs." Be that as it may, writing this story was valuable for an assortment of reason. It was the first step of a career; it proved I'd get better because I couldn't get worse; it acquainted me with rejection, and I didn't die from it. I revised "Eggs" two more times in later years. I called it "Counterman on Duty" and then just "Eat." And the story got better without getting good. Finally I abandoned it and put Herby, the protagonist, in a novel under another name, and there he is at last even though he missed out on *Collier's*

Eudora Welty once wrote that a writer should write not about what he knows but what he doesn't know about what he knows. I translate this to mean that the writer should try to understand mystery. And mystery, someone once said, is the basic element of all works of art. The only mystery about "Eggs" is why I didn't know it was awful. In time I did put some of my own mystery into the places I wrote about, and my fiction improved. I'm sorry my parents didn't get to appreciate what happened to me as a writer. My mother died while I was still trying to get my short stories published, and my father was at the cusp of senility when I finished my first novel. But he bragged about the book down at the State Supreme Court where he worked. He said it was about how 2,000 cows get swept out to sea in Puerto Rico. Actually, the book is set in Albany and doesn't have any cows. But you can see how, with that kind of imagination and critical apparatus in my genes, it was inevitable I'd become a writer.

Robert Stone

M ANY THINGS COME together to put you in a situation in which you find yourself a writer. In the house where I was growing up, there were many creepy books, but none of them was more creepy or more ghastly than one I particularly remember that had a great deal of dreadful gothic lettering and extremely frightening illustrations and a text of which I could make no sense at all, though I did puzzle out one particular verse. And as soon as I had puzzled it out, I realized that the book was far more creepy and dreadful than I could ever have imagined. The verse in it went, "As one who on a lonesome road doth walk in fear and dread, and having once turned round, doth no more his head, for he know that close behind him a frightful fiend doth tread."

And as soon as I read that, I realized what I was involved with. I took the book, and I hid it where I would never find it, but of course I experienced the first of many guilty urges that I was later to experience and I had to go and dig it out and read that again. And I had to ponder and wonder, "Did the writer of these verses actually mean me to feel the way I feel having read them?" Having read them, my hair would have stood up on end had it not already been standing up on end because of the crew cuts that we all wore in those days. When I finally understood that I had been meant to experience what I was experiencing as a result of reading those verses, and that unlike all the sensations that I'd experienced listening to the radio or going to the movies, this one seemed to go on and on so that I could never contain it, so that it had no bounds, I wanted to approach that force and take hold of it and to deal, of course, not only with fear but with love and the rest, and I tried to do that, and I'm still trying.

Pat Conroy

M Y FATHER, A Marine Corps fighter pilot, 220 pounds, six-two, a blunt instrument: a semiautomatic assault weapon. My father waged war against the Japanese, the North Koreans, the Vietnamese, and his family. My first memory: my mother trying to stab my father with a butcher knife while he was beating her. I knew this was going to be a long and involved life.

My mother – from the hills of Alabama. Her relatives were named this (and I give you the exact names): There was Jasper Catlit, Plumma, Clyde. There was an uncle in the graveyard named Jerrymire Peak. And I said, "Where did he come from?" and she said, "He was named for the prophet, Jer-ry-mire."

These two improbable people got together, had a marriage that produced seven children, six miscarriages. My sister called the miscarriages the lucky ones. In the dance of this particular family, in this horrible dance – you know, when I read Eudora Welty's thing that her mother and father sang to each other from the stairways – not my mother and father. This was martial art. This was a terrible, terrible union, but it was the one that caused me to be a writer.

The worst thing that happened: Dad was stationed at the Pentagon and a fight broke out between my mother and father when my sister had her birthday party, her ninth birthday party. I was eleven. A fight started. My role was to get the other six kids out of harm's way. So I rushed them out of the room. My second job was to get Mom away from Dad. I went roaring in. I was eleven. Dad could eat Ollie North for breakfast. I got between them. I looked over my head and saw the butcher knife I'd seen when I was a child. My mother connected this time. Blood got on me, my sister. Mom took us to Hot Shoppes and said she was going to leave Dad. She did not. What she did instead was wash my shirt and my sister's dress that had the blood of my father on it.

Later, when I asked my sister if it happened, she said no, it didn't happen. I said, why not? She said we didn't write it down. If it's going to be real, you got to write it down. My sister's book of poetry is coming out next year, published by Norton. My father made one mistake. He was raising an American novelist and an American poet – and we wrote it down.

William Styron

W HEN I WAS twelve and a half I attended a rural school in Tidewater, Virginia, about 150 miles south of here, which boasted a mimeograph newspaper called *The Sponge* – soaks up all the news. My first literary creation was a contribution to this journal, a short story entitled "Typhoon and the *Tore Bay*." This document has been preserved in my father's doting papers. Joseph Conrad was, of course, the author of a famous story, "Typhoon," and that was the inspiration for my own story, which I'm afraid lacked even the originality of a truly fresh title. *Tore Bay* was the name I christened the doomed ship of my little narrative after I found an English bay by that name in an atlas. Upon rereading "Typhoon and the *Tore Bay*" and comparing it with its model, I am relieved to say that while no plagiarism is evident, there is much déjà vu. The word "derivative" is perhaps too generous, "counterfeit" too harsh. Let us say this work of about 750 words is an unconscious parody and profoundly Conradian. Here are some brief passages to help render its special flavor:

A sickly green haze hung over the East China Sea. "Typhoon brewing," mused Captain Taggart darkly, with an inner shudder gazing at the barometer. 27.20 "God save the mark" he blurted aloud with another inner shudder.

The diabolical storm lashed the stricken bridge with a murderer's vengeance. The great ship was yawing and heaving every which way like a huge berserk animal. "We're bound to founder," Captain Taggart heard the mate say with a despondent shriek. "He is a despicable coward," Captain Taggart mused darkly.

"There are 400 helpless Chinamen down there in the hold," Captain Taggart cried. "We can't let them perish." The mate swore a vile oath. "Who cares about a bunch of Chinks. Let them all drown." Captain Taggart saw on the mate's twisted face a look of supreme evil.

At this point, my literary career was overtaken by a long and merciful silence. A diary that I kept faithfully during my fourteenth year reveals a fascinating detail about my intellectual development. It shows that while I went to and appreciated to one degree or another a total of 125 movies, occasionally seeing as many as two films a day, there is no record whatever of my reading a single book. Not even Conrad. Books came later. At age eighteen, I discovered Thomas Wolfe. In a recent notorious essay on Wolfe, a critic, Harold Bloom, wrote (I think I'm quoting exactly) that "the novelist had no talent whatsoever." This is a ludicrous misstatement, since Wolfe had prodigious talent, as prodigious as Shakespeare's or Homer's, except for the fact that, unlike Shakespeare's and Homer's, it was a talent that was arrested at age eighteen and, therefore, was the perfect medium for an adolescent like myself to discover the splendor of language and to be provided with the impetus for a desperate falling in love with literature. And so, for the next five years I read. I read passionately, promiscuously, eclectically, critically, and uncritically until my mind was dizzy and intoxicated with a thousand wonderful books. And then having written nothing ambitious since "Typhoon and the *Tore Bay*," I decided it was time to be a writer, and so, at the age of twenty-two, I sat down and began my first novel, *Lie Down in Darkness*.

Hortense Calisher

I THINK WE'RE ALL storytellers, and I would like to say just a few words about why I'm talking and you're listening. I'm a mixed American. When I grew up, I grew up in New York. My father came from Richmond, Virginia. He was born during the Civil War. He married a woman much younger than he, and when I was born – I was the first child of, you know, this ancient family – there were all kinds of accents in the house. There was Southern; my mother was German but spoke a very careful English. We had English people in the house, and I was never sure what accent was coming out of my mouth – and I'm not always sure at the same time now. What it meant was a little girl who listened and listened to language, especially the long strophes that Southerners seem to have.

When I came to go to school to be taught to read at five, it was found out that I could read and I don't really remember a time when I couldn't. There must have been a time when I was shaking rattles and so forth. But, I think something about the vocal thing in the house did it. It was a happy childhood – then it disappeared. For a while my mother got sick. My father was away on business. And I had that absolutely necessary thing to create a writer – an evil housekeeper. And she scared me blue, and nobody knew, so that at night I began to dream, half-dream. I was thinking about it the other night. I never was really asleep in those periods, but I dreamed of happier times, and I began to concentrate on language. When I got older, when I went to high school, I began to collect language the way you collect stamps, jewelry or baseball cards. There were books at home, but they were a marvelously dotty collection. I read

Dickens and Thackeray in the old *Harper's* for the Civil War years. But I never got them all because we had lost some of them, so that I never found out about what happened to the *Tale of Two Cities* until I was a grown woman. We had a strange collection of books. *The Memoirs of Ninon de L'Endos* was at one end and the war writings of Walt Whitman were at the other. After, when I got to college, there were all those riches, and I knew I was going to be a writer. I had known at seven. I had written a little book of fairy tales in a notebook and my Aunt Mamie came and said, "What's that?" I showed it to her and she laughed. That was the wrong thing to do. Maybe that's how one becomes a writer. Well, in college there were all the marvels and I read them and I wasn't scared, but it was a company, I think, that I was afraid to join in any way because naturally I wanted to be of some good company.

Then the war came, I married, I had children and I still did not write. I had written like crazy in college. I really didn't know why. I think I was still scared. I for a while traveled all over the United States. I didn't realize that I was learning what it was like to be an American. My then husband was an engineer, and the children and I dragged along behind him. I saw small towns. For a New Yorker this was a strange and marvelous thing. I learned to see all kinds of people. For a while I was a social worker and went into houses that I did not believe. I met all kinds of people. Still did not write. When my first child was born, I began, but I never sent it out anywhere, and I finally broke through what seems to me still a plate of glass that was between me and other people – when you know that you think you have a capacity and you haven't done it yet, it's almost a schizoid thing that comes between you and people. That broke, I wrote and I had found my vocation and I haven't stopped writing or talking since.

I think writers lead double lives. We are people who have to, in a sense, indoctrinate ourselves into living by recording as well and somebody asked me once what I felt about writing, and I said – and I still believe – I have to write as if my life depends on it, and of course, it does.

Eudora Welty

I 'D LIKE TO read a few little snatches from my writing story called "One Writer's Beginnings."

When I was six or seven, I was taken out of school and put to bed for several months for an ailment the doctor described as a fast-beating heart. I felt all right – perhaps I felt too good. It was the feeling of suspense. At any rate I was allowed to occupy all day my parents' double bed in the front upstairs bedroom.

I was supposed to rest, and the little children didn't get to run in and excite me often. Davis School was as close as across the street. I could keep up with it from the window beside me. Hear the principal ring her bells, see which children were tardy, watch my classmates eat together at recess. I knew their sandwiches. I was homesick for school. My mother made time for teaching me arithmetic and hearing my spelling.

An opulence of story books covered my bed. It was the "land of counterpane." As I read away, I was Rapunzel, or the Goose Girl, or the Princess Labam in one of the thousand and one nights who mounted the roof in her palace every night and of her own radiance faithfully lighting the whole city. Just by reposing there. And I daydreamed I could light Davis School from across the street.

But I never dreamed I could learn as long as I was away from the schoolroom and that bits of enlightenment far-reaching in my life went on as ever in their own good time. After they told me good night and tucked me in, although I knew that after I'd finally fallen asleep they'd pick me up and carry me away, my parents draped the lampshade with a sheet of the daily paper that was tilted like a hat brim, so that they could sit in their rockers in a lighted part of the room and I could supposedly go to sleep in the protected dark of the bed. They sat talking. What was thus dramatically made a present of to me was a secure sense of the hidden observer. As long as I could make myself keep awake, I was free to listen to every word my parents said between them.

I don't remember that any secrets were revealed to me, nor do I remember any avid curiosity on my part to learn something I wasn't supposed to. Perhaps I was too young to know what to listen for, but I was present in the room with the chief secret there was – the two of them, father and mother – sitting there as one. I was conscious of this secret and of my fast-beating heart in step together as I lay in the slant-shaded light of the room with a brown pear-shaped scorch newspaper shade where it had become overheated once.

What they talked about, I have no idea, and the subject was not what mattered to me. It was, no doubt, whatever a young married couple spending their first time privately in each other's company in the long, probably harried day would talk about. It was the murmur of their voices, the back and forth, the unnoticed stretching away of time between my bedtime and theirs that made me bask there at my distance. What I felt was not that I was excluded from them but that I was included and because of what I could hear of their voices and what I could see of their faces in the cone of yellow light under the brown-scorched shade.

I suppose I was exercising as early as then the turn of mind, the nature of the temperament of a privileged observer. And owing to the way I became so, it turned out that I became the loving kind.

I live in gratitude to my parents for initiating me (and as early as I begged for it without keeping me waiting into the knowledge of the word) into reading and spelling by way of the alphabet. They taught it to me at home in time for me to begin to read before starting to school. I believe the alphabet is no longer considered an essential piece of equipment for traveling through life. In my day it was the keystone to knowledge.

My love for the alphabet, which endures, grew out of reciting it but, before that, out of seeing the letters on the page. In my own story books, before I could read them for myself, I fell in love with various winding, enchanted-looking initials drawn by Walter Crane at the heads of fairy tales. In "Once upon a time" an "O" had a rabbit running it as a treadmill, his feet upon flowers. When the day came years later for me to see the Book of Kells, all the wizardry of letter, initial, and word swept over me a thousand times over, and the illumination, the gold, seemed a part of the words' beauty and holiness that had been there from the start.

Ever since I was first read to, then started reading to myself, there's never been a line read that I didn't *hear*. As my eyes followed the sentence, a voice was saying it silently to me. It isn't my mother's voice or the voice of any person I can identify. Certainly not my own. It is human but inward and it is inwardly that I listen to it. It is to me the voice of the story or the poem itself. The cadence, whatever it is that asks you to believe the feeling that resides in the printed word, reaches me through the reader-voice. I have supposed, but never found out, that this is the case with all readers – to read as listeners – and with all writers to write as listeners. It may be part of the desire to write. The sound of what falls on the page begins the process of testing it for truth for me. Whether I am right to trust so far, I don't know. By now, I don't know whether I could do either one, reading or writing, without the other.

Through learning at my later date, things I hadn't known, or had escaped or possibly feared realizing, about my parents – and myself – I glimpse our whole family life as if it were freed of that clock time which spaces us apart so inhibitingly, divides young and old, keeps our living through the same experiences at separate distances.

It is our inward journey that leads us through time – forward or back – seldom in a straight line, most often spiraling. Each of us is moving, changing, with respect to others. As we discover, we remember. Remembering, we discover and most intensely do we experience this when our separate journeys converge. Our living experience at those meeting points is one of the charged dramatic fields of fiction.

I'm prepared now to use the wonderful word *confluence*, which of itself exists as a reality and a symbol in one. It is the only kind of symbol that for me as a writer has any weight, testifying to the pattern, one of the chief patterns, of human experience.

Here I'm leading to the last scenes in my novel, *The Optimist's Daughter*:

She had slept in the chair like a passenger who had come on an emergency journey in a train. But she had rested deeply. She had dreamed that she was a passenger and riding with Phil. They had ridden together over a long bridge. Awake she recognized it. It was a dream of something that had really happened.

When she and Phil were coming down from Chicago to Mount Salus to be married in the Presbyterian church, they came on the train. Laurel, when she traveled back and forth between Mount Salus and Chicago, had always taken the sleeper. She and Phil followed the route on a day train, and she saw it for the first time.

When they were climbing the long approach to a bridge after leaving Cairo, rising slowly higher until they rode above the tops of bare trees, she looked down and saw the pale light widening and the river bottoms opening out and then the water appearing, reflecting the low early sun. There were two rivers. Here was where they came together. This was the confluence of the waters, the Ohio and the Mississippi.

They were looking down from a great elevation and all they saw was at the point of coming together, the bare trees marching in from the horizon, the rivers moving into one, and as he touched her arm, she look up with him and saw the long ragged pencil-faint line of birds within the crystal of the zenith, flying in a V of their own, following the same course down. All they could see was sky, water, birds, light and confluence. It was the whole morning world.

And they themselves were a part of the confluence. Their own joint act of faith had brought them here at the very moment and matched its occurrence and proceeded as it proceeded. Direction itself was made beautiful, momentous.

They were riding as one with it, right up front. It's our turn! she thought exultantly. And we're going to live forever.

Left bodiless and graveless of a death made of water and fire in a year long gone, Phil could still tell her of her life. For her life, any life, she had to believe was nothing but the continuity of its love.

She believed it just as she believed that the confluence of the waters was still happening at Cairo. It will be there the same as it ever was when she went flying over it today on her way back. Out of sight for her this time thousands of feet below, but with nothing in between except thin air.

Of course, the greatest confluence of all is that which makes up the human memory, the individual human memory. My own is the treasure most dearly regarded by me in my life and in my work as a writer. Here time also is subject to confluence. The memory is a living thing – it, too, is in transit. But during its moment, all that is remembered joins and lives – the old and the young, the past and the present, the living and the dead.

As you have seen, I am a writer who came of a sheltered life. A sheltered life can be a daring life as well. For all serious daring starts from within.

Larry McMurtry

I N THE BEGINNING, art came in at the ear, wafting to me from radioland, a wondrous domain whose happiest feature, from my point of view, was that it seemed to contain only three animals: Sandy, Little Orphan Annie's dog; Silver, the Lone Ranger's horse; and Scout, as in "Get 'em up, Scout," the faithful Tonto's equally faithful pinto. This paucity of fauna was welcome indeed because the world outside the screen door of our little ranch house in West Texas teemed with animals, none of them the chatty, vivacious creatures one meets in storybooks. On our ranch, unfortunately, beasts behaved like beasts. From an early age, I had to be forced outside, always to my peril. The turkeys were aggressive and much larger than me. The hens were irritable. The guineas went chittering along in neurotic packs. The peacocks screeched. The mules were sullen. The bulls so ominous, one's mind preferred to avoid thinking about them. Most frightening of all were the pigs, watching one cannily from their Hogarthian wallows. My pony was vicious and even my dogs unreliable. They constantly got themselves bitten by rattlesnakes but, faithful as dogs in Baden-Powell, they struggled on only to drop dead at my feet.

All this was bad, but the beasts of the barnyard paled in comparison with the beasts of the schoolbus, and in my first grade year the bus carried me ninety miles a day to education and back. I was the youngest, smallest, and most tormentable person on the bus and always arrived at school so terrorized that I would throw up my Ovaltine and be consigned to the sick room all day to await in fear and trembling the terrible bus ride home. I could see little in education at that point. Nothing could be worth those bus rides. Within two months I had woven myself a cocoon of illness that kept me home the rest of that year and portions of several others.

The real world was too hard. I wanted to live in radioland and I did, beginning my day with W. Lee O'Daniel and the Doughboys and ending it with Fibber McGee and Molly. At least I ended it with them if it was Tuesday. In between there were the bewildering passions of Stella Dallas. For years I assumed the city of Dallas was named for her. The patriotic genius of Captain Midnight and the folksy wisdom of Hackberry Hotel.

Then, to my indignation, World War II broke out, disrupting what had been until then a perfectly ordered world. The war meant constant interruptions. One could never be sure what would be on when. But I did like what I heard about hand grenades. If I could lay my hands on a few of those, I could blow the pigs right out of their Hogarthian wallow.

Then one day my cousin Bob showed up at my bedside. He was on his way to war and he wanted me to have his books. Nineteen in all. I accepted them indifferently. I was still happy enough in radioland, but one day – it may have been Dunkirk or the fall of Manila, I'm not sure – regular programing was interrupted for so long that I began to delve in Cousin Bob's box, coming up with a stirring tale called *Sergeant Silk, the Prairie Scout.* It was about mounties in Saskatchewan. It instantly sucked me in. Though I was probably six, I remember no book before that one. And I suppose it was on that day, when Captain Midnight was silenced, when Sky King couldn't fly, when the great horse Silver didn't gallop, when Fibber McGee and Molly's closet remained closed, that the literary life began for me.

Maurice Sendak

I T PROBABLY BEGAN on my grandmother's lap in Brooklyn way back when us thirty kids were always, it seems, recovering from one interminable disease after another. To keep me amused, my grandmother would pull the window shade up and down to reveal a series of real moving pictures. First up, and to my joy I watched my brother and sister making a sooty snowman in the backyard. Then down, a breathless pause, and up again and they were gone! It was all like turning pages of a picture book.

My first proper book, Twain's *The Prince and the Pauper*, was given to me by my older sister. It had marvelous illustrations by Robert Lawson. The fresh new book smelled divine and felt even better, all shiny and smooth with a brilliant inlaid picture on the dark red front cover. Thus began my passion for books. Not reading, but smelling, fondling, biting and luxuriously caressing. It felt and smelled so much better, classier, than the cheap paper books I had up till then – that funky sour stink issuing out of comic and big little books. I still like that smell and I still treasure that copy of *The Prince and the Pauper*. That experience directly led, or so it must for the sake of brevity, into creating books with my brother, Jack. Our collaboration began when I was seven and he was twelve. He wrote the stories and I illustrated them on shirt cardboard. Our masterpiece and swan song was the dramatic tale, *They Were Inseparable*. We were both in love with our sister, who was sixteen, and this story had to do with that dark passion. The plot, in brief: the brother and sister are madly in love and decide to get married. We were either very stupid or very naïve but, as I recollect, this tale was a great family favorite and when read aloud to the relatives my parents positively glowed. Anyway, somewhere deep in my brother's unconscious something finally warned him that the situation wasn't strictly kosher because, immediately preceding the wedding, the brother is in a terrible accident and as he lies dying and bandaged from head to foot (my favorite picture) the sister bursts into the hospital room, pushes aside nurses and doctors who attempt to stop her, leaps onto the dying brother, clasps the bundle of bandages and before anyone can stop them, they cry out in unison, "We are inseparable" and leap from the fourteenth floor of the Brooklyn Jewish Hospital – SPLAT! At this point, I would proudly hold up my shirt-cardboard depiction of that terrific death. So, it seems that as a small boy, I pasted and clipped my bits of books together and hoped only for a life that would permit me to earn my bread by pasting and clipping more bits of books. And here I am, all grown-up, at least physically, and still in the same old business.

Amiri Baraka

THE BEGINNINGS – words as notes and beats. My writing came out of me without too much formal grunting and extrapolation of the dry. I was first more interested in music naturally enough. African-American life is rhythm-wrapped. Its social context, its history, the living rooms and kitchens and churches and street corners pushing sweet blues afternoon and evening. We are abundantly chorded, and our syncopated walks harmonize us to the blue future like laughter from the only thing bigger and warmer than our hearts – our soul. I'd taken all kinds of music lessons, too. Thrice pianistic, trumpet, drums, plus drawing and painting classes, too. I guess our mama wanted us to be close to or well acquainted with art instead of not. I had bands, sang in choruses, hung out all night traveling light in and out of joints to hear Larry Darnell, Ruth Brown, the Orioles, Ravens, Little Esther, Lynn Hope, Bullmoose Jackson, Louis Jordan, Nat King Cole, Tuesday mambos at Lloyd's Manor, and later Bird, Diz, Kenton, Miles and his Monkness, Thelonius, Billy, and Ella. My parents always played plus my grandparents loved old blues. We had concerts of spirituals. Mama and my grandmama, Nana, put together a gospel chorus for the middle-class negroes at Bethany Baptist each and every Sunday. My grandfather used to promise me a silver dollar to memorize Weldon Johnson's "The Creation," and the slim volume with the fantastic Aaron Douglas woodcuts has always sat heavy in the breakfasts of my poetic sensibility. My mother, on the other hand, got me to memorize Lincoln's "Gettysburg Address," which I recited on his birthday annually for years in a Boy Scout suit.

But then, all of a sudden, it was college-going-away time and, after being the fly in the proverbial buttermilk at Rutgers, I found Howard and lifelong friends and Sterling Brown, who taught me the music as history and analysis and, you know what? I put my trumpet down. Although for sure there is nothing I love so much or identify my very soul so deeply with as music word, make no mistake. And even the first formal verse I loved was in the music, the blues, city and country. I used to walk down the halls of my high school reciting Larry Darnell quietly at the top of my voice – "YOU'RE RIGHT UP ON TOP NOW, YOU WANT TO BE FREE, WHY YOU FOOL, YOU POOR SAD WORTHLESS FOOLISH FOOL." It was poetry; the form and feeling of the blues that first moved me wordwise, like, [sung] "If you don't love me, tell me so, Don't tell other people, I'm the one to know," or "It's rainin' teardrops from my eyes," or "Yoooou made me lose my happy hoooome, You stole my love and now you're gooooone," or [dialogue] "You way out in the forest fighting the big old grizzly bear. How come you ain't out in the forest? I'm a lady. They got lady bears out there."

And with them add the Langston poems and *The Defender,* a copy of *The Rubaiyat* they sent my mother from the Book-of-the-Month Club, where I also got *Black Boy, Native Son, The Collected Poe,* and Frank Yerby. In grammar school I had a short-lived comic strip with a feature called "The Crime Wave." In my senior year, I took the only creative-writing course I ever had hanging out with two friends of mine who also wanted to be writers and imitating Poe and Yerby, terrified by Wright. Now, suddenly, I was writing some little jive sonnets and cellophane love jingles after Herrick and Shakespeare and Suckling. And then reading Joyce and Pound and Eliot and Stein, etc. An old high-school buddy, Alan Polite, I ran track with, a real hero athlete I looked up to and longed to know, to imitate, had gotten out of school and gone to the Village to live. Somehow he summoned me/us over to his all-white-with-yellow-trim Bedford Street apartment. He was a writer now, he said. I looked at the neat piles of legal pads, the walls of books, the smiling graceful woman his wife, now the writer Charlene Polite, and seeing that life and that look in his eyes and already idealizing him, I knew that's where I was headed. Yeah, that's where I wanted to go. And the music? Did I leave it? Hell, no. Check the writing, any of it. Music's still got me going.

Richard Bausch

I THOUGHT EVERYONE COULD draw. My twin brother could, my two sisters could. On the wall of my grandmother's living room in that big old house in Washington was a drawing my mother had done. I remember being astonished at the detail and beauty of it, seeing in its sophistication and delicacy exactly how much better she was than we were, taking pride in it and beginning to know this was not something just anyone could do. I remember that I thought everyone came from loud, boisterous, large-spirited families with a penchant for talk and for the telling of stories, too. And I remember that when I was nine and told my father that I wanted to be heavyweight champion of the world he reacted with a tirade about the corruption of the boxing business; it took me almost thirty years to realize what a gift that was, to be taken so seriously as a matter of course and talk about the things I might find to do in life. My parents believed we could do anything we chose; we never quite learned to dismiss anything as being out of reach. And we learned the love of words, of talk.

It seems to me now that there was a tremendous respect in the house for the power of words. It was almost atavistic. I grew to love what Shaw calls the majesty and grandeur of the language because I was fortunate enough to live among people for whom its power was visceral and immediate. For me as for them, although they may not even quite have known it, the phrases from Auden seem literally true: "Time that is intolerant of the brave and innocent and indifferent in a week to a beautiful physique worships language and forgives everyone by whom it lives."

Annie Dillard

WHEN I WAS ten growing up in Pittsburgh I ran into Kimon Nicolaïdes' book *The Natural Way to Draw*. This was a manual for students who couldn't enroll in Nicolaides' own classes at New York City's Art Students League. I was amazed that there were books about things one actually did. The idea of drawing from life had astounded me two years previously, but I had let it slip, and my drawing such as it was had sunk back into facile sloth. Now this book would ignite my fervor for conscious drawing and bind my attention to both the vigor and the detail of the actual world. All summer and fall the urgent hortatory book ran my life. I tried to follow its schedules. Every day, sixty-five gesture drawings, fifteen memory drawings, an hour-long contour drawing, and then the big one – the sustained study in crayon clothed, or the sustained study in crayon nude. I outfitted an attic bedroom as a studio and moved in. Every free morning I taped that day's drawing to a wall. Since there was no model – nude or clothed – I drew my baseball mitt. I drew my baseball mitt's gesture. Its tense repose, its expectancy, which ran up its hollows like a hand. I drew its contours, its flat finger tips strung on square rawhide thongs. I drew its billion grades of light and dark so that the glove weighed vivid and complex on the page and the trapezoids small as dust motes in the leather fingers cast shadows and the palm leather was smooth as a belly and thick. Draw anything, said the book. Learning to draw is really a matter of learning to see, said the book. All the student need concern himself with is reality. I could draw the mitt in forty-five seconds or in three hours. A given object took no particular time to draw. Instead, you, the artist, took the time or you did not. All things in the world were interesting, infinitely interesting, so long as you had attention to give them. By noon all this drawing would have gone to my head. I slipped into the mitt, quit the attic, quit the house, and headed up the street, looking for a ball game.

Brendan Gill

W HEN I WAS three or four, my choice of a future career
teetered back and forth between architecture and writing. I
lost interest in the practice of architecture when it turned out I would
have to take courses in mathematics, to which I was unsympathetic.
Especially distasteful to me at an early age was the discovery,
encountered in first or second grade in the course of learning
how to add and subtract, that when I subtracted one number from
another I could borrow from a zero in the upper row of figures.
Being New England born and bred, I knew in my bones that
borrowing was a sin. No mathematics, no architecture for me.

There remained the bewitching temptation of literature, especially
as it was made manifest in the form of metaphors. My mother died
when I was seven, but long before that sad event she had introduced
me to the magical nature of words by means of which they were
permitted to stand for several things at once. At a tea party, she served
ladyfingers and I remember asking her, "Are they really ladies'
fingers?" No. Nor did they need to be. They resembled ladies'
fingers and so were not ladies' fingers. How wonderful! Next came
the day when at a dinner party she served chicken à la king. Kings
existed in fairy tales. What had a king to do with that speckled dish
upon our table? As for the merrily lilting "a la," what on earth could
that be? *A la façon du revoir?* Oh God in heaven. Mother, tell me
more. And then my father and mother went to the theatre and sat in a
box. A box? Why on earth would grown-ups sit in a box, which was
something that I kept my toys in? No, no, my darling. Not that kind
of a box. And so my eyes became saucers. Yes, saucers! And my heart

began to hammer. Yes, hammer! And I perceived then and there and once and for all what my Hartford neighbor Wallace Stevens was soon to be setting down as the truth that every one of us in this room lives by, to wit: that words of the world are the life of the world.

Doris Grumbach

I ENVY PERSONS WHO began to write fiction only once. At last count I have begun four times, and if I live long enough I expect a fifth onset of the disease will come upon me. When I was four years old and had learned to read, I was under the impression that the act of reading was inextricably tied to writing, perhaps because my scrupulous mother made me write the words I had learned to recognize. One day, left to myself, I read a little book I had taken out of the public library. Then I carefully copied it out and brought it to my mother. I've written a book, I told her. She read what I had written. Then she said, "This is by Helen Bannerman, not by you." "I wrote it," I said. "No," she said, handing back *Little Black Sambo*, "you copied it, that's different."

This revelation stymied my nascent career as a creative writer for twelve years. It was revived only by necessity and in this manner. All the usual means of entry into college having been denied me by virtue of failing the English, history, trigonometry and civics regents given by New York State, and having amassed the highest total of unexplained absences in the records of Julia Richman High School, I decided to write a story to submit to the New York City short-story contest for high-school seniors because the poster said that one of the judges, Rudolph Kagy, was a professor at Washington Square College and wrote mystery stories under another name. My scheme was simple. I would write a short mystery story, win the contest and then appeal to the professor for help in circumventing the admissions committee of the college that had summarily turned me down. By another miracle, the plan worked. "A Man and His Dog," as the story was called, a title I think I took from either Chekhov or Thomas Mann, not having learned my mother's plagiary lesson very well, won the contest. Professor Kagy listened to my plight and interceded for me. I was admitted to New York University on probation and proceeded to be educated in philosophy and mathematics. From this experience, I learned that one wrote fiction only when it was necessary. Necessary, in this case, to effect a passage from high school to college. Thirty-seven years went by before my third beginning. It was 1962. Then the Berlin crisis had taken place. My husband was called up in the Army Medical Reserve and departed for training in Georgia. I was left with a tedious teaching job and children, but little to do in the evening after the dishes were washed. I was too tired to read; we had no television. I had never learned to crochet or knit or make quilts or paint on china, so I filled the time by writing a novel. It took six months to finish. I sketched in a second book. The Berlin crisis passed. I took the novel to New York and went to the publisher on my list whose address was closest to the 42nd Street train station. Wrapped in a box in brown paper, I left it with the receptionist. Two weeks later, *mirabilis*, an editor called to accept it, published it, and a year later the second one. But my husband had come home and my evenings were now occupied so I dropped fiction writing as the time filler.

Fifteen years later, I left a Camelot of a journalistic job, and having little else to do taught two days a week and filled the rest of my time with writing a novel, *Chamber Music*. Critically speaking, I'm not sure it was much of an advance on "A Man and His Dog," or the first novel or, for that matter, *Little Black Sambo*. But it, too, was published and started me on a sort of roll of three more novels.

Now it is almost four years since that spate of books. If I am to do it, I had better think about beginning again. I could, of course, pay attention to Longfellow who opined that "Great is the art of beginning, but greater is the art of ending," and stop while I am somewhat ahead. Or, I could listen to Lewis Carroll, who advised us to "Begin at the beginning and go on till you come to the end: then stop." I might take a biblical suggestion from Ecclesiastes, "Better is the end of a thing than the beginning" and try to improve on the fourth try. Most preferable, I think, is Winston Churchill's paraphrase of Talleyrand on England's role in World War II: "It is ambiguous enough to leave me entirely undecided." This is it: "Now, this is not the end," he said, "it is not even the beginning of the end, but perhaps the end of the beginning."

Stephen Goodwin

I THINK I FIRST realized that I would need to be able to tell a story when I was eight years old and lying on the sidewalk in front of the Catholic church in Bruton, Alabama. It was just after seven o'clock on a summer morning and I'd pedaled as hard as I could to reach the church in time to serve mass. At the age of eight this was as solemn an obligation as I could have, and I was afraid that I was going to incur the wrath, or at least the disapproval, of Father Horgan – a tall Irishman, a missionary priest, like all priests in south Alabama then, who had a voice like thunder. I wish you could have heard him begin the mass with those words – I can't do his brogue but I remember how it sounded when he said "*Introibo ad altare Dei*" in that brogue. Anyway, I feared I would be late. It was a weekday and not a Sunday. It was the only day of the week that mass would be said in our new church, the Church of St. Maurice – new, but still the humblest church in town. A little brick building with a little white cross at the peak of the rook. Before it was built, the Catholics in town – there were about thirty of us – used to meet in the courthouse, and sometimes mass was even said on the sideboard in the dining room in my family's house. My Catholicism came via my father, whose mother was Irish. She'd started out as a housemaid in Baltimore and ended up raising three children in New York and Paris. So there was a kind of sophistication, I think, for me at least, associated with being Catholic and a kind of glamour about the Irish. And on this particular morning, I was responsible myself for getting to church. Ordinarily my mother would have driven me. And she was a convert to Catholicism. She was from Pennsylvania, daughter of a Lutheran mother and a Jewish father who now lived in Bruton in the big house next to ours. I mention all this because my family was a tangle over religious loyalties and I was aware that we didn't, like so many other families in town, share the same convictions and beliefs from generation to generation. It was an enormous relief that I was on time. Father Horgan wasn't there; the church was empty and locked. I was breathing hard after that bike ride, my eyes were stinging. I think I felt a little queasy. I sat down on the steps and they were cool. I sat down, felt them, decided that I needed more relief and lay down on the sidewalk. I honest to God don't know why. I closed my eyes and I didn't hear the woman approach me. "Are you sick," she said. "Are you sick?" and I said, "No," but couldn't get up. "What are you lying there for?" she said, and she sounded very put out and angry. I'd seen her before; she lived near the church. And she said, "You're the Goodwin boy." I felt accused somehow, though I expected everyone in our town, a small town, to know my name. I believe I said I was just waiting for Father Horgan. She told me, "We never wanted this church here. We never did want it. It's a false religion, a false religion."

Those are really the only words I can remember about the flood of righteousness that washed over me in the next few minutes, which I took, rightly I think, as a condemnation of my faith, my family. I felt then the force of everything that separated me from the others in that town and knew that I'd never take for granted again who I was and what I was. The surprising thing about that to me when I think back on it is that I believed that I was called upon to make an answer and that the answer would have to include something about Catholicism, about the migration of the Irish and the Jews, and the stigma of being a Yankee there, something about the language, a good many other things that I suppose I'm still trying to figure out. But it never occurred to me that I wouldn't have an answer for her. If there was one thing my childhood had given me it was pride – not I hope the kind of pride that is a deadly sin, but the other kind of pride that Isak Dinesen defined as pride that comes from believing that God had some idea in mind when He created you. I believed that then, when I was a little kid. Now, when I start to write a story, it's what I try to remember.

Gloria Naylor

WHILE I AM by birth a native New Yorker, I've often mentioned publicly that I was conceived in Robinsville, Mississippi, because, for me, that conception was the beginning of my writing career. It was through my mother's genes that I inherited my passionate love of books. But since she was from a sharecropping family that could not afford the luxury of buying books, and the public libraries in the South were closed to black Americans, she would take her spare Saturday afternoons and hire herself out in someone else's fields to earn the money to send away to book clubs. And she made a vow to herself that all of her children would be born in a place where you could be poor and still read.

She kept that promise, and my earliest preschool memories are of being taken to a low brick building in the Bronx with dark walnut shelves that stretched high over my head, shelves that seemed to a four-year-old to almost stretch into eternity. And she told me that once I could write my name, all of those books would be mine. She would repeat this ritual with her second daughter and then the third. My sisters were average readers; I became an avid one. I was the shyest of the three, painfully shy, and fortunately I was taught early to revere a place that would become the repository of all my unspoken fears and my unspoken needs.

And today, with my own writing, that's basically what I'm giving back. Words that attempt to make some order out of the inarticulate chaos I have within. But writing for me is also about dreaming, and I grew up being encouraged to dream by a woman who, in spite of her very limited personal circumstances, somehow managed to find a way to hold on to a fierce belief in the limitless possibilities of the human spirit.

Joyce Carol Oates

I N A RURAL community in western New York State, in a region south of Lake Ontario, of small, unprospering farms and households, we had no idea that we might have been characterized in sociology's grim jargon as hovering somewhere around or below the "poverty line." There was for a child like myself a solace so precious as to be bound up with my very life, without which I am sure my life would have come to a radically diminished fruition. This was the world of the imagination, of stories told to me and read to me by my birth parents and grandparents, a world honored and even given a certain measure of permanence in the written word.

For writers, of course, begin as listeners, privileged listeners, wholly uncritical and appreciative of the voices that seem to descend to us out of air. It might be theorized that we who write, write in order to read what we have written and, reading it, to hear voices nowhere else accessible. We hope to recapture some of the magic that gradually departs from the world as we mature into it. So our delusions keep us going.

Later, in the 1940s, introduction to the children's room that was below the stairs in a sort of granite sepulchre that descends, of the Lockport public library on Main Street of Lockport, New York – which is one of the many Carnegie-endowed public libraries – was an introduction to a treasure trove that took my breath away. Shelves and shelves of books, each with its own transparent plastic cover, its bright, hopeful colors, so individual, so rich with promise, opening into unimaginable worlds, the interiors (as I thought of them) of other souls, opened by the profound mystery of language – that is, printed language. I would not claim to be, of the numerous writers in this gathering, the person most "redeemed" by the grace of the imagination, the culture of books, literacy, and free public libraries. But I'm sure there is no one who can count herself more blessed and more grateful. George Santayana once said, "Another world to live in is what we mean by religion." And so, too, the world of the imagination and the enlargement of human sympathy it provides.

Mary Lee Settle

W HEN I WAS four years old in Pineville, Kentucky, I knew
that the word "ice cream" and the word "Floko" meant
the same thing and that Bobby Lowe was my father. This was
embarrassing to my mother and to her best friend, who was Bobby
Lowe's wife. I was untimely ripped from Pineville when I was six.
People don't know when they make grown-up decisions that in the
back seat of a Chandler sedan may be a child learning too quickly
about the end of things. No one asked or imagined it, but Bobby
Lowe's last words to me were "Don't worry, Little Onion, you'll be
back in no time."

The town lay in a cup below Pine Mountain on the banks of the
Cumberland River. A county courthouse was the central and biggest
building. We lived in a cottage with a garden where the flowers had
names I like to say: cosmos, delphinium, marigold. Bobby Lowe
lived on Pine Mountain in a brown house with a whole mountain
where he worked his bird dogs. About once a month I ran away up
the hill, and I sat in the swing on his porch until he found me. He
taught me how to scratch a dog on its belly, to love silence, to carry a
gun broken over my elbow with the barrel toward the ground, the
scream of the panther, the whir of the grass.

Last year, for the first time, I went back. I drove through the
Cumberland Gap, past the sign that read "Pineville, Kentucky,
Population 2,600." There was the courthouse, but I was disoriented,
and then I saw the sign. On the corner across from the courthouse,
the Floko Drug Store. Two white-haired men sat having coffee.

One of the men got up to introduce himself. "I'm the druggist," he said, "Mason Cones. You're not Buster's little brother? Who are you?" he asked me. "I'm Mary Lee Settle. I used to live here." "Why, you're Joe Ed's little sister," the other man said. It had been sixty-four years. Later I drove my car to where our house had been. There was a concrete parking lot and a service station and then I went, six years old within, slowly along the street to the turn uphill to Bobby Lowe's house. It had been a quarter of a mile, a long way for a little girl. The swing was there, or another. It didn't matter. I sat there in a rented car. Bobby Lowe had been right. It was no time, sixty-four years later.

I went at last to say goodbye to Bobby Lowe, to the old cemetery that was on the next hillside below Pine Mountain. There was a narrow horseshoe of a road. I walked slowly uphill on the left-hand side. I looked for Bobby Lowe for nearly an hour under the green trees, through the uncut grass, from stone to stone, but he was not there. At the top of the horseshoe road, I turned to the right to go back downhill. A dog and a county beagle were playing among the graves. I spoke aloud, "Please, God. Help me find Bobby Lowe," a prayer that had echoed without my being conscious of it through all my years. The little beagle jumped up on my leg, wagging his tail. I petted him and walked on along the right-hand road. He followed me and jumped up again, then ran back to the left. I followed him. He kept checking back every ten feet or so to see that I was still there. At the end of a small footpath to the left, where I could just glimpse Bobby Lowe's house through the trees across the ravine, the dog stopped, turned to eleven o'clock from the path, and froze on point like a bird dog, and there, directly between his ears, I read the stone: "Robert Gibson Lowe." I was able, at last, to mourn and pray for both of us, and then I went back down the hill. The beagle stood against the sky with an immortelle, a plastic wreath, in his mouth. His other job at the graveyard seemed to be to move plastic wreaths from one grave to another, and that part of me which had been torn away was healed. And now I can accept where I am, who you are, what my life is today. I have been allowed at last to say goodbye.

Susan Sontag

I COULD TELL YOU about my bereft childhood with parents as remote as fairy-tale royalty living as far away as one could imagine. My father dying in China. My mother after her return to America – I was then six – continuing to be more absent than not. I could tell you about my precocious ardent relation to the written word, which had me reading books by the age of four – writers begin as bewitched readers – and beginning to write at age seven. At eight, one of my mother's suitors, in an unsuccessful attempt to win my vote, gave me a typewriter, and by nine I began to self-publish. I discovered in a magazine an account of a printing process called hectographing, so primitive even I could master it. My paper, which came out weekly or bi-weekly in some two dozen copies and ran to at least four purple-inked pages, consisted exclusively of my stories, poems, playlets, and bloodthirsty tirades against Hitler, Mussolini, and Tojo. I note that I began as a rather prolific writer and have been steadily devolving from that blessed state ever since. The childhood of a misfit, in large measure a voluntary misfit, in which other children seemed terrifying, school boring and depressive as well as terrifying, and being at home in bed with a book was not just the safest but the freest place to be. I had that familiar writer's childhood with all its bliss-ridden pathos. There was everything except the elementary schoolteacher or interesting older relative who befriended me, gave me books to read, encouraged my dreams of becoming a writer. I had no such mentor and I take pride in being a pioneer of my own self.

To speak thus, to evoke one's beginnings, implies of course that one has begun in obscurity, in provincial isolation, in anguish, in a delirious dream of emulation, that it is begun and one goes on. It is to be someone for whom beginnings are long past, to be recollected with rue, with complacency, with pride, with the distinctive fondness that one reserves for oneself. But I would rather speak of the fact that to be a writer, for me, is to be always at the beginning. I have never had what, it seems to me, most writers have – a sense of mastery. For unlike, say, the art of the surgeon, that of the writer does not, through years of practicing it, become less difficult. It doesn't get easier. Surprisingly, it gets harder. There are no uplands of accomplishment. The permission given to the self to be expressive steadily, unremittingly as a vocation, feels as if it could be withdrawn at any time. Each time feels like a new beginning, one that has to triumph over a lengthening set of obstacles and inhibiting forms of self-awareness and ambition.

I could hardly be more American. American not only in that I understand myself as self-created, American in that I respect nothing as much as self-transformation and that I feel myself perennially capable of a radical new beginning. Thus, my beginnings in the usual sense didn't interest me very much. What interests me is the beginning that I make quite unarmed, filled with anxiety and elation each day that I'm able to write, as if I were writing for the first time or, more precisely, as if I were at last writing something with which I am not too dissatisfied so that I can go on from this piece of writing to the next, to the real beginning.

Reynolds Price

I N A RECENT volume of memoirs, I spoke of the role of medical hypnosis in freeing my access to a horde of early memories that I thought were lost. Here I'd like to speak of another, more common means by which our crowded minds can ambush us unawares with a good or bad image from our buried past. The ambush, of course, is laid in dreams. A few years back, in a peaceful dream, I told myself a fictional story that nonetheless gave me a fact I'd forgot. In this case, a dream uncovered literally a useful, physical object from my child-hood, an object I'd long forgot. The fact that the object was never mine, but belonged to my younger brother, is maybe the strangest truth in the poem I made the next morning from the dream. I see it now as my mind's first try in middle age to set me at work digging my own past for good or bad, weal or woe. The poem is call "Found," for my brother:

> Here in my dream of Uncle Grant's shack,
> Grubbing for what in the packed fawn clay
> Alone no human or bird to watch,
> I find your old red square sand shovel.
> Neither of us can have seen it for thirty-odd years
> And surely it has either dissolved where you lost it
> Or survived reforging for an interim war
> Dissolute atoms in the plains of Korea
> The thicket southwood your Vietnam
> It had leached anyhow from my consciousness
> I had longed occasionally for toys of my own

The seven dwarves set of castille soap,
The pillbox of dried mud from Hitler's Mercedes
The boy-size Charlie McCarthy with hinged lips.
But hardly for yours; yours were weapons,
A footlocker armory of realistic guns, colts, lugers, Flash
    Gordons,
And you, Miles, gentler than the Dalai Lama
Despite your party renditions age four of "Don't Fence Me
    In" with cap pistol chorus piano by me.
Yet here my hands uncover this peaceful implement,
Realistic and real.
I stroke it, quick to recall, then reinter it,
Certain it will constitute treasure for you,
Another true self endured and found.
Awake tomorrow I'd bring you here
Actual site, the house long gone.
We'd crouch by the oak
My fingers hunt unerringly
You own it again.

Susan Richards Shreve

WARTIME IN WASHINGTON and my father brought home soldiers on their way to Europe. They drank bourbon in the kitchen, sailing stories back and forth, while I in the bedroom, expected to be sleeping, listened for the secrets whispered by my mother and aunt, who were putting on magenta lipstick, too cheerful for war. By night it was a carnival world, and I couldn't sleep for fear that if I closed my eyes, the clapboard house would tumble down.

We lived in a state of emergency. In the pale safety of daylight, I listened to soap operas on the console radio beside my bed, which was in the same bedroom as my mother and father's bed and my aunt's. Housing was scarce after Pearl Harbor. There was a shortage of heat.

During the day I had my mother to myself and after lunch, when I was supposed to take a nap, my mother would climb into bed with me, bringing a shoebox full of paper dolls with extensive wardrobes. She was a sweet and earnest woman, very fond of paper dolls. "Here," she'd say to me, handing me a yellow-haired woman dressed in a full slip, "this is your Helen Trent for today and I think she should be wearing fur, because it's January. And a cocktail dress." She handed me the bright red cocktail dress, half-length, and a fur. For herself, she chose a brown-haired Helen Trent with a bun, a long black dress and a cap. "Today she'll be going out with Ralph to a dance," she said. She took her own Ralph, who looked very like the Ralph she gave to me, an Arrow-shirt American with the permanent smile. "They have not yet fallen in love," she confessed, setting up her paper dolls side by side. She reached over to turn on the radio in the nick of time: "Can a woman find romance and happiness even after the age of thirty-five? The romance of Helen Trent."

This afternoon, as my mother had hoped, Helen Trent fell in love with Ralph, but not as passionately as Ralph fell in love with her. We did her story with paper dolls on my bed, and when it was over for the day, my mother turned off the radio, put away her own paper dolls and said to me, "Who do you want to be today? Ralph or Helen?" "Ralph," I said. And, secret conspirators, we played out the unwritten romance believing completely in the life of paper dolls.

FIRST LOVE

October 3, 1994

Pete Hamill

I THINK ADORATION PRECEDES love, and when I was a boy I started first with Captain America. It was really a guy named Steve Rogers who swallowed a secret formula that made him taller, stronger, and smarter – a kind of intellectual anabolic steroid – and went off to fight the Nazis and their ferocious agent, the Red Skull. Then there was Captain Marvel, really a crippled newsboy named Billy Batson who said the magic word "Shazam" and became taller, stronger, and dumber. His nemesis was Dr. Sivana, who called him the big red cheese, and convinced us that all scientists were both mad and funny. And then there was Bomba the Jungle Boy, who lived in a cave in the Amazon jungles with an old naturalist named Cody Casson. Bomba had lost his parents and Cody Casson had lost his mind. The Amazon was a little like Brooklyn.

These were my heroes, the people I admired as a boy during the war, but I can't say that what I felt for them was love. That came a few years later, when for the first time I got a marvelous newspaper strip named *Terry and the Pirates*. Written and drawn by Milton Canniff, it was a superb literary achievement, a kind of picaresque novel about the coming of age of a young man named Terry Lee who had somehow washed up on the shores of the South China Sea. The episodes were exciting, the characters finely drawn, the dialogue crackling and intelligent and adult. Nobody took magic pills or said magic words.

In *Terry and the Pirates* I first met the woman who inspired in me that mysterious, elusive, obsessive emotion we call love. Her name was the Dragon Lady. She was to my ten-year-old eyes amazingly beautiful, with an oval face, high Asian cheekbones, almond eyes, black glossy hair pulled back severely in a bun that somehow did not make her look like a schoolmarm. Sometimes she wore trousers, riding boots, men's shirts, military caps. Other times, indoors at night in darkened rooms, she appeared in deeply cut gowns, her shoulders as bare as John Singer Sargent's Madame X, and she made me feel funny, not Abbott and Costello funny, funny in a new, more mysterious way. But lust alone didn't explain my feelings about the Dragon Lady. She was also tough. Not hard, but tough in the way the best women in my neighborhood were tough. Those women lost husbands and sons in the war, but didn't resign in self-pity from the human race. They somehow learned to laugh again and went to work in war plants and hospitals and offices. They were not convinced of their own martyrdom.

The Dragon Lady was tough in other ways. She was kind of a bandit at first, and then during the war became a patriot, thus reversing the process I witnessed among some men in my neighborhood who lived off the black market. Whether fighting for herself or for her country, China, she was a leader, not a follower. She commanded battalions of men, giving orders, planning assaults on the enemy. She packed a gun. She depended upon no man, had no husband, no boyfriend. She had a thing going with a guy named Pat Ryan, but nothing much ever came of it. She acted as if marriage was a kind of surrender.

The Dragon Lady got in some terrible trouble, of course, but she never whined. If she couldn't fight her way out of a jam she thought her way out. Then she would vanish, her departures as mysterious as her arrivals. I didn't know all that when I first met her. That initial encounter was as usual a case of sheer physical attraction. After all, I lived in a neighborhood where girls were named Betty and Mary and Joan. They had freckles and red hair. They wore braces on their teeth. Not one of them looked remotely like the Dragon Lady. And because of that I began to obsess about her.

When I first came upon her, *Terry and the Pirates* had been in existence for ten years. I began to haunt the secondhand comic-book stores, searching out the old reprints, trying to get to the beginning of her story. Who was she really? What was her real name? I mean, she couldn't have been born and then her mother and father said, "Let's call her the Dragon Lady." When did she leave home? Why did she pick up a gun and become a bandit. She was a lady with a past, and like all jealous lovers, I needed to know about that past, at the risk of lacerating my heart.

I never got any answers. I patched together almost a full run of the strip, met some other Canniff women, and moved on. Canniff was too good a writer to provide his characters with résumés. The Dragon Lady was an existential hero. She was what she did. Action was character. I had to be content with my night visions: that face, that voluptuous body, that autonomous style.

At the end of 1946, Canniff walked away from *Terry* to do another comic strip. Around the same time, I started looking more closely at the girls with the freckles. They would never be the Dragon Lady, but they, you know, had their points. I entered my teens, and the toughest women I saw were the matrons in movie houses. There were guys in my neighborhood who weren't tough enough to be matrons. Matrons were almost all built like safes in white uniforms. They didn't have skin. They were covered with a kind of leather. On Saturday mornings they were charged with suppressing youthful savagery through terror. And on Saturday nights they roamed balconies like agents of the Inquisition, shining flashlights upon those hands under sweaters and unlocking belt buckles. The first great curse I ever heard was charged with tumescent desperation, cast as it was from the sweaty darkness of one of those balconies. It was a guy speaking for all of us. "The matron ain't got no mother!" he said. Neither, of course, did the Dragon Lady.

About ten years after the war, I was going to school in Mexico City on the G.I. Bill when I wandered into a movie house on a street named *San Juan de letran*. The movie was *Maria Caudelaria*, directed by the great Fernandez. It starred Pedro Almendariz and Delores del Rio. Two hours later I walked out convinced I'd been in the presence of the most beautiful woman in the world.

Ten years after that, working for a newspaper, I had lunch one day with Milton Canniff, who was a kind, intelligent man. By then the Dragon Lady had entered the language. Madame Nhu of Vietnam was called the Dragon Lady. The woman who owned my newspaper was called the Dragon Lady. Virtually every woman with any kind of authority anywhere was called the Dragon Lady. I asked Canniff how he had created her. He laughed and said, "Well, to tell the truth, I wanted to have a dame who looked like Delores del Rio. She was my first great love." And so the template is cut, the die is cast, the imagination is the supreme lover, from the Dragon Lady to Molly Bloom.

Rita Mae Brown

MOTHER DISAPPROVED OF him. Said he was lazy and "no 'count." When she'd really get mad at him she said if he was a mule she wouldn't feed him hay. But I watched him beguile her even as he beguiled me. Not even Mother, the only five-two linebacker I have ever met, could resist Mick's green eyes or his deep, throaty voice when he chose to talk. He wasn't talky though, which was a good thing because Mother liked being the center of attention. When my homework or chores dragged me down like fathoms of chain, I could hear her on the front porch taking a break from her relentless work ethic. Mickey visited with her while waiting for me to finish. People would pass by and Mother would bestow upon my boyfriend her assessment of their characters. Mrs. Mundes cruised by in a brand-new Cadillac and Mother whispered into his eager ear, "She's so good, poor thing." Then she'd laugh at her own opinion. Mrs. Mundes was holier than thou. But I suspected as I doodled on my school tablet that Mother was jealous because of the new Cadillac. If Mickey thought that he never said a word.

Mrs. Mundes dug a pool that summer to which all of Coffee Hollow was invited at the opening party. Mickey and I left in disgrace because when all the adults were yakking away I threw Baby Ruths in the pool. Actually we didn't leave in disgrace. We ran like scalded dogs. Because Mother was hot on our tails and she was fast. To make matters worse, Mrs. Mundes appeared at our porch the next day and Mother hauled me out for an apology. Mick of course was nowhere to be found. So I listened to how my generation was contributing to the moral and spiritual decline of America. Mrs.

Mundes's generation knitted socks for the doughboys in World War I, thereby proving for all time to come that they sacrificed for the war effort, whereas I threw Baby Ruths in the swimming pool. Swathed in purple as she delivered this tirade, I could hardly wait for her to leave. Mickey peeped around the porch and then disappeared. I could've killed him. As Mrs. Mundes waddled off, Mother whispered, "Looks like an eggplant, the old windbag!" And then, as if I'd grasped the full import, she commented on Mrs. Mundes's marriage, a union for which her husband lacked enthusiasm.

"Mislaid his love like he mislaid his keys."

"I'll always love Mickey," I eagerly piped up.

"Hah!"

"I will!"

"You're too young to know about love."

"I am not!"

She drew deeply on her Chesterfield, which was stapled to her lip. "Honey, let me give you a piece of motherly advice. If it's got testicles or tires it's gonna be trouble."

I pondered this, and then replied, "Mickey doesn't have testicles!" She laughed, and Mickey jumped back on the porch. He'd been underneath all along waiting for the Gorgon to leave. "Come here, you lazy good-for-nothing cat!" He traipsed over to her and she scratched his ears. Then he leapt onto my lap and purred like Mrs. Mundes's Cadillac on full accelerator. He did love me truly and totally. Later, Mickey as my sidekick, I rubbed poison ivy on Mrs. Mundes's steering wheel. People didn't lock their houses or cars then and I didn't get caught for that one.

Many years have passed since that summer day. But Mother was wrong to say I didn't know about love. I did. And I still love Mickey and pay honor to his memory, for I'm never without a big tiger cat.

After what Mother told me about testicles and tires I have had ample occasion to discover she was right about that!

Christopher Buckley

I WAS GOING TO tell you a warm and fuzzy story about a cocker spaniel, but our hosts took us over to the Supreme Court earlier today and the sight of all that marble and all that probity convinced me that I cannot stand up here and lie to you. My first love was a gun. A Browning .22 semi-automatic rifle. I know. I know. I'm not wild about standing up here in a Shakespearean Theater and telling you about all this. I'd much rather be talking about abdominal pain, which I learned at last night's PEN/Faulkner party is going to be the topic of next year's gala. So buy your tickets soon.

Let me point out that this was not an assault weapon. This was the sort of rifle that hundreds of thousands of red-blooded American boys cut their teeth on without growing up to be disgruntled postal workers. I don't know why they're so disgruntled. We're the ones whose mail is always late. Anyway, from the moment I first saw it in the catalog of sports, it was love at first sight. Before you lead to disturbing conclusions of a psychological nature, bear in mind that I was ten years old, not yet mature enough to appreciate more nourishing pursuits such as bra snaps, cigarettes, and grain alcohol with Kool-Aid. I begged and begged my father. He made me demonstrate safety consciousness with my Daisy BB gun for two years before finally he relented one birthday. I remembered great excitement when I saw on the box of cartridges that their range was one and a half miles. I vividly recall too the look on my father's face when I asked him how high the planes were that flew over the house on their way to land at LaGuardia Airport.

What a beautiful piece of work it was. It had been designed by the

legendary American prometheus John Moses Browning in 1910. I
was extremely disappointed to learn that it had not been designed for
the purpose of shooting Germans. This was the post-World War II
era. All our fathers had been in the war, which we knew from
watching *Hogan's Heroes* had been no piece of cake. Actually, this rifle
had been designed for "plinking" – a weeny sort of word to describe
shooting at inanimate objects like your sister's Barbie dolls, stop signs
and vigorously shaken cans of Coca Cola. Life used to be so much
simpler.

"What do you want to do today?"

"Let's shake up cans of Coca Cola and shoot them."

"Yeah, cool."

Browning's .22 never made it to war. It went instead to the
shooting galleries in the amusement parks. How many billions of
billions, as Carl Sagan would say, of steel ducks and rabbits went
down in front of its sights with a loud *blang! blang!* How many
millions and millions of women turned to their dates and said,
"Maybe you need glasses." I remember taking it out of the wrapping
and holding it for the first time, amazed at how sleek it was, how
beautifully engineered. It came as no surprise to me when a few years
later America landed men on the moon. But really! Four pounds,
four ounces. Thirty-seven inches long. I knew Freud was going to
enter in here somewhere. Blond French walnut stock. Eleven
rounds. Tabular magazine. Blow-back recoil. Actuated auto-loading.
And something called "take down," meaning that it came apart into
two pieces – something keenly appreciated by a twelve-year-old
who'd just seen *From Russia With Love*. And it had this unique
feature, bottom ejection, meaning that the hot brass casings ended up
in a shiny pile at your feet instead of bouncing painfully off the teeth
of the person standing next to you. It was really something.

Now maybe this is a guy thing. By and large, women tend not to
get warm and fuzzy over a piece of blued steel. I have known women
who were beautiful shots; like my wife, who was trained by the U.S.
government. One day there was a great big fat hairy rat in our
backyard. She took the air pistol, got down in a combat stance, just

like Don Johnson in *Miami Vice*, and she blew that sucker away. What is it exactly, I asked, that you do for a living. I never asked her what her first love was. I'm not sure I'd want to know. Plastic explosives, probably. So maybe it's not a guy thing. But I'm so glad to have had this chance to share this with you. I feel so much better. Probably shouldn't have even brought up the business about its being thirty-seven inches long.

Allan Gurganus

I was eight. I guess I sort of got molested, and I liked it. First love Cynthia Thorpe was twenty-two, taught third grade, wore wing glasses, spoke exquisite singsong, chain-smoked Kents, kept roses on her desk, sighed a lot. Probably a little trust fund somewhere. She had a slight limp only her lovers would notice. She'd just finished Randolph-Macon. She'd aced Creative Child 101: Problem or Promise? In the principal's dark vault she peeked at our IQs, she tasted mine like your very first garden's first snow pea ever. The sweetness is paradise. The crunch is your own body. In I walked: fifty-seven pounds of the desire to please, a constellation of freckles, one flannel shirt so new it blistered my neck. "You must be Allan." The eight-year wait for her had seemed eternity. Love is born with all its little fingers and toes, the fuzzy loverly side effects we know from songs, the roaring, cliff-edge-sick feelings that pushed me over facedown into whole Antarcticas of melting. The sight of what she wore each day would fill me with a sadness that was most of what there is of adult hope, our chances of making it as a couple really just a few points down from anybody's ever. True, her body weight was nearly three times mine. True, she was married and I had no pubic hair. But look, what relationship is ever perfect? By October we team taught. I worked in no workbook. I painted immense murals. I was busy being as multitalented as a trained seal on Ed Sullivan.

At Piggly Wiggly I saw my loved one, in the cart spaghetti and a huge blue box of Kotex. I dashed outside. Not her! Not her too! She kept me after school. Her red nails bolted our classroom door, lowered torn green shades, scooped me safe into her gorgeous lap. She brushed back my thick bangs – yes, bangs. Chaste kisses left wet check marks. She rocked me, singing "Row, row, row . . . life is but . . ." Sometimes I sobbed from pleasure. Then she cried. She asked if I'd pretend to be a blind boy and refasten her garter belt; her thigh – the ice tray my fingers stuck to.

"Allan dear, what if you could do anything on earth for people? What would you do, Allan?"

"They're so hungry, so many of them. But after feeding them, I guess I'd have to say that people can be hungry, Miss Thorpe, in the imaginations too." (And batted my eyes.) And oh, but she sighed so! Come spring I begged, "Flunk me! I need you to be my first flunk. If not for me then do it for our science corner." Instead, she sent me to a man teacher. He was hairy as a pig. He was mean. I caught her in the hall. I cried all night. At least she kept my murals up. And my new class looked downright web-toed with retardation. The point is, an eight-year-old can be as in love as poor Othello. If love comes, it comes complete, demeaningly addictive as oxygen is.

Last year, home to see my folks, dinner at the country club, I noticed a fat lady of seventy limping back to the dessert bar. Mrs. Thorpe hadn't seen me since I was nine. I slid over before her. She smiled. I saw it register. She put down her little white plate, and simply said, "You?" I nodded. "I hope," she said, "back then I didn't exploit you as they call it now. My first year in this snobbish town, I had a little mini-breakdown I think now. There was a miscarriage, Allan, I was lucky, really. I just hope I didn't . . ." Instead of being cool I blurted like some kid, "Oh, boy. But I loved you so much!" She placed one hand to her mouth, shook her head yes, gimped back to her family, the three fat lawyer sons.

Seeing her didn't make me feel so old. That's just it. I felt so young. Ever ask yourself why we keep doing this to ourselves? For forty years since her, to rerisk such addicting pain. Maybe love's too good to be good at. Maybe with love it's always the third grade. We're all forever getting molested and yet we stand here, don't we. Why? Because, basically, at least they notice us. We like it. Why? I guess, since Mrs. Thorpe, I loved so many and so well, and this recklessly for one, the only reason: because I could. Amen.

Thomas Caplan

T HIS IS A short poem with a very long title, which is:

"After the Profane and Sacred Diversions of
Public School and Grousmore, Ex-Lad Succumbs
for the First Time to Love in London"

Caring for Claire as Robert found out
Was rather a serious matter
For other men fancied her too.
After lunch in St. James
And a nip to his hatter
He passed a long hour in the barber's chair
Breathing lilac water and sizing up the competition.
He was a sporting man, he had ambition.
But his odds, he regretted, were long.
There was John who was younger and James who was older
George who was taller and Charles who was bolder
Whose hands seemed especially strong.
There were lean man with titles, Etonian voices.
Square ones with rather too-modern Rolls Royces.
There were even men who had not met her yet,
Athletes or merchant bankers from at least three generations
Who had either entered a room too late or left one too early,
Spent their lives in the wrong rooms or perhaps a different city,
But whose fantasies he knew would one day collide
With the reality of caring for Claire.

When the shampoo was lathered he had a word with the
   Barber
On the subject of hair.
The Earl of Nothing Much had more, she said, but his was
   better;
The Duke of No Place, less and he seemed wetter.
They, too, he feared, would one day care
For the girl a golden light illuminated.

He had detected in the behavior of many elderly men
Towards certain elderly women –
Lunching friends of his grandmother's
Ladies whose hair had been purpled –
Both the memory and continued perception of beauty
That had known its apogee in the thirties or twenties
Before the Great War in one or two cases.
Could it be that such emotions,
As distinct from those he'd felt for pin-ups,
Were not simply for the time being?
The men he'd watched had run their lives in races
And who had won and who had lost and who had taken
   places
Even a boy could read clearly and at once.
Their eyes showed triumph or regret
Their sudden glances down a knowledge of their best friends'
   deaths.
And, more than ever in this distant place of dying,
Young Robert came to see the point of trying –
Not *too* eagerly, but a little harder always than the rest.

Claire, for her part owned a greater problem.
Her decision from among so many choices,
Presented as large an opportunity for failure.
She wanted kindness, beauty, brilliance at their best –
But having a few years ahead of her,

Sought to let fate take its natural course.

Looking from the inside out,
She had no idea why Sidney, the head barman at Annabel's,
Thought, when he saw her, of Greta Garbo . . .
Of Muriel what-was-her-name –
The nymph they had all known, in Brighton,
In summer, in the early days.
Thinking from the inside out,
From the wrong pole,
She was not herself impelled
By her compelling force,
Which of course she had heard of
From an orchestra of poets from The House
And was, if truth be told, a little bored by.

She had, a while ago, ceased spending weekends close by
   Oxford
And taken to keeping a diary
In which she recorded the details
Of holidays passed, the Villa Contrito,
Of adventures with Francois or Johnny or Dieter –
Of a sand trek on horseback across the Sahara,
Although the last had occurred but briefly, and in a dream
She told the pretty marbled book
How men mistook her by her look,
How all the most exciting ones
Preferred to call her by her cover.
How pleasant Bob, though far from perfect,
Had tried at least to see inside.
Her hand revolted from her mind;
Her heart had never mastered penmanship
Wish me a man, she wrote, so kind –
And a true friend first, to be my lover.

Reginald McKnight

M Y FIRST LOVE was named Nancy Claire Anderson. She was four and I was four. Her parents and mine were stationed at Mather Air Force Base near Sacramento, California, in the late fifties and early sixties. I haven't seen or heard from Nancy or any of the Andersons since the autumn of 1961, the year she and her family moved from Mather to someplace else, I have no idea where. I don't remember what she looked like – I mean, her facial features. I do remember that she was a little shorter than I, a little darker-skinned, and had knees – it was sort of a dead heat between who had the knottiest knees – I'm not really sure. We played house in a variety of ways: Ricky and Lucy, Tarzan and Jane, her parents, my parents, Porgy and Bess. I drove, she cooked, we both went to work.

Nancy was a good deal more assertive than I and we almost always played by her rules. If Nancy said we were going to dance on *American Bandstand*, we danced on *American Bandstand*. If Nancy said I was a lion tamer, there I was in jodhpurs and a pith helmet. "Oh my God! A crocodile!" Jane would cry, and Tarzan would grab knife, go kill. If Nancy didn't get her way, she would pout. Nancy Claire Anderson wrote the book on pouting. She'd sit in something large and soft, a sofa, fold her arms and bounce steady as a pulse against the cushions. The girl wouldn't talk. The girl would not talk. I would have been less surprised to see Buffalo Bill and Howdy Doody do a musical tribute to Little Richard than hear Nancy reply to anyone who asked her what was bothering her when she was bouncing. Not a soul, not a word, with but one exception. Nancy would talk to me. She'd talk to me even when it was I who'd set her to bouncing. And sometimes I'd sit and bounce with her, but that always made her laugh, and her laughter would recoil, making her a thousand times more angry than she was to begin with, so I usually just sat next to her. I'd ask her what was bugging her and she'd say something like "Don't-want-cherry-jelly, Don't-want-cherry-jelly" or some such thing, and I'd sit there, usually hold her hand and make no reply. I'd listen to her thumping to the beat of windshield wipers and watch her till the rhythm slowed.

Soon enough Nancy would stop bouncing. We'd watch TV or play outside or eat peanut butter and cherry jelly sandwiches. Back then I didn't have a word for the way I felt about Nancy's letting me in and keeping everybody else out, but I later discovered that the word was close to something like reverence. I'm still not sure. It was a buoyancy in my stomach, a lambency in the chest. It made me blush. It tasted better than butterscotch. I thought of Nancy and the way I felt about her when my last love told me that my problem is that I'm a fixer – a person who gives reams of unasked-for advice and philosophy to anyone who even mentions a problem to him. "I don't want a remedy," she said. "I don't want you to tell me a story or quote something from the Dalai Lama. I just want you to sit and listen. Can't you just do that? Is it that hard?" Really, I don't know what's happened to me between Nancy and now. You'd think I would have learned from Nancy that reverence is a kind of wariness that allows us to behold those we love, merely behold them as they move to the rhythm of their own music.

John Casey

MY MOST RECENT experience with first love is not my own. I feel it through the first independences of my four children. Maude, first-born, at two shared my life, my boiled egg, and my bath. Maude, in bath: "What's that noise?" I: "That's the water pump." Maude: "Sing the water-pump song." We had songs for almost everything, but the water-pump request was out of the blue, out of Maude's blue-eyed certainty that I made this stuff up right then. She inspired me and I sang, "Water pump, you pump the water that fills the tub in which our Maude goes rub-a-dub until she pulls the fatal plug and the water goes glug-glug." Never composed faster, never better, really. But at eight my muse left me for a rock star and at fifteen for a lacrosse player. ("He has really big muscles, Dad! Bigger than yours!")

Second-born Nell had a tumult of early love, and I, early rebuff. When I was out of favor she allowed me to tell bedtime stories only if I sank out of sight and talked through one finger: "Once upon a time . . ." When she began to read I offered books. She said, "Oh no, here comes Dad with another book he loved when he was my age." I lost her to Judy Blume among others.

Third-born Claire came home and announced at the age of five that she was going to marry Benji. "I love Benji," she said. "Benji is really, really smart. Benji knows Hebrew." "Well," I said, "He's the rabbi's son." "Benji knows Hebrew, and . . . and . . . and . . . Benji knows Gaelic." That was love.

Fourth-born Julia, now four years old, still runs across the lawn full-tilt to be picked up, every sinew stretched out from her heart, and it makes me wonder, was I ever this all-out?

1942. The young men were at war. My father was in a Senate race, a tight race because some Massachusetts Irish were turning on one of their own for having voted for Lend-Lease for perfidious Albion. Someone in fact snarled at him, "Are you running for Congress, Mr. Casey, or are you standing for Parliament?" But our house is comfortable for the only boy. First sister Jane; Nurse Rita Quinn, whom I adored; and Struensi, a German cook devoted to my parents and grateful to have a job in 1942. She baked them a three-layer anniversary cake. At dawn I spied it on the pantry shelf, pulled out the drawers for steps, made my ascent, was feeding with both hands, when in came Struensi. She cried out, "Ach! You poor boy, you must want some milk!" I thought all life was going to be like that. Could there be anything better?

And yes, there was, because next door there was an apple orchard. The apple orchard belonged to a small convent, and every afternoon the young nuns came out to climb the apple trees, and every afternoon they called to me to come, and they scooped me up in their arms in the soft folds of their habits, pressing my cheek half against the hard white wimple, half against their own soft cheeks. They took me up into the trees afternoon after afternoon until the mother superior put a stop to it. The mother superior told me to go away, to stay away, to be a good boy. I still wonder if I was a distraction to the discipline of the flesh, which they were trying to maintain, because I was a child, or a little, little man.

After an evening like that there are two choices. I could try to be a good boy, or I could be a bad boy. Neither of which turned out to be near as good as playing with the nuns in the apple trees.

Elena Castedo

T HE WOMEN IN my family never thought it beneath them to see men as sexual objects. Wrapped in patriotism and romance, my mother had endless stories about pinups from Spanish history: well-built Romans; curly-haired philosophers; muscular knights of the Visigothic kingdom of Toledo; passionate minstrel singers of the Moorish reconquest; errant *caballeros* with swift arms and good legs; agile guerrillas from the hills; and droopy-eyed nineteenth-century poets. As tradition also dictated, on Sunday afternoons, friends of my parents came to visit with their sons in tow, ostensible targets for puppy love, and respectable matrimony later.

All this to no avail. My romantic life was launched due to the arrival in Chile of some alien and exotic elements. One came in a mobile book. The pages of the square little book, when flipped very, very fast, brought to life a hero with the intrepid name of Poapeiyeh. Twenty years later I learned his name was pronounced Popeye. Poapeiyeh smoked a professorial pipe, was strong due to a proper diet, and like any correct *caballero*, spent his time saving a damsel in distress. His damsel in perpetual distress had a Spanish hairdo and was skinny and hysterical, like all the women in my family. I didn't know what Poapeiyeh said because I couldn't read yet, and when I asked I was told he spoke in a foreign language called English. Fortunately, my mother didn't know that Seneca, Philip the Beautiful and El Cid had been wiped out by Popeye the sailor man.

Another hero came on Sunday mornings, when my father carried a rush-set chair to the garden and settled with a cup of *café con leche* and the paper. He handed me the comics, and thusly I met another object of my obscure desire: the Phantom. When it came to sexy, with that cute striped bikini, no chronicle, minstrel poem, or boy with hairless legs could compete with the Phantom. Older girls who played in our neighborhood square discussed whether, at the appropriate moment, the Phantom removed only the bikini or also the leotard. Careful inspection revealed no zippers in either one, but it underscored the fact that everything about the Phantom was magic.

And of course, in the twentieth century, when a woman thinks of first love, she must round up the usual suspects: movie stars. Nothing was as thrilling as the bright blue eyes set in peanut-butter faces of the gringo movie stars. No boy's crackling voice could match their vibrant bassos. No ordinary name like Juan or Manuel could compete with a name as euphonic as Tony Curtis. Sadly, our hearts were thrown into confusion when a teacher said the movie stars did not speak Spanish; their idiosyncratic, mellifluous bassos were the dubbed voice of a paunchy Colombian grandfather. Moreover, a girl in school who claimed to speak English insisted that we mispronounced the stars' titillating names. She said the euphonic Tonee Coortees was pronounced a slithery Tony Curtis; the bold Haamess Estiwirt was a pasty James Stewart; the virile Estiwirt Graanhair was a weary Stewart Grainger; the assertive Daana Andreoos was a sissy Dana Andrews; and that "queen" as in Anthony Quinn meant the king's wife. That did it – how could a mucho macho actor be called a queen?

And so, all the warm, tender and fickle parts that form my first love came from that powerful country occupying the torso of North America, up there, with that phallus called Florida pointing down toward South America. That is, all my first loves came . . . from you. Thanks for the memories.

Rita Dove

I T LOOKS LIKE they've let a poet slip into their midst – so I've decided to stay true to nature and read three poems – three very different takes on first love.

Every intense love feels like the very first, and the rituals of love are as important as the object of one's affections. This first poem is about the time-honored courtship ritual of the high-school prom:

"Planning the Perfect Evening"

I keep him waiting, tuck in the curtains,
buff my nails (such small pink eggshells).
As if for the last time, I descend the stair.

He stands penguin-stiff in a room
that's so quiet we forget it is there.
Now nothing, not even breath, can come

between us, not even the aroma of punch
and sneakers as we dance the length
of the gymnasium and crepe paper streams

down like cartoon lightning. Ah,
Augustus, where did you learn to samba?
And what is that lump below your cummerbund?

Stardust. The band folds up
resolutely, with plum-dark faces.
The night still chirps. Sixteen cars

caravan to Georgia for a terrace,
beer and tacos. Even this far south
a thin blue ice shackles the moon,

and I'm happy my glass sizzles with stars.
How far away the world! And how hulking
you are, my dear, my sweet black bear!

Movie stars are often the targets of our first love. For me, though,
before movies came fairy tales:

"Beauty and the Beast"

Darling, the plates have been cleared away
the servants are in their quarters.
What lies will we lie down with tonight?
The rabbit pounding in your heart, my

child legs, pale from a life of petticoats?
My father would not have had it otherwise
when he trudged the road home with our souvenirs.
You are so handsome it eats my heart away . . .

Beast, when you lay stupid with grief
at my feet, I was too young to see anything
die. Outside, the roses are folding
lip upon red lip. I miss my sisters –

they are standing before their clouded mirrors.
Gray animals are circling under the window.
Sisters, don't you see what will snatch you up –
the expected, the handsome, the one who needs us?

The frisson of first love can happen in the least expected moments –
long after one has been wooed, long after one has married. In this
final poem, a mother is breast feeding her child:

"Pastoral"

Like an otter, but warm,
she latched onto the shadowy tip
and I watched, diminished
by those amazing gulps. Finished
she let her head loll, eyes
unfocused and large: milk-drunk.

I liked afterwards best, lying
outside on a quilt, her new skin
spread out like meringue. I felt then
what a young man must feel
with his first love asleep on his breast:
desire, and the freedom to imagine it.

Alice Hoffman

FALLING IN LOVE for the first time is always dangerous, but when you're foolish enough to fall in love with a fictional character you can pretty much be assured it's going to be unrequited. Also, you're not going to be the first or the last, for that matter, to have been involved with this fictional character. He's got a string of women, some of whom have been involved with him for years, rereading him again and again. And in the long run he belongs to his author, heart and soul.

Tonight, I speak for anyone who has ever fallen in love with Heathcliff and survived. Heathcliff is not only the most romantic man in literature, he's the most dysfunctional. There are a lot of men who wouldn't be half as attractive if not for Heathcliff's literary precedent. Some men are interesting only to women who have read *Wuthering Heights*. Everyone else considers them sociopaths. So, tonight I just wanted to give a short list of men who ought to be most grateful to Heathcliff, and I think you know who you are:

Men who disappear for three years, then come back and expect to find you've waited for them.

Men who wear only black.

Men who marry your sister-in-law and still expect to date you.

Men who are more interested in their own pain than they are in you.

Men who'd prefer your tortured spirit to wander for twenty years, because if they can't have you, no one will.

One rainy summer when I was twelve, I did fall in love with Heathcliff and I have never recovered. For a young girl, *Wuthering*

Heights is an extremely radical text. It allows her to see herself in the role of a rescuer. It's the fairy tale reversed: the man who will destroy himself without her help, the man who is trapped in a tower of grief or drink or self-hate. The older the reader, the more *Wuthering Heights* has to offer. It's the most psychologically complex novel ever written about what women and men want. It offers no easy answers and it gives us a world of conflicting desires where heaven and hell can be the very same place, depending on who you are and what you want.

In my opinion, *Wuthering Heights* is the Book of Love, but it's also a brilliant cautionary tale. What happens to any woman who falls in love with Heathcliff is right there on the page. She dies of love. She's turned into a ghost. And yet Heathcliff continues to make readers fall in love with him. We're in love with him because of how deeply and how truly we know him. When we fall in love with him, we are falling in love with everything on the page: with the power of fiction, with the idea that a man like Heathcliff can be created by a gorgeous combination of passion and prose. If all people were fashioned by Heathcliff's author, if all were imbued with her consciousness, we would know them as deeply and love them as well. During that summer long ago, when the sky was gray each afternoon, and I cold not stop reading, when the words "Nellie, I am Heathcliff" seemed to stop time itself, I fell in love with Emily Brontë and have never recovered, and quite frankly, I never want to.

Mona Simpson

ONE NIGHT I was working on this piece and I took a walk and ran into an old boyfriend who asked me what I was doing, and I told him and he said, "Who was your first love?" And I realized, in that moment I guess, I wasn't his. So I told him the truth, which was that I was trying to write a very short fictional piece about first love and in fact this is in the voice of a young man.

I'd been in love a hundred times by the time I was twenty-five, all unrequited. What did it matter? Unrequited love lasted only slightly longer than its opposite. But I needed someone to think about in order to fall asleep at night, and so I could work as hard as I did. I promised myself if I practiced my painting long enough, work would win me love. So far work hadn't done that. It had won me a prize up at school though. I'd painted a portrait of my first wheelchair, which was thrown away long ago when I was a boy. I learned how to love by loving a thing, I wrote at the bottom in red. I was in love with Louise, but that was no problem yet. We were roommates. She kept a picture of her mailman father, the sole of one shoe three inches higher.

That night I dressed in a new jacket and the good pants. Thank God for the goddamn Gap. One thing about a wheelchair: shoes stay polished. They don't wear out. I celebrated my prize with a cappuccino before the ceremony and drank it outside on the steps. Then a woman in a suit passed fast, thighs flashing, and dropped a quarter in my cup. I was so startled I threw it at her, coffee arching through her legs, staining probably. "You little monkey!" she said. Pretty women can sometimes just change a $2.50 cappuccino.

I went into the student thing after, even though I hated this kind of party, where everyone was standing. I shoved a window open, leveraged myself up out of the chair, and sat on the ledge, the flurry of snowflakes lighting on my sweater and my hair. "I don't know if you remember me but . . ." It was Celeste, with the triangular legs. "I saw you won." She knew about the prize. I lifted the bottle to my mouth and threw my head back. I wanted her to see me out of my chair against the snow like this. I offered her the bottle and heard myself laughing for no reason. She backed away, dancing a little, hopping on one foot.

When the bottle was empty I rolled to the back bedroom, where coats were piled on a bed. My head was revolving not in a circle but in an oval. Back again every cycle passed one bad place. Then Celeste banged the door, collapsed on the bed, saying "I'm pretty wasted." She was wearing tights with a picture woven into them. She pushed her soft boots off with the fork of her striped toes.

"I remember that once you were giving me advice about moving here, and I like New York now."

"And New York likes you," she said.

I was lying on a coat and the button hurt me. My head was still revolving and I kept meaning to twist and move the coat, and then it was happening, what I'd wanted and thought about countless times, and now too soon.

"My ex-boyfriend's here. I thought it would be all right, but he's making out with somebody in the middle of the room." She kissed me and it was not what I'd imagined, but rougher. Her tongue sandpaper, like a cat's, and I worried about not knowing how. I tried to do what she did back. She was unbuttoning me, murmuring, and her hand moved on my buckle. I turned and looked outside for a moment at the stone ornaments on top of a building, the strange pure shapes of water towers. Her tights bunched at her ankles, an accordion mural, and I wanted to wait. It was going too fast, but my body flew ahead, complying without me. It was too soon and too late to master myself. Suddenly a flash of light from the door. "Oh, just my coat," the girl said. A tug, fabric scraped on my back, and then we were alone again. Celeste arched her head so I could see her neck. Beautiful. A noise left out of my chest, a long pulled rickety chain.

We were still on top of the coats. A piece of her hair was in my mouth. She sat on the edge of the bed and lifted her legs up one at a time, toes pointing, to pull up her tights again. I said, "Wait." "Shhh," she said. Then she kissed my forehead and after that she left; I felt a weight there, like a coin.

What I'd wanted to say was that she had to help me down. Now I'd have to slide, or wait for the next person. The years of my captivation I was stopped a thousand places. I waited in hallways, I waited in rooms, people said, "Just wait there, I'll be back." I became stationary. There was once, early before boundaries, when I was left out on a blanket in the sun; grass pricked through the thin wool and the buzz of the low world was balm on my skin. But I had not lived that way. I was an early crawler. Tonight I slid down using the bedspread, tossed my clothes to the chair first. But I sometimes still heard that alternate music: wheel marks on a white wall, people in attics staring out one window, beginning to love the dependence. I thought of the world outside, never Christmas, hospitals dotting the city always open and every night the same; Louise at home, probably fierce in a fit of sweeping, mad because she'd not come and now the party was over.

Years from now, Celeste will hear my name and I would hear hers, I thought. We would be part of a secret network of kindness, watching for each other's interests in silent ways. She knew, wild as I'd been on the windowsill with the bottle, that I was losing my virginity to her there on top of the coats. She had been like that, as if she were unwrapping a package.

Me and Louise that night in our beds, I always slept with my chair so I could touch it.

"Hey, what would you want if you could want one thing?" she asked.

"For years, all I've wanted was to walk. Now if I could have one thing, it wouldn't be that anymore."

"What would it be?"

"Same as you. I want to be an artist."

But that was a lie, too. An old truth that stopped being true only a few hours ago. Celeste's brisk act of curiosity and charity, proof of wildness and the variety of life to herself, had brought back a late train of a thousand memories. I loved to be touched. All I wanted now was Louise, and love.

Kaye Gibbons

I THINK I WOULD need an eternity to tell you about my first love the way he deserves to be talked about. I married him a year ago last Saturday and we have five children aged five to twelve, five dogs, two cats, three gerbils, and a land crab. My first love tells me I'm a good mom, even when I'm off somewhere like this having a swell time and feeling guilty. My first love makes me floss my teeth. My first love showed me Cavafy's poetry and he took my side in a protracted fight with a tailor about the exact size of my hips. He asked me out for a date every Friday night. He brings me coffee in the mornings and sets the table for breakfast the night before. He introduced me to malt whiskey. He is no doubt the only man in America to have ever filled Eudora Welty's ice trays. Each Sunday morning he reads aloud to me the summary of the week's episodes of *The Young and the Restless*. And each weekday he reads my hometown obituary column to me to see if there is anybody I might know or have known. He tells me stories that I've put into my books and he can make grilled cheese sandwiches, egg sandwiches, and Bloody Marys. He never lets me open a car, restaurant, or house door, and when we walk down the sidewalk he walks along the outside. He gave me the Mixmaster of my dreams for my birthday but this is not to say he keeps me battened down.

Speaking of Miss Welty, when once asked if living in the South necessarily made her a Southern writer she replied, "Listen, if your cat has her kittens in the oven, does that make them muffins?" Think about it. I believe she meant, does the South have the power to turn an outsider into one of its own? I happen to think not. But when I think about her answer I think also about the power of transformation, from kittens to muffins in her case and from girl to woman in mine. Even by thirty-two I was still a girl. My first love, through his power of transformation, saw me through the metamorphosis from little girl to woman. He gave me the confidence to come talk with you. A girl could not have done it. But he still approves when I fan about the house in *Far Side* T-shirts. He says nothing when I throw my clothes on the floor as if I still lived in a dormitory. He let me bring back five dogs from the pound and didn't make me take any back when we found out that one was pregnant and thus we had nine. I still have a puppy to get rid of.

When I think of him, I think of a catalog or collection of attributes all disparate yet bound by humor and the plain truth that we just like each other. I met him when he used to introduce me at Friends of the North Carolina State University Library meetings back home. I liked what he said, so I married him. He still introduces me, and I will keep marrying him again and again and again, every day and especially every night.

William Kittredge

I COME TO YOU from what I think of as another country, Montana, and I'm going to tell you a little cautionary tale. The far West where I grew up is gorgeous but sparsely populated and first love came to me very late in life.

Long ago, when I was a sophomore at Oregon State majoring in Agriculture, and drifting through classes in Agronomy and Soil Science which seemed to bear on nothing I cared about, close to flunking out of college, it came to me one winter night as I tried to fathom the intricacies of intermediate Algebra that I was, in a probably incurable way, quite useless. The young women we knew, boys like me, seemed to inhabit another county, for they laughed together and lived by rules which were incomprehensible to us. We thronged together in jock fraternities and ran with others of our kind in loud, boyish packs. We shouted and yearned for unlikely athletic careers. There were great walls of boisterousness between us. For weeks after recognizing my uselessness, I lived in intimacy with no one but my new companion, my ceaseless regret that I was, irrevocably, it seemed, what I was. Then it snowed, a great rare thing in the lowlands, snowflakes falling in the grey feathery light. By nightfall we were snowballing, chasing fate and here it came. We were ambushed from behind a wall of snowy lilac by a horde of hilarious women. How could this be, a thing so delicious, such attention happening to me? Then the snowball that broke my glasses and cut my nose brought her to me. She was dark-eyed and strong and utterly what I understood as gorgeous. "Lord!" she said, "Look at you." She folded my broken glasses into her pocket and took my hand. "Come on," she said. Her name, she said when I didn't ask, was Janet. "What's yours?" she asked. And then, as she studied me, waiting for an answer, I began to understand that despite all my incapacities, another life was possible.

Deep in that same night, Janet gone far away, back in the fraternity upstairs on the cold sleeping porch, my friend and I were awakened by news of a terrible accident. Two men I admired, captains of the football team, one a former roommate of mine, had been riding sleds towed along the icy streets at reckless speeds behind an automobile. They had, at an intersection, swung into the path of an oncoming pickup truck and been killed. Curled tight under my old Hudson Bay blanket (a gift from my father), shaking, I understood that I didn't know how to grieve for anyone but myself and I thought "She'll forgive me when I tell her."

Decades later, when our children were grown and we lived a far distance from one another, as we still do, I finally realized that probably the last thing that Janet was looking for that night in the snow was someone to forgive.

Lee Smith

T HE HOUSE I grew up in was one of a row of houses strung along a narrow river bottom like a string of beads, just up from the little coal town of Grundy in southwest Virginia. The river was named the Leviathan. We were not allowed to play in it because they washed coal upriver so its water ran deep and black between the mountains which rose like walls on either side of us, rocky and thick with trees.

My mother came from the flat, exotic eastern shore of Virginia and swore that these mountains gave her migraine headaches. Mama was always lying down on the sofa, all dressed up. She had chosen my father over the well-bred Arthur Bangs from Richmond – a man who went to the University of Virginia – and never got over it, according to Daddy. Mama suffered from ideas of aristocracy herself. Every night she would fix a nice supper for Daddy and me, then bathe and put on a fresh dress and high heels and bright red lipstick named 'Fire and Ice' and then sit in anxious dismay while the hour grew later and later, until Daddy finally left his dime store and came home. By that time the food had dried out to something crunchy and unrecognizable so Mama would cry when she opened the oven door, but then Daddy would eat it all anyway, swearing it was the most delicious food he'd ever put in his mouth, staring hard at Mama all the while. Frequently my parents would then leave the table abruptly, feigning huge yawns and leaving me to turn out all the lights. I'd stomp around the house and do this resentfully, both horrified and thrilled at the thought of them upstairs behind their closed door.

I myself was in love with Hayburn Owens, my best friend's father three houses down the road. Every night after supper, he'd sit out in his garden by the river and play his guitar and sing the old songs for Martha and me and every other kid in the neighborhood who gathered at this feet to listen. He sang "Barbara Allen" and "The Wagoner's Lad" as one by one the lightning bugs began to rise up from the garden and the river back – up, to the pale sky above the high dark ridge. I felt that my friend Martha certainly did not deserve such a father, for Martha loved only Elvis and every afternoon after school she'd drag me into her house to listen to her 45 recording of "Heartbreak Hotel," which we played over and over on her new hi-fi. My love for her father was enhanced by the air of mystery which surrounded him, for he was the only man in our neighborhood who didn't work. The very opposite of my own exhausted daddy. I understood my mother to say that the reason Hayburn Owens didn't work was because he had romantic fever. I was fascinated by this. I imagined him at home all day long while we were in school, strumming his guitar, black eyes smoldering with love and hopeless longing. But of course it turned out to be rheumatic fever, and in fact he died young when Martha and I were fourteen, and neither one of us ever got over it.

Martha married soon, a dutiful boy we both knew in high school, a boy who wore a pen-and-pencil set in his breast pocket and got rid of her after she worked to pay his way through college and graduate school. I didn't do much better, marrying disastrously for what I thought was love and, though it ended badly, I could not have done otherwise. Now I'm older, but I'm still not any wiser about love than I was then, on that river bank in the summer with my heart beating right out of my chest to think of my own parents upstairs kissing like crazy in the dark or Martha digging her fingers into my arm as Elvis' voice broke down at the end of Lonely Street, while Hayburn Owens played the old sad songs and fireflies rose like little lights above that slow black river.

Richard Wiley

I GREW UP ON the beach in Washington State back when a lot of poor people lived on the beach in houses stripped of their paint by the rain and the salty air. Before I was in the third grade, I may have had loves, but the only actual memory I have of my inner self back then is that of a boy living in stunned surprise, shocked by the world, dumbfounded by a strangeness.

In third grade though, two things happened that brought our current world into focus, making me want to stay a while. The first was when we started getting the vocabulary words in school. Here's the first week's list: glorious, remorse, coincidence, flotilla, debris, and fortuitous. I remember crumpling the paper up and pulling it open and going to my teacher at her desk. "Teacher," I said, "I don't know any of these words." "That's because they're new words, Richard," she told me. "Do you suppose we can get along with only the words we already have?" She pointed at my crumpled list and added "We get those words from the word room, Richard. From a library somewhere in Washington, D.C." After that, I remember the most profound feeling of possibility growing inside. I imagined people entering the word room with unruly ideas and coming out with words in which those ideas could be contained.

Now, soon after that, a kid named Gary from down the beach slipped on a rock and knocked himself out. He fell on a tangle of seaweed and kelp wrapped around a piece of driftwood, and when the tide came in, it took him on his rotting bed and floated him out into the bay. There was a fisherman out there trying to catch the riptide. The fisherman had a strike and cut his motor, his rod frowning severely against the grey Tacoma sky, when the tangle of seaweed floated by. First he worried he'd catch his line it it; then he saw Gary, his own youngest son, unconscious, everything but his shoes and his hair still dry.

Though this is a true story, I realize it's an impossible one for literature. It's too neat, too saccharine, somehow it's too sentimental. But when Gary's father brought him ashore, the story spread even as he strode with Gary over the barnacles and sand. Churches proclaimed it as the proof of God's goodwill and fishermen called it the catch of a lifetime, and Jerry Meeker, an old Puyallup Indian who lived nearby called it good luck. As for me, just as surely as Gary was knocked out by that rock, I was knocked out by the wild improbability and the incalculable odds, the fantastic timing of it all. I felt profoundly connected and when the story appeared in the newspaper I knew why. This is what the headline said: "Fortuitous Father Finds Son on Flotilla of Debris". It was a miracle as big as Gary's rescue. Three of my new words coming through the pages of the *Tacoma New Tribune*. And though I won't say that the rest of my words were there too, I did learn that the concept of coincidence floats in such a wide bay that in life, as in literature, we'd be fools to insist on seeing that bay's other side.

So my first loves were the sense I still carry that the English language can do nothing but live and expand and that we should embrace the miraculous even if it bobs up to us on a bed of seaweed and kelp.

One more thing. After his rescue, Gary got very smug and irritating. I grew to hate him, and one day I shot him in the stomach with my BB gun. When my father heard of it he rowed me and my gun out into the bay and I learned the meaning of remorse when I saw my BB gun sink away. The remaining word on my list "glorious," I didn't learn the true meaning of until I was well out of high school.

Cynthia Ozick

I F I WERE to go back and back, really back, to earliest consciousness, I think it would be mica. Not the prophet Micah, who tells
us that our human task is to do justice and do justly and to love mercy
and to walk humbly with our God, but that other still more humble
mica, those tiny glints of icy glass that catch the sun and prickle
upward from the pavement like shards of star stuff.

Sidewalks nowadays seem inert, as if cement has rid itself for ever
of bright sprinklings and stippled spangles. But the pavement I am
thinking of belongs to long ago and runs narrowly between the tall
weeds of empty lots; lots that shelter tiny green snakes. The lots are
empty because no one builds on them. It is the middle of the summer
in the middle of the depression – childhood's longest hour. I am
alone under a slow molasses sun staring at the little chips of light
flashing at my feet. Up and down the whole length of the street there
is no one. Not a single grown-up and certainly in that sparse time no
other child. There is only myself and these hypnotic semaphores
signaling eeriness out of the ground. But no, up the block a little way,
a baby carriage is entrusted to the idle afternoon with a baby left to
sleep all by itself under white netting. If you are five years old,
loitering in a syrup of sun heat, gazing at the silver-white mica eyes in
the pavements, you will all at once be besieged by a strangeness; the
strangeness of understanding for the very first time that you are really
alive and that the world is really true, and the strangeness will divide
into a river of wonderings.

Here is what I wondered then among the mica eyes. I wondered
what it would be like to become, for just one moment, every kind of

animal there is in the world. Even, I thought, a snake. I wondered what it would be like to know all the languages in the world. I wondered what it would be like to be that baby under the white netting. I wondered why when I looked straight into the sun I saw a pure circle. I wondered why my shadow had a shape that was me but nothing else. Why my shadow, which was almost like a mirror, was not a mirror. I wondered why I was thinking these things. I wondered what wondering was and why it was spooky and also secretly sweet and amazingly interesting. Wondering felt akin to love, an uncanny sort of love, not like loving your mother or your father or grandmother but something curiously and thrillingly other; something that shone up out of the mica eyes.

Decades later I discovered in Wordsworth's *Prelude* what it was. Those hallowed and pure motions of the senses which seem in their simplicity to own an intellectual charm. Those first-born affinities that fit our new existence to existing things. And those existing things are all things. Everything the mammal senses know, everything the human mind constructs, temples or equations, the unheard poetry on the hidden side of the round earth, the great thirsts everywhere, the wonderings past wonderings. First love is first thinking, bridging our new existence to existing things. Can one begin with mica in the pavement and learn the prophet Micah's meaning?

ILLUSIONS

October 5, 1992

Grace Paley

T HIS ASSIGNMENT, IT'S something like a school assignment where you try to figure what the teacher really has in mind. And you finally decide to go ahead anyway on your own and it's only a couple of days too late anyhow. So, illusion. A word that obviously has no meaning until it's over. That is, only when disillusion appears, digs in, under belief, blows it sky high, do you see: Why! It was an illusion!

Love illusions are very famous. He says, "I never really loved you. I mean, not really." She says, "What?" "Not once," he says, "in the last thirty-two years." "Not even that week in Santa Cruz?" He says, feeling the honor of truthfulness, "No." He says, "Not deeply really. No. It was an illusion, but not until disillusionment. Before that, it was a fact. It was love."

Another example. I was talking to a cab driver here in Washington a couple of weeks ago and I asked him if he'd seen the people on the Capitol steps who were fasting. "Who?" "Well, uh, Brian Wilson, the guy who sat down in front of a munitions train about a year or so ago and it just barreled over him and his feet were cut off." "Lord, Lord," he said. "Well, they're fasting until October 12, a witness for the five hundred years from the time Columbus landed and wiped out the native people. They think he wasn't much of a hero." "Why," he said, "what are those folks bothering about? Who cares? Who cares? Everybody knows there were people here when he got here. Indians. My kid knows it." OK, so there's no disillusion there, therefore no illusion.

A third. The most radical kids as I remember them during the

Vietnam War were the ones who were very patriotic in a real sense and who really thought that they felt the Constitution, loved the Bill of Rights. Half of them were Eagle Scouts. Then knowledge set in as far as they were concerned and, understanding, disillusion set in, and they thought that it was all an illusion before that.

Now, I look at this list of speakers, of illusionaries, of illusion makers, inventors, and I'm glad to see there are five women among the sixteen people speaking, telling, talking; three people of color; and I'm really glad, and that's how good-natured I am these days. Glad as I am though, I have to remember that I was on a panel last month with nine men and two women and invited to join a board of ten men and I'd be the second woman, so I think, since I'm just about seventy, what a long time everything takes, and if I can only keep my temper then I won't be disillusioned, and if I don't become disillusioned, that'll mean that all these years of struggle are not an illusion, but hard continuing fact, unimpeachable, day-to-day living fact.

Jim Lehrer

S OME OF YOU may be old enough or poorly educated enough to remember the works of William Sydney Porter, alias O. Henry. He is not big these days in the better literary circles. In fact, as I understand it, the only people who read him now, read his short stories, are seventh-graders in small towns in Kansas, Texas, Oklahoma, and Arkansas. But, nevertheless, he said something once that I deem extremely relevant to me and extremely relevant to our subject tonight.

O. Henry was a newspaper man in Texas, and then he became a banker, and then he went to federal prison for bank embezzlement. And then when he got out of prison, instead of returning to journalism, he went into full-time fiction writing. And somebody said, "Why did you do that?" And he said, "Because I wanted to tell the truth and I sure as hell couldn't do that in journalism."

For the record, and thank God, he was not asked how he found the earlier transition from journalism to bank embezzlement so easy and natural. At any rate, what he meant of course was that what often passes for the truth, but often is labeled the facts, what is often referred to and thought of as the real story, are in fact actually illusions and vice versa. And one could also say as a result of that, that I am truly qualified to speak about illusions because I have a full-time day job in the business of illusions. The pundit or the president or the presidential candidate or the senator, the secretary, the governor, the mayor, or the county judge says, each in his or her own way, something like, "I will not rest until I solve our crime, health, and budget problems by putting every citizen of this county behind the wheel of a new Ford pickup truck." The only real fact or truth in that statement could be that the county judge really did say it. The rest may very well be nothing but illusions. Did he mean what he said? Will he really not rest? What caused him to say such a thing anyhow? Who really is this guy? What kind of human being is he? Is he a person of mind and purpose? Or is he a person of emptiness and evasion? What is the real source of his thing about pickup trucks? What have been in his dreams or nightmares, if anything, about pickups? How does it fit into his feelings about his fellow human beings? About dogs and cats and other animals? About sex and music and other sensations? About motorcycles, buses, and other vehicles? And on and on the questions go as each layer is peeled away. For the most part, those questions, beyond the first two or three maybe, will remain unanswered by journalism. It is neither equipped nor expected to find and report those kinds of answers, and, believe me, that is probably just as well.

So that leaves the real truth, down and under those layers, the final truth, the whole truth to the fiction writer. And that, ladies and gentlemen, is why I try to do both at the same time. I spend my days laboring happily in the illusion business and my nights and weekends at home doing the same in the truth business. I, like O. Henry, try hard not to mistake one for the other, although, unlike O. Henry, I have never worked in a bank.

Robert Stone

A S WE MOVE further into the nineties it is occurring to many
people that we have wasted the entire past ninety-odd years
acting out or living down or otherwise discharging the ideas of the
previous century. It sometimes seems that there was no nineteenth-
century European notion so fatuous, so paltry, so homicidal or mean-
spirited that it wasn't embraced by some group somewhere as the
final answer to humanity's prayers, nor was there a cause so distasteful, so illogical, so absurd and self-negating that it wasn't seen by
entire nations as eminently worth the sacrifice of whole generations.
They thought it up, we lived it. The guts-and-glory decades where,
in the words of Humphrey Bogart, the problems of little people
didn't amount to a hill of beans in this crazy world. Find a logo, put it
on your armband, wear it, wave it in their faces, kill them all! *Viva la
muerte.*

It wasn't particularly the American century. If it had been we
should have much more to answer for. It was the movie century.
What films would we enclose in a time capsule to enlighten posterity
regarding the nature of our time? I propose a double bill. *The Triumph
of the Will* and *Duck Soup*. The pictures are complementary. Each tells
you all you need to know about the other. Hitler saying at
Nuremberg, "Those who impose upon the world another war will
be held responsible. They will be made to pay." Rufus T. Firefly
saying, "Either this man's dead or my watch has stopped."

Finally, not a moment too soon, the nineteenth-century ideol-
ogies have run out of gas. We may have a few years to ourselves to
dream up our own mischief. One of the unlikely comforts that has

survived with us is religion. Who would have thought that after all that operatic villainy and science fiction, its homely little candle would still flicker, the object of our sentimental regard. But it does because through all the ideological storms a fading remnant held to the idea of personal responsibility and awe before the fact of creation. It's not a moment of triumph, it's a moment of respite during which we may be able to say very softly, "Look, we've come through." I think it very rash of certain people in so fragile a moment to call for religious war. Religious war, jihad. Surely we ought to spare ourselves that. It won't be all flag-waving, sing-alongs and balloons. Religious wars require terrible cruelty, hypocrisy, and self-deception. One thing we ought to have learned from this ridiculous century is that religion thrives best in persecution, in the darkness, the wilderness, the silence of the heart. It fares least well when puffed up and vaunting itself. Religion does not require of its people a war; it requires that we watch and pray.

In late seventeenth-century Massachusetts, a pamphlet was published entitled "The Sovereignty and Goodness of God Together with the Faithfulness of His Promises Displayed Being a Narrative of the Captivity and Restoration of Mary Rowlinson of Mansfield." Mrs. Rowlinson was captured with her new baby by the Pequots during King Philip's War. Her entire family was killed, her baby died, and when he died she said, "There I left that child in the wilderness and must commit it and myself also in this our wilderness condition to Him who is above all." Mrs. Rowlinson concluded that God had caused her sufferings to mortify her pride, but he had done this out of love for her. He wanted her to know, she says, that all human nature is fallen, hers as well; that there is finally no distinction in creation between man and woman, English and Pequot, pagan, Christian; that overriding all human pride is the mystery of grace, the dread dispensation, she calls it. Instead of having a religious war, let's consider Sister Mary Rowlinson, our pilgrim mother, an American Job. How far her reflections seem from contemporary tub-thumping and vulgar religiosity, hypocrisy, and vanity.

Russell Banks

PERHAPS IT IS apposite here to quote the master illusionist, William Shakespeare, who, as Prince Hamlet, says, "Illusion, if thou hast any voice or use of speech, speak to me." Let the illusions speak to us. Call me Ishmael, don't call me Herman. Call me Holden, call me Huck, call me Tristram, but don't call me Jerry, Sam, or Larry. For writers, reading and writing are not very different, as Toni Morrison has said, and we authors no more want to hear from ourselves than you do. We, too, want to hear from the illusions, not the authors. Not those dull, rumpled folks, please. Most of us are depressives, superstitious ink-stained wretches who seldom venture from our cluttered dens, and when we do we come forward and attempt to pleasure folks with our company, we all too often drink too much and gorge on the canapés and leer bleary-eyed at the attractive young men and women refilling our glasses and passing the trays of iced shrimp. We stay too late and talk the hostess and host to sleep, and ourselves as well, and wake on the couch the next morning shamefaced, hurrying back to our cubby murmuring prayerfully, "Oh, illusion, if thou hast, any voice or use of speech, speak to me, speak for me, speak instead of me."

Our best use and our peculiar gift, if we have any, is our ability to sustain the precious illusion that the teller of the tales is not the author. I have, in the interests of sustaining and sharing this illusion, invoked dozens of voices to speak in place of my own. I've turned to middle-aged women, adolescent girls, William Hogarth's wife, a medieval coffin maker, and even a Haitian, not a one of whom could be confused with the author, this middle-aged bourgeois white man you see before you. And even if I spoke in the voice of a middle-aged bourgeois white man, he would not be me. It is how we bear witness to the witness; it is how we invoke and honor the other.

I recently attended an international literary conference in Boulder, Colorado, where, to everyone's surprise excepting the various security forces who accompanied him, Salman Rushdie appeared, as if in a puff of smoke, like a wry and world-weary, slightly rotund genie, speaking from behind a huge bank of microphones and a sheet of bullet-proof glass, asking us from the most threatened position possible, to please, please remember that the author is not the teller of the tale, that there are two distinct entities. That is the illusion. The absolutely necessary illusion which allows the tale – any tale – to get told at all. To conflate the two, author and narrator, artist and image, in Rushdie's case has led to a *fatwah*, a million-dollar bounty plus expenses on his head.

In this country, conflating the two leads mostly to idiotic, financially punitive tantrums by Congressmen, mild but nonetheless inhibiting forms of censorship, and a vice president who sends a toy elephant to the fictional baby of a fictional television character he probably wishes he hadn't insulted. At that conference in Boulder, the American author William Gass arranged to obtain and distribute a box of buttons with the words "I am Salman Rushdie" printed on them, and many of us, in the interests of solidarity with a fellow author under a death threat, but also in the interest of our favorite illusion, began wearing them on our lapels. I am not Salman Rushdie as you may have noticed, any more than I'm a middle-aged woman, William Hogarth's wife, or a Haitian, but by affirming in this most transparently artificial way the illusion that I am even for a moment Salman Rushdie, I'm able to bear witness to the unspeakable that Rushdie's every single day of his life must witness. This small illusion, four words, "I am Salman Rushdie," inscribed on a yellow tin badge, allows the author Salman Rushdie to speak where he is otherwise forbidden to speak. Here, for instance, where he reminds us that he is a prisoner of conscience, a hostage, a victim of religious persecution of the vilest sort and that we who remain silent are complicit.

Susan Richards Shreve

W HEN I WAS young, I fell in love with the work of F. Scott Fitzgerald, who, in *The Great Gatsby*, wrote the story of the illusion of the American dream. It was not just Fitzgerald's fiction I loved, but his lyrical prescriptions for living, which he, as an excessive member of a generation of acquisition and irresponsibility not unlike the one we have just left behind, failed to follow himself. There is a paragraph about illusions in one of his essays in *The Crack-Up* which struck me when I was in college and particularly tonight. It goes like this: "The test of a first-rate intelligence is the ability to hold two opposed ideas in the mind at the same time and still retain the ability to function." One should, for example, be able to see that things are hopeless and yet be determined to make them otherwise.

My parents were married on New Year's Day in 1938 in the parlor of my grandmother's house. No one, so I have been told, approved. My father was from the wrong side of the tracks in a small Midwestern town. He was a man of unknown genes, and for years my mother had been engaged to marry a splendid young athlete whose pictures in basketball shorts doing jump shots and lay-ups are in my attic. She agreed to leave the basketball player several weeks before the wedding, but my father, committed as he was to emergencies, found Donna, a tall voluptuous blonde in mid-December. On Christmas Day, a week before the wedding, he maintained that he was undecided about marriage. I think he made it up. My father saw my mother when she was twelve years old sitting on the veranda of her house with the quiet and contented air of the well-born, on the bottom side of the century, just after the first war. He decided about marriage then. He crossed the railroad tracks on Valentine's Day to bring her chocolates, which he gave to her father because my mother wouldn't come to the door. "He was too small and my friends would have laughed," my mother said to me. "Besides, he was younger than I was and didn't play sports." I expect my father found Donna just in time to protect himself with understudies in the wing, to seal my mother's commitment to this persistent dark horse.

I grew up in a time when this city was a small, sleepy, segregated city. We believed in the Norman Rockwell pictures of the perfect family, knew that our families belonged with them. We believed in unrevised history books that told us of our heroism, and in the dream that our lives would be better than our parents' lives had been. Things have turned out differently. Some time ago I found a five-year diary I had kept for a month when I was nine years old. Every entry in that month of January, the only month recorded, begins "We are all well and happy." Day after day, the coldest months of the year, we are all well and happy. It is no wonder, I thought, reading that diary, understanding the quiet desperation of the child who wrote it, I couldn't write beyond the first month of the first year. I must have sensed that the wonderful promises we had been given by the world we entered as children could not be kept.

The first thing I was told as a young writer was to tell the truth about the way things are, that writing is an optimistic act requiring hope about the way things could be. On my parents' way to Cincinnati, driving at night after the wedding ceremony and the disappointed relations, my father spotted a brown paper bag in the middle of the highway and stopped. "There's a baby in that paper bag," he said to my mother. "A baby?" my mother asked incredulously. "How do you know?" "Look, for heaven's sakes," he said to her, as though her sense of sight had failed her in an instant. "Can't you tell?" She looked; there were lights on the highway and headlights on their car so she could see the brown paper bag perfectly. It appeared to be a brown paper bag which gave no evidence of concealing a baby. But it did move she noticed, as my father rushed to rescue it from the middle of the road. Filled with a sudden and unfamiliar excitement, she began to believe that he was right and would return with a small baby, which he would dump from the paper bag onto her lap. She straightened her skirt in anticipation. "Well," she asked as he opened the door by the driver's seat, "what is it?" My father got in the car, tossed the paper bag in the back-seat, and turned on the engine. "Nothing," he said crossly, and drove off into the night with his new bride, headed for Cincinnati. "Why," my mother asked quietly, "did you think there was a baby in the paper bag?" "There could have been a baby," my father said simply. Anything, of course, is possible and so my reasonable mother agreed that, yes, there could have been a baby. "Besides," my father said to her later, "I couldn't imagine that it was simply an empty paper bag."

William Least Heat-Moon

I DREAMED THAT I dreamed that I stood before you in a peculiar theater and I began speaking of my dream. I fumbled with my notes. Should I read them or perform them? Before I could finish the first twisted thought, I went silent. All I could do was stand and wait. An embarrassment of silence. Then, seeing in you – or hoping I saw – a shared discomfort for this stage player who drops the ball like a center fielder who's sure he's got it – I tried again to speak. This time not so much to find a thought as to discover a cradle of words that might pull me from mortification, from dying on my feet in front of so many helpless witnesses. I dreamed I heard you murmur, "Thank God it's not happening to me. No one can fail after this guy." Further silence. As I lay in the tangled dream of a dream where I stood speaking these words, as if they had already happened, I began to take comfort in a notion that seeped in like damp into a dark cellar. Surely and soon I would wake to find, not an audience and klieg lights, but the familiar haven of night walls, real ramparts between me and some somnolent life that could stand me up here, a nude soul. And then I dreamed I awoke, got up from the tortured sheets, took pen and paper, and wrote the dream down and it ended in these words that I had hoped to open with: "From the *American Heritage Dictionary*: 'illusion,' from the Latin '*illudere*,' to mock." So, let writers admit there is no reality worth a damn in our lone imaginings. Let us subvert our self-serving belief that merely writing down a dream life gives it a reality worth speaking of. Let us affirm that the only actuality worth the agony of our dreaming is the one which can break the silences between us, the same reality which sets us at risk in front of others, for it is in the end a writer's public voice that opens us to the mockery in the word illusion itself.

Lee Smith

I STARTED TELLING STORIES as soon as I could talk. True stories and made-up stories, too. My father was fond of saying that I could climb a tree to tell a lie rather than stand on the ground to tell the truth. In fact, in the mountains where I come from, a lie was often called a story and well do I remember being shaken until my teeth rattled with the stern admonition "Don't you tell me no story now." But I couldn't help it. I was already hooked on stories, and as soon as I could write, I started writing them down. I loved writing stories, because everything in them happened just the way I wanted it to. Writing stories gave me a special power, I felt. I wrote my first novel at the age of eight on my mother's stationery. Its main characters were my two favorite people in the world at that time – Adlai Stevenson and Jane Russell. In this novel they fell in love and then went west in a covered wagon. Once there, they became, inexplicably, Mormons.

My best friend, Martha Sue Owens, and I published a laboriously copied-out neighborhood newspaper named *The Small Review,* in which we published newsworthy events, such as the following, from *The Small Review* of 1954: "Lee Smith and Martha Sue Owens went shopping at King's department store in Bristol, Tennessee, to buy their school clothes. Lee Smith got to look at her feet through a machine to see if her shoes fit." And then, the controversial editorial entitled "George Maguire Is Too Grumpy," for which I had to go and apologize to the neighbor across the street, and a poem by me comparing life capitalized to a candle flame. After school every afternoon, I'd walk across the river into town and go to my father's dime store, my favorite place in the whole world. I'd get to dress and undress the dolls and help Mildred work the popcorn machine and read all the new comic books the minute they came in. My favorite memory from childhood takes place at the dime store. It is a Sunday afternoon near Easter and the store is officially closed, but the basement is full of women working overtime to assemble Easter baskets. I helped for a while and then I'd got sleepy. The women don't pay me much mind. They are busy talking, and before long they've gotten off onto one of my all-time favorite topics, having babies. I hear all about a terrible britches baby, which is how they refer to a breach birth, and about a baby girl born with a veil and doomed to know the future in her breast. I sink down and down into a big box of pink cellophane straw, which drifts and settles until it covers me entirely, and when I look up all that I can see is a pink dazzle of fluorescent light. All I can hear is these women's voices telling stories. That Sunday afternoon seemed to go on for ever and ever.

This past August my father closed the dime store after forty-six years in business. All up and down that main street stores are closing. The Rexall drug store, Stinson's dry goods, the Lynwood Theater. The town is becoming a ghost town. On the last day of his going-out-of-business sale, my father went home and had a stroke. Five days later he died. This did not happen to Adlai Stevenson or Jane Russell, or any character I ever made up. This happened to my father, Ernest Smith, age eighty-four, on September 5, 1992. I cannot write any story that will change this. I cannot keep the dime store open or keep my father alive, but I know I will go on writing stories, for they're as necessary to me now as breathing. This is the only way I know how to live my life, and though I know it is an illusion, for nothing can stay time, I will fix on a piece of paper someplace, in some story, that Sunday dime store and those women telling about the baby born with the veil and myself looking up through the pink Easter straw into a future that held only light.

Tobias Wolff

ILLUSION IS WHAT we see instead of the truth. In the most important matters, matters of value and faith, we can't be sure which is which. I remember a late night in the summer of 1974 when Ward Just and I were discussing the question of religious faith, and to Ward I quoted old man Karamazov: "If there is no God, then who is laughing at us?" Ward answered with a line from *The Spy Who Came in from the Cold*: "I believe that the number eleven bus will get me to Hammersmith, but I don't believe it will be driven by Father Christmas."

We doubt, endlessly we doubt. We call doubt a pang, a shadow. Truly it is a shadow. It only leaves us when we are completely in the dark. But if we had the chance to be free of doubt, would we take it? Years ago, hoping to strengthen my faith, I went on a pilgrimage to Lourdes. I lived in the barracks with other men. During the day we worked in the dining halls, in the hospitals, at the baths, wherever we were needed. One afternoon I was driven with some other workers to the local airport, where we were to help a group of disabled Italian pilgrims embark for Milan. It was a hot, humid day. At first things went smoothly. We wheeled a number of people across the field and up the ramp into the plane. Then there was a mix-up. They closed the airplane door, forcing us to wait on the hot tarmac. I was with a girl about two years old. She was completely paralyzed and had tubes in her nostrils that drained into bags on the side of the gurney. She looked up at me calmly, too calmly somehow. I moved her into the shadow of the fuselage and made encouraging sounds and fanned her face with my hand. Still they kept us waiting. Then the flies discovered her. I couldn't keep them off; I kept brushing at them, but they became ever more relentless in their swarming. I was desperate with anger. My anger went beyond the situation. It was hysterical and fundamental. It had to do with the entire scheme of things. By the time they opened the airplane door again, I was weeping, though only I knew it. By now, all our faces were glistening with sweat.

Afterward I got on the bus back to Lourdes, and it came to me that something peculiar was happening. I had taken my glasses off earlier in the afternoon because they kept slipping down. They were still in my pocket, but I could see as well as if I had them on, could read license plates, and see sheep grazing in distant fields. I couldn't understand it. I rubbed my eyes, thinking it must be a lens of tears and sweat, but it didn't go away. I felt giddy and restless, not myself at all. Then I had the distinct thought that when we got back to Lourdes I should go to the grotto and pray. That was all: go to the grotto and pray. But I didn't do that. Instead, I went inside the barracks to cool off and fell into conversation with a very funny Irishman I'd gotten to know. We sat on his cot and talked and laughed and all the while I was aware of what I wasn't doing and what I wasn't telling him. I had no reason not to mention what had happened. He would have been interested, not at all derisive, but I didn't say a thing. We talked for a couple of hours then went to dinner and I never made it to the grotto that day.

Next morning I was wearing my glasses again. What happened? Maybe it was, as I first suspected, a film on my eyes. Maybe it was an illusion. I only thought I was seeing clearly. It would seem un-generous, ungodly, to make such a gift conditional and to take it back. Of course, there's no way of knowing what really happened or what might have happened if I'd gone to the grotto that day. What concerns me now is why I didn't go. I felt, to be sure, some incredulity, but this wasn't the reason. I have a weakness for good company, but that wasn't it either. At heart, I must not have wanted this thing to happen. If I had confirmed it, what then? I would have had to give up those doubts by which I defined myself in the world's terms as a free man. By giving up doubt, I would have lost that measure of pure self-interest to which I felt myself entitled by doubt. Doubt was my connection to the world, to the faithless self who took me in when faith got hard. Imagine the responsibility of losing it. Where would that lead? No wonder I was afraid of seeing so well.

John Edgar Wideman

I MAGINE YOUR FIELD of vision is a jigsaw puzzle with invisible seams, a vast flat screen resting on one laser-thin edge. What seems three-dimensional is in fact the play of illusion on a screen, puzzle pieces gathered from a box and assembled to render the pictures you see. You understand all this because one day you glance out and notice a piece is missing, and its absence reveals the black velvet backdrop upon which scenes are projected. The lost fragment is dog-shaped, a black, shiny emptiness revealing the screen's thinness, its arbitrariness. You are reminded how easy it would be to poke a finger through this New England winterscape of trees, hills, fences, rolling contours of white earth that appeared substantial just a moment before when you believed what you were seeing was real, whole, out there surrounding you, as safe a bet as you'd ever find to lay your money on. Then the dog moves. It is not a shadow-play dog, not the reflection on a wall of hands and fingers held a certain way to fool you. The black dog scampers swiftly toward you, and the door it enters swirls closed behind it, disappearing in a commotion of snow spray the instant your attention is seized by the sudden explosion of black limbs galloping, thick black torso hurtling, the metallic ting of nameplate and license plate looped to a cobalt collar. Details you don't register individually, but remember all at once as the suddenly familiar shape materializes, loping closer, drowning your wonder, your fear, when you had seen through everything to the mercifully dark ground where the pieces are arranged precisely so every one fits and the seams, like black lines drawn around people in comic books, fade into the story. A dog – our dog Crooker – with the crooked tail, bounds through the snow, raising in her wake little snow squalls, silent combustions of snow bumped from low-slung evergreen branches. The dog's motion brings me here again beside you, both of us looking back at our footprints, the only tracks this morning on the trail, except the dog's meandering criss-cross. We're ready to turn around. As we begin to retrace our steps the dog shoots ahead then brakes abruptly, checking us out, a motionless silhouette again, a black hole in the snow as if it could call into question again the orderly tide we're depending upon to carry us back where we started. We hold hands as best we can through clumsy mittens, two robots groping, not feeling, each other except as pressure, the blind correspondence of forms, coincidence of male and female, meeting in the dark, evolving ways to fit a love story.

A quarter-mile later I let go, stride away two long paces, turn my back to you, fumble out my business with one bare hand, and pee over the edge of the trail, mark the drifted snow with new alphabets. I watched the blue sky watching me. Think of being one thing, then another thing after this moment, think of absolute zero, substances freezing instantly and shattering like glass. Steel or flower petals equally brittle, fragile, exploding at a touch. Think of how I might gingerly break myself off and hand myself like an icicle to you and how you'd have to laugh even though the joke wouldn't be funny unless I could painlessly stick myself on again, no stitches, no seams, and be instantly healed and whole. I finish peeing and say out loud some of the silliness I've been thinking, pantomime a humble offering: "With this thing I thee wed." You laugh and look at me like I just might be crazy enough to try. And after all the sorrow this season, the holding on till the weather broke and dumped tons of snow. I realize your smile might be worth the risk; the metaphor is, after all, something to get carried away with.

Elmore Leonard

A GUY BY THE name of Harry Arno, sixty-six, who operates a sports book in Miami Beach – you place bets with him on football and basketball games – tells about an experience he had in Italy in 1945, during the Second War.

"May 29th we delivered a deserter to the Disciplinary Training Center and that was the day I saw Ezra Pound for the first time, inside one of the maximum-security cells he called a gorilla cage. It sat on a concrete slab about six by ten and was open on four sides so the rain could come in from any direction. They kept a spotlight on him at night and no one was supposed to talk to him. Hardly anyone there knew he was a world-famous poet." [He was being held as a traitor, for his radio broadcasts sympathetic to the Axis Powers.] "Finally they moved him to the medical compound and let him use a desk so he could write his poetry."

"His Cantos," Joyce [Harry's girlfriend] said. "He spent 40 years writing a poem hardly anyone in the world can understand."

"Once," Harry says, "I asked him how he was doing. This twenty-year-old kid talking to Ezra Pound. He looked at me and while he was still typing said, "The ant's a centaur in his dragon world. Pull down thy vanity." I said, "What?""

"I saw him again in '67 (in Rapallo), three days in a row at the same cafe, Ezra Pound and his mistress. One time I followed him to the men's room, got ahead of him and held the door open. As he reached me I said, 'The ant's a centaur in his dragon world.' He looked at me and walked right past into the can, didn't say a word.

That was okay, he had people bothering him all the time. They'd come and ring the bell, tourists, and Olga Rudge would tell them, 'If you can recite one line of his poetry you can see him.' "

[Harry shows photos of Pound in a biography he has.]

"Here, this is what he looked like when I last saw him. He was eighty-two then. Look at the hat. You ever see a brim like that? The coat and the walking stick; the coat's like a cape. The guy had style right up to the end, eighty-seven when he died in Venice, Olga there with him. Here's a picture of her. Good-looking woman, uh?" He handed the book to Raylan and watched him turn to the photos of the gorilla cages and the military stockade. "I went back there on one of my trips," Harry said. "You know what's there now? A nursery where they grow roses. Another time in Rapallo, you know who I saw? Groucho Marx."

That might have told Harry something.

"Harry thinks he's hip," [Joyce says] "If he is, he's Miami Beach hip. He's a bookie who happens to have met Ezra Pound. He comes back to Rapallo three or four times and finally, after seeing him in a cage, there he is again, an old dude now but still with that flair, the hat, the walking stick, a man who'd been dining at sidewalk cafés with his mistress all his life and Harry wanted to do it too."

[Raylan Givens, another character in the scene, says] "And the bad guys came and ruined it for him." [At the time Harry retires to Rapallo, in the dead of night, he's in serious trouble with his silent partners, the wiseguys.]

"Even if they hadn't come after him," [Joyce says] "it's one thing to sip Galliano on a nice day and watch the girls go by. But it can get cold and damp and the girls put on coats, the ones still around. He shouldn't drink anyway, not even coffee. Harry's too late for sidewalk cafés. He wouldn't last more than a few weeks, even with the sun out. He might be a romantic, but he's practical too, set in his ways. When he called and asked me to come? He tells me how much he misses me, he can't wait. And then he says, 'Oh, yeah, and bring me a couple bottles of aftershave.' His favorite, Caswell-Massey No. Six."

[And Raylan Givens says,] "That's aftershave? It sounds more like an east Kentucky coal mine."

This is from my next book, *Pronto*.

I'm not ordinarily aware of themes until reviewers point them out. (So *that's* what my book is about.) But if I'm not mistaken, illusions move the story in this one and might even be the major theme.

Gay Talese

ILLUSIONS AND THE Mafia. When average Americans think about the Mafia, they contemplate scenes of action and violence, of drama and intrigue and million-dollar schemes, of big, black limousines screeching around corners with machine-gun bullets spraying the sidewalk. This is the Hollywood version and while much of it is based on reality it also exaggerates that reality, totally ignoring the dominant mood of Mafia existence, a routine of endless waiting, tedium, hiding, excessive smoking, overeating, lack of physical exercise – no Mafia man has ever belonged to a health club – of reclining in rooms behind drawn shades being bored to death while trying to stay alive. With so much time and so little to do with it, the Mafia man tends to be self-consumed, self-absorbed, over-reacting to each sound, over-interpreting what is said and done around him, losing perspective of the larger world and his small place in that world, but, nonetheless, being aware of the exaggerated image that the world has of him and he responds to that image, believes it, prefers to believe it, because it makes him larger than he is, more powerful, more romantic, more respected and feared. He can trade on it, profit from it in neighborhoods where he runs the rackets and in other areas where he hopes his inflated ego will allow him to expand. He can, if sufficiently bold and lucky, exploit the fact and fantasy of organized crime as effectively as Federal crimebusters at budget time and the politicians running for district attorney and the press whenever organized crime is topical, and the movie makers whenever they can merchandise the mythology for a public that invariably wants its characters larger than life, tough-talking, high-living, big-spending, little Caesars, goodfellows and godfathers. No less than anyone else, the Mafia man is lured by the illusion, live the lie; it feeds his compulsion to travel first-class, to lease expensive cars he can ill afford, to stroll into courtrooms with a suntan he claims to have gotten while playing golf at Pebble Beach. It is essential to his status in the secret society to give the appearance of prosperity and power, to exude confidence and a carefree spirit, although in so doing the Mafia man's life becomes more pressured in the larger world where government agents are watching him, tapping his phone, bugging his home, seeking to determine the source of his illegitimate income so they might indict him for tax evasion. The Mafia man is consequently forced into an almost schizophrenic existence. While pleading poverty to Internal Revenue in an attempt to conceal his resources, he also attempts to impress his friends by picking up checks in restaurants and driving a new Cadillac or Lincoln (Mafia men drive only American cars) and by otherwise living beyond his means. For in reality he has no choice if he wants to maintain the respect of his colleagues in the underworld or indeed in the larger world of American capitalism where there has traditionally existed a grudging admiration for Mafia bosses, possibly because their success reaffirms every tycoon's belief in the free-enterprise system or possibly because the gangster's shrewdness and initiative remind some of America's leading industrialists, bankers and politicians, of how their grandfathers had begun. As Balzac said, "Behind every great fortune there is a crime."

Bette Bao Lord

A S AN IMMIGRANT child of eight, I had the illusion that I could already speak English. And so, along with my classmates at P.S. No. 8 in Brooklyn, I placed my hand over my heart, stared at the stars and stripes, and proudly proclaimed "I pledge a lesson to the frog of the United States of America and to the wee puppet for witches hands, on Asian, in the vestibule, with little tea and just rice for all."

Surely I mangled the words, as surely a dream was born. Today, voices just as confounding are raised. They speak for factions and divisions, ethnic chauvinism and racist fears; they mock the American dream. They cannot imagine our country greater than the sum of its parts. They cannot imagine the world wedded to our common humanity. If only I could have taken them by the hand that Christmas eve to the reopening of a church in Beijing. Ahead, flanked by gaudy Chinese pavilions, stands a giant gingerbread house decorated with white icing. In the air the tolling of bells badly taped. For a moment I think I'm at Disneyland. But as I study the people I sense a gravity, an expectancy, a soulfulness unlike those who gather to be amused. They are pilgrims, the night is cold, the moon is high, we are going to worship. Inside, every inch is taken by people stretched on tiptoes and scrunched, knee to knee, in pews overflowing. The decor is bewilderingly eclectic. Chandeliers that belong in grand hotels, garish paper flowers that bedeck Buddhist temples, sorry attempts at stained glass, mosaics reminiscent of mosques. Red and green and gold trimmings that tint Buddhist halls. Unlike other Catholic churches I visited at home or abroad, this one does not glow with mysterious solemnity, but is intense, almost screaming, with light. It is as if the congregation, after a forty-year absence, fears that God might pass them on this holiest of holy nights. The choir sings hauntingly, the tune is oh-so-familiar, but Silent Night and Holy Night in Mandarin sound oh-so-new. The processional enters, the white gowns on the altar boys are unhemmed, improvised. Some stop at the knees, some stop at the ankles, a few sweep the floor. And yet there's dignity about them that years of practice cannot instill. The priests are stooped, frail and nearly translucent from spending the best years of their lives in jails. The incense climbing upward toward the floodlights produces that special effect evoking scenes in movies when the presence of God is here. Surely for most it is the first time they are in church. Surely for most it does not matter what is said; it could just as well have been from the Torah or the Tao, the Koran or the Sutras, or perhaps just a simple declaration of the people, by the people, for the people. What matters are the intangible tidings cast by a rainbow of hope. I was there; it was not an illusion.

Ward Just

I HAVE A 200-WORD short story that I've adapted from a 50,000, word novella. It's a topical illusion.

Imagine a politician late at night talking to a companion. He's trying for once to speak the truth, but he's had a drink so things are a little bit off center.

Lecture twenty-three of the general introduction. Freud describes the artist as one who desires honor, power, riches, fame, and the love of women, but lacks the ways and means of attaining them. Frustrated, he attempts to satisfy himself by making fantasies which, according to the great analyst, represent repressed infantile longings. The fantasies of the artist and the fantasies of the politician are the same fantasies with the same goals – honor, power, riches, fame, and the love of women. Write a poem, run for office. In his secret heart, the politician believes he is loved. He is the wise creator of his own sweet universe, father to a constituency of children, and while some of the children are obstinate or disobedient, none of them is beyond salvation. So if the election is lost it is not lost because he was a bad person or disliked, or that his policies were bogus. No, he was denied full access to the electorate; he was not permitted to make himself fully understood; the press was hostile and his opponents spread damned lies and falsified his positions; there was slander; there was libel. And if the campaign was a success, there is frustration still. A small voice will wonder about those who voted the other way. What was in their minds? Why did they reject me? That is the small furious voice that knows that if there was honor enough, power enough, riches enough, fame enough, love enough, the result might be, should have been, unanimous. Don't you think?

Vasily Aksyonov

I N FRONT OF him was the Washington Mall with its set of memorials and its lavish spread of shallow ponds, where new broods of ducklings come briskly close to the reflections of solemnly soaring gulls. He stretched his limbs and thanked the Washington Monument for its convincing participation in the sunny, airy business day on the Mall. In the meantime, a Goodyear blimp was circling the Capitol firmament like a procrastinating Valkyrie. The grandiose and most reliable building of the National Archives was adjacent to the most slippery place, if not in the world, then in the town where Congressmen, lobbyists, White House and national officials, members of the diplomatic corps and the intelligence community, were making circles in a somewhat condescending challenge to the laws of friction, yet with a certain deferential bow to the laws of gravity. Did you stumble again? Never mind. All you have to catch in skating is the universal rhythm as are the rhythmical motions of swimming or swinging. A split moment of pre-dusk before the lamps around the Ellipse turned on. Cranberry, orange and pistachio in the great volume of the Virginia skies shown through huge crowns of chestnut and plane trees. Every now and then shadows of jetliner, like intelligent creatures, glided down to National Airport. Back to the residential area.

At the corner of Decatur and Mass, he stopped to make a bow to a huge magnolia tree. "Thank you, magnolia tree for a bit of additional harmony. In your person I make a low bow to all evergreens. Thank you for your implacable endurance, you evergreens. Without your invincible foliage General Sheridan would look like a deserter from the battlefield. Flora and fauna of Embassy Row, thank you for everything. Oh, thank you very much, northwest wind, fifteen miles per hour, for making a dashing Irish setter out of the smoke from a chimney at the Pakistan Embassy, and unleashing him to chase down his own tail over the roofs of the Moorish Victorian classic and colonial mansions and town houses. Thank you grey stone building filled with the enigma of Yugoslavian communism for giving me a chance to make a sharp turn to see the Dumbarton bridge with its four greenish-bronze buffaloes. Thank you beasts for your zeal in guarding in the installation which cost zero without you." Twilight was growing thicker, full moon was pointing out the farther destination, Georgetown. "Cabbie, double time to Master and Marguerita Street." "Yes, sir." Through his hussar's moustache the taxi driver started whistling the motley carillon. "This is a night of zezezing-zooiezezzin," whispered she into the density of his ear. "Did you get it?" "But, of course." They strolled along a narrow embankment trying to make themselves out as a decent couple of apparitions. Around was a world of olden times, the tiny windows and ajar doors of that lovely rudimentary capitalism. Here, one could see a colonial pharmacy which displayed yellowish balls filled with powdered hornets, various fungi, jars holding the fragile husk of dried seahorses, ground ginseng, pills made from spotted-deer antler, fish glue, snake gull, tiger bone, and other wondrous substances. They walked by like protagonists of a perverted version of a Theodore Dreiser story. The first thing they saw as they entered Au Pied du Couchon was a huge painting of a troika of cooks with knives chasing a pig which expressed no desire to be cooked. It was supposed to introduce the place in French style. Then they saw their friend who played jazz holding his sax like an embryo inside the concavity of his lanky body. Another friend accompanied with an energetic staccato on the thick bass strings. In top hat and with cigar between his corpulent lips, the guy looked like the bugbear of the class struggle. He pumped up his font and the audience under his conducted nose sang, trying to make it real and immediately asked itself, "Compared to what?" "Compared to Immanuel Kant," she screamed all of a sudden. "Oh, yes," responded the crowd. Zziingzooiezinzeezee. No one has ever seen before a decent female person astride a cajun broom flying over the tables toward the window and leaving up here with a train of glass particles behind. If it wasn't a manifestation of the socialist realism, what was it?

All this in public followed suit; we flew over Wisconsin Avenue toward the river and over the rough pebbled Potomac and over the Kennedy Center, a farewell trumpeting and bassooning of Mr. Beethoven's 'Eroica,' higher and higher until everything vanished in the clouds and the clouds themselves vanished in the clouds. Farewell, Washington, Knoshington, District of Columbine.

Awakening, Channel 4 News update, according to the latest research, the annual consumption of illusions in Washington, D.C. has reached a level 1.8 percent lower than a year before. People are getting less confident in buying illusions. Analysts are leaning to believe that the D.C. declining rate of illusions will be growing handsomely in the years to come.

OBSESSION

October 2, 1993

David Bradley

Y OU KNOW, DOING this assignment represented a research problem. I mean, where do you go to do three minutes' worth of research, on anything, let alone about obsession? Where do you find inspiration? I went to the video store. And in the clean, well-lighted aisles of my local Brainrotter, I discovered that the most popular films, which is to say the ones that weren't there – just the boxes were there – had obsession as a theme. Interestingly though, it seemed that the object of the obsession didn't matter. Obsession itself was the rub. Nearly every cassette box promised me a tragic tale in which some ungovernable demand was the flaw that led to a burnt-out BMW in every parking structure and a rabbit, rather than a chicken, in every pot.

Well, I thought, here is my news. In modern America, for all our supposed excesses, we loathe obsession. We fear it and generate graphic, cautionary tales against it. So I noted down a few phrases and went back to better work, in the course of which I happened on the following quote: "It was heard in every sound and seen in every thing. It was ever present to torment me with a sense of my wretched condition. I saw nothing without seeing it, heard nothing without hearing it, felt nothing without feeling it. It looked from every star. It smiled in every calm, breathed in every wind and moved in every storm. I often found myself regretting my own existence and wishing myself dead."

Gadzooks! thought I. That's an obsession. The trouble was, it was Frederick Douglass writing about his lust for freedom. This gave me considerable pause, for Douglass has always been one of my idols.

Well, not idol, a role model – I don't want to sound obsessed or anything. But when I was young, I wanted to grow up to look like him, and later though male-pattern baldness put paid to that ambition, I continued to admire him. But now I realized Fred Douglass had been an obsessive, wild for freedom long before he tasted it. And his obsession was destructive; his lust caused him to mock and assault his superiors, to default on lawful contracts, to abandon his pregnant lover, to defy the laws of state and nation. The message from Brainrotter Video was clear. It would never do now, in this America, to idolize a man like that.

Well, I'll compress the mental agonies that followed. Suffice to say I could not give Douglass up, and predictably I descended into madness from whence I began to judge the quick and the dead. The founders of this nation, for example, now appeared to me not as patriots, but zealots, risking lives, fortunes, and sacred honors to confront a power against which they had to go toe to toe because their heads would not have reached their opponents' ankles. Indeed, they challenged not merely a nation but the natural order of the universe – the Great Chain of Being – God himself. Nay, they declared, there is no chain. All are created equal. Clearly, these were obsessive madmen. And I in my madness loved them, not for their wisdom, but for their obsessive insanity. And I loathed the eight who regained their senses and with others framed a constitution that in the interest of domestic tranquillity compromised equality, and counted some men and women but three-fifths. And I became suspicious – yes, I'll say it – paranoid, about our current politics, this so-called spirit of compromise that is the antithesis of obsession. Pray tell me, citizen, what is so wonderful about consensus-building, about having everything on the table? What would we have been now if independence had been negotiable? Oh, we'd be covered by a national health plan, true. But we'd be British, or Canadians at best.

Today we seek the middling middle ground in everything, responding less to principles than to interest. Why, just last week I heard some government official say, "This is not a crusade. It's a pragmatic effort to see freedom take hold where it will help us the most." Is that what our rebellion has come to? Are we no longer the apostles of freedom to all, but brokers of freedom to those who are most useful to us? What's wrong with a crusade for freedom? I mean, we have crusades against tobacco. But I don't mean any of this. I'm not obsessed or anything. But since Fred Douglass doesn't fit the times, I thought I'd try Rush Limbaugh.

Robert Olen Butler

E VEN BEFORE I knew there was another part of girls that would one day whisper to me, that would call me over and over, there was the machine in my uncle's shoe store and there was Karen Granger, and she was on my mind all the time. And somehow I knew that I had to get her to put her feet in the machine.

My uncle's was the last shoe store in Granite City, Illinois, to put in an X-ray machine to check the fit. And as soon as it was ready, I went to Karen and brought her to the shop. She had on her black Mary Janes and white lace anklets, and she went up to the step and put her feet in the slots, and my heart was beating furiously as I stepped up beside her, for there were two view ports, and together we looked at the bones in her feet. I lifted my arm and I put it around her, cupping her far shoulder in my hand.

"Wiggle your toes," I said. She did. And to this day, though I am now forty-eight years old, there have been few moments in my life as intimate as the sight of Karen Granger's actual bones: her actual articulated bones with their shape visible to me, the shape that had been secret even when she stood barefoot in the grass of her front yard bossing me and giving me an excuse to keep my eyes cast down. She wiggled her toes in the green glow of the X ray, and she let me keep my arm around her and she began to hum softly.

As I think of her now it seems true, what I just said, that the intimacy of that moment with Karen Granger in 1955, in the eleventh year of my life, was rarely matched in all the years since. And yet, I did not think of her again for decades. She did not begin to hum again in my head until a few months ago, on a trip to Puerto

Vallarta, and then she came with a newspaper article on X rays and health, and I let the paper fall from my hand by my canvas chair on the beach. She came briefly with that and then much more strongly an hour later with the smell of shoe leather in a shop in the hotel, the smell and a glimpse of the bare feet of a slim blond woman wearing a towel knotted at her hip, slipping past me without a glance.

I can't remember what song it was that Karen hummed as I pressed her against me, though trying to remember it distracted me in the Mexican shoe shop. I did not look again at the blond woman, but fixed on the buckle of a sandal in my hand and I tried to make the humming shape itself into a tune. And now of course I understand it's not the tune I really want to know. I want to know why she hummed. Did she know her bones were beautiful to me? Did she feel the same intimacy? Did she wait for me to ask to put my own feet in the machine? This is the thought that bothers me. I wish now, wish devoutly, that I had whispered to her, "My turn," and I had put my feet in the machine, and she had seen my bones.

Barry Hannah

H AVING HELD A teaching job off and on for twenty-five years without dispatching a single piece of scholarship, I thought I might read for this high occasion a brief commentary on a passage by Samuel Beckett, the master of farewells. Especially since I had said deep farewells lately just here in the last two years, to my father, my mother, and our own dear cat Billy – a gentleman cat, gray and white, who took care of baby kittens not even of his own paternity, all sweet nine years of his life. Wounded by a horse I think, Billy could not even rightly meow, yet he curled there in the monkey grass at the back steps, or slept in the laundry basket with great optimism. Farewell again, Pappy, Mammy, and Billy, sic transit, Mr. Beckett too. Farewell again, old friend, quiet, strange and exact, who wrote:

> All the old ways led to this, all the old windings. The stairs with never a landing that you screw yourself up clutching the rail, counting the steps, the fever of shortest ways under the long lids of sky, the wild country roads where your dead walk beside you on the dark shingle, that turning for the last time again to the lights of the little town, the appointments kept and the appointment broken, all the delights of urban and rural change of place, all the *exitus* and *reditus* closed and ended. All led to this, to this gloaming where a middle-aged man sits stroking his snout waiting for the first dawn to break . . .

To which this writer says yes, with abundance, stroking my snout in wild thanks for the beautiful lonesomeness this life of writing has afforded me, and most grateful to my listeners. At a certain time in life, something falls inward. You can almost hear the shudder in your chest. You'll see many things for the last time. Almost everything becomes elegiac, so you must watch very carefully, my friends, and touch these things with tenderness.

Jayne Anne Phillips

W E LIVE ON a rural road in a forgotten place somewhere in the 1950s. My mother has gone to college nights until at last she has a job as a teacher of six-year-olds. Many of the kids are brought in on buses from the hollows and settlements that crop up along the dirt roads. Our own road is a concrete two-lane that runs past open fields and isolated houses. One of those houses is a narrow bungalow perched at the crest of a hill. It sits up on blocks, has no foundation. We call it the shed. My mother says it ought to be against the law to rent a house like that to anybody. But people move into and out of the shed. Or it is empty whole seasons, winters mostly, when it must be barely habitable.

My brothers and I go to the same school where my mother teaches but sometimes we ride the bus. This year, when I'm ten years old, the bus stops at the shed and two scrawny boys walk out alone. They climb onto the bus and stand still for a moment in the aisle, looking at the rest of us. They have the fragile, porcelain skin that seems to characterize neglected kids from the country, and sores at their lips, and ill-fitting clothes. But these boys have their hair slicked back tall, Elvis style, and their features are fine and sharp, like those of little foxes. They take us in with their pale blue eyes, scent the air. Then the older one, who must be eight, puts his arm around the younger, and they sit down. Soon I'm hearing about the little one, Nathan, from my mother. He's in her class. He's one of the two or three she takes to the lunchroom in the mornings before school even starts. She finds them something to eat, and the cooks look the other way. She takes clothes to school for Nathan, too. And towels and soap. He comes to school smelling of

urine. Sometimes he has accidents. She brings his dirty clothes home
and washes them, and takes them back to school. Somehow Nathan
knows who I am, that I am her daughter, and I see him standing alone
in the long noon hours, watching me.

My mother tells me Nathan's mother takes off for weeks, riding
around in a tour bus with some country singer. I've seen her
downtown on Saturdays, a woman the size of a little girl, petite
and foxish like the boys. She wears tight gold lamé pants, spangly
earrings, and her brown hair hangs below her hips. The kids seem to
take care of themselves. Apparently there's another boy, younger
than Nathan. Sometimes we see them all outside in the field behind
the shed, but we never see the parents.

One day Nathan has another accident in class and my mother takes
him into the teachers' restroom to help him change his clothes. She's
preoccupied, having left the inexperienced student teacher in charge.
She fills the sink with warm soapy water and hands him a washcloth.
Then she actually looks at him. She's seen marks on him before, but
today there's no mistaking the long bands of discolored bruises across
his back and hips and legs. She asks him, "Nathan, what happened to
you?" And he doesn't make up another story about falling off a fence.
He tells her in his soft flat voice, "Daddy beat me with a board." My
mother takes him back to class, then calls the county welfare office.
She tells them, "I'm not sending him back to that house. Either you
find a place for him or I'll take him home with me." In fact he does
come home with us. We give him chocolate milk and graham
crackers while my mother makes more phone calls. She convinces a
kindly older couple, Hank and Christine, friends of my father's, to
take Nathan, and they sign themselves up as foster parents.

I know a little about a lot of people in the town by listening to adults
talk. I know a little about Hank and Christine. They're childless. Hank
is big and ruddy with a shock of white hair. Years ago he had a problem;
he nearly drank himself to death. Now the town says of them, "She
stood right by him and for once it worked." It all seems to work
tonight. Hank and Christine come for supper as though we're all a big
family. Then they take Nathan home to their spare room, to a teddy

bear and a new coverlet printed with cowboys and clouds. Over the
next three weeks they take him to a circus in a neighboring town, and
shopping for a winter parka. He has a new pair of boots with stitching
on the sides, like cowboys wear. And at recess at school he stands with
his brother on the playground. He brings the brother over to me nearly
every day, silently, the two of them with their fists in their pockets. I
wonder if the brother is angry because Nathan was taken away, but he
doesn't seem angry. He inspects Nathan's new boots and seems eager to
talk, as though he wants to make a good impression. I think about the
first time I saw him on the bus, the look on his wary face and his arm
around Nathan. He had someone to protect. Now he's not sure.

The bell rings and the playground begins to empty. The boys go off
in different directions, the brother hesitating, shuffling his feet. The
look he gives me over his shoulder is one of such grudging hope and
uncertainty that I feel angry at my mother. Angry that she hasn't
rescued him, too. Rescued all the kids like him who after all only have
each other. But soon I hear that Nathan's back with his family, that
there wasn't enough evidence to keep him out of the home. Soon the
family moves on, disappears. The shack of a house stands empty again.

One day in the spring I'm riding my bicycle past and surprise myself
by turning onto the dirt track that leads across scrub grass behind
Nathan's house. I stand beside the rickety back porch, which is about as
broad as a sidewalk. There's a view of fields, and the stream beyond, and
the wooded hills. This is what Nathan saw, and over that way to the
right he saw my house, a big ranch house with trikes and bikes in the
yard, as far away as the moon. Strangely, there are no windows in the
shed at all, but there's a circular window with a glass pane, like a
peephole, in the back door. So I look though. It's months since they left,
but the floor is strewn with objects as though they ran out yesterday,
dropping things. A shoe. Torn magazines. A cot-sized mattress, ripped
and propped up so that its contents seem to spill out in a damaged froth.
I can see the woodstove squarely in the middle of the little room,
hulking, its awkward pipe piercing the ceiling. I look for something of
Nathan – the boots, or the coverlet, crumpled into a corner, no longer
sky blue – but nothing is there. He's taken it all with him.

George Plimpton

I AM OBSESSED BY fireworks. I have been so since childhood – astonished by the alchemic wonder of touching a match to inert matter and have it rise and perform its miracle of color and concussion in the night sky. I think my obsession is because I'm a writer, who, unlike the pyrotechnician, rarely has the opportunity to realize the effect of his or her work on a reader. The English novelist John Mortimer once told me of a writer friend of his who got on the tube at Piccadilly and discovered that the young woman on the seat opposite was reading a book of his. He knew that forty or fifty pages from where she was reading, there was a scene which would surely produce a laugh. So rather than getting off at Green Park, his original destination, he stayed on until the end of the line at Cockfosters, waiting for the laugh. It never came. The writer identifies with Mallarmé, the bemoan of the blank page that faces him or her every day, the appalling difficulty of decorating it with words. Compare that to the fireworks man who touches a flame to a fuse and within seconds the "oohs" and the "aahs" rise from the hillside from those in wonder at what he has done in the night sky.

And how fortunate he is with his black canvas of the night sky – the faint and insignificant stars, comets of minuscule aesthetic value, a moon which only shows its one face – and how eagerly he decorates it with man-made brush strokes, fat comets, rainbow-hued stars, mad whirligigs . . . doing better with the heavens than the gods themselves.

The Chinese, very likely because they discovered the earliest pyrotechnical ingredients, are wondrously imaginative in naming their fireworks. A tag accompanying a shell from the Orient will read "The Monkeys Enter the Heavenly Temple and Drive Out the Tiger." Alas, our more prosaic retailers change this to "Sky Monkeys." "Humming Birds Blossom over the Yangtze and Blot Out the Moon" is muted to "Colored Birds."

In my later years, the octogenarian phase, I would like to become a fireworks-shell namer, my fame such that I am called to China every autumn to name their newest produce. I step off a train in a distant province carrying a small suitcase. I am met by officials who bow very low. At the firing site a chair is brought out with a soft cushion in it. Dusk. And then the night sky comes with its miserable display of stars – insignificant, immaterial, no moon – the perfect canvas. I'm handed a pen and a sheet of rice paper. The first shell of the night flutters up, a comet tail, then a cascade of blue stars. I am lost in thought. "The Blue Ox Comes Down the Turnpike?" No, that will not do. "I am not inspired," I tell them. "Send it up again."

That night will be the only time I put pen to paper until autumn comes around and I am summoned once again.

Ernest Gaines

A N OBSESSION OF mine concerns a half-acre of land in south-central Louisiana. This plot of land is surrounded by sugarcane fields on all sides, some of the rows coming within twenty feet of it. This plot of land is where my ancestors have been buried the past hundred years, where most of the people I knew as a child are now buried. This is Riverlake plantation, Point Coupee Parish, Oscar, Louisiana.

The first fifteen-and-a-half years of my life were spent on this place. My ancestors for over a hundred years planted the sugarcane here, hoed the sugarcane, plowed it, cut it and, when it was time, hauled it to the mills. They, like too many others who worked this land, are buried here in unmarked graves because they could not afford the headstones.

A hundred years ago, the land was owned by one man who designated that the land would be a cemetery for the people on that plantation, but he did not give it to them, nor would he let them buy it. Today the land is owned by sixteen people who live all over the country and probably different parts of the world, some of whom I'm sure have never visited the plantation or know anything about the cemetery which lies there. Yet it is their land, and those who are buried there do not own even six feet of the ground.

Many rural cemeteries have been destroyed all over this country, and day and night I worry that the same fate may happen to this one. There is no law in the state of Louisiana that I am aware of that says it cannot be done. My wife and I and several friends from my child-hood are trying to find a way to get control of the land. We have contacted lawyers to work with us and presently we are keeping the place clean of overgrowth, because that is one excuse landowners and developers use to plow under cemeteries. "We didn't know that one was there."

At a recent interview, I was asked where would I like to be buried and I answered that I'd like to be in the same place where my ancestors are. The interviewer asked me what would I like on my headstone and I said, "To lie with those who have no marks." These are the people for whom I wrote letters as a child, read their letters because many of them could not read nor could they write. Many of them had to go into the fields before they had a chance to go to school. Yet they're the ones responsible for my being here tonight. Not only did they encourage me to stay in school, but they, and only they, have been the source of all of my writings. I've said many times before that my novels, my short stories, are just continuations of the letters that I started writing for them some fifty years ago, and since I've tried to say something about their lives on paper – their joy, their sorrows, their love, their fears, their pride, their compassion – I think it is only my duty now to do as much as I can to see that they lie in peace forever.

Francine Prose

I N MANY WAYS there is nothing more boring than obsession. That tiny pinpoint of white light glittering on the horizon, reducing the whole world around it to grayness and general blur. Its qualities are fixation, monotony, repetition. It's yet another psychoactive drug, like alcohol or LSD, that looks better from the inside than it ever does from the outside. Our best friends are tired of hearing about it, that thing or person we desperately want, that muddy center we poor, possessed oxen trudge round and round in circles.

The interesting exceptions are the obsessions of great obsessives – Joan of Arc, Napoleon, Freud, Columbus, Mother Teresa, Saint Simeon Stylites sitting thirty years on a pole in the desert – an extreme and very early piece of religious performance art.

And what's more interesting even than that is the mysterious way in which obsessions great and small are alchemically turned into art. Of course, this is a great mystery and defies explanation. Kafka wrote to his father, "Everything I wrote was about you," and it was everything, but only a very small part of Gregor Samsa's short, sad life as a cockroach. Marcel Proust building with tea cakes, and with a particular hat that a particular duchess wore to a particular party, a model of nothing less than time itself. How does he differ exactly from the little boy whose parents are sick with worry because he is maniacally building with Legos and never goes out to play with his friends?

Every artist is an obsessive. Some are eccentric, like Joseph Cornell. Some of us are hidden about it. Some wallow in it, like Kafka. We become obsessed with writers whose obsessions match our own, so one year it may be Colette, and the next, George Orwell.

Writers write from obsession, and to learn what their obsessions are. I seem, for example, to be obsessed with household pets and weddings, two subjects I think are beside the point in what I think is my conscious life. I always imagine Flaubert working for months to come up with the perfect gift for Emma Bovary to give her lover, Tolstoy breaking the printer's plates and rewriting *Anna Karenina.*

If there is an obsession that writers have in common, it's the obsession with truth and perfection, that maddened fixation on every word that is the hallmark of a real writer. Writers are like those screamers who yell at you in the street, shouting the same phrases, the same words again and again and again, convinced that someone will stop and reply if they can only just get it right.

Mary Lee Settle

T HE MOST COMMON obsession, one we have usually survived by the time we are twenty-one, is falling in love. Alas, with some of us, the experience goes on and on and on. It is not love. They are as different literally as day and night. Love is of the day, daily, survives in lovely light, reality, acceptance of one's fellow beings. Falling in love is alone and of the night, dreams, insomnia, hopes, fears, and above all, the question "Why?"

I do not propose to say anything wise about falling in love. There is little wise to say. I fall in love every three years. My husband is very understanding. At least I think he is. But his obsession is chess, which is after all a war game between partners in which you win by checking your mate. He can read the signs, though, from long experience – the staring into space, the waiting, the deterioration of the food from gourmet cooking to what we call "plates of stuff."

Like all falling in love, it begins with an image, evasive and uninvited. The lover moves into my mind as a squatter would move into a house, always at first unknown. Cruel? Oh, often. Like Jim in the song who doesn't send me pretty flowers and makes me, God knows, wait the lonely hours. Sometimes, not often, the image is like Juliet's beauteous flower, formed and glowing. But even that can be suppressed at first so easily by interference, demands, the human voices that wake us and we drown. So I begin to question this intruder, and go on questioning. Know, because it's happened before, that I have received a gift and a burden for which I have not asked. Like Jacob and the angel, I cannot let it go until it blesses me with the answer to "Why?" Why has it happened? What does it want of me? The months pass, sometimes the years – once twenty-eight years of this sustained illusion. The image has taken up residence, becomes familiar, more so than daily life. The physical horizon narrows to a single room, the dream horizon of my love expands beyond oceans, empires and time. And finally the questions are answered as well as I can. The work is done. I have been blessed and can let go.

The book is finished. I can reenter the human race, be quiet, content, love daily life, cook well and cultivate, as Candide learned, my garden.

I hope every time against hope, of course, that it will never, never happen again, which is as obsessive an illusion as the initial image. Sometimes I'm asked innocently why I chose to write. I didn't choose it. Like a lover, it chose me. Nobody but a fool, or an obsessive, would work so hard for such low pay.

Ntozake Shange

THIS IS AN obsession of a favorite character of mine. She appears in several things, in some stories and two plays and in the next novel in different manifestations. She only has the same name. Her name is Lilly.

I'm gonna simply brush my hair. Rapunzel, pull your tresses back into the tower, and Lady Godiva, give up horseback riding! I'm gonna alter my social and professional life dramatically. I will brush a hundred strokes in the morning, a hundred stokes midday, and a hundred strokes before retiring. I will have a very busy schedule. Between the local train and the express, I'm gonna brush. I brush between telephone calls. At the dance hall I brush. I don't dance on slow dances. I brush my hair thinking about anything but mostly I think about how it will be when I get my full head of hair – like lifting my head in the morning will become a chore. I'll try to turn my cheek and my hair will weigh me down. I dream of Chaka Khan, chocolate from Grand Central Station with all seven wigs and Medusa. I brush and I brush. I use olive oil, hair food, and Posner's Vitamin E, but mostly I brush and I brush. I may lose contact with most of my friends. I could lose my job, but I'm on unemployment and brush while waiting on line for my check. I'm sure I get good recommendations from my social worker: "Such a fastidious woman, that Lilly, always brushing her hair."

Nothing in my dreams suggests that hair-brushing *per se* has anything to do with my particular head of hair. A therapist might say that the head full of hair has to do with something else, like a symbol of Lilly's unconscious desires, but I have no therapist. And my dreams mean things to me like, if you dream about Tobias then something has happened to Tobias, or he's gonna show up. If you dream about your grandma who's dead, than you must be doing something she doesn't like or she would not have gone to all that trouble to leave heaven like that. If you dream something red you should stop. If you dream something green you should keep on doing that. If a blue person appears in your dream, then that person is your true friend. And that's how I see my dreams.

And this head full of hair I have in my dreams is lavender and nappy as a three-year-old's in an apple tree. I can fry an egg and see the white of the egg spreading in the grease like my hair is gonna spread in the air. But I am not egg-yolk yellow, I am brown, and the egg white is not white at all as actual hair, and it will go on and on forever, irregular like a Rastafarian man's hair. Irregular and gargantuan and lavender, nestled on blue satin pillow, pillow like the sky. And so I fry my eggs. I buy daisies dyed lavender and lavender lace table mats and lavender nail polish. Though I never admit it, I really do believe in magic and can do strange things when something comes over me. Soon, everything around me will be lavender, fluffy and consuming. I will know now a moment of bitterness through all the wrist aching and tennis elbow from brushing. I'll smile. No regrets. "*Je ne regrette rien,*" I'll sing, just like Edith Piaf. When my friends want me to go see Tina Turner or Pacheco I'll croon, "Sorry, I have to brush my hair."

I'll find ambrosia. My hair will grow pomegranates in soil rich as around the Aswan. I wake in my bed to bananas, avocados, collard greens, fresh croissants, Pouilly Fuissé, Ishmael Reed's essay, Charlotte Carter's stories, all just streaming from my hair. And with the bricks that plop from where a nine-year-old's top braid would be, I will brush myself a house with running water and a bidet. I'll have a closet full of clean bed linen, and a little girl from the Castro Convertible commercial will come and open the bed repeatedly and stay on as helper to help me brush my hair.

I am the only person I know whose every word leaves a purple haze on the tip of your tongue. When this happens, I say clouds are forming and I have to close the windows. Violet rain is hard to remove from blue satin pillows.

Elizabeth Spencer

THE OTHER DAY, while wandering about, thinking obsessively about obsession, I passed a perfume counter in a store, and there it was: Obsession. Trapped in an array of oddly shaped bottles – flanked by Passion in purple bottles on one side and Poison in black bottles on the other. This seemed a fitting arrangement as though a poet had devised it. Obsession. Passion. Poison. It's worthy of Baudelaire.

Martin Scorsese, remarking on his recent movie *The Age of Innocence*, saw its subject as obsession, which he described as an unattainable desire, a neverending torment. He might have added that literature, like life, abounds in obsession. Ahab was obsessed with that whale. Quentin Compson was obsessed with his sister's honor. Silas Marner hated to lose his gold.

Obsession is like a virus. You don't seek it, but if you catch it, how do you lose it? Clearly there is a dark side to obsession, a diabolical darkness may be at work. The devil may be in it, and if he is, he's winning. Down goes the *Pequod*, all souls but one drown with her. Quentin Compson kills himself. I began to wonder if any light side is possible.

Then I found Ray Lum.

Ray Lum, no part Chinese, was born in 1891 in Vicksburg, Mississippi. He was a mule trader. During the major part of his life, mules were so attached to the farming landscape that if you didn't see mules, you didn't know if it was really a farm. Ray Lum was a trader and an auctioneer. He made private sales and public sales. He ranged through the Mississippi delta and the hills. He knew everybody. His long life story is now in a book, a transcription of his very words, thick with his lived experience. This book is called *You Live and Learn, Then You Die and Forget It All.*

Through the decades of our century, Ray Lum dealt in mules, not only in Mississippi and nearby states but also in the southwest, and bought wild horses by the thousands in South Dakota to ship south for sale. He traded and he swapped. He made money. "I never saw any place," he said, "where it was necessary to lie to a man in horse trades, but you handle the truth awful careful sometimes."

His trade was his obsession. He never gave it up. At age eighty-five, during the 1970s, back in Vicksburg and sitting in his shop selling horse blankets and saddles, bridles, and brushes, he was still attending every auction in a wide radius, though they were mainly in horses now, as mechanized farming had all but finished off the mule trade. Ray Lum kept on because he couldn't quit. He bought up horses he couldn't even transport home, didn't need, and had no use to put them to. He would trade, acquire, and leave them there. He was obsessed, but he was happily obsessed. He did not have tunnel vision. He wore no blinders on his bridle. It's this that makes him different.

Ray Lum remembered all the people he found in any way remarkable. He could tell about them all. He came too close to an ostrich once and it kicked him harder than a mule. He held the bets for a fight between a monkey and a bulldog (no lady speaking in the Folger Shakespeare Library should tell you how the monkey won). On a street out West he saw Pretty Boy Floyd. He was careful to look the other way. On a drive approaching Abilene in his "good Cadillac car," he gave a wide berth to Bonnie and Clyde, who were driving so fast all four wheels had left the ground.

It was not in spite of his obsession but because of it that Ray Lum lived a rich, fulfilled, and loving life.

Why fall hopelessly in love with some trifling guy or some uncaring woman? Why spend your days lusting for fame and fortune when you can do something really rewarding? Don't go chasing whales or worrying about your sister. If you have a choice, choose mules.

Scott Spencer

S OME YEARS AGO, I wrote *Endless Love*, which I wrote from the point of view of a love-starved and then lovesick young man. Though nowhere in the novel is the word "obsession" used, I became, for a time, associated with the idea of obsession, and since then readers have found the theme of obsession in my work, as if I wrote about characters whose moral dilemmas could be cured by psychiatry.

Obsession is one of those quasimedical terms that have worn their way into the mainstream of language and can appear and disappear like the queen in a game of three-card-monte. It is part of the language of control, a word we use against those whose actions we seek to govern. Sometimes, it seems whether or not you're an obsessive depends on crossing a very thin line. Fail to get a date with someone after asking her out a couple of times and you're a suitor; ask her out a third time – you're obsessed. Sometimes it means you just aren't looking out for number one. Speak out daily for the rights of the homeless and be given a salary to do so and you're a lobbyist; espouse the same views daily from a picket line and you're obsessed. And sometimes it means you're living by some unfashionable credo, a degraded commandment. A man who says he will do literally anything to protect his family has a good chance of being described as a model father; a man who says we will do literally anything to protect that nice family who lives next door will probably find himself described as obsessed and may be directed to seek counseling. Collect string and you're an obsessive; collect Renaissance art and you're . . . a collector.

On the political level, we have seen the elusiveness of obsession's definition in the past couple of years. Whereas once anticommunism was routinely considered patriotic, even mandatory, this former mainstay of American political consciousness is now looked on as a kind of feverish derangement. A recent issue of the *St. Petersburg Times* (in Florida, not Russia) said, "The fall of the Soviet Union has freed the U.S. from a national psychosis. Our irrational obsession with communism dominated our collective unconscious as surely as any phobic disorder." The writer may be correct, but what we have here is not the sharpening of a political analysis, but a shift in power relations. Today we're selling light bulbs to the Hungarians and Mrs. Butterworth's Breakfast Syrup to Ukraine. Business with the Eastern bloc is Renaissance art, and now espousing anticommunism is like collecting string.

Calling an act obsessive is society's way of shouting *enough*. And now – in our codependent, dysfunctional age – the language of control is medical. Just as we label as paranoia the fears of those who are powerless and whose view of reality we do not respect, so do we brand obsessive those people whose passions are inconvenient, or too long-lived or too sexual, too costly, too dangerous, or too critical of the current consensus.

And it is here, in that vast public ward implied by the word "obsession," that the characters in my novels are forced to take their meals – with stalkers, rapists, and disgruntled former employees. Is it any wonder that I look forward to the time when the word "obsession" collapses under the weight it has been asked to bear, when it will become a diagnosis as antique as the vapors?

Louis Begley

THE CHILDREN WERE the first to notice. As soon as they saw me do it, they pointed with their fingers and tittered. Then they told my wife about it. I would hear them all laughing until tears ran down their cheeks, her laughter always the brightest, like a crystal bell, never failing to thrill me even when it's at my expense.

It became official on my fiftieth birthday. Visions of perfectly honed #2 Ticonderoga pencils had been dancing in my head. I had been hoping for a rechargeable sharpener. But as soon as the cake had been cut, before I could herd them together for a family snapshot, they presented me with the Stradivarius of brooms, a yellow ribbon tied around the bright red handle, a red one pleated in its head of blond straw. No explanation was needed. It was the perfect gift for a man whose obsession is sweeping.

How had it started? In Long Island. We had acquired a house with a summer room that looks like a yogurt factory. The floor was made of flagstones. At its edge, covering the native sand, were gray and white pebbles. For similar aesthetic reasons, the builder had sowed more pebbles in the space between the flagstones lining the part that leads to the pool. Only I was nimble enough to walk in and out of the summer room or on the path without disturbing the pebbles. Under the feet of my family or guests, the pebbles scattered, or, worse yet, invaded the surface of the flagstones. I watched warily for this breakout of disorder. At first I would brush the pebbles back to where they were intended to be stealthily, with my bare toes. Soon, I was no longer able to contain myself. Indifferent to my audience, I would neaten quite openly, sweeping the pebbles to the circumference of the summer room or the interstices in the pool path. The stooped, melancholy and stubborn figure – broom in hand – that's me, the solitary sweeper of Long Island's South Fork.

What does it mean? Clean sweep? Swept away? Sweep under the rug? None of these metaphors fits my grand obsession. To sweep is to restore order. To return to an imagined world of pristine innocence. So I ride my broomstick in search of a stasis of perfection where each thing, breathless and suspended, is beautifully just where it should be.

Thomas Flanagan

I WAS DELIGHTED TO have been asked back to PEN/Faulkner, which seemed to me one of those rare literary occasions which are both elegant and human. Ever since April, when PEN/Faulkner asked me to join with you and talk about obsession for three minutes, I have been able to think of little else.

I went first of course to the dictionary. Not the *OED*. I had misplaced the magnifying glass, and in any event, using it always arouses my latent feelings of social inferiority. A friend many years ago inherited a full set from his father, and I always imagine him strolling to his shelf while I crouch over microscopic type. I did go, though, to its admirable abridgment, the *Oxford Universal Dictionary*, where I discovered of course that all my life I had been using the word incorrectly. The word obsession derives, I was instructed, from the Latin *obsidere* and meant originally "to besiege," as a fortress is besieged or invested. And thence, says the dictionary, actuation by the devil or an evil spirit from without. And thence, finally, from that, the action of any influence, notion or fixed idea which persistently assails or vexes. But this ran very counter to my notion that an obsession arises from within and seizes upon the external. A man obsessed by the notion that he is the reincarnation of Napoleon is not influenced toward that big leap by a chance visit to Waterloo, or by marriage to a woman named Josephine; it is quite the other way around. His obsession leads him to seek out the battlefield that he may relive an old sorrow, and he pays court to a woman who bears the appropriate name.

I turned to *Webster's Third*, which of course dismissed the besetting activities of devils or spirits as obsolete, obs. Obs is an abbreviation which in *Webster's Third* always carries a chilling whiff of contempt. *Webster's* settles instead for "a persistent and disturbing intrusion of, or anxious and inescapable preoccupation with a feeling, especially if known to be unreasonable." This seemed even worse. Obsessions are indeed persistent but they need not be disturbing or a cause of anxiety, nor something from which one vainly seeks relief. Surely it all depends on the nature of the obsession. And the more I reflected on it, the more hostile seemed that word "unreasonable." Unreasonable to whom? It seems a bit nasty of external reality first to implant the obsession in the sufferer's mind and then to condemn that mind for accepting it. Dictionaries claim to be neutral judges of language, but in fact they are subtle casuists. And in fact they are subtle casuists directed against writers and artists in general, who believe that their central energies arise from within, and then confront them without.

After these two, I had no need to consult their lesser and more recent rivals, but something unreasonable and obsessive drove me on. *The American College Dictionary* speaks of the besetting or dominating action or influence of a persistent feeling, idea "or the like." One turns to a dictionary for precision, and is fobbed off with an airy wave of the editorial hand, "or the like!"

The American Heritage Dictionary is the most modern, with hundreds of line drawings and little reproductions in the margin. I had hoped, as I turned to the O's to find a drawing modeled upon Fuseli or Goya of an actual obsession, crouched upon a skull and battering for entrance. I was disappointed but was able to learn that of recent years, the verb "to obsess" has acquired an intransitive usage. For illustration, the *Heritage* turns not to Walter Pater or Evelyn Waugh or Vladimir Nabokov. Instead it goes right to stylistic headquarters, to Scott Turow himself, one of whose novels contains the line "She's dead but you're still obsessing."

After that, it took me the better part of two days to find the magnifying glass, but was it worth the effort and the dust? When the *OED* needs an illustration it turns to the splendidly named Hubert

Crackenthorpe, a decadent of the English 1890s and a justly forgotten one, who is quoted as having said, "The thought of death began to haunt him until it became a constant obsession." One does not quarrel easily with the *OED*, but surely all obsessions are constant? My task, fortunately, has only begun. Roget's and *Webster's Thesaurus* list among synonyms: fixations, fascination, phantom, craze, delusion, mania, infatuation, fixed idea, compulsion, and (perhaps Mr. Turow's contribution) hang-up. I am now in the process of hunting down these words and their shadings and colorations. It is a task before which everything else seems unreasonably to be fading away.

Maureen Howard

MY DEARS, I have never been what you suggest. The idea that I should be beholden to, let's say, the erratic splashing of a killer whale or wish to display upon my palms the bloody nail holes of the crucifixion, displeases me. Displeasure – the very word gives you a clue to the sort of unruffled woman I am. Neither sinner, nor saint; I've not known the corrupting passion of the mad captain nor the ecstasy of the little virgin bleeding, as it were, from the wrong place. Neither a loser nor a winner be: give me a pail of quarters, face me off with a one-armed bandit, I will not waste one coin in a frenzy of hope against hope that three identical cherries or lemons or limes will bing, bing, bing into place. Unless, of course, it is love – first, second or fourth – you intend by obsession, those hormonal overdrives, seizures of the heart we are prone to, more than passing fancy, passing nevertheless, within the natural order. If that's all you mean, I've been there, but I suspect you are after something else. Confession is begged by the unholy word. Idolatry? Witchcraft? I have no such history, and must conjure for you a harmless story.

Two girls, they shall be nameless, but in the days of girls at a girlish college sharing a room, both given to dreaming life into art, small life they knew: it was for them foreign films, gay posters of Lautrec and Mary Cassatt, the strenuous modern dance. Chekhov and Charles Trenez, Parsifal, twin-sets, Cinzano were all too lovely. In their flannel nightgowns they wrote – often late into the night – poems. You'd know it was poetry had you ever known them, moony and innocent as they were. One wrote heroic couplets, villanelles – an angular girl tucked up in smooth blankets, versifying in her loose-leaf notebook. Adept at enjambment, caesura, she won all the prizes with her poems which were of things – states and paintings, landscape, and the weather.

Across the room, a frowsy girl ate cookies in her bed. Propped with a snoutless bear, a napless creature, she sighed, laughed, rumpling her quilt, scribbling, erasing in a red book, a silly book it was, let me tell you, cheap red cloth embossed with improbable daisies and whatever was written on those pages, written with those sighs, hums, elicited a sucking of breath in pain or was it pleasure? The red book was never offered, never to be seen one girl to another, that secrecy an affront to the poetess with the prizes who wondered what faltering rhymes, dear-diary stuff might be hidden from her in the red book with its lock, yes the teeny lock with teeny keys secreted somewhere in the room like a child's game taunting here to find it, the red book the last thing she saw at night, the last thing she heard the feeble scratch of its key, its frayed edges the first slight of the morning mocking her own neat couplets or quatrains to be typed on a slippery, sleek Olivetti, until on a gray evening, alone, naked, come quick from the shower, the red blank book, for that's all it was, fell at her feet not like a lover, and she tore at the flimsy lock to see the smudges, crumbs on the page to find there (have you guessed it?) words spun free in their lines, the wild surmise, journeywork of the stars – without artifice and, yes, without things, not a trace of teddy bear or common daisy.

In a precarious balance, the girlish scale of things, it was like first looking into Chapman's *Homer*, Emerson opening, my god! *Leaves of Grass*; coming upon a sacred scrap of Amherst's blest spinster. Having broken the lock, to burn the red book? The ashes, the stench. Toss it then in the dormitory trash where its cover would scream for retrieval? No. Run in bathrobe and bare feet – cold, bitter cold – sink it in the sludge of Paradise Pond, wash away words, blank the blank book.

Frowsy still, rumpled – the woman reads from her collected words. They hang from the rafters. The great show, I am told, is to hear her proclaim from memory her earliest poems, each line soft and clear, exhibiting in the spoken moment the delight in her discovery of the lost book, the indelible words. You will have to make do with this transparent fable. I'm sorry if you wanted de Sade's sexual exhaustions, Loyola's gift of tears: I write grocery lists, my dears, thank-you notes, reviews, the occasional essay.

I have never been possessed by words.

HEROES

October 7, 1991

Sue Miller

P ITY THE HERO. He's the man of the hour or at least of the famous fifteen minutes, but he's about to be exposed, defrocked, caught sleeping with many women (none his wife), caught trying to cash in on his videotaped version of the truth, caught skimming the profits. It's discovered he has a criminal record, he drinks too much, he's padded his résumé, he's plagiarized portions of his published work. There's the perception of a conflict of interest. As a culture, we're quick to revile those we've idolized. We're all too ready to buy into disillusion, weary of the very idea of heroism, because so many of our contemporary heroes are revealed to have feet of clay, a streak of avarice, a pinch of priapism, the tendency toward needy self-aggrandizement. In fact, we take great pleasure in the deliciously prolonged, shocked, and self-righteous double-take at the discovery of those clay feet sticking out from under the idol's marble robe. We can lay the blame for this in a variety of places, on the press for raking up the muck in the first place, on television for having so reshaped our attention span that we need the frequent hit of muck in order to sell more cars or beer or deodorant or whatnot. But none of it would be possible without the blinded vision that refuses to look at those feet of clay in the first place. There's a kind of hagiography in our passionate embrace of heroes that leaves us, I think, uniquely vulnerable to cynical disillusion.

Literature has everything to say about this if there's anyone out there reading. It offers the correctiveness of ambiguity, ambiguity about the notion of what it means to be a hero. For serious literature through all time, when it's freed of responsibility to the state, or to the church, or to the idea of political correctness, has been at pains to demonstrate that being a hero is not a permanent condition, but rather a moment one rises to. Sometimes, in spite of everything one intends or wishes, from King Lear to Sethe in Morrison's *Beloved*, from the grandmother shot by the misfit in "A Good Man Is Hard to Find" to Lord Jim, it descends on unworthy and unlikely fictional characters like a moment of terrifying and sometimes unwanted grace. It shakes them, it changes them utterly. Sometimes it destroys them. A culture that reads literature can understand heroism as a mystery. It can forgive and pity its heroes. It can be ready to embrace the astonishing and redeeming possibility of heroic behavior everywhere in human life.

Tim O'Brien

This is a dazzling array of talent and I feel as if I'm on an all-star team, a literary all-star team, and I'm honored to be in the lineup even if I'm batting way down the order. I'm glad too that the event will raise money; I'm glad the money won't go for hair spray for sheiks in Kuwait, I'm glad the money will go in one form or another to writers. Writers can use it. I'm a writer, by the way. The reason we're all here, aside from hearing about heroes, is that America sometimes gets absentminded about paying writers. For instance, the guy who bats in my slot tonight for the Boston Red Sox makes twelve times what I do. He's not even an all-star. He doesn't get to give speeches. Now and then he gets to explain on television why he can't stop striking out. "No can see the ball too hot," he says. Anyway, I'll bet you can guess that the hero I want to tell you about tonight does not play baseball for the Boston Red Sox. The Boston Red Sox, I might add, often do not play baseball for the Boston Red Sox; they play for Baltimore a lot.

The hero I want to tell you about does not play baseball for Baltimore either. He's a dead old man – at least I think he's dead. Elroy Birdall was eighty-some years old when I last saw him and that was two decades ago. I was twenty-one then. There was a war on which I despised and thought was immoral. Certain blood, I thought, was being shed for uncertain reasons. I didn't want to die in that war. I didn't want to die. The war was named after a country called Viet Nam or Viet Naam, the pronunciation varying according to which president of the United States you'd happen to be listening to. I listened to four of them. All four got paid pretty well. They gave more speeches than I do and they were all-stars; they're in the Hall of Fame.

My hero, the old man, wasn't an all-star. He was just a tiny shrunken, bald old man in brown pants and a flannel shirt. His name was Elroy Birdall, and old Elroy was smart. He was hard to fool. Like the famous all-star once said, "You can fool some of the people all of the time, and all the people some of the time, but you can't fool all the people all the time." There should have been an extra clause in that statement to include Elroy Birdall. He hardly ever got fooled. I did get fooled for a while. The Gulf of Tonkin business fooled me; it fooled a lot of people, including many hundred members of Congress and forty-eight members of the U.S. Senate. They passed a resolution named after the Gulf of Tonkin. The resolution legitimized the war I didn't want to die in. Anyhow, twenty years ago, when old Elroy and I talked about the Gulf of Tonkin, he said a smart thing. The thing he said was this: he said "Crap." He said another smart thing: "There should be a law," he said "if you vote for a war," he said "you have to go fight in it in the front lines, or else you have to send your mother." "A law" he said.

Well, I'm sorry to be talking about these terrible things to you. America gave me Viet Nam. I spent twenty years giving it back. What happened was this: When I got drafted, I decided to run away. I lived in Minnesota, which is a state north of Mexico, adjacent to the Canadian border. Nobody in my generation had trouble pronouncing Canada. So I packed a bag and I drove north to a river called the Rainy River, which separates Minnesota from Canada. To think things over for a while, I stopped at a fishing resort called the Tip Top Lodge, which was just a bunch of old yellow cabins along the Rainy River. Elroy Birdall was the caretaker, and for six days in the summer of 1968 Elroy watched over me as I made my decision. He asked no questions, but he knew there was a war on. He knew that, he knew my age, he saw the terror in my eyes, he heard me squealing in my sleep, he knew Canada was just a boatride away. Even so, he didn't press me, he offered no advice, he fed me and gave me a place to lie low. Elroy, in the summer of 1968, was simply there, like the Rainy River and the late summer sun. And yet by his presence, his mute watchfulness, he made it real. He was a witness, like God, or like the gods, who look on in absolute silence as we live our lives, as we make our choices, or fail to make them. He was a hero. I wasn't. I went to Viet Nam.

Allan Gurganus

M Y NAME IS Allan and I'm a news junkie. The doctor told me to quit the six papers and even my four hours a day of NPR cold turkey. So bravely I go to Yosemite. Nature, a methadone substitute for the world tragedy I binge on. The Middle East, my kidney stones; the Iraq war, my six-week epilepsy televised. I blame myself and, everybody, once and for all, I'm sorry. Okay? It's great in the woods, green, no newspaper stands, less responsibility. I'm with a woman friend, platonic, I assure you, but that's calmer, you know, and we're both writing in an uninsulated cabin of thirty square feet, in a park newly deserted of tourists, out among redwoods, beautiful! Miles from a paved road, dull. My life's newsprint smudge lightens to almost daylight. Listen, I just can't keep helping everybody anymore, okay?

So two A.M., a darkness medieval and, it's true, I did a no-no and left our barbecue grill caked with chicken grease on the deck, and the ranger did say they got hungry with the tourists gone and just before hibernation and everything. Two A.M. something hits the back door so hard – and in my mammal bowels, I know, I just know. Wearing only Brooks Brothers boxer shorts, I tiptoe toward the deck's light switch. There's a small window over the sink and I hit the switch and I'm facing the broad chest of something brown black, on its hind legs, too tall for its head to even fit in the window. We're talking black bear, five and a half feet tall. The thing is hairier than even anybody at my Manhattan Health Club. I mean thick. "Honey," I called to my friend, "Think we got a bear here." And I at once bite my lip for saying first thing "Honey." Suddenly the "h" word. "My period just started," she called. "You know, I bet that's part of why it's here. They say their sense of smell is just . . ." Now she tells me. Out here in the woods, just asking for it. So I turn on everything loud – garbage disposal, Cuisinart, vibrators, everything. Too late for bribes, I switch on the radio. One station, an evangelical, ". . . and Lord, as we wander paths of sin, plague and tribulations will befall us, Lord." I turn it off. I grab a broom, I make threatening motions toward the chest but its head is too high to notice yet. The broom handle is royal blue and that seems important. How else can we make noise? Screaming? Yes, that will be easy, the screaming. I do that. And then it just walks around the deck, very confident on its back legs. I don't know, like Robin Williams. It looks like Robin Williams and begins working with the back door's lock. This friggin' thing is coming in! Well, a man's got to do what his testosterone suggests, and I don't want to take credit for what I tried next, but I had a woman near even if she was sending mixed signals. So I go ahead and I just do it! I dial 911. Then have the ultimate late twentieth-century experience, my brothers and sisters. For the first time in my life I dial 911 and nobody answers. Then I understand the heroism of our ancestors, then I understand it's not the news that's bad, it's the world. I leaned against a door bowing inward with bear weight. I beat it with the phone's suddenly colorful wiring and I hear a kind of native mantra that just wells up, heroic and helpful, out of me. It seems an ancient Lakota Indian term that means, roughly, "Do I need this?" "Do I need this now?" And I scream it at the bear over and over, my new mantra, "911," "911," "911." And that's when things got crazy, adrenaline, I don't know, but I'd fled west to escape the dark news, and even here it found me.

What's trying to get in and eat us is not just a beast, but *them*, you know, the bad news, the awful news. Is it Willie Horton? No. Let Willie in, I understand Willie. Willie wants post-prison sex and some revenge. How human! Look, I tell my woman friend, will you get under the down comforter and pull it round your waist, for God's sake, dancing around here just asking for it. No, it isn't Willie, it's sicker. It's yes, the entire Air Force helping John Sununu with his national priorities, getting his teeth cleaned and building his stamp collection. It is the House membership looking for unlimited checking and the proverbial free lunch. It's Dan Quayle in search of those phantom seventy IQ points and his nine Secret Service guys who have to take him white-water rafting anytime he wants. Oh God! It's Al Sharpton seeking pizza, flashbulbs and hair pomade. 911, 911, it's Senator Jesse having heard that some of the Mapplethorpe crowd is hiding out here right now, screwing at me with his Polaroid to check on it and to look, and to look, and to just look. Here's Barbara Bush hunting another Springer spaniel, her third, to write a ghost book for. What a vision of self-confidence. It's Marion Barry in search of hardened nose candy and Rashida. 911. It's Clarence Thomas, forgive the expression, Justice Clarence Thomas, lost in robes and now searching for the very thing that made him a shoo-in, got him picked, the central thing he lacks – a self. And worst, it is our ill-tempered president seeking Reba McIntyre CDs and the Grand Canyon. The guy who thinks our presidential seal looks best on golf carts, a man who has confused human opportunity with photo opportunity, a man who has mentioned the disease called AIDS in a single speech in three years. He's sure loud out there, that's a whiny guy door kicker, but no, after forty minutes of trying every window and thumping across the roof, turns out we're in luck – it's only a bear. And it got tired and went to the neighbors, who dialed 911.

Heroes are in short supply. Here's my advice. Know you are one. When you spy another one, be she a teacher or a game warden or a diligent phone operator, say so to that person. We are living in a darkening dark age, my loved ones. The icy shadow of the Capitol is felt around the world, and all across our land I see taking their place in the American sky a thousand points of night. My name is Allan and I was a news junkie. It's dark out here, it's cold, 911, 911, world without end. Amen.

T. Coraghessan Boyle

I THINK SOME OF you may find it odd that I've been asked to speak to the subject of heroes tonight, since I've spent the better part of my career knocking them from the pedestals, from Mungo Park in my first book to Natty Bumpo, to my current victim, John Harvey Kellogg, inventor of the corn flake. But, in fact, I have any number of personal heroes, those who have helped to shape my life in one way or another, for better or worse. Scores. Hundreds even. But given the time constraints here tonight, I thought I'd just share my short list with you.

My heroes. A short list.

Willie Mays. Muddy Waters. Davy Crockett. St. Thomas Aquinas. Woody Allen. Walter Pater. Arnold Schwarzenegger's mother, Mrs. Schwarzenegger. Joshua P. Whirlpool, the great humanitarian who invented the dishwasher, in case you're interested. Madame Curie. Paul Ehrlich. Albert Payson Terhune. Erik the Red. In fact, I'm very impressed by anyone who uses the definite article as a middle name, from Catherine the Great to Bozo the Clown to Ivan the Terrible. It's just plan inspirational.

T.S. Eliot. Jimi Hendrix. Hopalong Cassidy. Giacomo Puccini. Johnny Appleseed. Y.A. Tittle. Max Perkins. Erik Satie. Jimmy Witherspoon. Flannery O'Connor. Leontyne Price. Raiza Amenni. If you don't know him, by the way, he was hat maker to the late Ayatollah Khomeni. Washington Irving. Geronimo. M.F.K. Fisher. Oscar Wilde. Franz Kafka. Connie Mack. Florence Nightingale. David Bowie. John Singer Sargent. "Spoonbill" Rizzo. He was, of course, the great trencherman from Baltimore who, on a fine spring day in 1956, was able to down forty-seven pullets, bones and all, in less than six minutes, a record that still stands to this day. Dr. Seuss. Bob Dylan. Dylan Thomas. John Henry. Paul Bunyan. Crazy Horse. Breughel. Botticelli. Bellini. Smokey Robinson and the Miracles. Nikita Khrushchev. And Saxo Grammaticus. I have a confession to make here. He's not really one of my heroes, I just love the name.

And then, of course, in the animal kingdom we have Lassie, Rin Tin Tin, Sparky, Buck, Big Red, Silver, Trigger, Cheeta, Shamu, Orca, Ricky-Ticky-Tavi, Ka, Old Yeller, and Secretariat. And more humans, too. John Coltrane. Honus Wagner. Maurice Ravel. Algernon and Charles Swinburne. Shirley Muldowney. Mother Teresa. Salvador Dali. Gerhard Frobel. He, by the way, is the unsung hero who, through crossbreeding, was able to develop the beefsteak tomato. Ben Franklin — who couldn't help but be influenced by the man whose face appears on the hundred-dollar bill? Amelia Earhart. Ichabod Crane. Mamma Leone. Chingachgook. Randall Patrick Murphy. And Dr. Herbert R. Axelrod. He's the great ichthyologist who discovered a new species of fish in a puddle at the Jamaica airport on getting down from the plane. And I can't forget Johnny Powers, the man for whom the finest Irish whiskey in the world is named, if you except Tullamore Dew, that is. And, finally, Wally Stackowitz, my sixth-grade teacher.

Have I left anybody out? Well, that's inevitable, I suppose. They'll have to wait for next time.

George Garrett

I GREW UP IN a radical household. My father was an American radical, part populist, part prophet, and mostly a rare example of what, in our buttoned-up era, amid this glittering black-tie company, I would have to call a Neanderthal Democrat. Wholly compassionate, but without an ounce or inch of self-serving sentimentality, he was radical also in his complete integrity, unflagging open-mindedness, utter independence, and consistent unpredictability. Most groups and parties and factions were contemptible to him. Needless to say he was not a politician. However, in the early years of this waning century, he was an active member of the very new United Mine Workers.

Picture this much. A man who worked hard as a miner in the far West, then left that work battered and scarred, still physically powerful, but maimed and crippled enough to be fearsome to his enemies and embarrassing to his only son. Came south to Florida where he made himself into a lawyer and lived on to do many good works. Tried a multitude of cases with equal vigor and urgency before small-town magistrates and the august Supreme Court of the United States. Did not so much defeat as destroy the Ku Klux Klan in Florida. More than once had as much to do as anyone in electing and reelecting Claude Pepper to the Senate, and was, alas for Claude, dead and gone when Smathers, the protégé, betrayed his hero and ran against him. By persuasion and perilous example, he saved a major bank and all the deposits therein when our banks were collapsing like shacks in a hurricane. In my presence, he once single-handedly stopped a lynching. The intended victim was a monstrously evil middle-aged white woman. He saved her life for the courts.

Devoted his time and energy to *pro bono* work. And thus his actions and admirable principles precluded many common kinds of material comfort and any serious estate for inheritance. Often he put not only his own life at risk, but the lives of all the family as well.

It was a joyous, noisy, loving household. But I have rebelled against it every day of my life. I confess that at his funeral I was ashamed of the crowd, that mob of black and white, raggedy-ass poor people who had come to pay their respects. Where were the good-looking people? The people worth knowing? And what kind of a legacy was this, to be told over and over and over again, "We feel the exact same way as we did when President Roosevelt died?"

It has taken more than sixty years for me to earn the right to have these three minutes. I ought to be camouflaged by glittering jokes or anyway at least offering up an eccentric list of famous names as my heroes. But this evening I have a debt to pay, if not to settle.

Once upon a time, in a hundred and one cases, my father brought all the powerful railroads of Florida – the ACL, the Southern and the Seaboard, the Florida East Coast – to their knees. They sent high-ranking representatives into our living room to offer him more money than he could ever earn if he would just *not* bring and try any more cases against the railroads. I was afraid he would throw them bodily out of the house, something I had seen happen before. But instead, he heard them out and thanked them for their interest before he politely ushered them back outside.

"That's a whole lot of money and would surely solve a whole lot of problems for me," he told them, "but great God a'mighty, gentlemen, what would I do for fun?"

Old warrior, forgotten American untitled knight in rusty, dented armor, I'm finally able to salute you tonight, here and now.

Gail Godwin

I DON'T BELIEVE WE ever outgrow our need for heroes, but our specifications for them change as we change. Even when the day comes that we realize it's our turn to be the heroes, even when perhaps somebody actually walks up to us and anoints us with the unsettling phrase "You are my hero," still we go on looking for what we can't do without, the image or the memory of or the meeting with that vivid person who lived or lives on the same earth we do and whose example will be powerful enough to show us how to go on. Often mysteriously, our heroes make themselves available to us just when we're most in need of their particular gifts. Suddenly he's just there or she's just there. Our befitting shepherd, that very one who can set us straight, who will graciously pause in the timelessness of his or her proper work and take us by the shoulders and turn us around so that we, still so helplessly bound and beset by time, can see where our proper work leads next.

And that, it seems, is part of what I was doing in England last month, looking for the one who could take me by the shoulders and recall me to my proper work. There were three of us driving through the Avon Valley in Wiltshire under canopies of overgrown hedgerows, past fields of gathered hay and grazing sheep, as we followed slips of roads so inconsequential they don't have numbers on the map, squiggly little lines leading us to the villages of Dauncy, Eddington, and Bimmerton, places where a man had prayed and walked and written poetry some 350-odd years ago, and gotten married and served a tiny parish as its priest. And in his last months of consumption, written a guide book for clergymen that is still in print.

And composed exquisite poetry still cherished today for its precision of language, metrical versatility, and remarkable insights into the inner life.

One of us on our English trip was a priest, one of us was composer, and one of us was a writer. Three pilgrims who had all concurred with equal desire that we wanted to visit the places where George Herbert had lived and worked from age thirty-six to thirty-nine, those three last happy, incredibly productive years of his life. The priest among us had been here before and wanted to go again. The composer among us had just finished a rough sketch for a choral piece of Herbert's ravishing poem "Virtue," the one that begins,

> Sweet day, so cool, so calm, so bright
> The bridal of the earth and sky
> The dew shall weep thy fall tonight;
> For thou must die.

The question that was foremost on the writer's mind was "How can I best use myself up for the rest of my earthly allotment?" What better hero to respond to such a question than this captivating and deceptively simple poet whose art and ministry could not be separated, who found in his small geographic sphere a life large enough to set up his entire assets, once he had channeled them into the right discipline? And what was the discipline? Only to befriend, comprehend, then transpose into words. Words refined of all posturing and extravagance, the astonishing range of a fully human creature's active inner life, feelings ranging the whole gamut from insurrection, bafflement, grief, self-disgust, gratitude, anger, serenity, and joy. What was the discipline? Only to plumb every aspect of his surroundings, his given patch of mundane earth, until it yielded up via words again, words rigorously and prayerfully chosen to sparkle sensibly through centuries. Not just the literal replications of the things he saw and heard and did and felt, but the significant reality shimmering behind them. He refused devoutly to take the world for granted. He believed you should refuse to stop challenging, yet marveling at, the big mystery right up until the moment you breathed your last breath.

In the tiny church in Bimmerton where George Herbert served as rector and is buried, we found this typed-up piece of his verse encased in plastic and lying handily on a windowsill next to a small arrangement of seasonal flowers:

> Sum up at night what thou hast done by day
> And in the morning what thou hast to do
> Dress and undress thy soul
> Mark the decay and growth of it

Not bad advice for pilgrims in need of a current hero.

Patricia Browning Griffith

WHEN I THINK of the two women who lived on Plum Street, it is always a summer evening in the 1940s. They sit on the porch of their weathered Victorian house with a gallery that wraps around the side and sags to an end, with a trellis of morning glories that have gone to seed for perhaps thirty years, so that the blue is faded, like old eyes. My grandmother and great-grandmother are widows, both widowed twice. Between them they've raised eight children of their own and at least three others of relatives and friends.

When my great-grandmother was thirteen, she taught school and played the piano for the children to march in and out of the local schoolhouse. Her grandparents had come to Texas just after the Civil War with a few head of cattle that all died the first year. To survive the winter, her grandmother knit eighty baby caps to barter for food. In 1886, when my great-grandmother was seventeen, she graduated first in her class from a college where the cornerstone on the women's dormitory read "Dedicated to Female Education and Piety." After graduation, she received three proposals of marriage. She chose the man who didn't have consumption. He died ten years later leaving her with five young children.

My grandmother, Kate, was widowed before my mother was born. In a Sunday afternoon sandlot game, my grandfather, twenty-one years old, was struck in the temple by a baseball. He walked a mile home, said to his wife of four months, "I'm going to take a nap, Kate," and never woke up. This was Paris, Texas: the north star of Texas it was called. Twice the town had burned and been rebuilt. In 1916 the fire raged out of control, crossing the square in the old wagon yard and heading down Plum Street. Often my grandmother Kate described the panic of people fleeing the fire, a man running with a chicken under his arm. When the fire reached the end of their block, the wind changed and their home was saved. For weeks afterward, people left homeless slept on their wide porch.

With no word of complaint, alone and together, independent and proud, the grandmothers survived on modest pensions and by renting rooms. The roomers tended to move in and out, except for one woman with a variety of chiming clocks, who lived there until she died. Sometimes the roomers were common people, I was warned. Common people, Kate explained, are people who talk about their problems. Intelligent people, she said, talk about the world. Each Friday afternoon the insurance man appeared to collect for their burial policies. When Kate died three years ago, she'd already chosen and paid for her coffin.

They were great readers, these women, daily Bible readers. And each week Kate walked to the public library for more books. Sometimes I'd accompany her, up the block to where the fire had stopped, toward the square, past the Plaza Theater, where she would take us every Saturday afternoon to the movies, even after we'd quit sitting with her, because she called out to Alan Ladd, "Look out behind you." Past the square, stopping to pay a gas or water bill, she headed across town to the library.

Kate and my great-grandmother preferred novels with moral messages. Lloyd C. Douglas was a favorite. It was said that Great-grandmother reread *Green Light* every year. The Douglas books celebrate the moral benefits of secret charity, an idea whose time has passed us by. Once when there are extra relatives around, I'm allowed to sleep in my great-grandmother's room with her in her feather bed. There is a special luxury of the mattress that makes me sneeze, and the smell of snuff that my mother still insists was her only fault. I wake in the night and Great-grandmother is propped up in bed reading. I never before have known anyone to be awake in the middle of the night. It is like waking in the middle of someone's secret life, and to my wonderment her long white hair, which she wore knotted in the back of her head, is down, spreading like a thin white shawl over her shoulders, giving her the air of a young girl. I lie there in the peaceful quiet of Plum Street, where no one has stirred since ten o'clock, when Betty Jean across the street comes home from selling tickets at the Plaza Theater.

For some brief moments there beside my great-grandmother and that nearly silent hour, the distance of time seems removed as if we are girls together, as if we are part of something endless and beyond time.

Terry McMillan

W HEN I THINK of a hero or heroine, I think of someone whom I admire and respect, so strongly that they've carved a permanent place in my heart. This person has had such a positive effect on my life that, whatever it is they've done and however they've done it, is so deeply embedded in who I am or whom I've become as a person that I often find myself doing all kinds of things to let him or her know how much I appreciate it. In this case, that person happens to be my mother. Although she gets on my nerves half the time, if it weren't for her I probably wouldn't be standing here now. Since I was a little girl in Michigan, I've watched her swim through a variety of hells and come out like a gold medal-winner. She has singlehandedly raised five kids alone while I'm still struggling with one. I have never once heard her complain about how bad things were, but I did used to hear her thinking out loud, "I've got to figure out a way I can get some more money to pay this damn gas bill," or I'd watch her open the refrigerator and calculate how long before it would all be gone.

My mother had me when she was in the eleventh grade and never finished high school and by the time she was twenty-three, she had five kids. She used to always tell me that she didn't want me to make the same mistakes she made with her life. And even before women were being urged to go to college, my mother told me I was going whether I wanted to or not. "I'm not raisin' no illiterates," she used to say, and she meant it. She never once let on she was scared, even when I was old enough to know how scary being a mother can be. She pushed forward and did what she had to do to make sure that we were all taken care of. And she always put us first before her own happiness, before her own well-being, and in the forty years I've known her, I've never once heard her express a single regret.

A few years ago, my mother developed asthma, and she's had quite a number of life-threatening attacks since then, but it was only recently when I was at my home in Tucson that she called me downstairs to the bathroom and told me I'd better call 911. I thought she was faking, because a few minutes before she had seemed perfectly fine and she loves attention. By the time the paramedics got there, she was grabbing hold of my arm and trying hard to breathe, but she couldn't. I had never seen her have an asthma attack before and I was scared, so I yelled at the paramedics, "Can't you do something for her? Where's the damn oxygen? Help her!" I took her by the hand and told her not to worry, even though I was worried. I followed the ambulance to the hospital and prayed harder than I think I ever have. I watched the light from the back of the van in front of me and saw my mother's arms flail up every now and then, which gave me hope. When we got to the hospital, they wheeled her into the emergency room, and for the next two hours I sat there in that waiting room and literally relived my life with her. My mother is fifty-seven years old, and I thought about just how much she's given us and how I'm trying to pay her back for all she's done; it's just that I want her to know that she does not have to spend the rest of her life struggling, that she has earned the right to experience finally some kind of happiness, even if it just meant driving that 1985 Dodge Lancer, or having her own two-bedroom apartment.

When I was finally able to see her, she had all these machines hooked up to her; her blouse and bra had been ripped off and whatever they'd given her had puffed her up so, she looked like she had put on forty pounds in the last two hours. Her eyes were closed, but the nurse said she could hear me. I told her she was going to be all right; I told her that I loved her, something I rarely said, and that I was here. I also had to stop myself from crying, which would have scared her; I told her that she was going to have to get her hair done when she got out of here 'cause it was a mess. She pointed to her mouth and wanted to know where her teeth were. I told her they were in a plastic bag in my purse. Later on, when she was able to sit up and talk, she thanked me for responding as quickly as I did. She said, "When you was little, you used to be the same way; I could always count on you in an emergency to do whatever was necessary. At least you ain't forgot everything I taught you." And I just looked at her and said. "I hear you, Mama. Now, will you do me a big favor and for once keep your mouth shut and save your breath for yourself."

Amy Tan

M Y HEROINE DIED long before I was born, but she has always
been a thread in my life and sometimes a needle in my side.
She was a widow, she was a drug addict, she gave up her oldest son,
then her youngest. She was kicked out of her family, she became a
slave, she became a suicide, a tragic figure to those who knew her.
And now she has no grave, no marker to bear witness that she ever
existed. Although I knew she existed from the time I was a child, she
was the ghost who followed me around. She was my grandmother,
my mother's mother. In my mind, she was a solemn painting on the
wall above our piano. When I didn't practice, my mother would
scold me. When I sulked, my mother would tell me what it was like
to be a little girl, only eight years old with no mother to guide her,
and I would become scared, then I would practice and get bored and
look at the painting, wondering what it was like to have no mother,
no one to make me practice the piano.

When I was fourteen, and my father and brother were dying of
cancer, when the doctors said nothing could be done, my mother
warned me not to listen to people who had no hope for others. She
had us turn instead to my grandmother, the painting on the wall. She
asked her what our family had done wrong, perhaps in a past life,
perhaps in this one, and now what should we do. I think my mother
was again that little girl watching her mother die, closing her dead
mother's eyes, yet still believing her mother would come back one
day and together they could finally go home. When I fell in love, my
mother warned me not to sacrifice myself, and here she was not
talking about virginal hymens, but of myself, my spirit. I should not

keep quiet if he forgot my birthday or if his parents did not like me. And here I think she was remembering my grandmother, who became a widow dependent on her older brother, who later had no choice but to become the third concubine to the same man who raped her, who cried about her life to her daughter, my mother, who lost her spirit, then took her life. When I wrote my first book, my mother read my stories and believed my grandmother was my muse, for how could I know these things about my grandmother, my mother, and myself? My mother asked me, "Does she visit you often? Does she talk about me?" "Yes" and "Yes," I said, "and she likes my computer."

Until I wrote my first book, I did not even know my grand-mother's name. It was Li Jing Mei – rather, it is Li Jing Mei. She was born in 1889; my first book was published in 1989. She was thirty-seven when she died; I was thirty-seven when I was first published. These are small coincidences, perhaps meaningless to others, but these are the things I look for in my heroine, connections so I can create myths I believe in to give Li Jing Mei a personal marker that she did indeed exist, this thread of my life, who sometimes made me cry and cry and cry, then fight and fight and fight.

Charles Johnson

I T'S BEEN SAID frequently that ours is not a time of heroes, but of celebrities, people whom we feel we know though we have never met them, people who are mainly famous for simply being famous. Yet, I think I have been privileged to know one person who is a hero or approaches being a hero in the old sense of that term. In other words, someone who has served his community through actions or deeds that benefit everyone.

That person is a black man I met four years ago. I was on location for a PBS film I had written; it was a ninety-minute dramatization of a life of the oldest living American, a black man name Charlie Smith, who in 1977 was 136 years old. He was played as a young man by actor Glynn Turman, and as an older man by the late Richard Ward. These were the two principal roles in the film, which was called *Charlie Smith and the Fritter Tree* and which is now shown on the Disney Channel. If you ever see this movie, you'll notice that among its many characters, there is a minor character, a black outlaw named Railroad Bill. Railroad Bill appears in this film for about ten minutes before he's hanged by a lynch mob. The actor who played Railroad Bill had just completed work on a television series called *The Electric Company*. His name is Morgan Freeman. And when he appeared in my first film for PBS, he was obviously working far below his creative potential. But this is what Morgan Freeman was doing after he left *The Electric Company*. He was not, as we say, "hot," he did not have a leading role. Fans who were on the set or part of the production team did not flock around him at that time as they did around Glynn Turman and, to add insult to injury, Morgan Freeman's character had a peg leg, which meant that Morgan had to play all his scenes with one foot strapped behind his back. I don't have to tell you how painful this was, but Morgan Freeman, I noticed, did not complain about the pain, nor did he complain about the Texas heat (we were shooting in Texas) or about the fact that too few people in 1977 recognized the fact that he was one of the greatest actors in America.

What impressed me most about Morgan Freeman in 1977 was the quiet heroism required over a period of twenty years to turn in the finest performances he could manage on television, in motion pictures, and on the stage, regardless of the size of the role he was given. I'm talking about the kind of heroism that keeps a black person working when almost everyone around him or her is looking in another direction, when some are telling him that he cannot reach the heights in this profession because he is black. Although I have only met Mr. Freeman once, I have followed his career, and I must say that he is the only actor who has produced films that made me cry, twice, once for *Lean on Me* and once for *Glory*, a film about genuine black heroes during the Civil War, men who, perhaps like Freeman, performed services originally unsung, but ultimately recognized by all.

Beverly Lowry

A HERO'S A DREAM after all, a child's wish to be better than, stronger than, braver, more wonderful, more nearly exactly whatever it is the child wishes to be or do. The dream is a possibility, a perfectibility, of the most magical kind of pure enchantment, wishing we could be like, or just be, somebody else. In dreams, these are walking, waking dreams, we do that if we let ourselves pretend, play "I can fly." Our heroes then are out there, on a limb on the thinnest edge of the farthest possibility, doing whatever it is we wish them to do, whichever dance that is theirs to do. Our dream of them then is tribute and a kind of love.

When I was little, I wanted to be Sheena, Queen of the Jungle. She was adventurous and strong, hot-headed and a girl. Then I changed, I wanted to be a boy. I wanted to be my father for a while. Later on when I got older I switched; I wanted to be a male Southern writer for a time, mainly William Faulkner. Then I wanted to be a male Jewish writer, Malamud, Philip Roth. It took me up until my twenties to get over that. I read Doris Lessing, found that there was someone who wrote about women – smart women, dumb women, clever women, ambitious women, you-name-it women, but women. She took them seriously, took herself seriously, and I finally figured it out that was who I was and I could take myself as myself seriously as well.

In the room I work in, I keep picture postcards on the wall. I tack some of them up, some I just lean on bookshelves. I collect postcards and the pictures are of people I admire. Miss Welty's up there twice, Colette with her dogs, Faulkner looking grave, the Kodo drummers,

Calvin Murphy making a basket, Dwight Yoakàm (who's not really a hero, I just like to look at him). But the two people I spend most time looking at are not writers, but performers. One is Baryshnikov and the picture of him is his usual, in the air like a man escaped, as if he lived there. The other one is my real idol, not Sheena but Tina – Tina Turner – in full regalia sprouting black feathers from the back of her head, smiling her head off, wearing her black sequined dress. Have you seen this woman in performance? Now, there's art, there's love, there's generosity. That's the kind of way-out, high-art, magical exchange I'd like to get down in a book and in my life. Full tilt, page one to the end. In my car, I take her with me. We do "Nutbush" together, "River Deep Mountain High," "Proud Mary." I read her autobiography. She's helped me get through some dark times. There's a mantra I've devised after reading the autobiography. In a dark time, I say to myself: If Tina can get away from Ike, I can get through this; if Tina can get away from Ike, I can make it through anything.

James Salter

W HEN I WAS young, it was the end of the war, and there were heroes. In the spirit of the time, and in the absence of other ideas, I believed that heroism was only connected with war. That war was its matrix and, of course, much of literature, as glimpses became visible to me, describes things this way. For a long time, I so held. But in a fuller sense, I count as heroic those natures that are admirable and the achievements that go with them. Men and women who are also magnanimous, that is my own preference, whose view is broad and who do not complain, but rather, comprehend. For me, it is also someone devoid of the eagerness of self-reference.

I have two writer's heroes. The first was Robert Phelps, the critic, editor, and essayist, who died little more than two years ago. He wrote a number of books. The one for which he is best known is *Earthly Paradise*, a so-called autobiography of Colette. In fact, it is a collection of her own writing that mirrors her life, arranged chron-ologically, and made richer by autobiographical segments, for he was her great American nominator. More than anyone else, he opened the world of literature to me, or I should say the world of literature that counts. He was lean and soft-spoken, and had a wonderful smile. He was fond of cats, gin, and beautiful sentences. He had a keen sense of gossip, without which most conversation is flavorless, and great modesty. One of the things I remember is the hallway outside his Village apartment, where there was often a stack of books to be thrown away, those that, in going through his shelves, he found unworthy, not good enough to own. I admired this discipline, those standards. It is a really hard thing to keep, I don't know exactly what to call it, one's "honor" this way. In the writers he gave me to read, in the long conversation, the lines stuffed as it were in his pockets, lines of Joyce, Cyril Connolly, Colette, in his very being he was one of the most important influences in my life and in whatever I wrote afterward. He allowed me to believe.

The other hero, strange as it may be to hear a writer say this, was my publisher, William Turnbull, the cofounder of Northpoint Press, with which almost everyone must be familiar. He was, in many ways, difficult to know. Tall, austere and somewhat pedantic in speech, he was perhaps not lovable, but he was much loved. He established Northpoint Press for, I think, a worthy reason. He wanted to publish good books, to pay back in some measure all that books had meant to him in his earlier life. And for ten years he did this. And Northpoint became a legend. Last December he was diagnosed as having stomach cancer and given only a few months. They had a huge tribute and farewell for him near the end. He had to go into the hospital for blood transfusions to give him the strength just to be there for half an hour. He was in a wheelchair, too feeble to speak; a few words to friends, that was all. He said, without speaking, one of the most moving things possible; when he saw me he began to cry. It was really a memorial service, the kind one would like to have. Ten of his own writers read, and many more were in the audience, which was eight or nine hundred people. This was in Berkeley. They came because of what he was and what he had done. Living counts, but in heroism, so does dying. He died just five days afterward in his house at the beach, surrounded by his family, music he loved playing (it was Ella Fitzgerald), and he was wearing a button given to him by a poet, Gary Snyder. It was a Hell's Angels button, and I like to think of his wearing it and of its motto, which in a strange way, drawn from such an opposing view of things, stood for his life. It said, "Ride Hard, Die Free." That is a fine epitaph.

JOURNEYS

October 30, 1995

William Kennedy

T HIS IS A story about me going to Cuba because of Ernest Hemingway and not going bowling with Fidel Castro, and not going duck-hunting with him either. Because this is a three-minute story, I will apply Hemingway's iceberg principle of writing – seven-eighths underwater for every part that shows. Eliminate everything unnecessary to conveying experience, said Papa.

I've been writing about Cuba since 1957, when Fidel was in the Sierra Maestra and I was a *Miami Herald* reporter with an inside track on revolutionary doings. It was difficult to know who was a true rebel, a true fascist, a true C.I.A. agent, for they often overlapped. They still do. Because this is a three-minute story I will leave all that out and say only that I interviewed them all, and preferred the rebels. By the time the revolution triumphed I had quit journalism to write fiction. I will leave that out.

After his triumph, Fidel transformed himself from a hero into the enemy of the United States, and the subsequent Cuban blockade has kept us isolated from Cuban life ever since. Castro remains an inimical yet charismatic and unpredictable figure, but I will leave that out except to note that two weeks ago he upstaged everybody at the United Nations while wearing a blue suit.

In 1985 I reviewed a posthumous Hemingway book, *The Dangerous Summer*, and a Cuban writer, Norberto Fuentes, author of *Hemingway in Cuba*, came to Albany to visit me. We talked about Fidel and Hemingway and Gabriel Garcia Marquez, whom I knew and, for reasons of brevity, will call Gabo. Gabo spends time in Cuba and wrote the introduction to Norberto's book, and Norberto said I should go to Cuba and he'd get me invited. I had written *The Cotton Club* film script with a man whom, for reasons of brevity, I will call Francis Coppola, so I was invited to the Cuban film festival. The invitation was sent but took five months to reach me, so I missed the festival. But Norberto said come anyway, and in 1987 I did, with my wife Dana and my son Brendan. I will now leave out almost everything, except that lunch has ended at Gabo's house in Havana and I am sitting in a rocking chair, and Gabo asks me to move, for *El Comandante* is coming to visit and he likes the rocker.

El Comandante Fidel arrives and stays two and a half hours, keeping on his field jacket and his hat, and when he rocks in the rocker his feet leave the floor. We talk of Cuban Scotch whisky made with Czechoslovakian malt, and whether I am related to John F. Kennedy – no, he was from Wexford, I'm from Tipperary – and why Latin-American movies are not successful in the United States. The *Comandante* used to watch a movie on video every night but now is back to books, reading *The Adventures of Marco Polo*, and Defoe's *Journal of the Plague Year*. He also has one of my novels in his car. "Reading never dies," he says.

Now, I will leave out all that happened during nine days of travel through Cuba and come to the bowling part. It is after midnight, our last night in Cuba, and Gabo has called to tell me not to go out of our house because I will be having a visitor. Norberto and Gabo and others are with us when *El Comandante* arrives for what will be a three-hour visit, and I am now drinking his Cuban Scotch, which is a nice beverage but not quite Scotch, and we talk about the new Cuban film school that Gabo runs, and where I have given the first lecture, a discussion of *The Cotton Club* and the upcoming film of my novel *Ironweed*. *El Comandante* says he read that novel and liked it and thinks it the first novel ever written about a bum and that people will now look at bums in a different way. I say I hope so. He also says he has been reading my novel *Billy Phelan's Greatest Game* and likes the sports I write about, especially the bowling. In that novel Billy Phelan rolls a 299 game, one pin shy of a perfect game, and Fidel asks how can that happen? He himself has been bowling for years and his high game is 169. I tell him my uncle bowled 299, and I also bowled 299. The *Comandante* finds this not only awesome but also hard to believe. It is true, I say. Very, very true. He seems to believe me but changes the subject from bowling to shooting and how he broke an ashtray lying on its side from 400 yards. Also, he says, a million ducks come to Cuba every year, and he holds the record for shooting the most ducks with precision, and for shooting the most ducks with fewest cartridges: 101 ducks with 98 shells. He says maybe some day I might come back to Cuba and go duck-shooting with him and I say I might.

But that was almost nine years ago and I never went back either to bowl or to shoot ducks. Things went very bad in Cuba, and Norberto, because he knew the wrong people – two military leaders executed by Fidel – was kept in interior exile in Havana for five years. Then he tried to flee Cuba in a boat but was caught and went to jail, and I helped organize, through PEN, a letter to Fidel from several American writers, asking for Norberto's release. Norberto came out of jail and soon after went on a hunger strike, and I wrote an article about that, which he believes helped him leave Cuba. He now has asylum in the United States and last week his wife was allowed to leave Cuba and is also here. But that is another story and I will leave it all out, because the subject here is bowling, and shooting, and also how much luck goes into surviving a revolution, which is a question I asked *El Comandante*, and he said, "Luck decreases the merits of a man." But why he thinks that is so I will have to leave out, for my three minutes are up.

Jane Smiley

I USED TO FANCY myself a traveler. Once I hitchhiked through Europe for a year, and another time, preparing to do the same thing, only alone, I sewed my own backpack. When I got on the plane my traveling kit included everything in that backpack, about sixty pounds' worth, and a long-necked banjo in a hard-shell case. But now I dread travel, even of the most mundane sort. I actually hate to leave my house unless to go to the stable, my other house.

In one of the most poignant moments in Virginia Woolf's *The Waves*, Bernard realizes toward the end of his life all the places there are that he will now certainly never travel to. That indeed is mortality. So I go, but I don't like it.

This time last year I was on my way to Russia. I couldn't bear going. I prepared for the trip during the last week by bidding a last farewell to everyone and everything I held dear. I got on the plane in a funk and flew to New York.

My foreboding was borne out when I called home one last time before leaving the continent and discovered that my sixteen-year-old had totaled her car on the interstate. She was unhurt but shocked. I was on my way to Russia. All I could do was tell her I loved her and that she would be all right. I was shocked, too. I cried all the way to Frankfurt. I hated Frankfurt. I cried every night in St. Petersburg and hardly slept. I could think of nothing but going home and seeing my children and husband, riding my horse. I was far, far away, twenty-eight hours by plane. What if, what if. How would I get home if something happened? The six days seemed unfairly endless, a cruel and senseless separation visited upon me by alien powers.

Even so, even though I felt as though I was hardly paying attention the journey did its thing to me, the thing that journeys always do. It made itself as vivid as jewels in my memory. I can easily make myself sense almost every moment, from the banal tedium of our meetings with gray members of the old Writers Union to the yellow of the leaves on the trees outside the windows of Anna Akhmatova's room, from the brown autumnal gloom of the cemetery where Dostoevsky is buried to the imposing and surreal dilapidation of the Nabokov estate, a degree of dilapidation impossible in the United States and a testament to how little the Russians care about losing things. I recall the delicious broths and soups I ate there, as savory and fully flavored as anything I've ever tasted. I recall the exact dimension and winy colors of my tiny but elegant room in the Austrian-owned luxury hotel where they put us. The fact was, I think, my very resistance to the journey, my very rejection of how far away I was and how alien everything felt, brought it all into high relief, made each moment both painful and pleasurable, therefore memorable.

The joke was on me. Though I know now I longed to be home there, I now often long to be there, to see that light again, those November trees, those stones and streets that Gogol knew and Akhmatova and Pushkin. The strangest part is that I long sometimes for that solitude too, because the solitude created the journey out of loneliness and vulnerability, and strangeness and sudden fresh beauty. So journeys are one of those paradoxes, impossible to take and impossible to live without. When I used to travel all the time I liked it too much to really see where I was going, but now that I hate to leave home I love the journey more than I ever did.

Toby Olson

I WAS SITTING IN a train station, in a city, somewhere in a country, and across the large, half-empty space from me a woman sat, reading a book. Her legs were crossed, the book's spine rested on her knee, and she was gazing intently into the pages, as if she'd just opened a birthday gift, a box holding an intricate quilt and she was discovering what was there.

When I journey alone like this and sit in train stations, I feel like I'm nowhere. I could throw away my wallet, the labels in my clothing, even my fingerprints. Just walk into the outskirts of this foreign city and begin again. That's why I often bring a book along when I travel and sit in train stations and read like that woman. It's a way to go somewhere and stay put at the same time.

I have an aunt who is in her nineties, but still travels. When she goes someplace, then comes back again, she measures where she's been by shopping centers. Shopping centers are like train stations in cities, but she doesn't see it that way. This good place has a fine one, but that place has nothing to speak of and is therefore suspect. She travels because most of her friends have moved to Florida; they live in condoms down there.

She means condominiums of course, and she knows she's made that mistake. She's said it often in my talks with her, a twinkle in her eye, and now the mistake has become part of her story. Hearing her is like reading a book over and over and in the meantime anticipating reading it, because it is so good. I mean, the image of that. Her friends live very close to shopping centers, and I can see their postures as they crawl into the pink tubes of their thin rubber homes. She means condominiums, like a book says one thing but takes you on a different journey when you read it again.

None of this has been true.

There was no woman reading, no dank and foreign city. That train station was a local stop and I was riding the express reading a book about her, the story of a woman who had never been to Florida but had plenty of understanding, a constantly expanding mind, and who read a lot. Some thought her lonely, bookish, disconnected from real life, but it was clear in the story that it was they who were that. They were not such travelers, and because of that had no powerful focus through which to see her clearly.

But a woman can be a man, men can be children, and the old who read in soft, safe houses in Florida can be all of them. It has something to do with imagination, with memory and travel.

The train came out of a dark tunnel and into the sunlight just as I finished the last page. I put the book down on the seat beside me and looked out the window. Trees were passing, then a river. Then we came to the first houses at the outskirts of a new city. They were row houses, condominiums, and because of the sun's slant I could see into their pink windows clearly as the train slowed, approaching the station.

People sat in chairs, on couches, all reading books. And I saw a woman standing at a window. She was looking out and watching the train I was in pass by. She'd been reading, but now held her book like a fragile and prized possession, open, as one might hold up a quilt for warmth near a drafty window, against her chest.

I was headed for home, and even as I saw her she became an image in the mind only, though just as vivid that way after she was out of sight.

The train eased into the station, but it was not yet mine and I could stay put. So I reached down for the book I'd just finished reading, lifted it up into the light, and began my journey again.

Michael Chabon

I SUSPECT MINE MAY have been the last American generation to be fed that beautiful canard "The City of the Future." I grew up there. It lay in the middle of tobacco county, about forty miles from this room. There were no glass domes, no mile-high spires, no atomic hover cars dotting its skies. Columbia, Maryland, was the outgrowth of a different brand of American dreaminess. It was, like me, a product of the loopy and tumultuous thinking of the late 1960s. It boasted large, well-tended swaths of public greenbelt, schools without classrooms, free public transportation, a single ecumenical worship center shared by all faiths, streets named for the works of great poets and novelists, and – most wondrously of all – the City of the Future was integrated. On the street where I grew up, there were more black families than white; on the next street over, the reverse was true. I tackled, head-faked, ate dinner with, teased, admired, quarreled with, lusted after, learned to dance from, had crushes on, watched television and eventually drank beer with black girls and boys from the time I was six until the day I left for college.

And as far as I knew, the same was true for black and white children everywhere in the United States. When, in our classroom-less schools, we studied the history of the civil-rights movement, it was exactly, for me, like studying the Second World War. A terrible conflict had consumed the efforts of people I considered to be my personal heroes, and then the good guys had won. For proof of this I needed to look no further than my best friends, my neighbors, my favorite teachers – many of whom had dark skin. Frederick Douglass, Harriet Tubman, Dr. Charles Drew: In the city of the future, in

1973, a young Jewish boy could look at the lives of these people and feel connected to them, indebted to them – in a very real way, descended from them.

As soon as I left Columbia, I began the journey that has landed me at last in the very capital of the American present: Los Angeles, California. On our block in the leafy and genteel old neighborhood of Hancock Park there are no black residents. I have, if you stretch the definition of the word to an absurd thinness, one black friend. He lives way over in Pasadena and I haven't seen him in months. And a few years ago I realized that in the course of this long and disillusioning journey, I had myself in some measure become, to my shame, to my absolute wonder and horror, a racist. For to qualify as a racist I don't think you must cruelly slur, stereotype or discriminate against people of another race. You have only to feel completely disconnected from them. You have only to look at them in a kind of almost scientific surprise, as I looked at the African-Americans I passed in Los Angeles in the days after the Simpson verdict, and realize you have been passing them by in just this way, for months, for years at a time. They were here all along, thinking what they think now, believing what they now believe, and somehow you failed to notice.

It's when I regard this failure of mine, this blindness, this apartheid of consciousness under whose laws I have gradually come to live, that I see just how far I have wandered in journeying the forty miles that separate this theatre from Columbia, Maryland, that separate the man, around whom 100,000 humans can suddenly materialize like ghosts, from the child of Tubman and Drew and Ms. Rosa Parks, that separate the endless present from that fleeting, long-vanished future.

Alan Cheuse

THE AUTOMOBILE RIDE that I took to reach this place this evening through a city filled with purpose, office workers headed home, others unhoused moving from one nonplace to another, others refugees, some like ourselves, hurrying off to various celebrations or jobs that would take us deep beneath the streets or into hangars where large turbines make the electricity that feeds our need for light, the light falling to earth, the wind catching the leaves and spinning them upward before the final fall, the flushing of blood through my veins, rushing all around through the system of tubes and shoots to reach my heart and lungs and brain and all around and back again. The images of journeys that rose up and fell back into the general buzz and hum of my natural confusion. These voyages of fluid and thought, of energy and aspiration. The lungs moving outward and expanding with air, then settling back to rest and expanding with air, then settling back to rest and beginning again. Pause, and begin again. Will flying fly? Will singing have a song? Pause, and begin again. Coursing back in my mind to a moment at school when I read those lines of Kenneth Patchen's and found them so profound. And now what do I think? My mind is a moil of movement and rest, movement and rest. Thinking now of the course of migration and emigration that brought my father to this country, walking back along the trail from France to Russia that sent his mother's great-great-grandfather hurtling toward his future, the Mongol horsemen galloping toward the west, flanking my future from another compass point, my mother's father living deep within the Pale, her mother's embryonic life beginning in deepest New

Jersey. All these rivers of blood and time that travelers journeyed within and upon, the mind lapsing back to a time before what we know as time. Chemicals in water and air itching to bond with their attractors in space. Simple-celled animals leeching toward the nourishment they desire. Fins moving in water and wings to air. Apes turning to their mates. Adam cleaving to Eve and Eve to Adam. Hands reaching for stones for shaping tools, reaching to lay stone upon stone, building, moving in, then feeling an old desire to move with the season, migrating outward across strange rivers where fish leap high to catch insects large as hands. Hands holding bows that send arrows flying to their marks. Hands tinted on the palms with fresh dye flowing toward cave walls. Hands that work bows across the luscious gut of cello strings. Hands moving at the behest of a traveling pen. Fingers at the keyboard. Nouns longing to mate with verbs, yearning to make that passage from being to action, or are nouns, like the whizzing, whirring, whirling atoms that comprise things themselves – rock, stone, tree – are these nouns a journey each within themselves? The words make their passage across the page like time, as Augustine suggested, moving toward eternity. Sparks flying between poles. Lightning tunneling from heaven to earth. Spit leaping from the throats of those who hate. Lips of lovers mapping the passage to the lips of the beloved. Eyes making their voyages, meeting, catching. Hands, hips, sperm setting out on a night journey upriver, the child growing in time. The births, the deaths, the loves, the hurts, the pain, the wounds, divorces and madness, the wars, suffering, traveling, the healing, the heart, the electric course of the mind, the lungs, slowing all this while with the whole breath of things. The air, the light, the hope of motion, the automobile ride across the city at dusk, wondering as always how I can ever make sense out of anything. Carrying with me this baggage, these words making their way now across the distance between us, hoping they find with you temporary shelter.

Maxine Clair

THERE ARE FEW things as personally rewarding as journeys, yet they seem to fall so flat when we try to describe what happened to us along the way. It's sort of like an ad for a feature presentation that turns out to be slides of somebody's trip to the Everglades. Well, I'm telling you right up front that I've got slides. I've filed each set according to the degrees of gratification from most to least. I'll flip fast and show only one, my number-one set:

The first one is of me. I'm on my way. I'm wearing one of those green, backless numbers. That's my mother. She's plying me with crushed ice. My husband was out of town and so he isn't in the picture. That sign – can you make it out? – it says "Delivery Room" but it's really the universal sign for "One-Way Street." What I don't know here is that I will do this three more times. Each soul that finds its way through this body will be like a separate country that I must find my way across. Each will have its own language, its own spectacular mountains, active volcanoes, and vernal places. Each will have swamps and seas as calm as oil.

This one is of son number one, pedaling his very first tricycle. When he grows into a flower he'll be a bird of paradise.

I'm downright fat in this one, walking through the same door in a different city, and my mother isn't there. It's another son, this one more like a bouquet of baby roses, all bud and thorns, but give him time.

And here a few years later, still another son – the sunflower – wild and radiant, hard to miss.

You've seen one like this before, but this time it's a girl, and her trip has been taxing, If she were a flower she'd be African violet – stunning, fragile – quietly insinuating herself into the land.

Here's me sitting on our kitchen counter reading *The Yellow Wallpaper* on a sunny afternoon. The four of them are making their own peanut-butter-and-jelly sandwiches at the table and making their own towers and tunnels with the jars.

This one seems out of place. It's the five of us at the dinner table. That's son number one. If this were a video you would catch the attitude in his voice. He's saying how nobody else's mother goes out on dates, and when his brother – the one with the fork in his hand – points out that Mrs. So-and-So down the street has a "friend", number one says that that's because *Mr.* So-and-So is dead, and "Dad's not dead," he says. "He's just divorced from us and living somewhere else."

This one is of me with *Webster's Collegiate* in my lap. I'm looking up the word "heartfelt," or was it "patience"?

At first glance at this one you think "adorable, so handsome, so intense." Look closer. He's swallowing a worm and he's grinning.

This one is of us ready for church. I have just buttoned my daughter into her cute pale blue outfit. That's not blood down her front. It's red shoe polish. She wanted her Stride-Rites to shine.

There she is in her plaid jumper, her hair in braids with a riot of barrettes, her first book bag slung over her pink Huffy bike.

Here it's autumn and we're out back. I'm supposed to be teaching them touch football, but tackle is all the boys know. See how the oak tree blazes? I never fell. I've got the ball. They're hanging on, and their weight holds my feet on the ground. I've thrown my reading aside on the stoop: *Wouldn't Take Nothin' for My Journey Now.*

This is me on the phone disowning number two the time he locked the principal out of her office.

This is me on the phone to the poison control center with my finger down number three's throat.

This is me calling 911. The skewed angular thing attached to my daughter is her arm.

This is me holding the phone that cannot ring again until the bill is paid.

This is us on leftovers night – lasagna and mashed potatoes.

This is me with *American Heritage* this time. I'm looking up the word "endure."

Now here's my son number two, the thorny one who locked out the teacher. We're at his baccalaureate. He has earned that piece of paper he's got rolled up in his hand. He's asking me why I cried the whole time.

Here's my son number three, seeking his fortune, painting sunflowers on blue jeans for a fee.

This is Miss African Violet, skipping school to be with her friends.

Here's son number one, away at school. Far away.

Here's the girl who wanted to marry him.

Here's the guy he ended up with.

Here I am, practicing my smile in the mirror.

Here are the five of us that winter in the backyard. I'm trying to get them to stomp the word "Joy" into the snow. They're trying to get me to make a snowball.

This is the Cross pen set they chipped in for when I got my MFA. An investment, they said. Make us rich.

That's my first-born son, my six-foot bird of paradise and me – two faces on a park bench in April. I'm holding on to him, he's crying. The test has come back positive. Let me flip back to the slide of him on his first tricycle where he's pedaling fast.

There's number two! That's New York, in front of Spike Lee's place. He's the young businessman come full bloom.

There's number three on MTV, my son – would you believe – doing a commercial in his sunflower jeans.

And that's my baby girl with her book bag, heavy with Torts and Civil Procedure.

Finally, here are the five of us playing touch on Christmas Day. I asked for an *Unabridged*. They've given me a Coach bag instead, and a walk-around telephone. But, thanks to them, I know the definitions by heart.

That's the end of the set. Don't worry if you fell asleep. They say it's the way of journeys. You'd have to have been there.

Barbara Kingsolver

MY GREAT-AUNT ZELDA went to Japan and took an abacus, a bathysphere, a conundrum. That was a game we used to play. All you had to do was remember everything.

Then I grew up and went to Japan myself. It was 1992. I was warned to expect a modern place. People said, "Take appliances, battery packs, cellular technology," but I arrived in Kyoto an utter foreigner, unprepared. Yes, there are electric street cars. Also golden pagodas and more invisible guidelines for politeness than I could fathom. When I stepped on a streetcar, a full head taller than everyone, I became an awkward giant. I took up too much space. I bumped into people. I crossed my arms when I listened, which it turns out is brazen. I didn't know how to eat noodle soup with chopsticks and I did it wrong. I never expected in the sweltering heat that a woman should wear stockings, but every woman in Kyoto wore nylon stockings. Coeds in shorts on the tennis courts wore stockings. I wore skirts and sandals; people averted their eyes.

When I went to Japan I took my attitude, my bare naked legs, my callous foreign ways. I was mortified. The Japanese language accommodates no insults, only infinite degrees of apology. I memorized the direst one. "*Sumimasen.*" It means "I wish I were dead." I needed this word. When I touched a palace wall, curious to know its substance, I set off screeching alarms. "*Sumimasen!* Wish I were dead!" In the public bath I couldn't get the hang of showering with a hand-held nozzle while sitting fourteen inches from a stranger. I sprayed my elderly neighbor with cold water. In the face. "*Sumimasen!*" She just stared, dismayed by the foreign menace.

I visited a Japanese friend, and in her small, perfect house I spewed my misery. "Everything I do is wrong!" I wailed like a child. "I'm a blight on your country."

"Oh no," she said calmly. "To forgive, for us, is the highest satisfaction. To forgive a foreigner, ah! Even better. You have probably made many people happy."

When I went to Japan I took my abject good will, my baleful excuses, my cringing remorse. I couldn't remember everything so I gave myself away, evidently a kind of public service. I prepared to return feeling empty-handed.

On the runway in Osaka Airport we sat in a typhoon, waiting to leave for Los Angeles. Suddenly our flight was canceled. Air-traffic control had been struck by lightning. No flight possible until the following day. "We are so sorry," the pilot said. "You will be taken to a hotel, fed, brought back tomorrow." Disembarking, we found an airline official posted in the exit port for the sole purpose of saying to each and every passenger, "Terrible, Terrible. *Sumimasen.*" Other travelers nodded with indifference, but not me. I took the startled gentleman by the hands and practically kissed him. "You have no idea," I said, "how thoroughly I forgive you."

E. Annie Proulx

T HE BEST PART of a journey is coming back home. You open the door in darkness, the lock that sticks, with the sleet rattling down and the wind tearing at you. The house is cold, freezing cold, but you soon have a fire going and the water turned back on and the teakettle roaring its brains out, and over the chairs and the sofa you spread your rumpled clothes and broken tooth-brushes, guidebooks and ferry schedules, baggage-claim checks and leaky cosmetic bottles, presents for friends that looked suitable in the distant shop but are now unmasked as tourist junk, such items as eucalyptus-leaf bookmarks, hand-knit stockings in four shades of puce, and pudding bags – I have never taken a journey without bringing home a pudding bag – souvenir spoons and those ill-written books on local grist mills that make up the contents of your luggage.

But after twelve years in the same house and forty-eight years in the state of Vermont, last January I decide to move to Wyoming. I sold the house, and somebody else now wrestles with the lock that sticks. I gave all my furniture away. This was to be a westward journey with books and only books.

The most difficult part of the move was packing the books, thousands of them. It was a grand chance to weed them out and I went at it savagely, day after day, sorting, stacking, and when I was done, 411 boxes of books were marked for shipment to Wyoming. During this labor I telephoned the local librarian and told her to expect a windfall.

"I'm going to donate some extra books [I didn't want to say

'discard' or 'cull'] to the library." I said a few were first editions in fine condition, with dust jackets.

She sounded excited. "Oh my, yes, we'd be delighted to have them."

The next day I loaded the culls – I mean extras – into the pickup and drove down to the library. "Here you are," I said, and thumped the box down on her desk.

She looked inside. She looked at me. "Is that it? Seven books?"

"I know it's a lot, but I was ruthless."

She picked up one of the books, its bright dust jacket catching the neon light overhead. "*A History of Celtic Pudding Bags*," she read in a sour voice.

"It's a first."

She took up another. " 'Uncorrected Proof – Not for Sale.' *Dreams of Ripe Tomatoes: The Journal of a Baffin Island Gardener.* You know," she said, "you know, this is not quite what we were expecting."

There was a silence. "I see," I said.

I made that bloody trip west with 412 boxes of books, and I'm glad I kept the history of the Celtic pudding bags. It's one of my favorites.

Susan Minot

The Road

I drove a road once every day
a summer working far away.
One night at nine
the longest day of the year
I drove the way I always came
by olive groves flung down a hill
and cypress trees in dense black rows
and a walled-in graveyard – still.

Everything was still,
and yet I felt it move,
the clouds as pink as unripe figs
and the sky as smooth as the man's
eyelid I had recently been kissing.
The strange light came down
and settled in me.
An evening mist snaked forward.
Lightning cracked the bruised green sky
then everything was yellow,
then all the birds were shaking
with small sharp cries.

Something rushed over the dashboard.
Wind filled the car,
and vineyards moved like rippled waves
with movements from afar.
Inertia overtook my arms.
My wheels spun off the earth
and I was every rock and tree.
I touched the top of every leaf.
I felt the crease in every fold.
I tasted the long day's heat.
I thought of people I had known.
their faces clear and good,
and all the tales I had not told
and all the tales I would.

It may sound shrill to say
but on the spine of that hill
on the year's longest day
I felt all hope and all despair.
I was aware of the deepest root
of every tree.
I became the road
and it me.

It was the birth of a star.
It was the end of the world.
It was just a dusty car
which the gods were hurling.
My eye was like a pearl
which someone was peeling
and over it rolled
the sight of every shroud I'd ever seen
and every man I'd ever kissed
and every tear I'd ever dropped
and every other road I'd strolled.

I felt that I had been a place
too beautiful to bear.
The car flew like eternity.
The wheels tore up my hair.
I felt that I would never stop.
I'd always go and go!
And then the light began to fall.
A sharp curve made me slow,
and hope went flying past me then
to places I don't know.

My eyes are different
since that ride.
My heart let go its load
and into its place poured the dust
when I became that road.
It seemed the longest stretch of road
and yet it was quite small,
just a little path from here to there
beside a crumbling wall.

Kate Lehrer

I WAS NOT THINKING of journeys when I began my sprint up the ladder for a high dive, my first ever. But that wouldn't stop me from being Esther Williams. The morning was just right, dry Texas heat that didn't singe, but reassured, invigorated.

"Atta way, Katie! Fast and neat!" a boy yelled. We'd been waiting for all the other would-be swans to take their plunges.

I was already over halfway up. I didn't look down. No need to think too much about how high I'd climbed. I wasn't much of a diver and doubted I'd ever been a fish. Swimming provided a good way to work off a phys. ed. requirement, stay cool, get a tan; and the summer season ended with this last exam – if you could call a high dive an exam.

But it was time to get on with this. As with life, the sooner, the better. I was eighteen and ready to see everything, do everything, be everything. I flew up the last few steps. And I was on the diving board, and giddy. Almost like I'd made my graceful glide. Maybe I'd been a bird. Birds soared and dived. Yeah, I bet I'd been a bird. So why was I still gripping the ladder rails? Birds didn't do that. Letting go, I straightened up and took a couple of tentative steps.

"Come on, Katie" our swim coach called. I took another step and reminded myself I had once thrived on dares.

"There she is, Miss America" some wise guy sang out, and a few others began humming.

I cursed myself for wearing my one-piece red suit with the built-up cups, but being what was called a good sport, I instinctively smiled down – and dropped into a crouch. The chorus grew louder, then faded when they saw I wasn't clowning. I couldn't move or talk.

The coach yelled, "Don't try to dive. Just jump!" In my squat position I inched forward a little, then stopped again. The group had grown quiet. No more "You can do it, Katie!"s. No more razzing, either.

I crept to the end of the plank. No place else to go. A class bell rang but I couldn't jump. Now the coach threatened to flunk me. NO! I was a collector of gold stars. Gold stars hide loss. Once more I called on my ever-ready will, but it was suddenly sick of this game. Even failing didn't matter. I was no Esther Williams. I was no bird. Just some lumbering land-bound creature and a coward at that. Beginning a slow, clumsy crawl backwards to utter silence, I imagined those faces watching in contempt or pity; but I didn't much care.

As with most journeys, the final destination wasn't exactly what I'd planned on. Only a long time later did I understand that, for me, writing a book is a little like climbing a high diving board: getting up there with an elegant design, yet not knowing whether I'll be a swan or a fool. Even so, I've learned to close my eyes, hold my nose, and jump.

Walter Mosley

THE SIMPLEST JOURNEY is that trek across distance, any kind of distance, and over time. A trip, a vacation, an exploration of new territory in the interest of science or curiosity or even in the interest of self-preservation. There is a destination, and in trying to reach that destination there are certain expenditures: time, money, physical exertion, maybe blood, maybe life, maybe you never get there, at least physically. But this kind of journey is usually its own reward. Someone else will discover that cure or climb that mountain, build on your experience by following the trail you blazed. This kind of journey, be it intellectual, physical or spiritual, is condoned or supported by the society in which the travelers live.

There is another kind of journey, and that's that excursion that leads away from the imagination of the people in charge – you know, the kings and the presidents and priests, people like Galileo and Darwin and Joan of Arc fall into this category. They take us some-place that others don't want us going and they take their lives in their hands by just imagining a different way. These kinds of journeys are what we learn about in school. They're simple to understand, if not to undertake. You start here and you go there, and that's easy. But what if the destination was in question. What if you said that you wanted to go to a certain place and the guy next to you says "But you're already there. All you have to do is open your eyes." Or even worse, you don't really even want to be there, you just think you want to be there.

I'm a member of a group of people that say that their destination is a place in the mainstream publishing world. I and my fellow travelers want to see people like us, people who aren't of white and European descent, in decision-making roles in the cultural backbone of America. We want to be editors, designers, publishers, publicists, and sales people. We want to be at Simon & Schuster and Random House and Harcourt Brace and Bantam, Doubleday, Dell, just to name a few.

When I tell people that the first stumbling block in our journey is their racism they say "No. No, we're not racist. We eat with Jesse Jackson. We hang out with Nelson Mandela. When we were young, we journeyed down south and marched with Martin Luther King." Some of them also talk about the sexual activities of their children. When I tell people that our destination is further limited by the arcane hiring practices that exclude my group they say "We'd love to hire young non-white people but those men and woman can easily find jobs in the financial sector." (As if white kids couldn't.) And then I say, "But the few young people that do make it to these trainee desks feel alienated by an almost all-white world that doesn't believe in the intellectual validity of the whole of non-white literature." Then I'm told that I don't understand, that publishing is a business and everyone has to cut it on their own. Then I say that the doors are closed to senior professionals in publishing who are not white and I'm told that they will gladly hire a qualified individual if they meet such an individual.

My journey is not across time or distance. I'm standing in front of the closed door of a man who says that he's my friend. All I want to do is walk across the threshold. All I want to do is go up in the elevator and go to a place that is at least partly mine but I can't make the journey because the destination is denied.

Octavia E. Butler

F OR ALL BUT the first ten years of my life writing has been my
way of journeying from incomprehension, confusion and
emotional upheaval to some sort of order, at least to an orderly list
of questions and considerations. For instance . . .

At the moment there are no true aliens in our lives – no Martians,
Tau Cetians to swoop down in advanced spaceships, their attentions
firmly fixed on the all-important Us, no gods or devils, no spirits,
angels, or gnomes. Some of us know this. Deep within ourselves we
know it. We're on our own, the focus of no interest except our
consuming interest in ourselves.

Is this too much reality? It is. Yes. No one is watching, caring,
extending a hand or taking a little demonic blame. If we are adults
and past the age of having our parents come running when we cry,
our only help is ourselves and one another.

Yes, this is far too much reality.

No wonder we need aliens.

No wonder we're so good at creating aliens.

No wonder we so often project alienness onto one another.

This last of course has been the worst of our problems – the human
alien from another culture, country, gender, race, ethnicity. This is
the tangible alien who can be hurt or killed.

There is a vast and terrible sibling rivalry going on within the
human family as we satisfy our desire for territory, dominance and
exclusivity. How strange: In our ongoing eagerness to create aliens
we express our need for them, and we express our deep fear of being
alone in a universe that cares no more for us than it does for stones or

suns or any other fragments of itself. And yet we are unable to get along with those aliens who are closest to us, those aliens who are of course ourselves.

All the more need then to create more cooperative aliens, supernatural beings or intelligences from the stars. Someone we can trust to listen and care, someone who knows us as we really are and as we rarely get to know one another, we just need someone to talk to, someone whose whole agenda is us. Like children, we do still need great and powerful parent figures and we need invisible friends. What is adult behavior after all but modified, disguised, excused childhood behavior? The more educated, the more sophisticated, the more thoughtful we are, the more able we are to conceal the child within us. No matter. The child persists and it's lonely.

Perhaps someday we will have truly alien company. Perhaps we will eventually communicate with other life elsewhere in the universe or at least become aware of other life, distant but real, existing with or without our belief, with or without our permission.

How will we be able to endure such a slight? The universe has other children. There they are. Distant siblings that we've longed for. What will we feel? Hostility? Terror? Suspicion? Relief? No doubt. New siblings to rival. Perhaps for a moment, only a moment, this affront will bring us together, all human, all much more alike than different, all much more alike than is good for our prickly pride. Humanity, *E pluribus unum* at last, a oneness focused on and fertilized by certain knowledge of alien others. What will be born of that brief, strange and ironic union?

Denise Chávez

*M*ERCADO day. My elderly divorced parents are trying to be friends. We sit in my mother's old blue Toyota, the one that only goes forward, not in reverse, with the car doors opened. Our legs dangle over our seats. We peel the skin of mango fruit joyously, without words, eating. It is *mercado* day, market day. We've driven to Juarez, Mexico; forty-two miles away from my home town in Las Cruces, the city of ever-present crosses. My mother sits in the front, my father in back. I am at the wheel. We just finished our lunch, *asadero*, a type of farmer's cheese, blood sausage, avocados. Earlier I'd asked the vendor *"Cuales estan listos?"* "Which ones are ready?" He hands me three ripe avocados. I later buy my *tortillas de maiz "las de deveras,"* the real ones, the ones from the woman who pulls them from her straw basket and then wraps them in paper soft as old handkerchiefs. We are thirsty. Our shivering, dripping hands lift orange Fantas, Sprites and ice-cold Cokes from the dispenser in the center aisle. The paid *mariachis* serenade us with *"Guadalajara, Guadalajara, tierra quemada."* Oh, this burnt earth of hot July, 117 in the shade. My parents bicker in the background. The shoeshine boys and their shiny wooden boxes perch on the stairway watching us eat. Our wet, sticky hands cannot wipe away traces of this last holy meal. Afterwards I drive through Juarez, confidently thinking, "I understand the way Mexicanos drive. They drive like me." I'm not afraid. I'm safe. It's when I leave the *mercado* that my terror begins. My parents are now both dead. They will never drive again. *En el nombre del hijo, mercado* day. *En el nombre del hijo* mango day. *En el nombre del espiritu santo*, sausage day. I step on the gas. I'm not afraid. I understand the way Mexicanos drive. They drive like me. *Guadalajara, Guadalajara, tierra quemada.* Oh, the voices of this burnt earth. *"Aguacates! Queso fresco! Dulces de camote!"* My mothers" favorite candy was made of crystallized sweet potato. My favorite is made of cactus, bisnaga. *Aguacates! Queso fresco! "Por favor, Senorita. Algo para la familia, por favor."* "Psst! Hey, lady! Land, you wanna buy?" "Later," I say, *"Despues."* Later, not today. I recalled our feast later in the rain. Later, much later. The *mercado* in Juarez; July, 117 in the shade. *Mercado* day. Mango day. Blood-sausage day.

A SENSE OF PLACE

October 1, 1990

Eudora Welty

I T'S A GREAT pleasure to be back here and to be back at such a grand occasion, and I'm deeply, deeply honored to be here. As you know, our subject is "place." Place in the practice of writing our stories provides a stage, sets the stage, where it allows and prompts the characters to unfold. All of us are writers here, and we all do this. And there is a precedent: the Book of Genesis. It tells us that God created the garden of Eden first. When Adam and Eve were made, it was all ready for them. The Garden of Eden, the apple tree, the serpent, and the angel waiting in the wings. Place was first. Indeed, for the writer of fiction, place gives testimony and endorsement to his fictions in a truth. Take Faulkner. Wouldn't we know in a place like Yokna-patawpha County, Beat Two – I think it's Beat Two – there would be Snopeses? Snopeses didn't make Beat Two. Beat Two with right good will made Snopeses after Snopeses after Snopeses. Just as its better, older, and declining neighbor made Compsons of Sartorises and defeated, and brought them to an end.

We're surrounded by our own story. We live and move in it, we continue in it. Place conspires with the artist; it may be a very deep conspirator in the very processes of art. One place, Ireland, awoke the genius of Yeats. It went on murmuring and repeating itself and confiding to Joyce and persecuting him through a lifetime, until he got it all written down. Today Ireland keeps its profound moral dialogue with the poet Seamus Heaney.

Place has worked upon genius in different times, different ways. Always, perhaps, place may focus a gigantic, voracious eye on genius, and bring its gaze to point. The act of focusing itself has beauty and meaning. Focus brings to the work of a writer awareness, discernment, order, clarity, insight. They are like the attributes of love.

Does putting value in a place mean that what results for the writer is regional? Regional seems to me a careless term, as well as a condescending one. Because it fails to differentiate between the local raw material of life and its outcome as art. Regional is an outsider's term; it has no meaning for the insider who's doing the writing. Because as far as he or she knows, he or she is simply writing about life. Jane Austen, Emily Brontë, Thomas Hardy, Cervantes, Turgenev, themselves, did they confine themselves to regions great or small? Are they regional? They knew from the start of time it has not been so. It is through place that we put out roots wherever birth, chance, fate, or our traveling selves set us down. But where these roots reach toward, every time, is the deep and running vein, eternal and consistent and everywhere purely itself, that feeds and is fed by the human understanding. That vein is searched for by the human imagination.

Whatever our place, it has been visited by the stranger; it will never be new again. Whatever our theme in writing, it is old and tired. It is only the vision, the single, individual vision, that can be new. But that is enough. And that is mystery enough. And place has helped to provide it for us.

Norman Mailer

I 'VE HAD THE pleasure of thinking about what a sense of place means, and it occurs to me that it is as large as one's birthplace or the country one adopts. And it can be as small as a mood that has a ground, or as small as a thought that takes place in a room. In fact when thoughts do take place in a room they have a wonderful sense of place. At any rate, what I love about it is that, when you're writing, there's nothing more difficult than to come up with a good description of place. Writers often feel that sometimes they do what they do through their work, and once in a while they get a gift from the various powers either up there or coming up from below, and we've never asked where the gift comes from, whether on high or below; we're just happy enough to get the gift, 'cause writing can be a dreary activity. Anyway, when we get that good sense of place we're happy with it. And it doesn't happen that often. So I thought I'd read from something I wrote once which wasn't wholly infelicitous.

There was a week when the weather never shifted. One morose, November sky went into another. The place turned gray before one's eyes. Back in summer the population had been thirty thousand, and it doubled on weekends, when it seemed as if every vehicle on Cape Cod chose to drive down the four-lane state highway that ended at our public beach. Provincetown was as colorful then as St. Tropez, and as dirty by Sunday evening as Coney Island. In the fall, however, with everyone gone, the town revealed its other presence. Now the population did not boil up daily from thirty thousand to sixty, but settled down to its honest sediment: three thousand souls. And on empty weekday after-noons you might have said the number of inhabitants must be thirty men and women, all hiding. There could be no other town like it. If you were sensitive to crowds, you might expire in summer from human propinquity. On the other hand, if you were unable to endure loneliness, the vessel of your person could fill with dread during the long winter.

Martha's Vineyard, about fifty miles to the southwest, had lived through the upsurge of mountains and their erosion, through the rise and fall of oceans, the life and death of great forests and swamps. Dinosaurs had lived on Martha's Vineyard, and their bones were compacted into the bedrock. Glaciers had come and gone, sucking the island to the north, pushing out to the south again. Martha's Vineyard had fossil deposits one million centuries old. The northern reach of Cape Cod, however, on which my house sat, that long curving spit of shrub and dune that curves in upon itself in a spiral at the tip of the cape, had only been formed by wind and sea over the last ten thousand years. That cannot amount to more than a night of geological time. Perhaps this is why Provincetown is so beautiful. Conceived at night, for one would swear it was created in the course of one dark storm, its sand flats still glistened in the dawn with the moist, primeval innocence of land exposing itself to the sun for the first time. Decade after decade, artists came to paint from life. Comparisons were made to the lagoons of Venice, and the marshes of Holland. But then the summer ended, and most of the painters left, and the long, dingy undergarment of the gray New England winter came down to visit. One remembered then that the land was only ten thousand years old, and our ghosts had no roots. We did not have old Martha's Vineyard's fossil remains to subdue each spirit. No, there was nothing to domicile our specters, who careened with the wind down the two long streets of our town that curved together around the bay, like two spinsters on their promenade to church.

Bobbie Ann Mason

I'M A NATIVE of Kentucky, but after college I lived in New York and then Connecticut, and then Pennsylvania. This year I moved back to my home state. My five cats are from Pennsylvania, and they weren't interested in moving to Kentucky. My white cat, Lolita, hated moving. She broke through the screen and escaped from the house the day after we arrived. She didn't know where home was, and so she was lost, out there in the weeds and the woods, and we haven't found her. She may very well be headed back to Pennsylvania. Two of our cats, Bilbo and Alice, are old and placid and they didn't seem to notice anything about the move as long as they had turkey and giblets and their familiar bed. Another cat, Albert, who is a very careful cat, spent many weeks sizing up the situation before he would venture out into the new property. But Kiko, the fifth cat, loved moving. He loved everything about it – he loved driving down the highway, he loved motels, he loved exploring our new home – Kiko's always ready for any new adventure; he identifies with Daniel Boone.

I've read that certain scientists who've studied cats in the wild have drawn a distinction between two sorts of cat populations. They call them residents and transients. Some cats stay put in their fixed home ranges, and others are on the move – they don't have homes. These scientists had always thought that the cats who established and held their territories were the most successful, the strongest, while the transients, who wander through, just looking around, are the losers. But in their studies the scientists began to wonder if maybe it's the transients who are actually the most successful because they have the greatest curiosity and a flair for adventure.

Some people are residents and some are transients. Some people can't be tied down, and others would have to be sawed down like a tree before they'd leave town. And now our growing American rootlessness is making a lot of people uneasy. Where is home? Where do we belong? Who are we? We go on vigorous genealogical quests to link ourselves with some bits of ancestral meaning so that we can understand who we are, and where we've been, and what place we've arrived at. Really, we've always been a nation on the move. We travel around and everyone asks, first thing, "Where're you from?" The question seems more urgent than ever. And more interesting: Where is that place we long for? We can sense it, but we can't find it. We keep looking for it: cruising and touring, getting a sense of this place and that place, until we're numb from the exhilaration and get the names mixed up, and can no longer remember whether the snapshots we took are of New Zealand in summer or of Oregon in winter.

But our transience, although it holds many dangers and has caused us much trouble in our history, is also our strength. If we go out and look around, then we can gain a deeper knowledge of our place of origin. It's a mistake to romanticize home, and deepen our roots so deep we can't get out. Nothing was ever so quaint and cute and wholesome as what the nostalgia merchants make of the rural American past. Nostalgia's a false direction to our rootless feeling, I think. I think dislocation is a dizzying reality, full of possibility – it's like reading, browsing in a library, getting a glimpse of fascinating new worlds. We can read a book, many books, each with a distinctive sense of place the writer has created. We trust the authority of the author to create for us that sense of place we can't always see from the tour-bus window or find in the Americana shop. If the writer can use his or her craft and imagination to pull off the illusions of a place we can believe is real, then we feel like we've really been somewhere.

John Edgar Wideman

I'M GOING TO read to you the end of a story called "Welcome." It's about a man who's having difficulty with the fact that he's lost a child and having difficulty about coming back to this place, which is very much like the place I grew up. He's talking to his sister; the only other thing you need to know is the man's father and son were named Will:

When I do finally catch him he tells me how hard it is to face these homeward streets. Like the world is washed fresh after rain, right? And when you step out in the sunshine, everything is different, Sis, anything seems possible. Well, think of just the opposite. Of flying, or driving for hours on the turnpike and getting off in Monroeville, and then the parkway, and already the dread's starting. The little boy feeling of fear I used to have when I'd leave home to deliver newspapers in Squirrel Hill and all the houses up there: big, and set back from the curb, and wide spaces between them, and green lawns, fat trees, and nothing but white people in those huge houses. I'd walk softly, no place up there really to put my feet. Afraid my big black footprints would leave a trail anywhere I stepped. That kind of uneasiness, edginess, till the car crosses Braddock Avenue, then blam, the whole thing hits me. I'm home again. It's the opposite of a new shiny world because I feel everything closing down. Blam. I know nothing has changed and never will. These streets swallow me alive and hate everybody and that's how it's going to be. Takes me a day at least to get un-depressed behind that feeling of being caught up again and unable to breathe, and everybody I love in some kind of trouble that is past danger, worse than danger, a state I don't want to give a name to, can't say because I don't want to hear it. Then I sort of gradually settle in, you all remind me of what's good here, why I need to come back, how this was home first, and always will be.

Last night I was driving to cop some chicken wings – you know how I love them, salty and greasy as they are, I slap on extra hot sauce and pop a cold Iron City, pour it over ice, hog heaven, you know. I'm on my way to the Woodside Barbeque, and I see a man and a little boy on the corner at the bus stop, on Frankstown at the bottom of the hill across from Mom's street. It's cold cold cold. I'm stopped at the light, so I can see the little boy's upset and crying. His daddy's standing there looking pissed off, helpless, and lost, staring up this hill for a bus that probably ain't coming for days, this late on a weekend. Daddy's a kid himself, and somehow he finds himself on a freezing night with an unhappy little boy on a black windy corner and no bus in sight, not a soul in sight like it's the end of the world. And I think, "Damn, why are they out there in this Arctic-ass weather?" The kid's shivering and crying in his skimpy Kmart snowsuit, the man not dressed for winter either, a hooded sweat-shirt under his shiny baseball jacket. And I see a woman some-where, the mother, another kid, really. The guy's returning the boy to his mother or her mother, or his, and this is the only way, the best he can do. And the wind howls, the night gets blacker and blacker. They'll find the two of them, father, son, man and boy, frozen to death icicles, in the morning, on the corner.

I think all that in a second, the whole dreary storyline, characters and bad ending, waiting for the light to change on my way for chicken wings. On my way back past the same corner, I see the father lift his son and hug him. No bus in sight and it's still blue cold, but the kid's not fidgeting and crying anymore, he's up in his daddy's arms, and I think, "Fuck it, they'll make it. Or if they don't somebody else will come along and try, or somebody else try to make kids, a home, a life, that's all we can do, any of us." That's why home was here, because lots of us won't make it, but others will try and keep on keeping on. And if I'd had just one wish in the world then, it would have been to be that father or that son, that moment when nothing could touch them.

William W. Warner

REMEMBERING LAST YEAR'S gala, which had as its theme a writer's beginnings, and trying to think what to say tonight about a sense of place, has forced me to the realization that very little in my upbringing seems to have pointed toward writing about natural places or natural history, which is what I attempt, or writing much about anything for that matter.

I was born and grew up in New York City, in the East Sixties, in a house that was without great books, without a father, and for some periods of the year, without a mother. *In loco patris*, I had only a highly irascible stepgrandfather. Col. George Washington Cavanaugh was his name, and he liked to be known by all of it. His most frequent utterances to me, apart from constant reminders that I was no blood kin, went something like this: "Your father was a bum, your mother's trotting around with every gigolo in Europe, so I suppose the spring can rise no higher than its source." Now you might think he was laying a genetic malediction, a genetic curse on me, but I always welcomed this little speech, because I knew it was a signal that the Colonel, as my brother and I always called him, was going to ease off or even grow a little mellow. "Yes, it's true the spring can rise no higher," he would repeat, "so I suppose I shouldn't have at you all the time." There might then even follow some awkward attempts at playing a more fatherly role, such as advice on how to prevent piles, a matter of great concern to the Colonel and none to me. Or, when I was a little older, the abrupt question: "Young man, tell me, have you ever deflowered woman?"

But there was one thing the Colonel did for us for which I'm eternally grateful. Come June, every year, he took the family, such as it was, to a place called Spring Lake, a summer resort on the New Jersey coast. Now, there was much about Spring Lake that I didn't especially care for: a fancy boardwalk, well-ordered streets neatly paved with gravel, great hotels with long porches and double rows of rocking chairs, and an institution known as the Bath and Tennis Club, where my contemporaries spent most of the day playing blackjack and sneaking cigarettes.

But at one end of the well-ordered streets, beyond the boardwalk and the great hotels, was an immense space. I think I began to wonder about it – or more precisely, what lay on its other side, before I could say its name. No one, least of all the Colonel, played that little game with me of digging a hole in the sand to see if we might come out in China, on the other side of the world. Rather, my older brother gave me a more exact geographic problem to ponder. "Look here," he would say, pointing to a map and running his finger along the fortieth parallel, "there's nothing between our beach and the coast of Portugal four thousand miles away. Just the Atlantic Ocean." He was right, of course. There is in fact not a headland, not an island, not even a rock between the New Jersey coast and that of Portugal. Well, suffice it to say that this bit of knowledge overwhelmed me. In fact, I began to stare for long periods out across an ocean that changed its face almost every day, and to dream about when I might have a boat of my own, to row out beyond the farthest breakers and explore it. I also took to walking along the beach, often with my brother, until one day we discovered another world of water, known by the prosaic name of Wreck Pond. It was in fact what biologists call a complete estuarine system, in miniature. At its ocean side was a tide-scoured inlet constantly changing its course, a shallow bay, a labyrinth of marsh-grass islands and ultimately, well inland, a freshwater stream fed by a mill pond bordered by pin oak and magnolia.

Thanks to Wreck Pond, we could do everything from dip-netting for crabs or catching small fish, to stalking the mud flats and the marsh grass looking for shore birds, muskrat, raccoons, even an occasional mink. Wreck Pond and the Atlantic Ocean: what a relief they offered from the Bath and Tennis Club. What an escape from the Colonel. These were our places, our private world of neverending discovery.

No wonder perhaps, that many years later, after you've journeyed out on that ocean and discovered more wondrous things than you ever imagined, or found an estuary so rich and varied as the Chesapeake Bay, you have an urge to tell people about them. In fact you want to say, Hurry, this time is short. See these things — better, do something about them before they are inalterably changed by the hand of man. (Yes, even the Atlantic Ocean is being over-harvested.) So you sit down and write, trying to convey this sense of it all. Finally, if you feel you've succeeded to some degree, you naturally want to thank everyone who helped you, without exception. That, in my case, I have to admit, includes the Colonel. So I will say it now, with words I seldom, if ever, uttered in his lifetime, namely: Thank you, Grandpa. You got me into all of this. And thank you too, Grandpa, for getting me out, in another sense, at a very critical moment. You remember the day my brother and I got through the surf, out beyond the farthest wave and were being rapidly carried toward Europe by a stiff west wind in a totally unseaworthy boat of our own backyard construction. You did, after all, call the Coast Guard.

Blanche McCrary Boyd

I HAVE ALWAYS HAD a certain amount of trouble understanding where I am. Maybe this is because I grew up in South Carolina. Maybe it's because, as a neurological examination revealed last summer, I have some mystery marks in my brain. Maybe I'm just absentminded. There's an old joke about a college professor walking down a hallway and dragging his hand along the wall. And he collides with a secretary. "Excuse me," he says, "which way was I going?" The secretary points and says, "That way." "Oh, good," he says, "then I've had lunch." Now, I'm a lot more likely to forget where I'm going than I am to forget lunch. But even when I was little, my mother would say, "Honey, you're in another world." I felt guilty about this when I was little, but as I got older, I began to say "I wish I were."

I grew up in Charleston, in the late fifties and early sixties, a time of racial confrontations, of sit-ins at lunch counters, freedom rides, integration of churches. I didn't have to watch a whole lot of television to figure out that, as a white Southerner, I'd been born onto the wrong side of this conflict. It's hard to be a teenager and think that what your family and your culture stand for are morally wrong. So, when I was eighteen years old, I left my hometown as if it were a burning building. I couldn't wait to get away; I couldn't wait to belong nowhere. And for a number of years I lived fairly happily in generic California apartments. You know, the kind that have white walls and white drapes and they were built five years ago. And later I lived in New York City, which is a good choice for displaced persons.

But no matter where I was, the world divided for me into South Carolina and not South Carolina. No matter where I was, home-sickness dogged me. And no matter what I wrote, the characters always ended up in South Carolina. This struck me as limited. How important could Charleston, South Carolina, be? And within that context, how important was the little bit of it that I knew? So, when I was thirty-three years old, I went home again, to palmetto trees swaying in moonlight, to the salt smells of marshes, to live oaks weighted with moss, and old plantations nestled now against shopping centers. I went home to humidity, to air so thick and wet and warm that people move slowly, speak slowly. And I went home to good manners, to folks too polite to blow their horns in traffic jams. I went home, that's what it amounts to. That's what my sense of place was. The world was South Carolina, and not South Carolina. Home, and not home.

I'm forty-five years old now, and two years ago I bought a house in Connecticut. I think that's growth. I can look out of my picture window and tell that the trees are not live oaks. I'm amazed by their leaves falling, stunned by winter snow. But when I left South Carolina that second time, I took my sense of home with me. I have it here with me tonight.

I am standing on this stage, in Washington, in America, on the planet Earth. I am held here by gravity, as the Earth spins at more than a thousand miles an hour, as the solar system hurtles through space. In space, I see a lot of unidentified bright objects. Do you know that's what the neurologist actually called those mystery marks that they found in the pictures of my brain? "Unidentified bright objects." UBOs. That's right. When all of this first happened, I was pretty terrified. And my mother phoned to comfort me. "Oh, honey," she said, "you might have had those things all your life. They might explain everything." Now, after many more tests, the doctors seem to agree that the marks in my brain are inexplicable, but harmless. "I know what they are," I told my doctor. "They're stars," I said.

Ellen Douglas

M Y NEIGHBORHOOD, WHAT it meant to me writing, got dislocated, or I got dislocated, the day I saw the first pictures of the Earth from space. Saw Earth as a neighborhood, the only place we have. Nothing before had shown us how small it is, how suspended in darkness, how fragile, and lit up by the sun like a soap bubble, but floating in the void. Always before my neighborhood had seemed solid. People had moved among buildings, sat under trees. I myself had played as a child under a tree so old that it was supposed to be the council oak, a place for the Natchez Indians before it was a place for us. Its limbs so long and heavy they were propped with steel beams against crashing of their own weight. But now the council oak was on a bubble, whirling through space, it weighed not so much as a feather.

Trees seem so solid, so permanent where I live. Green-black magnolias with leaves as thick as shoe leather. Dark cedars, weighed down with moss, heavily perfumed. Oaks, with their great boles and powerful stretched arms. I knew that I had been lucky to live in such a place, for I knew that most Americans these days, most people in the world, are blown about like Saharan dust. Place is transformed before one can draw a breath. But my great-grandmother would still recognize our place, would know the lilies blooming by the door, might have planted them herself. Would know the shards of glass embedded in concrete along the top of the redbrick garden wall against intruders. But now all these – trees, flowers, wall – float away on the fragile bubble that is our place.

Such terrible knowledge opens chasms at the writer's feet. I could no longer trust my neighborhood not to pop, and vanish, whirling us away with it. Easy to see, looking at the bubble, how it could dissipate in the void. A meltdown. The ozone pierced. The final choking dust of poison. The weight of too many billions of people; the loss of too many billions of trees. In the face of such knowledge, to write fiction? To keep on writing? Oh, it's not our mortality, we've always had to face that. Or close our eyes. But to lose the place all lives have sprung from? What to do? What to say about that possibility?

Maybe, since I continue to write, I do so out of habit. Voice sounding its puny locust song, "keeping on talking," as Faulkner said. But my impulse here, tonight, is to do what fiction says it must not do: to sound the tocsin, call us all to arms against the destruction of the world. And to celebrate, too, to rejoice at the sight of our bubble, all blue and green, and swirling clouds. To proclaim the miracle of it: our neighborhood, hanging there, alive in the black void.

Shelby Foote

I DON'T REALLY UNDERSTAND the choice of subject under discussion here tonight. As sense of place is at once so large and so limited, as if we were swimming-pool contractors, and the question is whether we should put water in those pools. Still, I suppose the nature of the proposition can be explored.

Eudora Welty, with her accustomed poetic brevity, has referred to the scene of a novel as a gathering place, which puts the emphasis where it belongs, on the people involved, without neglecting either the backdrop or the curtains. And she is also suggesting that the writer would do well to shore up the flooring stoutly to make sure it doesn't creak or buckle under the actors and acrobats when they perform their various jigs and contortions. Another Mississippian, our pre-siding spirit, William Faulkner (though William would have run barefoot over broken glass to avoid just such a gathering as this), emphasized the writer's need for being thoroughly familiar with the scene whereon the action is played out. He was, he said a Southern writer because the South was what he grew up with and knew. Anything else would have required research, which was something he could not abide, and later proved how right he'd been in his assessment by writing his fable, which suffers from the ailment Flaubert found in his own salon beau, "The pedestal was too large for the statue." In other words, sense of place can be overdone by overdoing the research. And in still other words, I have tried for about a minute and a half, and got nowhere.

Marita Golden

W RITERS ARE ALWAYS headed or looking for home. Home is the first sentence, questing into the craggy terrain of imagination. Home is the final sentence, polished, perfected, nailed down. I am an American writer, and so my sense of place is fluid, ever shifting, ever salt. The spaciousness of this land reigns and pushes against the borders of self-censorship and hesitation. I have claimed at one point or other everyplace as my home.

My people were brought to this county in an act of grand theft, actually. With no return ticket. Part of a perverse, stunning, triangular trade-off of culture and identity. Launched in the middle passage we have sojourned from Accra in Ghana, Ondo in Nigeria, to Tougaloo in Mississippi and Oakland in California. Our sojourns have required few passports, and we have indelibly stamped, reshaped, and claimed each place we have called ours.

Like their creator, my fictional characters reject the notion of life lived on automatic pilot. The most important people in my books see life as a flame, something that when lived properly bristles and squirms, even as it glows. In the autobiography *Migrations of the Heart*, the heroine, who just happened to be me, came of age in Washington and began the process of becoming an adult person everywhere else. If you sell your first piece of writing in Manhattan, give birth to your only child in Lagos, experience Paris in the spring – yes – with someone you love, and return to Washington after thirteen years of self-imposed exile to write the Washington novel nobody else had (and you thought you never would), tickets, visas, *lingua franca* will all become irrelevant. When all places fingerprint the soul, which grasp is judged to be the strongest? In my novel *A Woman's Place*, one woman leaves America to join a liberation struggle in Africa. In *Long Distance Life*, Naomi Johnson flees 1930s North Carolina and comes up south to Washington, D.C., to find and make her way. Thirty years later her daughter returns to that complex, unpredictable geography and is sculpted like some unexpected work of art by the civil-rights movement.

I am a Washington writer, who keeps one bag in the closet packed, just in case. I am an American, who knows the true color of the nation's culture and its heart, a stubborn, wrenching, rainbow. I am Africa's yearning stepchild, unforgotten, misunderstood, necessary. Writers are always headed or looking for home. The best of us embrace and rename it when we get there.

Larry L. King

I F YOU LIVE long enough, and I have, your sense of place or your place becomes illusionary. In a changing world, our special places are not exempt. The rural Texas where I grew up in the 1930s and 1940s simply does not exist anymore. It exists only in memory or on pages or stages where a few of us have attempted to lock it in against the ravages of time. And it is, of course, a losing battle. Attempting to rhyme my work of an earlier Texas, with the realities of today's modernist urban-tangle Texas, that place where, as my friend Edwin Trake has written, "southern California collides with Georgia on a vast sheet of concrete," well, I sometimes feel that I am writing about pharaohs.

My friend Larry McMurtry a few years ago stirred up a Texas tornado with an essay in which he charged: 1) that Texas writers were producing many words but damn little literature; 2) that we stubbornly insist on writing of old Texas, vanished Texas, the Texas of myth and legend while 3) shirking our responsibilities to write of the complexities of modern Texas. Hardly had the anguished cries of the wounded faded away on the Texas wind, until Mr. McMurtry himself delivered a novel called *Lonesome Dove*. A cracking good yarn, if a bit long on cowboy myths and frontier legends. And decidedly short of skyscraper observations or solutions to urban riddles. But not only did my friend Larry McMurtry have a perfect right to change his mind, I'm delighted that he did. Because any place shorn of its myths and legends, you see, runs the risk of winding up as New Jersey.

I spent my formative years in Texas, my first seventeen years, before random relocation arranged by the U.S. Army. Uncle Sam sent me to Queens. I must admit, Queens failed to grow on me. But from it I discovered Manhattan, which did grow on me, and with much the same passion and ego with which General MacArthur vowed to return to the Philippines, I vowed to return to Manhattan. And one day did. But before that, in 1954, at the age of twenty-five, I came to Washington to work in Congress. My objectives being to end war for all time, balance the budget, eliminate red tape, fashion a perfect social order from the existing political chaos. That work is still ongoing.

New York and Washington offered themselves as measuring sticks against the only world I had previously known. They made me aware of cultures I had not even suspected; they permitted me to look at my natural habitat with fresh eyes and even spurred me – yes – to leave my native place. I have now tarried here in what I call the misty East for almost forty of my sixty-one and a half years. This has sometimes led to a confusion of place. I strangely feel like a Texan in New York and Washington, but when I return home to Texas, I feel like a New Yorker or a Washingtonian. So if my native place has been guilty of change, then so have I. Yet when I set out to write there is little of ambivalence. The story speaks patterns, and values that pop out are from an earlier time and of my original place. I fancy myself a guide to the recent past, one who passed along a certain Texas path and tried to leave behind signposts saying "Here's what I saw, and heard, and felt in this place in my time." In an age when the past seems not much value, to say nothing of being unconnected to the present in too many people's minds, I think that is not a bad function for the writer. It's often that a lot of writers who report their native places to be faulted by some critics and by some friends (and please let us never confuse the two), for revealing home-precinct wars, and perhaps doing it too gladly. I hope I am guilty of that charge. If not, then I've wasted my days. No writer of any worth can look at his native place or any other as if wearing blinders or as if in the pay of the chamber of commerce. Perhaps what I am trying to say was better said by Mr. Faulkner's Quentin Compson, reconsidering his native South after painful refurbishings at Harvard; when asked by an inquisitor why he so hated the place of his birth, he blurted, panting in the cold air, Mr. Faulkner tells us, the iron New England dark, "I don't hate it. I don't hate it! I don't!" Me neither, Quentin.

Paule Marshall

I T WAS A four-story, narrow-bodied, turn-of-the-century brownstone in Brooklyn. A house with a tall, imperial stoop, a boxwood hedge around the grass out front. And high-ceilinged, dark-paneled rooms that were always faintly redolent of the lemon-oil furniture polish my mother applied religiously. Outside stood a huge, barren, chestnut tree. And all the years we lived in that house, that miserable tree failed to produce a single chestnut. Lots of leaves in the summertime, but never a chestnut to roast over an open fire in the fall. Number 501 Hancock Street: My family leased and managed it for years. When I was a little girl, its hallways seemed peopled with ghosts. The Scotch-Irish family who had lived there before us were still rattling around. So, too, the ghosts of the tenants to whom we rented out the upper floors. They came, and as quickly went, driven away by my mother's rules and regulations. "Stop ringing down the bell. Don't play the radio so loud. Turn off the blasted light in the hall – you think I'se family to Mr. Edison?" Her West Indian voice flailed away at them.

The nerve center of our part of 501 was the basement kitchen. Some fine talk went on there among my mother and her friends. They were all immigrant women from small islands in the Caribbean, and they seldom ventured beyond the tight little island they had created for themselves in Brooklyn. Yet their talk took in the world. The raged against the Italian invasion of Ethiopia in 1935. They debated the merits of Marcus Garvey's master plan of repatriation to Africa. They denounced their one-time hero, F.D.R., when he interned Japanese-Americans during World War II. Because of the talk, the West Indies and Africa, too, became, in my consciousness, places to which I also belonged, by virtue of blood, longing, and choice. 501 Hancock made possible for me an expanded sense of place and self.

The old house is still there, although scarcely recognizable. The present owners have painted the reddish-brown sandstone a leprous white and have allowed the boxwood and grass to rampage over the yard. The desecration doesn't matter, though, because 501 has been elevated over the years into the realm of memory and the imagination. Besides, I can still sometimes smell the lemon-oil furniture polish, see that old tree outside, and I like to think that the ghosts, especially those of my mother and her friends, who used to talk their talk in the basement kitchen – "Talk your talk, girl!" they would exalt each other. "In this white-man world you got to take your mouth and make a gun." I like to think that these women, dead for many years now, are still alive and well in my work.

Peter Matthiessen

THIS IS SORT of going to be a sense of place lost. It's the impression of the Hudson River Valley from the point of view of a man who comes back there after a half-century away and feels so alienated from the development that's been happening there that he spends most of his time down by the railroad track, near the river.

In the sunny silence of the railroad track he sits on the warm trunk of the fallen willow, pulling mean burrs from his city trousers. From here he can see across the tracks, to the river and the Palisades beyond. Perhaps, he thinks, those sugar-maple yellows and hot hickory reds along the cliffs welcomed Henry Hudson, exploring upriver with the tide four centuries before, in the days when this gray flood, at that time blue, swirled with silver fishes. A train comes from the north, quickening by, no longer dull coal black as in his childhood, but a tube of blue-and-silver cars, no light between. In childhood he could make out faces, but with increased speed the human beings were pale blurs behind the glass. And nobody waves to the man on the dead tree by the railroad tracks.

The tracks nearest the river are abandoned, a waste of rusted rails and splintered oaken ties and hard, dry weeds. Once across, he can see north, to the broad bend where a shoulder of the Palisades juts out from the far bend into the Tappan Zee. A thick new bridge has been thrust across the water, cutting off the far blue northern mountains. In his childhood, a white steamer, the Hudson River Dayline, might loom around that bend at any moment. Or a barge of bright tomato-red being towed by a pea-green tug, both fresh as toys. In his lifetime, the river has changed from blue to a dead gray-brown, so thickened with inorganic silt that a boy would not see his own feet in the shallows. An ancient car, glass shattered, rust-colored, squats on the shore. And a grit beach between concrete slabs of an old embankment is scattered with worn tires. Years ago, his father had wondered at the sheer number of these tires, brought by forces unknown so very far from the roads and highways and dumped in low woods and spoiled, sullen waters all across America. As if, in the ruined wake of the course of empire, the tires had spun away in millions down the highways and rolled off the bridges into the rivers, and down into deep swamps of their own accord.

But the horizon is oblivious, the clouds are white, the world rolls on. Under the cliffs, the bend is yellow in the glow of maples, and the faraway water, reflecting the autumn sky, is gold and blue. Soiled though they are, the shining woods and glinting water and the bright steel tracks, the high golden cliffs above, with their tight driveways and sealed cars, their plump, vigilant houses, wall-eyed with burglar lights, a-tremble with alarms. For a long time, by the riverside, he sits on a drift log worn smooth by the flood. Withdrawn into the dream of Henry Hudson's clear blue river, of that old America off to the north, toward the primeval mountains, off to the west, under the shining sky.

Geoffrey Wolff

I 'M GOING TO read from the first chapter of my new novel, *Final Club*. This is a novel, it's the world where I've been living these past few years, so I'm going to forgive myself for missing it. The time is 1956, it's late autumn, and a Seattle boy, eighteen years old, is heading east on a train to a great university that will try to teach him, in that awful malediction, to know his place. Poor boy, he's just met a girl, also eighteen, and now his heart's full and wide open to the world and chance.

Before first light the *Empire Builder* slowed, passed yardmen at their switches lit by glowing oil pots. Here was sere, forlorn Malta. Nathaniel saw this country as alien and hostile, unmeshed with his own wherever was his own. He wanted to belong to some society beyond the community he had left on the margin of Puget Sound. He wanted to be the wide world's neighbor. He didn't know how to articulate this want, but he knew there should be a place for him out there, east of here. He wanted to have begun an adventure. He imagined the beautiful girl he had kissed and smelled, and he hoped she felt some of the feelings he felt. The stationmaster stood in the front door on the Malta depot staring balefully at Nathaniel as the *Empire Builder* resumed its eastern way. The windswept little shacks seemed to Nathaniel hopeless. He wondered what it would be like to wake up in such a place as Malta, to make it through the day all the way to dark. To lie down there knowing you would wake there, unbroken cycle, no more to be expected than what you already knew. To know that tomorrow would be no different from today, no more than today.

He opened a book his grandfather had given him, and the book was published by Charles Scribner's Sons, bound in dark green cloth without a dust jacket. It was *The Great Gatsby*. The sleepy boy began to read, and by Wolf Point on the nothern edge of the Missouri River, Nathaniel was with Nick and Daisy and Tom and pretty Jordan in West Egg at a pretty party where peoples' voices sounded like money. The *Empire Builder* was slowing for St. Paul. Here was F. Scott Fitzgerald country. Here was Nathaniel's first sight of the gathered tribe of boys and girls sent east to become gentlemen and ladies, bond salesman and post-debutantes. They were being seen off by clots of tanned moms and by bluff, red-faced men wearing, like their sons, pink-soled white bucks or saddle shoes and Brooks Brothers blue buttondowns. A couple of girls coming aboard wore beaver coats. It was a comfortably warm late afternoon, but Nathaniel was not so innocent that the fur coats puzzled him. He had just had a glimpse, he realized, how another world made its intricate orbits.

Alone in his compartment, he read. He was at the end now, and Nick Carraway was recollecting where he'd come from and how it felt to go back. It was difficult for Nathaniel rolling east to share Nick's nostalgia for a reverse journey in a contrary season on those parallel tracks yonder. The *Empire Builder* rocked explosively as a long-haul passenger train blew past, shaking the windows. It was a shock to feel this imposing rush, and Nathaniel looked up from the pulpy pages of *The Great Gatsby* into the other train's windows. He saw flashes of faces hurtling west into the burning forests he had left behind. He read on. He read: "And when we pulled out into the winter night in the real snow, our snow began to stretch out beside us and twinkle against the windows, and the dim lights of small Wisconsin stations moved by, a sharp, wild brace came suddenly into the air, and we drew in deep breaths of it as we walked back from dinner through the cold vestibules, unutterably aware of our identity with this country for one strange hour before we melted indistinguishably into it again." So Nathaniel read on to the end and found he was surprised that he was weeping. He wasn't weeping for Gatsby's death, or for what became of the new world when it grew middle-aged, or for the impostor's broken dreams. He was weeping for love of beauty, and in particular for a beautiful girl it seems Fitzgerald had known before that girl existed. He was weeping old, old, tears, the tears shed when a drunk put a nickel in a jukebox and heard a song sung to him alone about his sweet baby, his broken heart. Such tears had dropped in Babylon and in the fertile crescent, in Troy and Provence, in Rome, and the Seattle-Tacoma metropolitan area.

A LESSON

October 2, 1996

Francisco Goldman

I NEVER LEARN ANYTHING. In one ear and out the other.
Everyone says so. Wondering what lesson I might write on, it
came to me – all those voices over the years, parents, teachers, lovers,
friends, saying, Frank, you just never learn. When I phoned my
girlfriend in Mexico and told her I might write on how I never learn,
she was enthused. She said, I'll write it for you. I'll fax it right up!
She's always claiming she knows me better than I know myself
because my self is one of the things I refuse to learn about. You wake
up innocent as a newborn babe every day, said another old friend, an
old love. And I remembered how when she unexpectedly broke up
with me she delivered the most stinging rebuke imaginable. You're
just like Ronald Reagan, she said, always looking on the bright side,
which is of course an obvious symptom of never learning anything. I
asked around and all my friends unanimously agreed that I never
learn. I asked one, Is it because I'm stupid or stubborn? He answered,
Yes. All this led to a bout of wounded introspection. My life passed
before my eyes in a way that three minutes can't convey, but okay, I
ended up agreeing that I really never learn.

Last week provided plenty of proof. Having messed up my foot on
a bad Stairmaster in Mexico, my doctor told me to switch to a low-
impact exercise such as a stationary bicycle, but I much prefer
bouncing up and down to just sitting there pumping my knees,
so last week I remounted the Stairmaster (that was a Mexican
Stairmaster, I told myself, and this is a New York one) and within
days I was limping and using a cane again.

I always get in trouble in thug bars. Everyone's always saying, Why haven't you learned to stay out of those places? Last Thursday night I went into one again and nearly ended up in serious thuggish trouble, the kind of trouble I'm too old for now. Youth doesn't last, but you can be immature forever. Philip Roth's Mickey Sabbath says that. Yes, that's part of the problem – stupidity, stubbornness, innocence, blind optimism – all those things I hope my writing is not. Does that mean my writing is wiser than I am? Faulkner said a novel is a man's secret life, his dark twin. Maybe I can live with that, but it doesn't mean I have to be dumb as a post about everything else, does it?

I make the same mistakes in every relationship. I won't go into that. But I did have some small victories over myself last week. I finally learned how to insert Spanish accents on the computer, and I learned that I'll never really learn what makes the great writers great, which is fine. You may think you can. You may imagine you've internalized some lesson from a favorite writer in a way uniquely your own, but then, as I did last week, you pick up a book in search of a moment's inspiration or perhaps even to self-regardingly rub noses with a pro's prose style, and realize that a writer's mastery seems more mysterious, beautiful, and bewitched than ever. I'm grateful to PEN/Faulkner for providing me with this unprecedented opportunity for self-examination. I only hope I've learned something from it.

Alice Adams

SOME TIME AGO I knew a young woman with what was said to be a very good job on a newspaper, which she hated. Against all advice, she quit that job in order to write a novel. Along the way, she had a hard time; big debts and occasional fill-in lowly jobs, during which everyone clucked and said, She should have learned her lesson by now. However, she wrote her book and it was a considerable success. She got both good notices and money.

At that time no one said anything about learning a lesson but probably she did. She learned that it is better to do what you want to do and probably are good at. And as I began to consider "A Lesson," it seemed to me that these words almost always have a negative, punitive cast. If a woman repeatedly falls in love with alcoholics and the third such loses his job, the lesson mutterers somehow fail to notice the fourth alcoholic who joins AA and pulls himself together. The man with the weakness for beautiful women is scolded – won't he ever learn his lesson? – whereas I once knew a man whose specialty, as he put it, was ugly women. Although a couple were also mean, no one suggested that he learn a lesson, but ugliness can be quite as character-deforming as beauty sometimes is.

My own lesson, derived from years of experiences, is that most advice should not be taken. Received opinion is apt to be wrong. I feel that this is particularly true for writers. A long time ago my college writing teacher told me that I was very nice; I should stop writing and get married! I think he meant too nice to be a writer, but it may have been a more general idea about women. Somewhat later when I had married but had not stopped writing, a shrink told me that I should stay married and stop writing. What he saw was that I was expending enormous time and effort in writing and sending out stories that no one wanted. I had no money. It was time I'd learned my lesson, which once more I refused to do, and finally a magazine accepted the story for $350, for which I concluded that all my stories from then on would be accepted. I got a divorce and planned to support myself and my son by writing, having learned one and only one lesson, which was simply to keep on writing.

Richard Bausch

T HE YEAR BEFORE and the year before that and the year before
that I had flunked algebra, bereft of a single ray of understanding, the way a math idiot would flunk it, or a foreigner without
a word of English, or, say, an infant. This was my second time, third
time through. I was seated next to a round, beady-eyed, strangely
frenetic boy who busily scribbled in his notebook all through the first
class. I thought he was taking notes, though I couldn't imagine what
there was to take down. Our new teacher, Mrs. Croft, was gently
reminding us that there would be an assignment of problems every
night and that we must keep up. To this day it seems absurd to me
that we would actually make up problems for each other. Finally,
when she had to pause to say something to another teacher at the
door of the classroom, I asked this kid what he was doing. Creating a
new number system, he said. With a sullen, perhaps even fiendish
smile. I looked at him; he looked at me. We were for the moment in
a state of unrecognition that I venture we'll obtain if and when we are
ever visited from distant planets. I said, You're . . . What are you
doing? He went on writing, It's quite simple, you know. When I
screwed up the courage to ask him if he might help me with the
algebra he smirked. Not on your life! And that was that.

So the first day was like all the other days, where I sat with my
mouth open watching the numbers and letters as Mrs. Croft wrote
them on the board: a foreign language. She spoke softly about what
was ahead. Every single reference to the subject at hand was opaque
to me, as unfathomable as pelagic depths, and it seemed also to be
rather perversely unnecessary, as if some school administrator in a

board meeting somewhere had said, I know! Let's mix letters with numbers and really confuse the little bastards! Except there was the round kid with his pencil feverishly scribbling the numbers and the symbols, utterly happy and absorbed with the figures he'd created, the world he was residing in or decorating or planning to destroy. Who could tell? And every class day Mrs. Croft wrote the numbers on the board, showing us how x and y could add up to something, how under certain conditions it always added up to the same thing. And she would step away from the board and look at us, this gray-haired lady who had been in England, we all knew, during the war, and she would say, Class, do you see how beautiful this is? This is always true. You can depend on it. All the time, every time. And somehow just standing back from it to contemplate its symmetry and shape made me begin to see it more readily. Of course it was mostly a confused fog, and yet there were those glimmers that this was a value. This mattered. This had shapeliness and order and was something a woman like Mrs. Croft, a world traveler, understood in a different way than all my other teachers.

She was sixty perhaps, maybe older. She had a soft, grandmotherly voice with a hind of the Midwest in it. Once during a session where she was explaining some algebraic concept now lost to my memory, she stood at her desk, the talk in her fingers, gesturing, talking, and I noticed that the front of her dress below the cloth belt was wide open. She noticed this not two seconds after I had, perhaps having marked the look on my face at the knowledge of what I was seeing; her undergarments. She glanced down at herself and then settled quickly into her seat and kept on talking without the slightest change in her voice and with no hesitation at all. In every class I had ever been in I was a troublemaker. The class clown. And I'd have gloated over this and made jokes about it with friends if it were any other teacher, man or woman. I'd have gotten big mileage out of it. But I didn't. I sat there hoping no one else had seen. No one had. I've kept it to myself all these years, thirty-five years.

And that year, very slowly, algebra began to seem to me something like a beautiful mystery whose secrets I might actually if very slowly and haltingly begin to grasp. I got through the year struggling, faltering, but more and more convinced of the intrinsic value of the pursuit through this gentle and good teacher's repeated pauses to make us see the larger picture, the orderliness of it. I got a C in algebra that year. A miracle of course. Maybe even a kindness. In any case, whatever I learned about algebra is gone but the example remains: sympathy, understanding, the almost beatific consciousness that the truth is speakable and knowable and can be conferred. The belief that the arts of civilization are intrinsically good.

Once in spring the band was playing out on the football field during class and many of us had turned our attention to it. Oh come on, darlings, Mrs. Croft said in that soft, caressive voice, Children have studied their numbers and letters with bombs falling around them. I'm sure you can do it with a little band music in the air. Somehow I knew from her face as she said this that she had been there with those children under the noise of the bombs. She had been their teacher, too.

Susan Isaacs

S ILENCE. WE WRITERS of a fiction need peace. Getting past "Once upon a time" requires concentration. First it's our jobs to provide our characters with their moral compasses, their ethnicities, their politics, their sexuality. Then we have to furnish their wardrobes and hang the wallpaper in their bedrooms. You think it's easy creating entire universes? We've got to have quiet. But the minute our first book is published, what happens? Whammo! We are pushed out of silence into a rocking, roisterous celebrity culture. It's no longer just the Fitzgeralds and the Capotes who become media stars. All of us become stars. Okay, maybe not supernovae, but at least starlets at Bread Loaf or on *Entertainment Tonight*. I have watched a poet sign his name for his fans with all the humility of a soap-opera star at a strip-mall opening. I have known a novelist who demurred, then consented, to read her book for audiotape, and after that she read from her work-in-progress at one benefit and then at four more and became incensed when not solicited to a sixth. Her work-in-progress is still in progress. But forget that poet, that novelist; I have seen myself shopping for a month for an outfit to wear on the *Today* show, giving up a week's work to prepare breezy patter for Oprah. It was exhilarating. I was as breezy as hell. But before I could dream too long about becoming a regular Oprah guest or having my own talk show (on PBS naturally because I'm literary), I was taught a lesson. I was being interviewed by the book-review editor of a large newspaper, my twentieth or thirtieth interview of that book tour. "Tell me about your father," he commanded. "Wow," I thought, this is penetrating. None of the predictable "Where do you get your ideas?" questions for this guy. I tell him about my father, an amiable man who taught me how to fish and make bookshelves. "No, no," the editor said. "You're not being forthcoming with me. What did your father have to do with you being here today?" So I say, "Not too much. He was an electrical engineer. He didn't read much fiction." "An engineer?" "Yes." "Then you're not Antoinette Giancana, *Mafia Princess*?" I said, "No, I'm Susan Isaacs, *Almost Paradise*." Not concealing his disappointment, he leafed through the stack of press releases on his desk and, coming up to mine, sighed and began the interview again.

A good lesson, but four novels later I had forgotten it. Home from yet another book tour, having twisted my kishkes into knots showing reporters how lighthearted and witty I am, I now view myself as a lighthearted, witty celebrity. I am recognized. They like me. So I'm in a Hamptons restaurant that features everything on popped oats with pygmy vegetables on the side. My handsome, silver-haired husband, the lawyer, sits across from me. Our knees touch. His hand brushes mine en route to the rosemary olive bread. A romantic dinner, except the woman at the next table keeps staring at us. I am annoyed by her rudeness and gratified by her recognition. Staring, I pierce a tiny zucchini and she announces to the people at her table, "My favorite writer." She has that brash, outer-borough, cigarette-and-Diet-Coke voice, like mine minus a few thousand Virginia Slims. Now she turns directly to us. "What was the name of your last book?" I'm momentarily speechless. "I read it," she tells me. "I just can't remember the name." And just as I'm about to tell her, she all but bats her mascaraed lashes at my silver-haired husband and sighs, "Joseph Heller."

That sent me back to where I belong, to silence, but I'm here tonight, and if Charlie Rose calls again or Long Island Cable Vision, will I perform? Will I play the tambourine for the Rock Bottom Remainders, debate at the Y, and read against hunger and censorship? Will the silence of my office begin to become oppressive? Will I ever again be blessed enough to get another lesson?

Robert MacNeil

WHEN I WAS a child some things were a mystery to me, probably longer than they should have been. Consider a winter morning during World War II at Tower Road School in Halifax, Nova Scotia. It was late 1943. I must have been twelve and still well shy of puberty. We were lining up in class to have some exercise corrected by the teacher, Miss Smith. I liked Miss Smith. She was young and, by any standards, good to look at. A child spends many hours a day looking at his teacher and I had given her close attention. She wore tight skirts and close-fitting blouses on a figure that did credit to both. She wore stockings with 1940s seams down the back and high-heeled shoes. Her eyebrows were penciled in dramatic curves and her lipstick was a scarlet signal. That signal was received by the soldiers manning the antiaircraft battery built right beside our school. We had frequent air-raid alerts and often saw the men on the ack-ack battery racing up the wooden tower to man their guns. When the all-clear came we watched them hanging around, smoking and ogling Miss Smith through the classroom windows. There was, I discovered, ogling and Ogling, and there was corporal punishment. For certain violations of public morality, you were strapped on the hands.

The classroom was hot in winter. Little fresh air got in through the small ventilation holes in the storm windows. The radiators hissed and the dominating smell was of wet wool as the snow dried on our pants and the girls' lisle stockings. We were lined up by the radiators that morning when I became aware of the girl ahead of me, June Parker, aware in a different way. She had long, honey-blond hair and was always neatly dressed. She smelled delicious, an enticing medley of soap, arrowroot biscuits, and graham crackers. What did I feel at that moment? Curiosity? Overcome by something, I suddenly reached out and lifted her skirt. I had a momentary glimpse of dark blue bloomers when Miss Smith cried out, "Robert MacNeil!" I looked up and found her eyes blazing at me. "Go to the cloakroom!" I obeyed meekly and was strapped three times on each hand while Miss Smith said with great passion, "Let this be a lesson to you! Don't you ever (*thwack*), ever (*thwack*) do such a thing again!" I took my stinging hands back to my seat to meditate on my wickedness and the lesson, but what was the lesson? Two days later the object of my depravity, the biscuity June Parker, invited me home after school . . . to her basement . . . to practice for a little play. Alone.

Jill McCorkle

I DID NOT COME from a long line of literary women, but I did come from a long line of creative ones; the difference being that their finished products did not wind up on the library shelves but instead were promptly eaten or washed threadbare or simply given over to the air in the form of a story. A story told might sound something like this: "You won't believe what happened to Theresa Payne Hook, but first let me remind you that it was Theresa's daddy who owned the hardware store that used to be where the A&P is now. He was a Methodist and was the first person to have a color television in town. Some people thought he'd burned down his own business but it was never proven, but what we all knew is that he was never quite right after his wife – not Theresa's momma, she had an early stroke – left him and went to Chicago." By the time you finally get around to hearing what actually did happen to Theresa, I learned early on that it wasn't nearly as rich as all that had been pulled down from the sides, the history and the details that proved that each and every life and situation is unique and worthy of attention. I always thought that this was a Southern way of telling a story, but then I met my mother-in-law, who grew up in Brooklyn, and she does it beautifully. Then I thought it might have been a gender thing, but I can't quite think about the art of storytelling without acknowledging my dad, a man who was the king of "what if." He saw each and every possibility. He could see hope within the hopeless. He could also take the most benign situation and introduce horrors guaranteed to spur paranoia and make you eternally grateful for your own reality.

I was once in a hotel room in Georgia with my parents, and I happened to look off to the side, where my dad had gone out on the balcony to smoke his pipe and I noticed that two legs of his chair were out on the balcony and two were in the room, and I went over and I said, "Are you coming or going?" and he said, "Well, you know, I was all the way out there and then I started thinking, What if the guy who was responsible for my balcony was having a bad day. What if he was depressed, alcoholic? Maybe he was just having a bad morning and he forgot to insert the steel beams in the right places." He said, "This way, if this balcony starts to shake at all, all I have to do is tilt my chair backward and I'll land safely in the room."

Needless to say I've always read the card on the airplanes and always know where the fire exit is. But this is the same man who taught me that if you just sit out on the beach and stair at the ocean, or close your eyes and think about life, somebody will come by and ask you why you aren't doing something: "Why are you being so lazy, just sitting there?" And he said, "But you put a fishing pole out there and they'll leave you alone," and he said, "And the real trick is, if the blues are running or you really start pulling them in, you stop baiting your hook." It's only been in recent years when I stopped and wondered why I write that I came to see all of these lessons I had always taken for granted. I try very hard now to build a life around those moments when I can stop baiting my hook.

E. Ethelbert Miller

WHEN YOU'RE THE baby of the family there are often too many lessons to learn. Before I went off to college my mother took me aside and told me not to let any girl tell me it was mine. It took me until almost graduation to understand that mother was providing me with the first lesson in sex education. The lesson of denial. If you were young and growing up in the Bronx in the early sixties, you learned your first lesson as Bill Nazaroski touched third and headed home and the New York Yankees lost the World Series. I was listening to the radio and the static of heartbreak filled my world, and there was no tomorrow, only the approaching winter and the promise of a new season. My father and I never discussed sports. We never played catch or went for long walks. I don't remember my father's arm around my shoulder, yet his presence was in the air I breathed. Years before I read articles in books about black men and the crisis of the African-American family I would accept my father being home as the place where all fathers resided. All my friends had fathers, and they were men who worked or men we hid from when we did something wrong. Some men, like my father, were quiet at family gatherings, and I wondered what they were thinking, but being the baby of the family I never learned their secrets. Only once did my father reveal what might have rested behind his heart. I must have been eleven or twelve, and we were watching television, and he confided in me that he could have walked out of the house and left my mother. He said it in the way a person thinks about changing the channel. This was years before my mother would give me advice about women and I had no way of understanding what my father was saying. I do recall the next thing he said, like a man catching his breath: "You always take care of your family. You place your family first." Perhaps what we were watching on television had no resemblance to our lives, other than how I might one day watch a baseball sail over a fence and understand that games are won and lost but the love of a father for a son is what endures.

Faye Moskowitz

"*MIR SOLL SEIN,*" my mother would say in Yiddish when one of us children were sick or hurt. *"Mir soll sein für dir"*: It should happen to me instead of you. Years ago, when my own son Frank was about five, he became gravely ill with spinal meningitis. For days his small body, limp and feverish, lay curled up on a cot in a closet-sized isolation room. Whatever else was happening in our lives at that moment, our ambitions and daily concerns, house, work, even the welfare of our other two children, fell away in the face of our terrible grief. Hourly we were on a kind of automatic pilot, my husband and I, asking what we thought were intelligent questions of the doctors, giving out bulletins to anxious relatives, advising each other to eat, get some sleep. Had we been able to step back and look at ourselves we might have said how proud we were of how well we were holding up. But one day our pediatrician pulled us out into the hospital corridor and told us that Frank would have to undergo yet another diagnostic procedure, this time a painful spinal tap. We both fell apart then. I remember we leaned against opposite walls of that narrow hallway, so devastated we couldn't even touch each other. To see our child suffer, nothing in our lives had prepared us for such agony. *"Mir soll sein für dir,"* I said, though I knew then as I know now that I could have said *"Mir soll sein"* until the end of time and I would not have been able to absorb one moment of my child's pain, so we both did the single thing we could do. We took turns holding our son in our arms and let him feel the blaze of our love leap like silver lightning from our bodies to his.

Lynne Sharon Schwartz

W HEN WE WERE little, we made things from whatever came our way. There weren't fancy toys like now, and one thing we loved to make was a rubber-band ball. First you balled up a bit of newspaper very tight, rolled it around in your palms, got it nice and round, bigger than a marble, not so big as a golf ball; let's say a large strawberry if you could imagine that round, and tight was very important. You know how rubber bands keep turning up? Around lettuce or asparagus? Brand-new pencils and envelopes? In the old days a piece of fish in wax paper. People saved them, not knowing what to do with them, but a rubber-band ball is a wonderful thing. We would wrap each one around the ball of paper, doubling or tripling it, depending on the size; it was best to start out with a few strong, fat ones. And at first it looked like nothing, a clump of paper with a few rubber bands around it. Then after a while, you needed time and patience, there'd be less and less of the paper peeking through till – here was the best part – you watched it transforming into a real ball. The work seemed to go faster once the thing took shape. You kept on going, adding more and more, till suddenly there was a good firm ball you could bounce or throw. It bounced like a dream, as high as you ever could wish, such a lovely thing. So I thought, here I am with time on my hands; I'll make one for our little girl. I started collecting rubber bands and wrapping them around tin foil. It's lighter and holds together better. We didn't have it back then. I imagined her playing with the ball I had made for her, bouncing it on the sidewalk just the way I used to do. But then I imagined, What if she dropped it and it rolled into the street where the cars are, she dashed out after it and a car was coming. I tell you, my heart started racing. I couldn't walk. So I didn't make the rubber-band ball after all. I couldn't with what I had pictured in my mind. I had to throw it away. I was so relieved she wouldn't have it.

Deborah Tannen

I APPROACHED MY PARENTS' door with a key clamped in my hand. I have a key to their home though they don't have a key to mine. I ring the bell so they won't be frightened if they hear me come in, but I use the key in case they don't hear the bell. My mother greets me at the door. My father appears in the hallway after I've hugged and kissed my mother. It's taken him longer to rise from his chair. He isn't carrying the cane he finally agreed to use after his last fall. He stumbles, but the wall catches him. When I see him making his way toward me everything inside me rebels. Who has taken my father and put this old man in his place? My father in my mind never walks up stairs but sends them flying behind him two at a time. He is steady as a pillar. When I was a child I'd watch for him to come home from work. When he appeared at the end of the street I'd run to him. He'd scoop me up, lift me high off the ground, press me to his chest, then softly put me down. We'd walk the rest of the way home at my little-girl's pace, hand in hand. I loved the feel of his huge, callused hand, a big safe house around my fragile little one. What does this old man stumbling along the hall have to do with my father? I once asked, "Daddy, what is it like to be old?" "I can't tell you," he said. "I don't feel old. Inside I feel like I'm still eighteen. When I pass a mirror I think, 'Who's that old man?' " This is what I think when I see him coming toward me down the narrow hall. Old was my grandmother, my father's mother who visited on Sundays when I was a child. When I greeted her at the door she bent to me, but instead of kissing me she'd thrust her big round chin at my face for me to kiss. Her body had an acrid smell. I walk toward my father and reach him in the middle of the hall and kiss him. He has my grandmother's smell. Age has drawn his lips in and pushed his chin out. My mother whispers, "The older he gets, the more he looks like his mother." I take my father's hand, now stiff and thin. We walk together at his pace to the living room. As we sit and talk, my grandmother retreats from his face, allowing my father to return. So long as we sit and talk, I have my father back. I think there's a lesson in this, but I haven't learned it. If my father is old, he's not my father. If my father is my father, he isn't old. I want to flee the stumbling acrid-smelling body to hold him in my hand. I want to hold his hand forever so he will never fall.

Christopher Tilghman

M Y LATE STEPFATHER, the historian L.B. Morrison, believed that many of the difficulties in modern marriages could be traced to the decline of the cocktail hour. In his view, Theodore Roosevelt was the most interesting man who ever lived, and James Gould Cozzens' *Guard of Honor* was the best American novel since the war. He felt strongly that the Northern Spy was the best apple for baking but he preferred the McKeon for his apple sauce, not that he actually did any of this cooking. When he died a year ago last April, L.B. Morrison left behind, as all of us will, a library of opinions. Call them for this evening mini-lessons. They were the fruits of eighty-seven years of living, thousands of separate truces with an over-whelming multiplicity of choices, each one narrowing the field of play somewhat. Whether born of instant decision or of long reflection, these opinions made life easier for him: "Don't waste your time with Chopin. Be distrustful of the French." Does an opinion exist if it is never expressed? I would think not. Unspoken, they can only be prejudices. Opinions are gifts, welcome or unwelcome: fashioned and packaged for delivery blooms a gay chrysanthemum or a bloody rose. They are let go like bombs or like kites. One would feel a deep sadness for one who died, leaving no opinions behind, no small monuments. Every time I drink a martini made with Bombay gin I toast my stepfather. As it happens, L.B. Morrison also left behind a considerable body of written work, biographies, the many-volumed set of T.R.'s letters, essays on technology, on solving the problem of directing naval gunfire at sea, on building canals. When he died he was at work on what he called a synthesizing volume, a work about poetry and policy that derived, I'm afraid, from a certain amount of disillusionment and pessimism about the modern age. But he did not live to finish this work, and I suspect that was for the best. Instead the events of time began to rob him of his vocabulary, his memory, his opinions. Toward the end he had to be reminded that he loved the New York Knickerbockers, that he disliked ice hockey and anyone, professional or prep-schooler, who played it. He spent his last few months at a nursing home, baffled by this unexpected turn in his life.

My mother spent many hours a day with him, a comfort to the end. During this time I asked her what she did with him, what they talked about, and she answered, not surprisingly, that she was reading to him. I asked her what she was reading, expecting that it might be from *Anna Karenina*, his favorite book, but it was not that. What she was reading to him was his own books, his own glorious window into himself as a younger man. I can picture this scene, the bright nursing home room overlooking Mount Monadnock, L.B. gaunt, stretched under a blanket, attentive but unmoving except for his eyes; my mother cheerfully mouthing the words he'd written so many years before. L.B. loved a good sentence more than anything else in the world, and of the many good sentences out there, he loved his own the best. My mother comes to the end of the piece. Perhaps it's my favorite essay, one on the steam vessel, "The Wompenowak." She asks perhaps if he'd like her to go on. "No," he says, "no more today. But wasn't it good? Wasn't that awfully good?" What he had in the end was what he had given away.

William Gass

L ESSON HERE, GOD said. You think this Bible of mine is the blue book of happiness? You think life is made of blue-ruled pages? You think there's chapter and verse on what's good for you? Less'n you think I think so, lesson here. Hear about my lack of a lesson plan. I've had too many prophets lately in the last couple of thousand years, anyway, cutting a piece of my pie in the sky, borrowing a cup of sugar, stealing a cask of holy water, carving up cloaks, rubber-stamping stigmatas on badly washed palms to prove they'd paid admission. Makes me want to puke elixir! Well, lesson up! Because I'm weary of changing my script because some Cheapside charlatan had got even a bit of it right, just I guess by damned dumb luck, so I've decided that there won't be any more lessons to be learned or plans made. Divine Providence is out of a job. I'm downsizing my staff too. The dominions of angels I'm franchising to another nova. Up here everybody's orbs are dim so when Ezra puts his hand on the Ark of the Covenant once again as it was written, I won't strike him dead for defilement like I did the last time to teach his heirs and buddies a lesson. I thought I'd taught Adam and Eve a lesson, but they didn't listen, didn't learn either. Ate of the tree of knowledge of good and evil and only got the evil part by heart. I'm doing away with tenure too. Everything will be mortal. The hinges of the Pearly Gates will rust and squeak like a trapped mouse. Cloud Nine will lose its fluff and go down five points. Even the fires of Hell will flicker out. I've learned my lesson if no one else has. It's no fun being God if you can't even get cream to rise to the top. I am lessening. Look at me, meagering. And soon shall be less, really less, like the "less" in Leicester, and every one of my royal words, the sun will dim, less, less, and it will all come back to me, the "le", the "l" itself, which is, it turns out, the same shape as the "I". What a stroke of luck. Lesson's up! I'm gone. So long.

Mary Gordon

I DON'T KNOW WHETHER this is a lesson or a story or a question or a series of questions, but perhaps the best lessons come to us in the form of stories or questions or both. In any case, this lesson came to me in a moment of crisis, again as a good many lessons do, the moment of crisis being that I had to fly to London in two weeks and I discovered that my passport had expired. The lines for the Passport Office in Rockefeller Center wound around the block that day in June. As a matter of fact, they wound around the block twice, so I decided to go to what is known as a designated Post Office, which reminded me of a designated driver and didn't make me feel confident. The nearest one to my house is the Manhattanville Post Office on 125th Street. I joined a much shorter line there. I stood behind a young black woman who was accompanied by two women friends. All of them were anxious. the line was short, but still long, and we began talking. She explained her problem. It was her third attempt to get a passport. She was unable, for reasons our acquaintance was too brief to warrant an explanation for, to locate her birth certificate or to obtain a new one. She had been told that she could bring only a couple of kinds of evidence to corroborate her identity – a driver's license or a tax bill. She explained that she didn't drive and she didn't pay taxes. She said she had a social security card but she was told that that meant nothing. It wasn't good enough. She was told she had to bring someone who was related to her who had both a driver's license and a tax bill. She said she didn't have any relatives who both drove and paid taxes so she was bringing two close friends. She was hoping that would be enough. Her anxiety affected me, and the root of the anxiety was the contingency of all our identities, the difficulty of making clear to the outside world that we are who we say we are; that this thing called a name, by which we assert that we exist and have since the moment of our birth in a way that if it is not unitary is at least consistent, is something that can be ripped out of context and rendered useless. And what in the America at the end of the Millennium was the context? Cars and taxes. Driving and wages. But it could be anything, and the context could, it occurred to me, rather easily be lost. I have a driver's license and I pay taxes, but it is not unimaginable that one day I will not, or that the context could one day be something that does not include me – the ability, for example, to use the Internet. I was reminded of the movie *The Net*, that starred Sandra Bullock. Sandra's a hacker who has no human relations except with her mother who has Alzheimer's and doesn't remember her. She stumbles on a virus that the bad guys are planning to use to destroy the world. To render her no longer credible they use computers to scramble her identity. All her documents say that she is not who she says she is, but a criminal. Her mother is her only human connection and her mother has lost memory. No one will believe she is who she says she is. No one believes she is whom she believes herself to be. The lesson for me in the Post Office was this: Who are we outside of our context? How would we get another person to believe us without the corroborating evidence of money or socially recognizable activities? I learned this lesson. How fragile is our place in this world. How dependent are we on things we may not even have thought of as important. How impossible it might be one day for any of us, with a twist of the dial we might not even have noticed, to assert that we exist, that we are someone whom a name describes.

Ward Just

T HIS IS A lesson about the relationship of the journalist to the
facts. It's called "The Nursery."

A magazine writer is trying to convince a Washington lawyer to
grant her an interview. She wants to write a cover story about him.
He's a political lawer who doesn't own a law book. He doesn't even
have a Rolodex. What he does have is a very, very long memory.
Surely no one in this room knows such a lawyer. He's a fiction. I
made him up. Now he's being obtuse because he doesn't know what
sort of cover story she wants to write. Will it be a real cover story or a
counterfeit? So at last the exasperated reporter decides she must
instruct the lawyer on the relationship of the reporter to the facts. If
she does this skillfully then naturally he'll consent to the interview
which will lead to the cover story which in turn will make them both
famous.

"The nursery." Virginia sighed. Alec had misunderstood, as
civilians had a way of doing, even worldly civilians who supposedly knew the score, so she tried again, speaking now in her
reasonable corporate voice, the one she used with her editors in
New York. She said, "We inhabit the world of facts. At best the
reporter has a supervisory role. You had supervision over the facts.
They were in your care and you could release some and detain
others. You could polish the shoes of this fact and comb the hair of
that fact and slash the throat of yet another, but you could not
create them. They were conceived elsewhere and put in your
charge, like children enrolled in a nursery. You had them on loan

and you released them and then they were gone. Any mischief they created was their own responsibility. It was true that ancestry was often an issue, a source of understandable confusion and resentment. Not every fact came with a family tree. Some were aristocrats, others mongrels. Still others were orphans, parents and place of birth unknown. You were always careful with the orphans. Some of them had unstable personalities leading to violent tendencies. They were unreliable, yet they too were often victims and deserving of sympathy." On certain specific occasions the reporter was encouraged to give approval or to withold it, forcing the children to take responsibility for their own actions, so when it came to matters of fact, it was a question of the gene pool . .

Gish Jen

YOU KNOW, EVERY writer begins by trying to figure out what it is that he or she can do and every writer unfortunately finds this out the hard way, which is to say by discovering what it is that he or she cannot do. You do do this by trial and error and it's painful and often prolonged. In my case it's particularly painful and prolonged. And you'd think for all that pain that you would remember what you had learned but, you know, education seems designed for us to forget it and so I have forgotten the first thing that I learned as a writer, which is that I cannot write poetry, and for this occasion I have quite foolheartedly written you a poem. This is a limerick cycle – a new art form, and it is a kind of meditation on the fact that all the lessons of old were all addressed to the wise.

In my innocent youth I could never surmise
Why the lessons of old were always to the wise
When in fact it was obvious
That it was only the lobbyist
In the teller that did attempt to disguise
The plain truth, which was namely, to wit and in sum
That the tale was aimed at the foolish and dumb,
The great whomsoever, who not being so clever
Could not, for example recall when pride comes.
Was it before a fall or after?
And didn't it goeth?
These were the things the author did knoweth
And did tell with the aplomb of a Godlike someone

Down whose neck no Derrida did bloweth,
And yet whose words were to the wise.
A diplomat we might judge him
If not a more common sort of rat
Though who knows, in his day
He might too have seen an NEA bite the dust
And concluded quite ruefully, that he'd better think
How to stroke the hands that fed him
A lesson that brings us right back here to Washington,
For in this our own time, we can write laws and books
    sublime
But if we would eat we must study Bill Clinton.

CONFESSIONS

October 27, 1997

Tony Kushner

I HAVE NOTHING WHATSOEVER to say on this subject. That's
my confession – I have nothing to confess, nor any thoughts
about confessing. I don't read tabloids and I don't watch talk shows
and I'm not a Catholic and I've never been accused of a crime more
serious than demonstrating, so no one's ever asked me for a confession, nor are any to be forthcoming. I do all sorts of shameful secret
things, appalling, abysmal, wretched, degraded, marginally criminal
things, but that's none of your business. Mind your own business.
Leave me alone! I'm a playwright, for God's sake. I don't traffic in
first-person-singular. The fact that I've already used the first-person
pronoun eleven times in this paragraph nauseates me. It's "I" disease.
I want to see my "I" doctor. I long for some chilly objectivity. I'm
not a stable enough character to confess. I say "I" a lot, but there's no
"I" home. I lack sufficient core consistency. I am sure of this and so is
my analyst. Just ask her. It's true.

It's ironic but not unexpected that the most strenuous objections
to the new national mania for confessing come from the political and
cultural right. It's not unexpected because public confession is
unseemly and the right has better manners than the left. The right
has politesse. This is Washington, so you know what I mean. Did you
see Al D'Amato at Hillary Clinton's fiftieth birthday party? What was
he doing there? They must loathe Al D'Amato, the Clintons, but still
they invited him to the birthday party. This shows good breeding.
Good breeding says, "Don't confess. Keep it to yourself." Or, as J.
Randy Taraborrelli says Frank Sinatra said once to Marilyn Monroe,
"Toughen up, babe, or get the hell out of here." This is what good

breeding says about confession. "Toughen up, babe, or get the hell out of here." Frank's not conventionally who we think of when we think of good breeding, but you know what I mean. The right has no business despairing of the culture of confession. The right in the short run is responsible for it, however much it demurs from direct participation. When you make of the entire planet a playground for rampaging individuals, ideological blinkers blind drunk on an unapologetically zoo-loony ethos of ego anarchism run amok, well, what do you expect? Unending individualist striptease, "I" disease, a deluge of autonomous, hermetically sealed, ego-distended individuals just dying to unburden themselves: "I did this, and I did that." And this is what really riles the right, what really makes conservative nostrils flair in offense: "This was done to me. My secret is that I have been forced by oppressive circumstances to keep secrets. My resistance is to reveal more about myself than you could possibly want to know." In the homosexual community these days there's a great debate on the subject of confession. Polite, conservative homosexuals – and this is Washington, so you know what I mean – think that we homosexuals confess, and confess far too freely, to our political detriment, but it's hard to find the brakes. When I tell you I'm a homosexual I'm confessing something that's none of your business – my sexual preference, something about what I enjoy in bed, but since you have made it your business, I must confess. And being forced, out of sheer spite I want to add horrible details. I want to make the squeamish among you crawl under your seats, wishing you'd minded your P's and Q's, but it's too late. You can't stop me now. I'm confessing. I want to make the signatories to the majority opinion in *Bowers* v. *Hardwick* certain that they'd never come to my fiftieth birthday party even if they were invited. I want to make them wish they'd never agreed to hear the case in the first place, so that eventually I can go back to my business, which is making up imaginary people, and you can go back to your business, and the dark disgusting things we all do, so long as they're consensual and adult, can go back to being transacted under the cover of night as good breeding dictates, as they were meant to be.

Barry Lopez

O ne day in April 1939, a man named Emerson Quilt dropped a letter addressed to him on the sidewalk in front of a stationer's store in Great Barrington, Massachusetts. A few moments later he was run over by a city bus. The letter, unopened, was retrieved by a clerk at the stationer's, and for some weeks after was displayed in the window. On April 14, the letter was claimed by a young man named Edison Pickerel, who'd watched those several days while the letter went unclaimed. Mr. Pickerel, an uncle of mine, was then vacationing in the Berkshires. When he returned home to Escondito in California, where he lived, he carefully filed away the letter and its unopened envelope among papers in his desk. In 1954, a young boy left alone in my uncle's house for an afternoon, I was rooting through the desk, in search of I don't remember what, when I came up upon the letter. I read it twice, and must confess I was not up to understanding several parts of it. It was essentially an admission of guilt on the part of the letter writer, a young woman named Norma Henderson. Mr. Quilt was a businessman of some sort, and Miss Henderson, writing him from Evanston, Illinois, describes the process by which she embezzled $18,000 from his Great Barrington office between 1935 and 1937, when she was in his employ. The parts that I didn't understand had to do with a sexual undercurrent in the letter, a contention that she might just as easily have blackmailed Mr. Quilt for what he'd been up to with her as embezzled from him. She had to do something, she wrote, for the sake of her self-esteem, and thought embezzlement preferable as it wouldn't put his tastes at risk before his community. Now, here's the stranger part. The letter evidently contained a check for $1,000 payable to Mr. Quilt, the first installment of what Miss Henderson meant to be a full restitution of the funds. What happened to the check? My uncle cashed it. And by introducing himself at the Post Office that day as another Emerson Quilt, needing a temporary address to receive funds from his sister in Evanston, he succeeded in securing and then cashing seventeen more checks, each for $1,000. I know this because I heard my uncle drunk and melancholy one night confess the ruse to my mother. It was the money she used to put me through Stanford. When I learned of it I began a search, both for Mr. Quilt's heirs in Great Barrington and Miss Henderson's kin in Evanston. I actually found Miss Henderson and made my complicity in the fraud, however innocent, clear to her, as well as my desire to make restitution. Mr. Quilt's only living relative was a Roman Catholic priest with a small parish in Baton Rouge, and one day Miss Henderson and I sent him a check for $18,000 – not, I must confess, much of a financial burden to me at the time. In the spring of 1988, I finally met Miss Henderson. When I asked, tentatively, what exactly was it that Mr. Quilt had done with her, she said she couldn't tell me. She'd confessed the sins long ago, she said. It was history and best forgotten.

Kathryn Harrison

T ONIGHT'S WAS AN invitation I really couldn't turn down. I was just so grateful that anybody thought I might have anything left to confess. This confession is made to my grandmother, my mother's mother, who raised me and who lived with me at the end of her life. She died in 1991.

I'm sorry, but I didn't have you buried. The plot you bought in California lies empty, a patch of grass mowed twice each week, a polished granite headstone left blank, unwritten. For a month I kept your ashes in my study, not in a fancy urn but in the white cardboard box in which the crematory packed them. One afternoon, the door locked even though no one else was home, I opened that box to find another of molded black plastic whose seams I pried at with a knife until they yielded. Inside was a plastic bag held closed with a red twist tie, the kind bakeries use. Your ashes weren't the soft cold gray I'd imagined, confusing them with what remains in the fireplace the morning after a blaze, but included recognizable pieces of bone, some large enough that I could observe the elegant tracery of your marrow's canals. They looked like lace: some white, others the color of rust. I'm sorry, but I couldn't not touch you. I was tentative at first, but then I dug my hand into the bag and sifted through the dust of you. I found a little coin stamped with a number, the one assigned your corpse at the crematory, and put it in my desk drawer between the rubber bands and the paper clips. My fingers coated, dropped dust in their wake, a residue that settled into a ghostly film under the pens in their tray, and that remains there still. I sucked one finger and felt the grit of your burnt bones between my teeth, licked the others, and my palm as well, and then I dipped my wet hand back in the bag and licked it clean once more. I'm sorry, but I couldn't let you go, not without this last consummation. Not without overcoming those bereft days in the hospital when you left me alone at your bedside, when, eyes closed, you spoke not to me, but to your mother, your sister, your father. They lived in a past we didn't share. Of course it's dangerous alchemy to eat your own dead, and now, remembering the taste of you, I wonder how I stopped myself, how I resisted taking more of you inside me. Instead, on a bright, windy day, I spilled what was left of your body into the Long Island Sound. The light made the surface of the water shine so intensely that I couldn't really see it, and the wind threw one last stinging handful of you back into my face.

David Ignatius

B ECAUSE I WRITE novels about spies, my thoughts on this evening's topic turn naturally to the polygraph, the neomedieval device used by our intelligence agencies to discern truth from falsehood and extract usable confessions. Surely, you're thinking, such an apparatus might have some value in the literary world, which like the spy business seems to attract people who are at once truth tellers and polished liars, and I'll get to my literary lie-detector in a moment, but first the spies. Real spies have to take lie detector tests all the time, yet reasonable people might wonder why the intelligence agencies continue to use them, given all the evidence they aren't scientifically reliable. The answer, I gather, is that for all their shortcomings, polygraphs work remarkably well as torture devices, especially with the sort of upstanding, law-abiding Americans who join organizations like the CIA and FBI. People who are hooked up to these machines confess to the most remarkable things. A CIA officer once told me about a colleague who confessed to having sex with a dog. The odd thing was, it wasn't actually true, but the spy in question figured that if he confessed to that the agency wouldn't worry about anything more mundane, and he was right. He was promptly cleared for the most sensitive work.

Polygraph operators know something that writers also know, which is that notions of truth are sometimes a matter of cultural conditioning. Our culture celebrates honesty, thus middle-class Americans who believe in telling the truth will sweat bullets when they try to lie on a polygraph exam, but there are many cultures where dissembling and concealment are the norm, and people in these cultures rarely tell strangers the truth about themselves, their finances, their business activities, their allegiances. To do so would be dangerous, and, worse, impolite. In such cases telling lies does not cause measurable anxiety. Often, as the polygraphers will tell you, it's telling the truth that makes people sweat. A CIA man once described to me his efforts to recruit one of the leaders of the triad gangs in Hong Kong. The man seemed willing enough, so he was duly strapped to the polygraph and asked a series of questions about his activities. He passed the test with flying colors; the needle never moved. But later it became clear that he had lied about almost everything. What a magnificent storyteller he must have been, our sort of chap entirely.

And that brings me back to the literary world. We novelists believe in telling what we like to call "the larger truth," but the essence of our craft is the ability to tell believable lies and create a world that is close to the literal truth but not so close that we'll get sued. Often, as we know, what seems most real in our books is what's entirely imagined and what's actually true seems least believable. But in this technological age we writers need help, so tonight I want to propose my literary lie detector, a device we can use as we begin work on a book to discern literary truth from falsehood. We might begin as the police do, by reading the writer his rights – reprint rights, foreign rights, movie rights. Then we'd pose some basic questions: In your fiction, are you getting even with the right people? Do you remember every unkind word in reviews of your last book? And if not, why are you lying? Have you thought, even for a moment, who might play your characters in the movie version? Are all your lies intentional? Do you know the truth you want to tell? If you can answer yes to all the above questions, you're ready to take a seat at the literary lie detector and start typing.

Willie Morris

I HAVE SEVERAL BRIEF and esoteric confessionals, none especially philosophic, nor for that matter existential, but they matter to me, to my wife, Joanne, and our three cats, who live on Purple Crane Creek in Jackson, Mississippi, which overflows in the rains.

My longtime comrade George Ames Plimpton's great-grandfather, Adelbert P. Ames, a distinguished Yankee general in the Civil War, was the radical reconstructionist governor of the great and sovereign state of Mississippi, acceding to power by the naked bayonet in A.D. 1867. I confess that my great-grandfather, Major George Harper, whose own grandfather as first territorial governor of Mississippi arrested Aaron Burr, was chairman of the state senate committee that eventually brought impeachment against Plimpton's great-grandpappy, who swiftly fled Mississippi for the North, so my friend George, everything comes full circle.

I readily confess to the strange mercurial neighborhood where I grew up in my small town of 8,000 people, Yazoo, Mississippi, in the Delta. I likewise confess that Yazoo is an Indian word that means death. I further admit to being an incorrigible name-dropper and place-dropper. I grew up in the 600 block of Grand Avenue. One block south of me grew up Haley Barbour, future chairman of the National Republican Party. Across the street from Haley, right across from Haley, was the ineffable Doralee Livingston, one day to be first runner-up for Miss America. Half a block west of me grew up Mike Espy, destined to be the first black elected to the U.S. Congress since Reconstruction and later the U.S. Secretary of Agriculture. Half a block east of me grew up the legendary Zig Zigler, whose inspirational books sell more copies than John Grisham. Zig gets $25,000 a lecture. Zig lived in an impoverished shack so close to the Illinois Central tracks that when the midnight Memphis-to-New-Orleans freight train came by they had to open the kitchen door to let it through. Zig got his start selling hot dogs at country funerals. As for Haley Barbour, as for Haley, he was a little younger than we, and when his teenaged Barbour brothers and cousins and the rest of us got together in the neighborhood park for our bone-jolting games of tackle football, I herewith confess that we used Haley as our blocking and tackling dummy, which may be the reason he grew up to be so damn tough or at the least shall we say resilient, or Republican.

Two blocks east of me in the black precincts of Brickyard Hill grew up Willie Brown, fated to be the greatest defensive back in the history of football. Another block down from me grew up Hershel Brickall, one day to be editor-in-chief of the *New York Times Book Review*. Four doors down from me grew up Jerry Moses, a future Major League catcher for ten years. Next to Jerry, he alone of these neighbors of an earlier generation, grew up Col. John Quekemeyer, aide-de-camp to Gen. "Blackjack" Pershing in France in World War I. Col. Quekemeyer once had a perfervid affair with Gen. Douglas MacArthur's first wife, and later was appointed commandant of West Point, although I do not think the two occurrences were in any way related. How to explain this unusual little faubourg, outlanders often ask me? My explanation, I confess, is that it had something to do with the quality of the indigenous sour-mash bourbon. I myself had very little to do with the phenomenon of our vicinity, but maybe the juxtaposition of such people helped make me the crazy neighborhood laureate.

Another confessional: I confess to being the last remaining white Democrat in the state of Mississippi. No, I'm a little wrong. There are three of us remaining white Democrats there, one in Itta Bena, I'm told, the other in downtown Alligator. There may be a fourth in Belzoni, but she is inaccessible. At any rate, the four of us are afraid to communicate. My beloved grandmother, Mamie Harper, child as she was of the Civil War and impoverishment, told me years ago when I was a little boy that the only thing protecting Republicans in Mississippi was the game laws. That day is long gone; however, I do confess to being both friend and unabashed admirer back home of my old friends Rosie and Thad Cochrane and Tricia and Trent Lott, and I'm proud of that. When the Mississippi Republicans were organizing an enormous banquet for Haley Barbour shortly after he was elected chairman of the national GOP, their organizers asked me if I'd sign my book, *Faulkner's Mississippi*, which I did in collaboration with the great photographer William Eggleston, which they wanted to present to Haley as a gift. I said I'd be delighted to do so on one condition – Haley must read my inscription out loud. They graciously assented. Before an audience of several hundred Republicans he read my words: "Dear Ol' Haley, I'm proud of you. Good luck in your new position, but not too much good luck, because may I remind you, Haley, that whereas you are the leader of the party of Thaddeus Stevens, William Tecumseh Sherman, and Ulysses S. Grant, I remain a faithful member of the party of Stonewall Jackson, Jeb Stuart, Jefferson Davis, and Robert E. Lee."

One more almost ineluctable Vatican City confession: I helped get John Grisham, who sat in on my writing classes back then at Ol' Miss, his literary agent. Soon I plan to go to Grisham for my 20 percent finder's fee. I always wanted to buy Arkansas.

Howard Norman

A S A WRITER I confess to being most interested in characters whose lives are animated by not being able to forgive themselves for whatever transgression they may have committed or how bad they felt about it. In 1959 in Grand Rapids, Michigan, my best friend was Tommy Allen, fifteen years old, who already drove a car. He epitomized beatnik cool – slouch, pompadour, black chinos in all weather. He was so fully resident in this persona, it was as if Sal Mineo had imitated him. That summer, Tommy and I were unofficial assistants to Mr. Penny Oler, librarian and driver of the city's bookmobile, a lumbering blue bus fitted with shelves, benches, card catalog. Many late afternoons, Penny Oler parked in front of his own apartment. "Unscheduled stops," he told us, but necessary, because he and his wife, Martha, were "trying to have a baby." Their apartment was across a field from what us kids called "the polio pond." Remember, this was 1959. On the cover of *Life* magazine had been a boy locked in an iron lung. In our neighborhood, rumor had it that if you swallowed even a drop of this pond you'd contract polio. What childhood security, that a source of evil was actually avoidable.

On a sweltering day in mid-July Penny Oler said, "Mind the store." He stepped from the bookmobile, propped open the hood disappeared into his building. Only a few moments had passed when a young woman, fifteen, maybe sixteen, sauntered into the book-mobile. Her face was flushed, her hair was wet. The visible damp press of her swimsuit beneath her shorts and white blouse. Tommy said, "We've got a bus problem, is why we're stalled here. You can't take a book out." She nodded, and then began to browse the aisle. The word for Tommy and myself was mesmerized. "What are you boys doing inside in this heat?" she said. "Just across the field's a pond. Nobody's there. Oh, my mom would kill me if she knew I went swimming with two boys and no lifeguard." I blurted, "I'll go," then saw a look of horror cross Tommy's face. Can it be that in the throes of certain circumstances all faith requires desperate action?

Tommy was out the door. He slammed down the hood, flew back inside, and then we were hurtling down twenty-eighth Street to nearby Blodgett Memorial Hospital. Now to my mind, then and now, in performing such a bold act without fear of consequences, Tommy had ennobled himself, ennobled me by sheer proximity. Tommy maneuvered the bookmobile up to the Emergency entrance, a nurse, attendant, and doctor rushed on board, and Tommy shouted, "She probably swallowed polio water. It might be too late. Do something!" These of course were medical people. Tommy's hysterical command could only seem a cruel charade. The attendant grabbed Tommy by his black T-shirt. Hospital security, then the city police, were summoned. In juvenile court, Penny Oler testified that the radiator had overheated, was why he'd parked there. Marsha Eldersweld (we'd learned her name when first spoken by a clerk) shrugged and said, "I don't know why he got so excited," both a lie and not a lie, or something like that. Tommy did not lie, but the truth of his actions were based on the lie of the polio pond, of course. As for me, I betrayed my friend. I could have said something, anything, to suggest that the incident rose above merely the indictable evidence of delinquency. I could have said, "He was trying to save her life," and yet I managed only to provide the chronology rather than the plot, and then, and then, and then what happened was the court stenographer wrote it down, Tommy went to the juvenile home, and I did not. He might have anyway. Nonetheless, I do not forgive myself. . . .

Tina McElroy Ansa

W HEN I RECEIVED the invitation from PEN/Faulkner and read the topic for this evening's discussion, my mind, like that of all good Catholic girls, went immediately to the confessional of my youth. I thought at first of talking about my experience with the sacrament of reconciliation (that's what it's called now), but I wanted to talk more about what's called confession in the 1960s, about the power I felt of calling the priest – Father McCartney in my case – out of sixth-grade study hall to hear my confession because my very soul was in danger, mortal danger of dying in the state of sin. I remember blithely doing this without any thought to what I was doing, mostly because I loved the confessional. But then I thought, you know, what kind of confession is that? But I loved the smell of the tiny confessional in my home parish, the smell of forgiven sins. That's what I always thought it smelled like. And I cherished the intimacy of that shiny wooden cubicle at the back of the church. How I loved to go to other churches because I didn't know the confessional and it felt and seemed different to me. But then I thought about it and decided I should go deeper – to go deeper and talk about what I really consider a confession, because I believe that God loves me best. I really do.

I know that sounds like something from the New Testament, you know, John, baby of the apostles, who thought he could lay his head on Jesus's breast. Why? Because God loved him best, and he wrote about this. I know I should be shocked at this kind of statement, this kind of statement of presumption, but I'm not because I believe the same thing. I believe that God loves me best. And to make that kind

of confession is not a small thing. Until I went away to college I was
taught by nuns, who felt it was their duty to regularly expound to me
on the unseemliness of identifying myself on the phone as, "Hello,
this is Tina." "You're not the only Tina in the world, girlie," they
used to tell me. Irish nuns taught me. They would be shocked and
dismayed at my confession of such flagrant assumption, because I
believe God loves me best. You're not the first people I've shared this
confession with. I have a writer friend with whom I've shared this
intimacy. In fact we say it to each other all the time – in times of joy
and peace, in times of survival and triumph, on best-seller listings and
when little old ladies we don't even know write us letters full of love
and encouragement – he looks at me and says, "Oh Tina, God loves
us best!" But I have to confess even here that I lie, because I look at
him and go, "Umhmm." But God doesn't love him best. God loves
me best!

You know, I ponder how I got to be this way; what gave me this
power of belief that God loves me best. I am of course the baby of the
family and used to attention, being in the middle of attention. I was
reminded recently that my mother said I used to dance during
commercials on TV, so I'm used to being loved best, but even
now my sister will look at me and say, "Tina, you expect people to
love you, don't you?" And I'll look at her and say, "Well, yeah!"

How did this happen? It is a question for our time in history on this
cusp of a new century. It is a serious concern when we have a
generation of our children who are fascinated with the culture of
death. We hear rappers saying, "I'll meet you at the crossroads," and
our children are dancing to this. We have a generation of children
that we call "throw-aways" and "latch-key children," many of
whom are engaging in more parenting of their parents than their
parents are engaging in parenting of them. How did we get this way,
and how did I grow up thinking God loves me best? I think it's
something that we truly need to think about for this generation of
children. How do we get them to believe, as someone made me
believe, God loves them best.

Robert Pinsky

T HE POEM I'M going to read you is confessional in two senses.
One is that it tells something that I was ashamed of at the time.
I haven't been a very autobiographical writer. Recently in little dribs
and drabs. The fact is that I had mental illness in my family when I
was a kid. It was a sort of a lower-middle-class milieu in which to say
"You ought to go to a psychiatrist" was an insult. Years later I went
to teach at Wellesley College, and everybody was seeing a psychiatrist
or married to one or was one or all three. That, it comes in incidently
in the poem. The other sense in which the poem is confessional
should appear from the title. I've got an interest in the idea of the ode,
which I take to be a poem addressed to someone or to some entity,
involving epithets and so forth. This poem is called, "To Television."

> To Television
> Not a window on the world
> But as we call you
> A box, a tube.
> Terrarium of dreams and wonders
> Coffer of shades
> Ordained cotillion of phosphorus
> Or liquid crystal
> Homey miracle
> Tub of acquiescence
> Vein of defiance.
> Your patron in the pantheon would be Hermes
> Master dancer, quick one, little thief

Escort of the dying and comfort of the sick.
In a blue glow my father and little sisters sat
Snuggled in one chair watching you.
Their wife and mother was sick in the head.
I scorned you and them
As I scorned so much.
Now I like you best in the hotel room
Maybe minutes before I have to face an audience
Behind the doors of the armoire
Box inside a box
Tom and Jerry are all so brilliant
And reassuring.
Oprah Winfrey, thank you.
Thank you.
For I watched Sid Caesar speaking French and Japanese
Not through knowledge,
But imagination.
His quickness.
And thank you.
I watched live Jackie Robinson stealing home.
That image, oh, strung shell
Enduring fleeter than light, like these words we remember
   in.
They too are winged at the helmet and ankles.

Alice McDermott

W E CATHOLICS CAN'T get away from this. This is a fragment called "Reconciliation."

The priests assigned to the girls' academy were usually in decline. They were paused between heart attacks or ravaged by alcohol, or teetering on the brink of some fatal diagnosis – Hodgkin's disease for Father Ludlam, leukemia for Father Jim, MS, lupus. The assignment was easy enough. They would be there for holy days and first-Friday masses for the once-a-semester reconciliation and the occasional religion-class visit, where the girls, upper-middle-class, most of them, smart, most of them, dirty blond and white-toothed and a healthy ten pounds over their ideal weight, would laugh eagerly at any old joke and take conscientious notes. None of the priests was so far along that there was ever any danger of his keeling over in the hallway, but neither was there ever any surprise when one was suddenly replaced by another, or when the morning announcements included prayers for the repose of the soul of Father So-and-So, our former chaplain. "You senior girls are sure to remember him."

Father Bart took up the assignment that autumn. He was young, no more than 30, dark-haired and slight. He appeared on the altar for the All Saints Mass, and for the first few minutes the girls watched him carefully. His youth reassured them. He seemed fine. He might even be handsome. In their pews in the small chapel the girls moved from foot to foot, let thin hymnals fall against their chins. But his sermon voice, the breathy "Hi" with which he began gave him away. Filing out of the chapel, a senior girl whispered, "probably AIDS." They saw him next for Reconciliation, which was held in the sacristy, the two folding chairs placed face to face having long ago made the dark confessional box obsolete. The first few girls returned from their whispered conversations – they had deceived parents, undressed for boys, caved in to adolescent despondence – with the news that Father Bart had an odd bruise on his cheek and wore bright red socks and wanted them to actually do something for their penance, like call a grandparent or volunteer at the library, or show kindness to some classmate in need, someone like shy Lauren perhaps, who now rose from the pew to go to him.

She had been scalded as a child by a toppled coffee urn, a scar that ran down the side of her neck and across her chest and over her left arm, ending in a shiny white triangle that covered the back of her hand like a bride's pointed sleeve. Her face had been spared; there was that. There were turtlenecks and uniform shirts for most of the year, and the fortunate brevity of the state's summers, so the despair, the anger she carried up the stairs of the altar and into the sacristy where Father Bart waited in his red socks was something new. Her body was changing, but rather than the blossoming of new flesh that she had imagined, the new breasts breaking through the taut, shining skin, fresh petals from a brown shell of a bud, there was only more of the same, a stretching, a reshaping of the damaged flesh, not a shedding of it, not a transformation. She had imagined a transformation, an answered prayer that would have eliminated from her first undressing, her first time, whether she did it out of love or impatience, the inevitable apology and explanation, the inevitable strain that she and whoever he was would feel pretending not to see. Reconcile me to that! She climbed the steps and entered the sacristy, where Father Bart, dying, crossed his ankles and leaned forward and waited to hear.

Madison Smartt Bell

I 'M GOING TO admit to a wicked desire. I would like to have a suitable fireplace, over which I could hang two portraits – one of Nathan Bedford Forrest, the other of Toussaint L'Ouverture. To casual observation, the pairing of those two icons would produce a terrible discord. Toussaint L'Ouverture, arguably the greatest black liberator of all time, and Bedford Forrest, a slave trader, the Confederacy's greatest cavalry general and leader of the reconstruction Ku Klux Klan. If you turned your back on those two portraits you might think they would be apt to start tearing each other to ribbons, like the gingham dog and the calico cat.

Weirdly enough, however, the black commander and the white one had a lot in common. Both were superb horsemen, superb cavalry commanders. Their military genius was much alike, based on extraordinarily rapid movement of small and nimble forces. Both were capable of daredevil bravery when there was no other way, yet both were contemptuous of gallantry for its own sake, and preferred the exercise of Machiavellian cunning to a reckless use of force. Tactically and militarily, the major asset for each was total unpredictability. Both were capable of ruthlessness. Both understood the uses of terror. Still, Toussaint and Bedford Forrest were patriarchal commanders with a familial relationship to the men in their command. In their dealings with civilians they were capable of charity and compassion. Both at one time had been owners of slaves. Both of them, I think, believed in freedom, though most likely they would have defined it differently.

Barely sixty years of history separate Bedford Forrest from Tous-

saint L'Ouverture. If they had met, I think they would have understood each other. If they had met as enemies, they would certainly
have respected one another. They might perhaps have had a liking
for each other. Under the right circumstances it is conceivable that
they might have been allies. As things stand with us now, it is very
hard to imagine Toussaint L'Ouverture and Bedford Forrest sharing
space in the same room. I would like to hang their portraits in my
parlor, but whom then could I invite?

Mary Karr

It's an honor to stand before an audience devoted to celebrating a fiction prize, particularly in a year when I and my feckless little memoir have partially been blamed for the death of the novel, a charge I would like to publicly deny just right here. They have been bitching about the death of the novel since Hemingway, which believe it or not was before I was born, so I'm fairly sure that whatever has happened to fiction is not my fault. It's not unusual in history to see one literary form favored while another is sort of looked down on. Memoirs, however, have been low-rent since St. Augustine and remain so today. In the eighteenth century the novel was the corrupt form, partially because it was made up of fancies, so the way memoirs now are supposed to be sort of low and base because they're real, novels were once low and base because they were made up. They lacked the moral purpose of sermons and epistles and the formal rigors of poetry. The surge of interest in reading novels through the nineteenth century had less to do with any innate virtues in the form and far more to do with the direction its practitioners took. By the nineteenth century, poets were writing about fairies and increasingly arcane personal mythologies, while novels were delving into grittier aspects of among other things urban life, so while journalists last year were griping about the death of fiction, or about the novel being plowed under by memoir, DeLillo and Pynchon and Jim Crace were quietly going about their work, which differs from mine in one significant way: No journalist called any of them to wail about the racks of unreadable Harlequin Romances and science-fiction thrillers that their genre spawned. It's not a question of genre as we know, but of quality.

Most confessions published this year will be bad, as most novels and poems will be bad. Any recipe for instant production that the marketplace issues — write a thousand-page novel, or a dirty realist story, or a steamy memoir — will drag ugly books in its wake. No form is *a priori* exalted or wretched, just as no subject is. No seal of approval is guaranteed. The best new writing this year may be fiction or memoir, poetry or a Nike ad. We cannot predict the country from which beauty will arrive. At the muddy mid-range of quality, we will quibble about virtues and sins, perhaps as though they are endemic to certain forms, but at the highest level of quality, at the level, say, of a *Stop-Time*, beauty will surprise us. And we'll all by God know it when we see it. That's what we're here to celebrate, and that's what I bow my head to.

Amy Tan

M Y MOTHER HAS Alzheimer's disease. Often her thoughts reach back like the winter tide, exposing the wreckage of a former shore. Often she's mired in 1968, the year my older brother and father died. This was also the year she took me and my younger brother across an ocean to Switzerland, a place so preposterously different that she knew she had to give up grieving simply to survive. That year, she remembers, she was very, very sad. I too remember. I was sixteen then, and I recall a late-night hour when my mother and I were arguing in a chalet that tinder box of emotions where we lived.

She had pushed me into the small bedroom we shared, and as she slapped me about the head, I backed into a corner, to a room that looked out upon the lake, the Alps, the beautiful outside world. My mother was furious because I had a boyfriend. She said he was a drug addict, a bad man who would use me for sex and throw me away like leftover garbage. "Stop seeing him!" she ordered. I shook my head. The more she beat me, the more implacable I became, and this in turn fueled her outrage. "You didn't love your daddy or Peter! When they die you not even sad." I kept my face to the window, unmoved. What does she know about sad? She sobbed and beat her chest. "I'd rather kill myself first than see you destroy your life!" Suicide. How many times had she threatened that before? "I wish you the one die! Not Peter, not Daddy." She had just confirmed what I had always suspected. Now she flew at me with her fists. "I rather kill you! I rather see you die!" And then perhaps horrified by what she had just said, she fled the room.

Thank God that was over. Suddenly she was back. She slammed

shut the door, latched it, then locked it with a key. I saw the flash of a meat cleaver just before she pushed me to the wall and brought the blade's edge to within an inch from my throat. Her eyes were like a wild animal's, shiny, fixated on the kill. In an excited voice she said she was going to kill me first, then my younger brother, then herself, the whole family destroyed. She smiled, her chest heaving, as she asked me, "Why don't you cry?" She pressed the blade closer and I could feel her breath gusting on my face as she ranted, hoarse and incoherent. Was she bluffing? I wasn't afraid. If she did kill me, so what? Who would care? While she rambled, a voice within me was whimpering, "This is sad, this so sad."

For ten minutes, fifteen, who knows how long, I perched between these two thoughts – that it didn't matter if I died, that it would be eternally sad if I did – until all at once I felt a snap, then a rush of hope into a vacuum, and I was crying, and then I confessed, "I want to live. Please let me live."

Since that day I've wondered if my mother really meant to kill me. I needed to know, yet I couldn't ask. Not until now. Now she remembers me differently. Now she recalls that I was a good girl, so good she never had to spank me, not once that she can recall.

REUNION

September 28, 1998

Allan Gurganus

M OM SWORE MY very first whole word was "Udnuhdnu-hudnuh." Daddy always promised us a car and a college education. He was so Republican, Mother followed him everywhere, whispering, "He didn't really mean that." We chose the college, but Dad, what vehicle and when. Used cars became his right-wing portraits of his children. My brother the potter got a VW van that, celebrating on Quaaludes, he rolled, totaling it in Boulder. Dad must never know.

A business success, Pop smoked his pipe with all the pedantry of James Joyce scholarship. He used the cheapest shag. It smelled of furniture polish, burning wetlands. Discount aftershave. Dad broke in all his gift cars first; this aged alpha animal's pipe scent got kilned and stamped "Factory Option" into the very chrome of all he gave.

I planned moving to New York. I really needed wheels now. Mom and I watched Dad out scrubbing his latest favorite, a silver Japanese-cloned Corvette, sort of, but somewhat steroid-deprived. Just slick enough to make some semi-successful, newly divorced dentist think he might, at the light, attract, say Monica. Mom said, "He means that sports car for you, hon." "Mom, that's not a sports car, that's a Datsun." "Well, he thinks it's a sports car." Basically, you want it or not? "Go out, say one nice word, it's yours, but not too nice. See, Ed sees that as weak and this once, until the key is in your hand, lay off the atheism, honey. Stay free of your same-sex free love, okay?" Okay. O Findley, o politics. The key Pop offered me was gold and spelled Datsun. Well, it was brass actually. "Son, you go up there, have a goddamned ball, show them what our tribesmen are made of, hear?" "Yes, sir." He had scrubbed this car like someone ending welfare as we know it. I sped north. On the roof, huge stereo speakers wrapped in black plastic made my advance seem somewhat Mickey Mouse. True, the price was right, but this plastic steering wheel, hoping to seem walnut, instead resembled congealed fat. The dashboard's gleam tried for NASA but never left the launch pad of F.A.O. Schwarz. I eased ten feet into Manhattan when a yellow cab clipped me, whole front fender gouged a *Z* for Zorro. Odd, the worse my Datsun looked, the more mine it felt. Its aerial got snapped off that first night, a snow pea. Spray paint bled all over it. As I succeeded indoors, its street suffering came to seem an animal sacrifice. *The Coupé of Dorian Gray*. Dad's tobacco stink was settling down into a doable aroma when Mom phoned at three A.M., "Honey, he's dead. His heart, on the sixteenth hole." I left the key with a friend, she'd move my road warrior during the funeral trip. When she finally led me where she'd left it, a new green Mercedes sat there. I tried the gold key anyway and set off such alarms. Odd, I grieved Dad doubly now. Was my love of New York demolition derbies some part of his odd plan? In memory of him, I kept the gold key on my heavy ring. Three years later I'm returning on a bus trip from the home of P.T. Barnum. Just as our driver insists we mustn't ask for any stops besides Grand Central, I spy a car legally parked, front fender *Z*'d for Zorro, in red. I gallop up the aisle, gold key held vertical, explaining, begging, jumping up and down. Our driver says, "Folks, in a neighborhood this chancy, let's say we wait for him, make sure this kid gets back." And they cheer. The door's unlocked, ashtray full of lipstick butts. On the floor a child's toy. Key somehow fits. I gun the thing and chuck the evergreen deodorizer out the window. Honking at my convoy escort, I scratch off like such white trash. Yeah! On the West Side Highway I buzz all windows up, not down, and hoping, slow at this speed, a smell. His smell refinds me. It's wood smoke now and frankincense and Wildroot Creme Oil. The sweet shag of the mean old alpha animal. And before flashing lights find my rearview mirror, I grip my almost walnut wheel and, three years into his death, drive my father's pleasant living smell 110 miles an hour. My remembered father's name is the name of all males, his name, King Udnuhdnuhudnuh.

Larry L. King

I N MY TIME and place, reunion has always been preceeed by the word family. In Texas, family reunions rated right up there with Wednesday-night prayer meeting and Friday-night football. My mother's people, the Clarks, simply could not make it without a three-day gathering of the blood line annually. So that improbable brag might be made on ingenious progeny. Sons and daughters. Grandsons and granddaughters. Even generations yet unborn. The Clarks fancied themselves to be genteel people. And so politely pretended to believe all brags submitted. Even if determined to the last in number, to top them before the final benediction. On my father's side, conversely, the Kings could not gather their blood, without also spilling some. Where the smiling and orderly Clarks arrived bearing gifts of pot roast, fried chickens, pies and cakes, the rowdy Kings poured out of their old jitneys or pickup trucks, while rattling cans, breaking bottles and ho-hawing enthusiastic invitations to wrassle, pull hair or knife fights. Indeed the King family reunion at Lake Sweetwater, Texas in the summer of 1949 was so spirited and required so much public attention that the Nolan County sheriff officially discouraged future King gatherings within his jurisdiction. Having much experience with the law, the Kings took him at his word.

These poor opposite family reunions provided a thoughtful lad with educational opportunities. From them I concluded that iced tea was a calming beverage, the Clarks drinking it by the gallons, while the Kings touched it not at all. I still insist mine was a logical, youthful conclusion, if limited in scope. But the highlight of the annual Clark reunion was the annual inspections of the nine Clark girls, as they call themselves to the grave, to see how they were respectively spared from the ravages of cancer. Each of those long lives of women had been eaten up with cancer from an early age. Some had recovered from six or seven or eight bouts of the dreaded disease. Though most were lucky enough to be reafflicted in time for their brother, Dr. Floyd E. Clark, to examine and prescribe orange juice and occasional bed rest for their disease at each new reunion. When Uncle Floyd died, the reunion cancer doctor became my first cousin, Dr. Stanley Gilbert. Dr. Gilbert examined bare feet, or arms or knees or necks – the Clark girls always having cancer in decent places – and in the old tradition, prescribed orange juice and bed rest. He sent each Clark girl home happy, in the conviction that she probably had but a few months to wait to greet Jesus. And they would joyfully rush out to buy new crutches or walking canes, so as to better spread the terrible good news in their home neighborhoods. Dr. Gilbert did a miraculous job, keeping alive the most persistent cancer patients, my mother and my Aunt Bessie, until the ages respectively, of eighty-eight and ninety-two. Aunt Jessie did die of cancer at age sixty-nine, although the surviving Clark girls ascribed other causes of death, so they wouldn't be obligated in the final few family reunions to resent Aunt Jessie's great good luck.

John Casey

W HEN I DIPPED into my twenty-fifth-year college-reunion report, I found one old classmate exuding fulfillment that he had been elected commodore of his yacht club, another guy proud of his second home in Blissful Valley, Vermont, only minutes away from Virgin Powder ski run. But I was even more depressed when I found my own entry, a hastily written, left-wing screed. There were some active people, but they apparently hadn't written in. Barney Frank was in that class, as was Ted Kaczynski.

I went to the reunion even though I thought the best reunions were in dreams or with ghosts. But it turned out dreams and ghosts had forgotten these three tidbits. I'd also gone to law school at Harvard, so I walked past Langdell and remembered this: In 1965, the day after I got my degree, I ran into an old law professor. He said. "So, Casey, and what high-priced Wall Street firm are you off to?" I said. "I'm going to go live in Iowa and write a novel." He said, "Good God, man, we might as well have admitted a woman!"

Twenty-some years later, I enjoy the benefit of a reunion. Times do change. Then I ran into one of my old college roommates, someone who had changed my life. When I went to college, I was an East Coast prep-school kid. My roommate, Hancock, was from Cicero, Illinois, and knew he was going to be in theater. He was outrageous, hungry, defiant, and enthusiastic at a time when cool was cool. He made me act in his plays as a way to cure my stutter. It worked, but only in plays. I was still too shy to ask a certain girl out. "I can't say Diana," I said, "it's the 'D.' And she lives at home, her father is Professor Gilmore." Hancock said, "You're an actor. Your line is, 'Is Miss Gilmore there?" I dialed. Even more terrifying than Myron T. Gilmore was his wife, and it was she who picked up the phone. I heard her many bracelets jangle to her elbow. She said, "Hello." I said, "Is Miss Gilmore there?" She said, "Which one?" Oh dear.

At a reunion you discover that some embarrassments have a shorter half-life than you ever thought. Hancock and I used to go to all the plays that came to Boston. Balcony seats were sold at a student discount at the tobacco store in Harvard Square. Hancock would ask me to go, usually saying, "That is, unless you have to go to one of your Fly Club dinners." There were still vestiges of that world described by J.P. Marquand and more uneasily by John O'Hara. That Franklin Roosevelt had belonged to the Fly Club cut no ice with Hancock. Bertolt Brecht was the man for him. So, one day Hancock and I went to buy theater tickets. I leaned on the counter to write a check. I felt lips on the back of my neck. It couldn't have been Diana Gilmore, but perhaps someone . . . I turned, hopefully, and I saw a round-faced man in a porkpie hat. "Hi," he said, "I like you." The store clerk looked up. "You again, I warned you." The man pulled his porkpie hat over his ears and said, "Don't tell my mommy I've been naughty again," and ran out. The clerk said to me, "Can you show me some I.D.?" I said, "Hancock, Hancock, why didn't you say something." Hancock said, "I thought that was the Fly Club secret handshake." So you come to a reunion to possess the past and let it go. To find out how early your life really started and how late you really began it.

Thomas Flanagan

W HEN I WAS growing up in Greenwich in the 1930s one of my ambitions was to write a reunion novel. There was a great vogue for them in the late thirties. In its paradigmatic form, it centered on a tenth or twentieth college reunion, but the paradigm could mutate to center upon a family funeral, a hurricane that draws a sundered community back to its roots, the survivors of a shattered regiment of a lost war. I cannot remember exact titles, but they ran along the lines of "Weep No More, Bitter Is the Wine." There was a brief vogue for titles based upon syntactical inversions and sounding, with luck, like the King James Bible or at least Pearl Buck: *To Plague the Locusts, Shadows on the Terrace, View from Harvard Yard*. Never the view from M.I.T. Engineers seemed not to indulge in lyrical laments, lost opportunities, and youthful ideals turned sour. There was always a scene in which the narrator, a transparent surrogate for the author, stood apart from the others, preferably on a knoll, and watched the academic procession, a chill New England spring wind fluttering their gowns. He experienced loss, disillusionment, and a hard-earned and not unattractive bitterness. I could hardly wait to write my reunion novel.

But something, perhaps what E.M. Forster called the spirit of English prose, whispered to me that there was something inescapably farcical in the idea of a world-weary high-school teen. The narrator was going to have to have some commerce with the world if he was to be convincingly weary of it. The only contemporary in Greenwich who shared my early craving for fame was Truman Capote. And Truman already had an agenda in which Spanish moss and oak trees convincingly shrouded a lack of experience (This is, I think, the appropriate venue in which to confess that it was I who persuaded Truman to read William Faulkner. For better or worse. It took a while. His first reaction to *The Sound and the Fury* was "that is one silly book.")

In my first semester in college, my efforts to at least look world-weary were frustrated by the college's tradition that, until Thanks-giving, all freshmen must wear green beanies. By June I was able to observe an actual reunion and was surprised by the rude good health of the alumni. By my calculations, I had most of them wiped out years earlier in the great crash of '29. Leaping from the high windows of brokerage houses or at least selling apples on street corners, and certainly unable to afford the fare from the Bowery. But there they all were, sipping bourbon and singing endless choruses of a song about the British general after whom the college had been named. His career had apparently been spent on the endless slaughter of French-men and Indians. And it was rumored, though not in the song, that he had disposed of the Indians by distributing blankets impregnated with smallpox. There were rival claimants for this, but I filed it away in case my bitter narrator on the hill ran out of world-weary things to think. Why he had to be world-weary did not detain me for a moment. Like all beginners, I accepted without question the con-ventions of the genre. The ironical truth is that many of my classmates were destined not for the tedious obscurity the genre demanded but for singularly impressive futures: a poet of the first rank, federal judges, scientists, two directors of the CIA. I would have had to raise the ante sharply and argue that even success of that order is allowed as judged by the exacting standards of my narrator. A few years ago a friend began a review of a novel by Joan Didion with the words "Can nothing cheer this woman up?". My hero also was to be in the grip of a Byronic world-weariness, the male equivalent of Didion's heroines of whom we learn from laconic sentences. But my hero was several old generations earlier. Just showing world-weari-ness wasn't enough in those days; you had to evoke the justifying experiences, and I was in need of experience. It came to me abruptly the following December in the form of our entrance into the Second World War. I set aside forever, fortunately, my reunion novel and set to work imagining my war novel. I had a chance to spend several years in the Pacific aboard a destroyer minesweeper. It provided me with what I clearly recognized as experience, but I spent my time trying, without much success, to imagine how Ernest Hemingway would feel and write about it. I was trying to imagine his experience of my experience. I was not alone in this. Across oceans and continents, thousands of young men were doing this. And not only the young. Hemingway himself was trying. It was not until a few years later, after I had walked away from my "young man on Madison Avenue" novel, that I faced reality and reported for duty at graduate school. I had at least achieved the experience of realizing that a writer's deepest experience comes from the shaping of his craft and from what he reads. Cervantes reading chivalric romances, and Stendahl reading Cervantes, and Flaubert reading Stendahl and Hemingway reading Flaubert. Our own "first-hand experience in life" is important in its way; after all, we have to write about something. But our true experience comes from the experience of language and structure and our struggles with pages, paragraphs, sentences, words. Logan Pearsall Smith, a minor writer, who remained minor because he worried too much about paragraphs (you can't win), said once, "People say that life is the thing, but I prefer reading." It is a shocking, a self-belittling thing to say, despite its small hidden coil of vanity, but we all know what he is talking about.

A few years ago, I actually went to a reunion, my fiftieth. My classmates, despite a terrifying process of aging, of which I had miraculously been spared, seemed a civil, well-mannered lot. It was a weekend of startling clarity. I glanced up toward the chapel one afternoon and in the middle distance saw a lingering undergraduate looking down toward us with what seemed an expression of condescending compassion.

Maureen Howard

WELL, IT'S A fantastic reunion. It stars two great American writers, Emily Dickinson and Gertrude Stein. And I've called it *Gert and Em at the Book Fair*. Em wears white. The marketing people insist upon white. The maiden's dress. But no head-shot, book-jacket promo of our poetess, only the one daguerreotype in which she wears black, with a black and white ribbon around her neck. Spinster hair pulled tight, pat, pat. The eyes look elsewhere. Elsewhere is inward. It's sad to say she does not look at us so we prefer the faked portrait in which she is doctored up in a theatrical white frock. We do wonder how they managed the transformation before the miracle of cybergraphics. Managed to produce our Em as this wistful Pierrot, so that now she sees us. This girl, who was so evasive. Emily cannot duck the expectant gaze of the audience. In her signature white, she is led to the podium as to slaughter. Will she be a draw at the book fair? Will she make nice with the critics? Take questions? Will she sign stock? We are appalled when she is asked to read, read out loud, and says, "I do not cross my father's ground to any house or town." We have outed her from the spare little bedroom with its dull view of college steeples and church spires. I do not cross. How dare she limit this running! And when flashbulbs burst brighter than the coarse fluorescence of the book fair, she swivels from us, trips away, gives us her backside, the negative black serge of her dress. The sparse knot of her hair as she repairs to the greenroom. We need not despair. The audience is agog, agape with Em's scandalous performance. They stomp, they whistle in thin air for another round of the disappearing act. And it occurs to us, the managers, accountants, security guards, editorial assistants, the cruel agents greedy for foreign rights, the Chardonnay peddlers, and ringmasters who run the book fair, that we will never get the confessional memoir from this faded middle-aged woman. She will refuse us the steamy, family story of lust. Surely not hers, lust in the afternoon and the heartbreak of the guys who could read neither the bold dash nor the eccentric capital letters of her poems. Not really. Emily will not sign on as victim or tattle. Though we had the contract in our pocket. Thank God it's a double bill.

Gert strides to the platform, abandons the mike. She has chosen the Spanishy costume, the one in the Picasso portrait. The hair is later, the grizzled buzz cut. Gert plops, legs apart, as in the Joe Davidson bronze, to tell it like it is. "What does a comma do?" she asks. And we know she has all the answers. "Commas are servile, and they have no life of their own." We see now that many in the audience have brought along their children and their dogs to get a look at Gertie. They cheer and bark when she pulls on her small straw hat, knit for her in Fiesole. When the important literary thinking is being done, she says, who does it? I do it. Oh yes, I do it. A wave has started in the upper balcony, *Gert, Gert, Gertie*, bounces off the astrodome. We have cordoned off the entrance to the book fair. The curious push against the barriers, grasping at souvenirs, rubbery, tender buttons, Beanie Babies of her little dog, basket. A strand of Alice's petit point wool. Working the audience, Gert is beyond a press agent's wildest dreams. *Gert, Gert, Gertie*: the chant is deafening. "I always, as I admit, seem to be talking," says our celebrity. "But talking can be a way of listening. That is, if one has the profound need of hearing and seeing what everyone is telling." We are amazed at her perfect timing as she rises to lumber offstage, her words lost in the din. Have we listened to what she was telling? In the greenroom. Em dabs rosewater on her temples. Gert says, "I don't believe we've met." "Meeting is reunion," says Emily, "I always knew you would come." "Reunion is meeting," says Gert, "I always knew you were there."

Kate Lehrer

H E SANG ALL the way from the open-ended cotton fields of East Texas to the lush treescape of Louisiana. Our mothers were taking our families to fishing camp, and he must have been fifteen. Already with his deepset eyes and lean, angular face, its ready smile, he's in the process of becoming tall, dark, and just enough handsome. I wished I weren't nine years old. We had a lot in common, only children, single working mothers, his divorced, mine widowed. I remember that summertime's happiness: his family's easy banter, the wraparound sleeping porch, the cookouts, the games, and everywhere James Oliver Trosclaire's songs, his sheer energy. He played ball with me. We fished as water lapped against our boat, motor purring, pace leisured on the moss-draped river. I hope those days held enchantment for him too.

When I was twelve, his mother Lois invited me and her neighbor, my oldest boyfriend, to dinner with James Oliver and his friend Patty. The glamorous couple flirted with each other and tried to make small talk with two mortals tongue-tied by such older sophisticates. After dinner they glided around the room to Artie Shaw's music. While my partner and I worried how best to two-step without bumping glasses. I would never attract the likes of James Oliver Trosclaire. Besides, he was about to leave for college. He thrived there, his mother later reported. Freshman football, lots of friends, lots of girls (though perfect Patty still held his heart). When the Korean War broke out, he enlisted, became an Air Force gunner. Except for news of his adventures, the war floated by me. Then Lois received word that her son was missing in action. His plane shot down. For six weeks my mother and I stayed with her in case they found the plane. In case they found the crew. In case. Only the Democratic Convention on TV distracted us, Lois and Mother's passion comforting me. When Stevenson won, the war would be over. When Stevenson won, James Oliver would come home. Stevenson lost.

Lois sometimes thought she saw James Oliver on the street. A surviving crew member thought he might have lived through the crash. Lois went to Korea, discovered nothing. So she negotiated her life, served her community and her church. Put in caring years as a social worker. Her sense of humor and delight in small pleasures returned. She relished her friends and watched the rest of my growing up with amusement, and with enormous generosity and understanding. Later she treated my husband as a son. Any residual bitterness over her loss she directed only toward those in government who failed to find her own son. What would he have become? I have no idea. He was a life-loving life-giving force. Lois always believed he would return. So did I. He didn't. I can only bring them together through the resurrection of their story.

In setting down their story, something happened to me as well. I freed myself from a sadness I was unaware I still harbored. I reclaimed his life. James Oliver and I had our reunion.

Willie Morris

ONE RECENT SUNDAY I drove my dear friend Eudora Welty along the dirt and gravel of backroads of my native Yazoo County, Mississippi, some forty miles north of Jackson. My wife, JoAnn, was in the backseat and Eudora was ridin' shotgun. The sinister, kudzu-enveloped terrain could have been right out of her fiction. Like a child dwarfed by the stark bluffs, she gazed into the bleak sunlight and misty shadows. At the crest of Bosky Hill, a narrower and darker byway, I said, "Eudora, let's make a left here and drive down Paradise Road." She replied, "We'd be fools if we didn't."

Surely, we'd be fools if we didn't have a PEN/Faulkner reunion like this one from time to time. Reunions. Allow me to tell you of a mesmerizing one I had in the great and sovereign state of Mississippi this summer. A reunion of profound emotion and remembrance. Warner Brothers was filming, on location, my book *My Dog Skip*. Boys and dogs have been allies since caveman days, of course. And Skip, naturally, was the smartest and most loyal dog who ever lived. He was my brother. He could drive a car and play football. Operating as a tailback out of the old Tennessee Volunteers single-wing formation. We were even in love with the same girl, Rivers Applewhite. Shortly after my book came out, my fellow Mississippian Trent Lott took me aside at a conference and said, "Willie. I know Skip had to have been a Republican." "No," I replied. "Skip was a Jeffersonian Democrat."

The Hollywood people zealously used all the faithful appurtenances of the World War II era in the filming, including the victory

garden in our backyard with the scarecrow replica of Hitler that Skip
was constantly attacking. I've never known a dog so down on Hitler.
So as I watched the filming, I mystically felt I had returned from
somewhere exceedingly far away in a Wellsian time machine trans-
ported precipitously to my childhood days as if by some arcane and
elemental act of nature itself. "Time, he is a tricky fellow," Lewis
Carroll said. And observing the actors depicting my long-departed
kin was a déjà vu of the most impressive kind, a reunion of the glands
and the senses.

One day I was following a scene from a distance and was drawn to
several figures sitting together in rickety baseball bleachers. There
were Kevin Bacon, playing my father; Diane Lane, playing my
mother; the little actress playing Skip's and my girlfriend, Rivers
Applewhite; and yes, the Jack Russell terrier named Enzo playing my
dog, Skip, himself. And I divined the supple whisperings of my
vainglorious heart: you've come back to me, all of you. And when
the gorgeous Diane Lane later approached me and asked for some tips
on the relationship between my mother and me back then, which she
might use as an actress, and would I demonstrate, I said, well, "I
remember I kissed my momma a whole lot."

They had eight dogs playing Skip because Hollywood can apply
makeup to dogs just as they can to people. They had puppy Skips,
adult Skips, old Skips, including the dog named Moose who stars in
the sitcom Frasier (so popular among the eastern intelligentsia). But
the main Skip in most of the scenes was Moose's son Enzo. One
afternoon, out of what must have been the most poignant and
precipitant canine recognition, Enzo, whom I'd not yet even met,
sighted me sitting in a chair behind the camera. He looked up at me
momentarily, then jumped onto my lap and began licking me on the
face and nose. It's been a long time, old Skip, I said to him. I miss you.

Thus, as we reunite this evening inside the deepest beltway, I
earnestly beseech each of you to go see My Dog Skip when it's
released next year. Please encourage all the U.S. Senate to go. All the
House of Representatives, all the Supreme Court, all the gang at Sam
and Harry's, and all of Judge Starr's investigators and deputy in-

vestigators and associate investigators and assistant investigators and
intern investigators and all the beleaguered folks he's investigated,
everybody he's put on a witness stand, and every single soul mentioned in the 8,268,046 pages of testimony in all those cardboard
boxes hauled to the Capitol. I ask for the simple, pristine reason that
the dog Enzo and I are getting 2 percent of the box-office gross. If
you promise to do so, I'll help out the Ford Motor Company and pay
for our next PEN/Faulkner reunion. We'll have it at the Catfish
Haven Cafe in downtown Yazoo City. Enzo will be there, too. He
also reads Faulkner.

Grace Paley

S O THIS IS about reunions. Okay. Some years ago, it was at my
husband's fiftieth at Harvard, he's a kind of snobbish guy and
never would have done a normal thing like going to it, but I'd been
invited to talk to the Phi Beta Kappa, so he really had to. I knew
enough about his class to know that lots of men in that yearbook
would not appear because they were dead. They were dead of old
age, and of their early patriotic participation as young lieutenants in
the Second World War and in some cases the Korean War. The next
important war was the American war in Vietnam. And it was thought
out, energized, and delivered to the American people by survivors
really, many of that class, Bob's fiftieth, as well as age-mates from
other Ivy League schools. The Gulf War really belongs mostly to
Yale.

As has happened for centuries and centuries and in other cultures,
the surviving fathers do feel obligated to prepare a new war for their
young sons. It's the gift of manhood. Because I'm old and I hate to
leave this world in worse shape than I found it, the burden of my
talking to these youngsters was really about not emulating their
brilliant elders. It was about suggesting, maybe if they're going to go
into chemistry or something, maybe they don't have to invent
napalm, they could probably do something a lot nicer. And that
they really had choices and should consider that fact. But it was also
about human and perhaps male, braininess, the way it was getting an
awfully bad name. Certainly not the whole story, I pointed out. The
gene in charge of smartness will not be considered an important
gene for the continuation of the human race. I can imagine my

granddaughter visiting me in some nice home for the extremely ancient and sad people. And she'll say about my adorable great-grandchild, "Grandma, don't worry, he's gets an A at school only once in a while. He'll never be brainy enough to destroy the world."

Ntosake Shange

M Y PIECE IS called "Reunion, or: A Bit of Manumission." I want to see my people. The ones who live and the ones living in spirit. I've got $5 from the Bank of the Commonwealth of Virginia, $10 from the bank of South Carolina, a Texas treasury warrant worth another $5 and a genuine $100 bill from the Confederate States of America, dated February 17, 1864. I know what Enoch, John, and Lucy cost. Actually, I know what a whole lot of people cost. For instance, Louisa and child James, $1,700. Phoebe and child John, $1,600. Carolina, $200, Miranda and child, six years, $1,600. Now I know my papers are in order. As a Fourteenth Amendment person, I've got something akin to freedom, but I've got no proof. Nothing I can hold in my hand and say, "Hey, I'm a free African with the right to travel, own property, get married, and drink water somewhere."

The first time I slipped past the Mason-Dixon line, I slept with my momma. I guess most little niggers sleep underneath their mothers as long as we can, but without those papers, where I can lay my head, causes me tremendous anxiety. A grown nigger that's able-bodied and fertile, I lay up in Charleston, round from the slave mart, drinking myself a mint julep, beguiled by the canopy and the evening breeze. When dream time come up on me, some David Niven-looking planter come pullin' me out of my bed talkin' 'bout how I know better than to be layin' in a white lady's bed, with my palm woven mat right at his feet. Well, I slapped this ruffled son of the South with all my might and my hand fell empty. Sneers branded red and swollen on my cheek. My nakedness and empty hand, bare feet shamed with no papers. What was I going to do? Nothing to let anyone know I am a free soul.

But slavery fell off me like sins run from angels, and I remain empty-handed, broken down in the mystery of what makes me free. Where it goes to and who can come takin' my freedom again any old time, any old body like somebody like Ken Starr. Scribble my words in some plantation ledger, a diary of the day's activities left me lower on the list than the fate of the rice crop, cows, horses, and such. Rosetta, $17, Rena, $1,200, Flora, $800. I'm further down the account than mares and pigs. Not so accurately observed as the daily silverware. A blemish on my body means less than a scratch on a quarterhorse. If I walk around without my freedom papers you know I must be a fool.

Now listen carefully, 'cause I might not repeat this again. I am not out of my mind. Cross-country jaunts are not inexpensive, and I do want to see my people, but I'm not goin' bankrupt trying to buy my freedom back. I've got here in my hand a Criswell note of the Confederate States of America with "the personification of the South striking the union down." This $10 note cost me $1,200 United States of America currency today, 1998. I want to walk the Confederacy with my manumission papers up my sleeve or in the bottom of my shoe 'cause slavers, pattyrollers, bushwhackers, even the New Orleans police and the Los Angeles police just this year are apt to grab my purse, dump everything, and claim I am an unidentified black female and take me wherever. But I'm convinced this particular personal odyssey can be accomplished. I have no issue about paying for myself in South Carolina, in Texas, in Connecticut, Oklahoma, Virginia, wherever my people are from or were from. Whatever currency my value is recognized in, I am ready and I am determined to have the last bit on myself. I can't pay with my freedom, it cost too much already. Nevertheless, $5 in South Carolinian currency, circa 1832, which was worth nothing in 1865, is now going at $48 United States of America currency, 1998. And I still want to see my people, alive more than those living in spirit. I am still free, I know that. I'm coming home to see them free, no doubt about that. Besides, any one in Carolina low country will attest to the truth of the fact that Geechee girls carry razors in the roof of our mouths or in the soft, fleshy pockets of our cheeks. So there's no doubt about it whatsoever, I get to go home free, one way or another, I told you. I want to see my people.

Lee Smith

RECENTLY, I CAME across the journal I kept over thirty years ago. The summer I went down the Mississippi River on a raft with fifteen other girls. Girls, not women. In the summer of 1966, nobody would have thought to have referred to college girls as women. My journal featured lots of exclamation points and idealistic statements, as well as an outline for the entire coming year. The first three items in the outline were: 1. Finish novel. 2. Graduate. 3. Get married. End of outline.

Curious about the girl who wrote those words, I decided to track her down for a little reunion. I went back to Memphis, and sure enough, I found her right there on the first page of the *Commercial Appeal* for June 13, 1966, in a two-column photograph, a bandana tied stagily around her head, grinning at the camera. Arrogant as hell. Ignorant as a post. But as I stood there, on the bank above Mud Island, I finally recognized her. Looking out at the great river, I remembered exactly how she felt. Oh honey, I thought, remembering. Inspired by reading *Huckleberry Finn* in our American literature class at Hollins College, we'd launched the *Rosebud Hobson* at Paducah, Kentucky, and headed 950 miles down the Ohio and Mississippi Rivers to New Orleans. The *Rosebud Hobson* was a forty-by-sixteen-foot wooden platform, built on fifty-two oil drums and powered by two forty-horsepower motors. Our captain was a retired river-boat pilot named Gordon S. Cooper, age seventy-five. We painted rosebuds all over the raft and sang "Goodbye, Paducah" to the tune of "Hello, Dolly" as we left. In fact, we sang relentlessly all the time, all the way down the Mississippi. We sang in spite of all our mishaps and travails, the tail of a hurricane that hit us before we even got to Cairo, sending the temperature down below forty degrees and driving us onto the rocks. A diet consisting mostly of tuna and donuts. Mosquito bites beyond belief. And rainstorms that soaked everything we owned. If anything really bad happened to us, we knew we could call up our parents collect and they would come and fix things. We expected to be taken care of. Nobody had ever suggested to us that we might ever have to make a living or that somebody wouldn't marry us and then look after us for the rest of our lives. We all smoked cigarettes. We were all cute. We headed down that river with absolute confidence that we would get where we were going.

In between stints as cook and navigator, I was writing a novel. I had it all outlined. And every day I sat down cross-legged on deck and wrote five or six pages of it on a yellow legal pad. I followed my outline absolutely. In creative-writing class, I had learned how plot works. Beginning, middle, and end. Conflict, complication, and resolution. Huck, our inspiration, was an American Odysseus off on an archetypal journey. The oldest plot of all. According to the archetype, the traveler learns something about himself, not herself, along the way. What did I learn? Not much. Only that if you are cute and sing a lot of songs people will come out whenever you dock and bring you pound cake and ham and beer. And keys to the city. And when you get to New Orleans, you will be met by the band from Preservation Hall on a tugboat and showered by red roses dropped from a helicopter, paid for by somebody's daddy.

For me, and most of us on that raft I suspect, it was the only journey I ever made that ended as it was supposed to. Subsequent trips have been harder. Scarier. We have been shipwrecked, we have foundered on hidden shoals, we have lost our running lights, the captain is dead. I can't stick to a traditional plot anymore. Such a plot may be more suited to boys' books anyway. Certainly the beginning-middle-end form doesn't fit the lives of any woman I know. For life has turned out to be wild and various, full of the unexpected. And it's a monstrous big river out there.

Denise Chávez

M Y FATHER LIFTS me high. He still lives at home, he hasn't divorced us yet. It's my eighth birthday. I'm wearing a white ruffly dress with lots of petticoats mother has made for me. When Daddy lifts me high, the lace rubs up against my legs, making me itch. Behind us is a giant pinata. Daddy bought it in Juarez when he went there to drink. We didn't go that time, but it's all right now, Daddy's home. The Oregon mountains are behind us, my father blindfolds me with a soft red scarf and whirls me round and round. I'm dizzy. I can't stand. I don't want to tell him that the scarf has slipped around my eyes and I can see. All the little cousins are waiting for the pinata to break, but it doesn't. Not with me. You see those pecos there, those points. No, no, not there. That's the rabbit ears. If I could fly I would go to the rabbit ears and beyond to the blue room. It's the place I visit nights when I'm alone and in bed. No one knows about this place. I go there through the secret door in the hallway closet just below the shelf where my mother keeps her father's *papacherros*, death mask. In my dreams in the blue room, my father stands in front of me in a blue polyester shirt and long droopy John Travolta leftover lapels. A white plastic belt and high-water white pants. Only his trademark ugly *Juarez que viva Mexico* teeth are missing. My daddy's been dead three years, but he looks really good. Not as I remember him in his old VA-filled chair, covered by a brown laprobe, beautifully hand-knit by his sister Elsie. My father was a lawyer. He argued good and loud. But he wasn't a good husband. "Ah, talk to your daddy," my mother used to say, "tell him to do something about those false teeth, those horse teeth." He used to have beautiful teeth. What happened?

My daddy comes to me in my sleep to tell me that he's doing fine, "Ah, baby, look, I can walk. I don't have those *pinales*, the diaper. They're gone." Who is that woman with my father? I don't know her. Are you June, his first wife? The one I could never get him to talk about? Oh, my daddy is a bad dresser, the same old cardboardy, wide, ugly belt. The same old gold chains that aren't gold. The arms plumper, the giant smile full of real teeth. Hello, Daddy, I love you. I'm fine, I'm really fine, Daddy. Oh it makes me happy to see you looking so well, so complete. You aren't feeble, your sister's ugly comforter covering your thin, bird legs. Your arms riotous with the sores that you spent all day picking. Nothing else to do but watch television in your finale. Take a nap, wait for me to take you for a ride. Later calling out to me, "Denise, don't let me die!" "Oh, but we all have to die, Daddy," I say and you agree. But not before the visions of you in a candy store as a young boy. You in the bright red car riding out past the pecan farms to Chopas for red enchiladas with an egg. Now crossing the Rio Grande, the river you love and left behind in shame when you came to Washington. Georgetown law school, a poor *Mexicano* in the twenties. Can you believe it? Your family back home in the barrio in Chiva town on Mesquita Street where the goats ran wild. Now all your dead sisters, your brothers, your mother and your father stand in front of your hospital bed. Your fellow Knights of Columbus have come to say hello. Your old drinking buddies stand to one side. Many women who you've loved wait outside the door. "Oh, he was handsome, a good lover," says one. Shame on her, I don't want to know. Your first wife, the second, the many women come into the room. You try to remember all those names. Names. Too many names. "Don't tell me I say," I'm your daughter. You were an alcoholic, a womanizer, a man who abused too many women, all sort of relatives. Numerous strangers and many dogs. But, you are still my daddy. You lift me high, so high and I lift you. I feel that I fly over the mountains and beyond to my blue room. You are the one who said, "You are my baby, my *machita*, my little girl." I hold you now. I lift you up, your face glows in the day. Red velvet sun. You are content, unperturbed, at ease. Silly

Daddy, I don't care who she is, I don't know her. It doesn't matter anymore. You had a life before me and you have one still and it is very comforting to know that you still love and have found distant love.

Kaye Gibbons

I AM SO PROUD to be back here, in that Southern proud sense of the word. Since my visit here four years ago, I have been a good Southern woman, getting bigger, stronger, blonder, more adept at managing shoulder pads. So I was going to talk about my mother. The year that NASA figured out how to put a man on the moon, my father finally divined the mysteries of installing indoor plumbing. Before, we all bathed at the kitchen sink in a row. Bathing, as Dolly Parton says, "down as far as possible, up as far as possible and the possible." (My husband said that was a cliché so I went ahead and tried to get around that by saying it was a cliché, that's good). My mother, named Shine, which is exactly what she did in her life with a renowned, though erratically paid, bootlegging husband, had been raised better. Raised better in the South, in a Southern blue-haired gentility. Her mother, a cross between Jessica Tandy and Nero. But as a grown woman, my momma deserved daily better than she got. I have to know why and how she survived until the day she told my sister, "I don't think I'll be here tomorrow."

My reunion with my mother is in a new book, her life story. I anticipate a literary reunion with her, with both a mixture of hope and dread. In the summer, some stranger told me, my mother always wore a wide-brimmed straw hat. I want to go back out to the strawberry bed planted by the eventual time-overgrown outhouse, and simply put, take the straw hat off her head and remember the color of her eyes. My mother, I do remember this, created fictions that enabled me to live. One thing I remember her saying, she always told me if I ate ice cream (and we ate ice milk), after eating fried fish, I would die immediately of ptomaine poisoning. I believed this until I was waitressing at eighteen at a fish place and watched a couple eat catfish, ice cream and then miraculously walk out of the restaurant. Then I knew the truth that Momma never had money for dessert, so I want to reunite with her in that kitchen, in that spartan kitchen and split a half-gallon of Chunky Monkey.

In the literary reunion I wish I could fictionalize her own world and give her things my father could not provide. A facial, a stack of novels by the bed and a nightstand to put them on, tortoiseshell combs, and a Cadillac. But I am bound to rejoin her in her true home with all the heat, clay dirt and sad certainty that her life would not be any other way. Again, and finally, simply put, I want to take off the straw hat and watch her shine.

ENDINGS

October 18, 1999

Herbert Gold

I T WAS SUGGESTED that I write something funny, but the subject of the endgame of an old writer didn't seem funny, so I thought I'd dress funny and you'd get your laughs before I begin. This is a story that I'm working on, a piece of it. It's about an old writer, a veteran of World War II. His wife is named Karen. Farley's, they refer to as the coffeehouse where he hangs out and tries to accept the adulation of the young.

The novelist and combat correspondent had heard a rumor that all men die and many grow older, but in his heart he knew it was just an unconfirmed story, at least in his case. His best-seller of the early fifties, later available in paperback at thirty-five cents, was still fresh in many minds – his, Karen's, and that of a certain professor at Trenton State whose Ph.D. dissertation, "S. Fictor: Novelist Faithful to His Mission," had narrowly missed publication. It came close to being accepted for the Twain Series of American Persons of Letters, but was fully available on microfilm. The world would catch up with Fictor again in due course. Yet there was a sense of injustice – yes, even sadness – at present neglect. Fictor admitted to an occasional relapse into melancholy in private, never in public, usually with Karen in the middle of the night, when he awakened and couldn't get back to sleep. "Darling, darling," Karen murmured in her dream, "just you wait. Okay?" Sometimes even during the day his many espressos seemed to cause a little prostate irritation, frequent trips past the pile of old magazines and yesterday's newspapers to the unisex bathroom at Farley's. He tried to remember to drink lots of fresh tap water. He didn't believe in the high-fashion bottled waters. It was too late to start worrying about impurities when he had drunk from shared canteens in liberated France, his mouth where the mouths of his buddies had fastened, and no bad results that he could recall. "Not even a zit on your lip," asked Lillian, one of his young protégées at Farley's, "no herpes?" "Not even," he said, "and hey, do me a favor and call it a cold sore, don't get stylish on me. Okay?" In the Fictor backyard – it wasn't a garden – he had set up a picnic table from Sears. Sweating in his khaki shorts, T-shirt, he sat on an inflatable tire-shaped rubber pillow – hemorrhoids – and stared at the sheet of paper in his Olivetti Letera 32. Fictor owned three Olivetti Letera 32s; they were easy to buy at garage sales and at Goodwill. These days everybody chose to write badly on word processors. It was forgotten that you could write just as badly thumping at a manual typewriter. Steam-powered, as he liked to explain. He scratched his chest hairs. He ran his hand through the sweaty tangle. The chest was still sound, though a little fleshy where new hormones were taking hold. Then he toweled off, would head out for coffee, pick up an early edition of the afternoon paper, in case something was happening in the world. Fictor's rule: no television before evening, and then some conversation with his sweet wife, who never tired of Fictor's treasure stories, evoking those difficult and challenging times which had been so full of hope.

Fictor not only remembered every moment of the war, which he reported as Yank's youngest combat correspondent. Every hour of the Battle of the Bulge, but also he could reconstruct day by day the struggle against Franco and fascism in Spain, in which he didn't fight. He was a schoolboy then. Yet an odd thing. His life since 1946 seemed to be one long sleepy time, interrupted by the furious months of writing. And here it was, a half-century later, and he was still the fighter he had always been, only heavier, slower, resembling a turtle when he looked in the mirror, his head ducked between sloping shoulders, hair sprouting where it didn't used to grow – not really like a turtle except in his stubbornness. Once Karen asked, "Are you a sentimental person?" And he answered, "Is that what it looks like to you? Look again. It's called not giving up, dear lady."

Jane Hamilton

I 'M HERE IN praise of middles. As much as the amorphous middle can be praised. That long beige corridor, but with doors, doors on every side. Door number one, door number two, door number three. And behind each one could there be – is there – an argument, a dining-room set, a secret garden, a marriage, a box of Tide, the big emptiness, a moment of love? Could it be that in our life, this real life, the corridor goes on for ever, generation after generation, world without end, end without end? For every action there is a reaction, reaction, reaction, the ripple out and out and out.

In storytelling the endings have an awful job, to pretend to hold that interminable middle, to bring all of the middleness to a screeching halt. No ending is nearly always a bad ending, and no good ending truly ends. It might be that there's no finality we can get a glimmer of except presumably and eventually our own, that greatest of mysteries to ourselves. How and when, and will we have dignity or make a mess of it? Will there be anyone at our side? Will it matter once we are in that final bubble of our own aloneness? Will we have one instant of firm knowledge that this then is what an ending actually is? The real ending of the story of our lives is that someone, somewhere, has the privilege of doing the difficult job of getting up the next morning, taking the walk down the hall – the intelligent body one hopes will do its work – and through the next door. Is there enough coffee? Daylight has come again.

If not endings, what? Shifts, transformations, the caterpillar to butterfly. Pauses, illuminations, and moments, briefest moments of conclusion. The slipperiest of moments, proved from the diploma, the divorce papers, the eviction notice. The Berlin Wall comes down, concluding fifty years of visible separation. Monica's book hits the remainders table, concluding two years of national insanity. Elvis is dead and yet he lives. In black ink, the bard says three hundred years later, "My love may still shine bright." Death is an end, so they say, but how does this simple story come to be?

In the overwhelming middle of giving birth I look around: a husband, midwife, doctor, nurse — no one there who can help me. "Father," I cry to my own father, ten years dead, "where are you? Can't you please come here just for a minute? Oh, where are you?" And there he is, as always at the ready, his dear face before mine. How has this happened to a matter-of-fact Midwestern woman of Puritan stock, about to give birth to a daughter? How is it that I am telling this to you tonight, years and years later? What has possessed me? These are sorts of questions of the overlooked middle, the unsung middle, the essential middle, the forever-ticking heart of the story, the place where characters do their mysterious work of living.

We're preparing for the big ending, December 31 — so we think. In the middle of the country, in the middle of Iowa, in midsummer, I happened on a Vedic astrologer in the middle of the bagel joint, who informed me that by the ancient, the real calendar, the millennium has already ended. It was over in 1993. We missed it, guys. In truth, and without knowing, we are, as always, at the beginning of another long middle.

Oscar Hijuelos

W HEN I WAS a kid growing up in New York City without too much access to outside information, in that age of the 1950s before 200-channel televisions and Internet porno, faith healers, dial-a-psychic, MTV, endless and largely banal news-programing, et cetera, the ideas I had about the world came mainly from three sources. The first was my own family, Cubans who had come to the United States in the mid-1940s, for whom life, unbookish, and uncluttered except by work and relationships, was largely a mystery to be unraveled, bit by bit, day by day. And then there was what I learned from the neighborhood: tales of tragedy and love passed about in its scatological language. My third source came from my Catholic church and school, where the Old and New Testaments were taken quite literally. I can remember a morning when one of the more sensitive nuns read us selections from the Apocalypse, and how I truly believed that one day fantastic beasts and plagues were to be rained down upon mankind at the end of the world. An event that, as a kid, with a fearful fascination, I thought I might live to see.

Oddly, that moment seemed to arrive one autumn afternoon. I was in the fourth grade or so, and abruptly around two some kind of unusual meteorological event took place over New York City. The skies darkened, as if it were night. I don't think it was a solar eclipse, and to this day I have no idea what it was. But suddenly, in the midst of an arithmetic class, midnight descended, and our nun instructed us to kneel down before our desks to pray. For the end of the world was at hand. Expecting multitudes of angels bearing down to flutter down through the clouds bearing torches, we said our "Hail Mary"'s and waited to hear the trumpets. A few of the kids trembling, some sobbing, and others, like myself, harboring skepticism. And then it passed. The sunlight returned, and without any subsequent explanations, except for the nun saying, "That is how the end will begin," we children went back to our lessons. And while it was obviously a minor event, for I have never heard about it again, that afternoon has remained with me ever since. So, in one sense I can say that I have experienced an expectation of the world ending. And the funny thing for me is that some part of my psyche is awaiting the end of the millennium with the same feelings of dread, and fascination, and skepticism.

Even so, I feel that the plagues have already arrived in a less dramatic but gradual manner. It seems that the quietudes of life have been overtaken by noise, the information overloads of the media, and, to cut this short, by many other things, societal obsessiveness with surfaces, how one looks, endless health when people are healthier than ever before, with corporate-directed versions of hipness, which is not really hip at all, and with money. I hope of course that all this is a passing phase and not a prelude to everything that will inevitably unfold.

Chang-rae Lee

I F YOU WERE to come over to my house, you would see, written all over, the most strange and lovely language. It's the handiwork of Annika, my daughter, in ballpoint pen, and Magic Marker, in crayon and grease pencil. She's nearly two and a half and knows exactly the purpose of these implements. I find her scrawl everywhere. On my writing desk and on my computer keyboard. Downstairs on the kitchen door and along the toe moldings of the dining room. She tags the novels in the bookcase, particularly the author photographs. She dots our calendars and appointment books with hot pink highlighter. Her chalk dances in sea green across the walls of the garage, out on the blacktop rings the trunks of the shade trees in what looks like a mad Cyrillic, or the scansion of some invisible verse. All this is wonderful, of course, even if some mornings I'm confounded by the markings I find on my body in the shower, as if someone's stolen out of her crib and tattooed me in the night. I've begun to think that she's trying to tell me something with all this new work of hers, besides that she's here and there and there, that she's fast becoming. She's also telling me something about me starting, really starting, a new book.

I finished my most recent one a bit more than a few months ago in a headlong fury. The darn thing was already two years late. And for various reasons, a moved-up publication date, a book tour, full-time teaching, the usual rounds of "they want to make a movie" talk, I wasn't quite able to enjoy the true ending of it. Not the literal ending, the last pages and words, but the "*après* write," as it were. That wondrously easeful period following the busy finishing of a story, the throttled-back, wound-down undisturbed repose that, at least for me, must be sweetest time in the writing life. The period needn't be long; no doubt it shouldn't be. But be it shall and must. For if it isn't tasted in its fullness, if not duly savored, the desire for its moment lingers, fattens, until all one does is try to re-create the feeling of that special ending time. It's quite easy, it seems, at least for me. There's yet another compelling recipe in the newspaper to attempt, whose ingredients I will happily fetch at four different stores. There are those innumerous lightbulbs and batteries and fuses to replace, which I go and buy and then carefully test one by one. And of course there's always a quick nine holes to play at the county course, an hour's drive away, which become an even quicker eighteen, until dusk swiftly falls for the season has changed.

I'm sure this is how a proper ending to writing a book should be. This is how it ought be done. And though I'm not so worried yet, or so anxious, about not writing as I should be – I even have a new story I think I like – the notion occurs that perhaps I've been too commemorative, too nostalgic, even mournful in my retroactive bask. That I've been living too deeply in an ending ideal. Being caught up as ever in the proper dispatch of last acts, I'm a romantic this way. Terribly sentimental, and part of me wants a neverending, a lengthened moment in which the writing at least feels perfected, self-assured, complete. But these days when I'm on my little errands around the house, I know I'll have to pause before wall or door. For I'll see my daughter's newest glyphs, almost fresh to the touch. And then the commissioning pen or nub of chalk that's left behind, right there, beneath. "Pick it up," I think I hear, "pick it up."

Claire Messud

T HIS SUMMER, FOR the first time, I joined an outdoor swimming pool. It was a joy to don goggles and cap like a space
alien in training and plow up and down every few days through the
hottest months. After Labor Day the pool was miraculously empty.
The children were gone back to school, the tourists vanished also.
Only the most faithful continued our pilgrimages to the water,
smirking conspiratorially at one another across the concrete deck.
We were the real swimmers. The ones who would swim to the last
possible day. Then I had to go out of town, not once but several
times. My swimming schedule was disrupted. The weather turned
windy and wet, and then cold. It dawned on me then that the end of
my swimming had come to pass without me realizing it. I had frog-
kicked my last lap of the year utterly unaware. In the same way, so
many times in our lives we travel to a beloved place without knowing
it will be the last visit. We speak to a friend without knowing it will
be the last conversation. Many of us will eat our last breakfast blithely
oblivious to the fact. In reality, endings are often hasty, and illusive.
It's arguably better that way.

In one of my favorite novels, Italo Svevo's *Confessions of Zeno*, the
protagonist, who is constantly quitting smoking, enjoys each cigar-
ette infinitely more because he firmly believes it to be his last. But in
real life, when we're aware of an ending we're likely to be self-
conscious and artificial. Endings may be inevitable but they don't feel
real. In fiction, on the other hand, in the world of *Confessions of Zeno*
say, endings are the heightening of reality – they are a certainty, a
culmination. They are part of fiction's delight. A novel, simply in

order to lie between covers, must have one. An ending that is in some way inscribed in its beginning. An ending that will give shape and meaning to all that has come before. Endings are what make novels significant, as life, so sloppy, fails to be. There are marriages and deaths. There are happily-ever-afters. The soothing pleasures, for example, of Jane Austen's weddings. There are apocalyptic endings, like the last sentence of Lampedusa's *The Leopard*: "Then all found peace in a heap of livid dust." There are inspirational endings, like the closing words of *Anna Karenina*: "My reason will still not understand why I pray, but I shall still pray, and my life, my whole life, independently of anything that may happen to me, is every moment of it no longer meaningless as it was before, but has an unquestionable meaning of goodness, with which I have the power to invest it." That'd be nice. There are the endings of self-conscious narrators that engage us directly and remind us of the arbitrariness of ending it all, like the close of *Notes from Underground*: "He could not keep his resolve and went on writing, but it seems to us two that we may well stop here." And then there are those endings that resemble most closely the ongoing drift of real life, like the memorable (to me anyway) last line of Tanizaki's *The Makioka Sisters*: "Yukiko's diarrhea persisted through the twenty-sixth and was a problem on the train to Tokyo." As Tanizaki knew, an ending, of course, is very rarely simply that; there are always beginning and middles bound up in it. Even when an ending appears bleak we can take solace in Shakespeare's wise reminder from *King Lear* that "The worst is not, So long as we can say, 'This is the worst.' " Or in more common parlance, "It's not over till it's over." And as with me and my summer swimming, when that moment really does come, we probably won't even know it.

Francine Prose

S OMETIMES, RARELY, THE stories and novels we are writing, or trying to write, take pity on us after all those months, or years, they've so cruelly made us suffer. Suddenly sympathetic or contrite, our stories end painlessly, accommodatingly, just as we all wish to. In our sleep at a hundred, or like the dear relative who tops off an extremely long and perfectly healthy life by spending one night in the hospital and leaving us every penny. These compliant, considerate stories do precisely what we would hope. Gracefully changing cadence so we know the end is near. Resonating back through the entire fiction without the tiniest taint of gimmick or contrivance. In short, they do everything except perhaps what we really desire, which is for them to be as good as the ending of James Joyce's "The Dead," or F. Scott Fitzgerald's *The Great Gatsby*, or John Cheever's "Goodbye My Brother." But, like thoughtful people, these kindly stories are regrettably rare. More often fiction refuses to go gently into that good night, and rages, rages, rages . . . well, against the writer. We think our heroes should jump out the window, and he won't get off the couch. We want our stories to end as Chekhov's do, with the merest shrug. And they demand a flat-out pedal-to-the-metal car chase.

The difference, obviously, involves the gap between what we want and what the story, which almost always knows best, understands about its own needs. But when we reach a standoff, when we simply can't finish a story, I have found that there's nothing to do but put the story aside until some compromise can be reached, or until our "real life" generously gives us what we have been missing. That is

to say, what we can steal to use as an end to our story. Here is my
favorite example of an instance when life came through in just that
way. I was writing a sad story for which I'd decided, perhaps wrongly,
that I needed a redemptive ending. But it was one of those sad times
when nothing redemptive was happening. Nothing even remotely
redemptive came to mind. So I put the story aside and waited until
one autumn morning. This was years ago. We were living in the
country near a reservoir. Our children were young. Returning from
driving our son to nursery school, my husband spotted a giant osprey,
flying above the road, struggling to carry a huge fish in its claws.
When at last it dropped the fish, my husband noted which light pole
it landed near. He stopped, turned around, drove back, and found the
seven-pound bass, whose eyes were still bright when he brought it
home and carried it up to my study. At first, I screamed. Then I said,
"Dinner." And then I had the end of my story, which ends
improbably, but magically, with a fish dropping out of the sky.

Richard Selzer

I N A FORMER life I was a doctor, and I've witnessed my share of unhappy endings. I've spent the greater part of my life trying to prolong the lives of my patients, and as a result I now find myself temperamentally reluctant to kill off the characters in my story. In a review of one of my books I read that among my other sins I am guilty of terminal sentimentality. I confess – that's me all right. I come from a family of weepers, in whom lachrymation can be brought on merely by saying "Once upon a time." We know what's coming. In a wretched orgy of sentimentality, a sort of sequel to *Little Women*, Louisa May Alcott gathered all her courage and killed off Jo March. It was a gentle death; as Beth put it, "the tide went out easily." Reading that at age eight I outwept Niobe, and doubtless would now if I had the nerve to read it again. Ever since, the only death I can dwell upon without soaking a handkerchief is my own. May the tide go out easily.

I've taken to rewriting other people's stories to give a doomed character another chance. Take Charles Dickens's novel *A Tale of Two Cities*. As you will remember, Charles Darnay is married to the lovely daughter of Dr. Manette. He's also an aristocrat, and therefore an enemy of the revolution. Having been seized and thrown into the Bastille, he's awaiting execution. One the day before he is to be guillotined, Sydney Carton, a lookalike who has led a life of rascally and wanton pursuits – a wastrel – goes to the Bastille and in an act of excruciating gallantry trades place with Charles Darnay. For the reasons why, I refer you to the original text. Suffice it here to say that the last lines of the novel are the last words of Sydney Carton: 'It is a far, far better thing that I do, than I have ever done,' and so forth.

And that was supposed to be that, until I rewrote the ending of *A Tale of Two Cities*. Sydney Carton has just uttered his immortal speech and has knelt, placing his neck to receive the dreadful blade. An expectant hush falls over the crowd. All at once a commotion breaks out in the immediate vicinity of the guillotine. Cries of anger and outrage are heard. *"Zut alors! C'est affreux! Merde! Cochon!"* And many other obscenities are exchanged by the executioners and the revolutionary guards. It seems that the guillotine is broken. The blade cannot be released. It is stuck. It is as though the instrument itself has rebelled against taking the life of so heroic a man. Poor Sydney Carton, lost in a vision of his own glory, is oblivious to the melee. Blows are struck, muskets fired. Being French, the crowd is over-come with emotion. At this demonstration of sympathy by an inanimate instrument of execution, the very one that had been meant to perpetrate the deed, singing "La Marseillaise" they surge over the barricades and attack both executioners and revolutionary guard. All at once Carton feels himself being lifted to his feet and carried away into the midst of the throng. A cloth soaked in chloroform is placed over his face; he inhales deeply – once, twice, thrice – and loses consciousness. When he awakens he is on board a ship. A beautiful young woman is kneeling over him, cradling him in her arms. "How long have I been here?" he asks.

"Three days," she says.

"Who are you?"

"I am the wife of Charles Darnay, the very man whose life you saved."

"Where are you taking me?"

"You are to come to live with us in England. We shall have a ménage à trois."

"Vive la France!" exclaims Sydney Carton, and rests his head against the young woman's breast. (The only trouble is that I have since learned that chloroform wasn't discovered until 1834.)

In the matter of endings I prefer a bit of ambiguity. There's nothing ambiguous about a corpse. It's dead. Here's what happened: I was ten years old and my mother had taken me to a performance of

Macbeth performed in upstate New York in Troy by a traveling troupe. And between the acts we had gone backstage to greet a friend of hers who was playing one of the witches. There, on a stool, in her royal robes, sat Lady Macbeth eating a corned-beef sandwich. When later she appeared in the sleepwalking scene rubbing her hands and wishing that the "damned spot" would get out of them, I knew it wasn't blood. It was mustard! This experience impressed upon me the wisdom not to reveal everything but to sustain a bit of ambiguity. Some mysteries are not meant to be solved, they are meant to be deepened.

Anita Shreve

October 18, 1999

F OR THIS OCCASION I have written a sort of poem. I am not a
poet but a novelist, which I think will be immediately apparent.
For want of a better title I have called this "Millennium Day."

> Your mother's quilt has a sweet smell
> I remember a boy with arms as thin as wood
> My father wore a uniform
> My mother slept at noon
> My daughter walked across a lawn
> and all endings were contained within that ending
> My father asked me not to tell my mother
> and I did
> I am the first daughter
> or the second son
> We love each other more than we can say
> It will mean nothing to me on the day
> Youth slips silently between the folds
> Our child is old, with words
> I do not understand his dreams
> Our wars, your gods
> I see you with the sight of years ago
> You are a boy with arms as thin as wood
> I promise to remember you
> As if I could
> As if I could
> All memory is unraveling now

Great schemes are thinning by the hour
Where is your face?
His hand, my breath, her flower
All meaning is unraveling now
This thread of life
That thread of lust
We will leave this place
And not come back
And in our dreams it will turn to dust.

Calvin Trillin

T HIS IS A poem, "Oh Y2K, Yes Y2K, How Come It Has to
End This Way?"

Now every day, to our dismay
We're told of yet more disarray
That Y2K may put in play.
A double zero on display
In some computers could convey—
Since they are lacking thought, per se—
A false impression they'd obey,
Concluding in a faulty way
Which century it is that day,
And thus unleash, without delay,
The cyberbug called Y2K.
Then life won't be a cabaret.

Oh Y2K, yes Y2K.
How come it has to end this way?

If circuits sizzle and sauté
The cables into macramé,
Those passengers then in Taipei
With reservations for Bombay
Could find themselves in St-Tropez
Or on the road to Mandalay.
And ferryboats to Monterey

Would dock on time, but in Calais.
Caudillos off on holiday
Could all end up with Pinochet.

And in a brief communiqué
The Pentagon might have to say
It cannot fight the smallest fray
Because it has lost the dossier
Of soldiers to be told that they
Must leave the service, come what may—
The list that lists each Green Beret
Who privately has said he's gay.

Oh Y2K, yes Y2K,
How come it has to end this way?

The lobbyists who work on K
See all their loopholes go astray
And benefit the F.P.A.
And thinking this is like Pompeii—
A doomsday in the U.S.A.—
Militiamen in full array
Go underground and say they'll slay
Whoever tries through naiveté,
To take the food they've stored away
Or criticize the N.R.A.

Then A.T.M.s begin to spray.
Fresh twenties fall like new-mown hay.
The traffic lights all go to gray.
A clebrator slurs "Olé!"
As cars begin to ricochet
Like balls caroming in croquet
And, slyly slowing his sashay,
He just escapes a Chevrolet.

There's darkness on the Great White Way.
Nearby, a fussy fat gourmet
Who's had some quail and duck paté
And finished with marron glacé,
Sips cheap Hungarian rosé
That in the dark, the sommelier
Mistook for rare Courvoisier,
And says—in French, of course—*parfait!*"

Oh Y2K, yes Y2K,
How come it has to end this way?

But maybe it will be O.K.—
As peaceful come this *janvier*
As water lilies by Monet,
As lyrics sung by Mel Tormé
Or herds of grazing Charolais.
For just such peacefulness we pray.
We say, "Oh *s'il vous plait*, Yahweh."
But still we're scared of Y2K.
There's no one who remains blasé.
No awesome monster's held such sway
Since King Kong grabbed the fair Fay Wray.
We try to keep our fears at bay.
But one fear makes us say, "Oy vey!"
And here's the fear we can't allay:

God's thinking of pulling the plug,
And not with a bang, but with a bug.

First published in *The New Yorker*

Edward Albee

W ELL, HERE I am . . . waiting. I wish they'd hurry. I know what my job is; I'm ready to do it – *eager*, when you come right down to it. I *do* wish they'd decide when it's *time* for me, though. I feel naked, and sort of ridiculous just . . . hanging around, whistling in the wind, as the writer put it – not the writer I'm waiting for, but . . . another one.

If you're an ending . . . which is what I am, in case you hadn't guessed – if you're an ending you have to wait around until the writer *gets* to you, so to speak. An ending can't just . . . be there without everything that goes *before*.

I mean, we endings are the whole thing, when you come right down to it. You can have an absolutely splendid book – or play, or whatever – absolutely splendid, full of great characters, exciting plot twists, thrilling dramatic confrontations, love, hate, loss, betrayal – all the stuff books – and plays – are full of – but without a proper ending the whole thing falls apart. Without *me*, there's . . . *nothing*.

I get impatient, though. I want to jump in and get myself over with . . . dot the final I, cap the stone, zing that final period, make it all cohere, become . . . inevitable. I can't wait to do my job. But, of course, you have to put up with the author. Now *mine* – this guy who's writing his way toward me – though he's certainly taking his time about it: 622 pages so far, twelve major characters, sixty-seven minor ones – so *far* – isn't a bad *writer* from what I can tell. This is his third novel. He got over the abyss of "the second novel" by not *writing* it. Damn clever, I thought; puzzled a lot of the reviewers, but more does than they let on. He isn't a bad *writer*, and I've been interested in what he's doing while I've been waiting for him to *get* to me, but I don't know how *close* he's getting and how I'm going to turn out. Cynthia's done with her affair with the Semiotics professor and I smell revenge coming but I can't be certain what that *means*. And what are we to make of that diamond-studded dildo that was introduced on page – what was it? – 312 and hasn't been mentioned since?!

And how does all this relate to *me*? I've got a reputation as one of the best endings around, and writers have been aiming at me for a couple of hundred years now – Meredith, Hardy, Turgenev, Pirandello, Nabokov – you know: the big guys – and while I don't *mind* being used by – well, this fellow who's writing his way toward *me* isn't going to be up for the Nobel Prize, or even the National Book Award, you know – a quick trip to the remainder table may be more like it – and he may even make a quick ninety-degree turn and not use me at *all* – that dildo has me suspicious – but . . . I wish he'd get *to* it, you know – get to *me*.

I was at a conference the other week, and I was talking to a couple of beginnings and one rather fat exposition, and they all admitted I could be one of the best endings around, and one even said that whenever he found himself getting going he wished he could be confident he'd get to *me*. But . . . it's the uncertainty, you know? The not knowing!

I mean, a book you know right off from the first page who's going to be the ending doesn't have much suspense going for it, but shouldn't you sort of have . . . an intimation, kind of, somewhere around the middle?

This guy – this writer – I don't know where he's going, and if he's not going to use me I'm going to take off!

Oh, wait! That *dildo's* back!!

Rilla Askew

I CAN TELL YOU the day the end of the world started. April the twelfth, 1945. I believe I'm right on that. That was the day President Roosevelt died for one thing, not that that was the end of the world, though some thought it, but what I mean to say, it was a sign. That same day the skies over the heart of this nation turned black, spat out a hundred tails of a cyclone just a-whirling and a-twisting right up the middle of the country. One of those tornadoes come over the mountain and hit Bogey, wiped our little town off the face of the earth. Now that was the end of something. I thought then it was the Second Coming. I was standing on the porch, had my guitar propped on the swing, the sky turned a weird yellow green, clouds way up high, swirling, and then all of a sudden everything went dark. I mean, black as midnight under an iron skillet. Not a breath of air. The hairs on the back of my neck stuck straight out. I heard that roar, looked up, here come the tail of that tornado dancing up over the top of that mountain. They say a tornado won't go up over a mountain, but I'm here to tell that a tornado will do just whatever it gets in its crazy mind to do. And that black funnel come riding up over Red Oak Mountain, rode it straight down the other side, coming right for us. I hollered in the house and said, "Mama, grab the kids and y'all get under the bed." I completely forgot I'd bought her that new wood-veneer bed. Wasn't six inches off the floor. She told me later she's praying, "Lord, Jesus, if you'll just save us I promise you I'll make him go right out tomorrow and buy us a bed we can get under." She did too. Had to. We never did find what went with that bed.

I's reaching for the screen door when it hit, and boy howdy, here I went just a-sailing. Twister lifted up my house and set it down a mile away. My wife and my two children hunkered down on that bare swept floor. Teacherage was flattened, the schoolhouse broke down into little sticks. Mr. Roosevelt was bleeding in his brain in Warm Springs, Georgia. We were bleeding all over Bogey, Oklahoma. What was left of Bogey, Oklahoma, which was nothing – just piles of rubble, a few goats and some trees. Miss Inetta Jones sitting on the outhouse throne behind the teacherage. That's true. That cyclone lifted up that little wood privy from around her and blowed it off toward Walls. Blowed all the hairpins out of her hair. Left that schoolteacher just sitting there with her drawers down, and her hair down. They'll do some strange things. Blowed all the feathers off Slape's chickens. Blowed my guitar plum over Podo, left it on the Assembly of God church roof – not a scratch on it. Nobody ever came back and built at Bogey again. Coal companies come in right after that and started stripping. And that little farming town is just gone.

But you listen to this: This is every bit true. The president passed away at 3:35 P.M., Eastern war time. That's in all your records. Now, what time was that in Oklahoma? Four 4.35 P.M. Buster Adams found the schoolhouse clock over at Shady Point the next evening. And what time was it stopped at? Four thirty-five. And it wasn't just our little community that was hit neither. There was fourteen towns struck in Oklahoma, Arkansas, Missouri – just a bunch, a bunch of storms. But I don't guess any of those other towns got wiped off the earth. Except Bogey. But, like I say, that was just a sign. April the twelfth, 1945. That's the day the tribulations started. Right there near the end of that war. We didn't notice it because we thought the worst was over. Two weeks later, Hitler was dead. Scripture says that in the last days the sun will darken and the moon will turn to blood. I didn't see no red moon, but what was the earth then in those days and ever since but a bloody planet. Fifty-eight countries at war with one another. Before the summer was out we had dropped that bomb. What I think is that war just cracked open the century, broke it in half like you'd pop a wishbone. It was just so much killing. Just a feast of killing. Kill, kill, kill. The earth couldn't hold all the dead. That's how come the tribulations started. Lots of believers think they're going to get out of it but I hate to tell 'em it's too late for that. We're in it. You don't have to watch TV to know it. But if you do watch TV you'll know it for sure.

Judy Blume

I N HER LATER years my mother, who enjoyed knitting for her loved ones, confessed to making bargains with God. He would not take her in the middle of a sweater. She was cagey about it though, always having new wool on hand to begin again the very next day. When I started to write I also made bargains with God. He, or she – because by then I had read Erica Jong – would allow me to finish my book before, well, whatever. And when I came to the end and sent it off in its plain brown envelope, I was filled with hope that this might be the one to make me a published writer. But just in case, the next morning I was back at it. I was in my twenties then and in a hurry; in my family life was short.

I grew up sitting *shivah*, shaped by death. Alternately fascinated, terrified, consumed by the ultimate ending, I developed my very own personal relationship with God that had little to do with organized religion. I believed deeply, as only a child can, that I was responsible for my beloved father's well-being, and that only I could prevent his untimely death. The year I was nine my father was turning forty-three, the same age his brothers had been when they had died. I secretly called it the "Bad Year" and invented a series of ritualistic prayers I would recite at least ten times a day, more if necessary, anything to protect my father, to keep him healthy and safe from harm. And it worked for a while. My father survived the "Bad Year" and lived for twelve more, then died suddenly on a sunny summer afternoon. I was twenty-one and had long given up the magical thinking that led me to believe I could save him, or anyone else. He was the last of seven siblings, none of whom lived to be sixty. Endings have always been hard for me.

Though I rejoice at writing that final line in a book, much as my mother did with the final row of each of her hand-knit sweaters, and I weep with relief at finding myself at the end at last, after months or sometimes years of struggle, I know that before long a melancholic funk will hit me and I'll go through a period of mourning. Parting with my characters is like saying that final goodbye to an old friend. Oh sure, they're still there for me if I want to pick up a book and thumb through the pages, but they're no longer part of my everyday life. Each time I have to learn to let go all over again, to send them out into the world without my protection. Lately, I've been allowing myself longer and longer periods of time between books. Now that I've passed my sixtieth birthday I'm in less of a hurry. I probably shouldn't admit this because my mother, if she were here tonight, would urge me to get back to work, and quickly. Then she would raise her finger and whisper a reminder, "You never know who might be listening."

Lorene Cary

I T'S THE END of September, the end of summer, and I'm riding my old olive-green bicycle north on 22nd Street with my five-year-old daughter in the child seat, going to kindergarten. Zoë weighs thirty-eight pounds; two more pounds and she'll be too big for the seat. We're riding fast so as not to be late, when I see a girl who couldn't be older than eight or ten skating down the middle of the street, between two columns of traffic. Drivers blow their horns and swerve. I bump us onto the sidewalk, out of the confusion, and I slow down in order to ride parallel to the child. We are separated by a line of passing cars, and years.

I could never ride this bike fast enough for our older daughter. More than anything Laura loved to cruise fast downhill. Now she snowboards. Nine years later Zoë prefers the slow side-to-side rhythm when I'm pumping hard to power up an incline. At the beginning of school Zoë drew her family, four of us, her daddy the biggest in the center. All with great swollen fingers on our out-stretched hands because she can't yet draw them smaller. We look like a wacky vaudeville troupe ending a show. She said we're hiking. We study the picture to make ourselves see what she sees. Sheer movement, lives entwined. "We are on our way to the land of endless day." I had just discovered Yeats when deconstruction came. Just settled into the union of dancer and dance when the two were ripped apart. Words peeled away from action, leaving a raw spot, a telltale – pardon the expression – sign.

With the school just a couple of blocks away, the girl on skates pitches forward. Ending means nothing, theoretically. I watch and wait. Somehow she gets up, rights herself, skates on. We stay with her. "Laura could skate in the street, right," Zoë says to me about her older sister. I remember standing behind Laura in the rough surf, trying to block the slap of the waves, and the pull of the undertow. "Don't touch me, Mommy," she shouted, "but don't let me fall." Now Laura listens to a band that punches the edge of my cultural envelope out. "Thirty seconds to the end of the world, let's call it quits. Thirty seconds to the end of the world, throw it all away. Ten seconds to the end of the world, five seconds to the end of the world, *pfft*". The light turns red, ankles flop in nearly to the ground, and the child slaps her skates against the curb cut to stand demurely behind orange-sashed safety guards and the gym teacher. I cross the street to her, ask her name. I tell the gym teacher that it's a miracle she's alive. I've dimed on her and she's upset. The teacher makes her put on her shoes and reassures me that he'll call her parents. Meat don't beat no steel, and yet we're both alive. I zip the last block under a shiny blue sky, and time shuffles itself so that for an instant I'm riding one endless, seamless movement. My father lets drop his steadying hand. I hold the bike in my body poised. I turn corners, lean at sharper and sharper angles to defy the earth's certain pull – roll fast and carefree, away from my mother's voice commanding "Care." Two more pounds and my child will be out of the child's seat. No doubt, we'll give it away too. Nothing is ours to keep.

George Garrett

I BEGIN WITH TWO propositions: first, that the commercial is the dominant art form of the twentieth century; and that the obituary is the sincerest form of fiction.

Here is one, a commercial with text only. You will have to use your imagination to enjoy the visuals and the music.

(Voice over)

Enjoy a happy ending in the hands of Fantasia Obituary Agency. The bad news is, of course, that you have to be dead, that the ending has already arrived. There is nothing to be done about that except, with the benefit of the best simile a high-class undertaker can give you, to grin and bear it.

The good news is that from the moment of your demise – in fact, well before that – Fantasia Obituaries is hard at work on your case.

Our basic service makes sure that you will get the maximum post-mortem buzz. After all, you probably have spent most of your real life trying to create and preserve an image. Do you want to throw it all away just because you are now among the dearly departed?

Nobody knows how much, if at all, obituaries may count in the afterlife, if any. But even as they can smoothly polish up your past, they may very well influence your future status. Don't take a chance on oblivion. Instead plan to take advantage of Fantasia's always impeccable timing. We make sure that you don't have to jostle for space and attention, head to head against Nobel prizewinners, movie stars and heads of state. All our clients are celebrities when we get through with them. Your friends will be proud to have known you. Your enemies will be glad you are gone.

Someone – there's always an unreconstructed cynic in every crowd these days – someone wants to know if we ever have to tell, like . . . you know, any little lies in a full-fledged deluxe Fantasia obituary. The answer to that is it all depends on what your definition of the word "lie" is.

Don't worry about it. Permit the guys at Fantasia to take care of your legacy. Let Fantasia preserve and maintain your reputation, keeping it bright and shiny in perpetuity while you sleep the sleep of the just.

The end.

A NOTE ON THE TYPE

The text of this book is set in Bembo, the original types
for which were cut by Francesco Griffo for the Venetian printer
Aldus Manutius, and were first used in 1495 for Cardinal
Bembo's *De Aetna*. Claude Garamond (1480–1561) used
Bembo as a model and so it became the forerunner of standard
European type for the following two centuries. Its modern
form was designed, following the original, for Monotype in
1929 and is widely in use today.